HOSTILE WITNESS

A Josie Bates Thriller
Book 1

By

REBECCA FORSTER

Hostile Witness

Published 2004 by Signet Fiction

ISBN: 061559591X
ISBN-13: 9780615595917

For Steve

PROLOGUE

Today California buried Supreme Court Justice, Fritz Rayburn. Governor Joe Davidson delivered the eulogy calling the judge a friend, a confidant, and his brother in service to the great state of California. The governor cited Fritz Rayburn as a man of extraordinary integrity who relentlessly pursued justice, continually uplifted those in need and, above all, protected those who were powerless.

It was a week ago today that Judge Rayburn died in a fire that swept through his Pacific Palisades home in the early morning hours.

No formal announcement has been made regarding who will be appointed to fill Justice Rayburn's position, but it is speculated that Governor Davidson will appoint Rayburn's son, Kip, to this pivotal seat on the California Supreme Court.

KABC News at 9 O'clock

CHAPTER 1

"Strip."

"No."

Hannah kept her eyes forward, trained on two rows of rusted showerheads stuck in facing walls. Sixteen in all. The room was paved with white tile, chipped and discolored by age and use. Ceiling. Floor. Walls. All sluiced with disinfectant. Soiled twice a day by filth and fear. The fluorescent lights cast a yellow shadow over everything. The air was wet. The shower room smelled of mold and misery. It echoed with the cries of lost souls.

Hannah had come in with a bus full of women. She had a name, now she was a number. The others were taking off their clothes. Their bodies were ugly, their faces worn. They flaunted their ugliness as if it were a cruel joke, not on them but on those who watched. Hannah was everything they were not. Beautiful. Young. She wouldn't stand naked in this room with these women. She blinked and wrapped her arms around herself. Her breath came short. A step back and she fooled herself that it was possible to turn and leave. Behind her Hannah thought she heard the guard laugh.

"Take it off, Sheraton, or I'll do it for you."

Hannah tensed, hating to be ordered. She kept her eyes forward. She had already learned to do that.

"There's a man back there. I saw him," she said.

"We're an equal opportunity employer, sweetie," the woman drawled. "If women can guard male prisoners then men can guard the women. Now, who's it going to be? Me or him?"

The guard touched her. Hannah shrank away. Her head went up and down, the slightest movement, the only way she could control her dread. She counted the number of times her chin went up. *Ten counts.* Her shirt was off. Her chin went down. Ten more counts and she dropped the jeans that had cost a fortune.

"All of it, baby cakes," the guard prodded.

Hannah closed her eyes. *The thong. White lace.* That was the last. Quickly she stepped under a showerhead and closed her eyes. A tear seeped from beneath her lashes only to be washed away by a sudden, hard, stinging spray of water. Her head jerked back as if she'd been slapped then Hannah lost herself in the wet and warm. She turned her face up, kept her arms closed over her breasts, pretended the sheet of water hid her like a cloak. As suddenly as it had been turned on the water went off. She had hidden from nothing. The ugly women were looking back, looking her over. Hannah went from focus to fade, drying off with the small towel, pulling on the too-big jumpsuit. She was drowning in it, tripping over it. Her clothes – her beautiful clothes – were gone. She didn't ask where.

The other women talked and moved as if they had been in this place so often it felt like home. Hannah was cut from the pack and herded down the hall, hurried past big rooms with glass walls and cots lined up military style. She slid her eyes toward them. Each was occupied. Some women slept under blankets, oblivious to their surroundings. Others were shadows that rose up like specters, propping themselves on an elbow, silently watching Hannah pass.

Clutching her bedding, Hannah put one foot in front of the other, eyes down, counting her steps so she wouldn't be tempted to look at all those women. There were too many steps. Hannah lost track and began again. *One. Two…*

"Here."

A word stopped her. The guard rounded wide to the right as if Hannah was dangerous. That was a joke. She couldn't hurt anyone – not really. The woman pushed open a door. The cock of her head said this was Hannah's place. A room, six by eight. A metal-framed bed and stained mattress. A metal toilet without a lid. A metal sink. No mirror. Hannah hugged her bedding tighter and twirled around just as the woman put her hands on the door to close it.

"Wait! You have to let me call my mom. Take me to a phone right now so I can check on her."

Hannah talked in staccato. A water droplet fell from her hair and hit her chest. It coursed down her bare skin and made her shiver. It was so cold. This was all so cold and so awful. The guard was unmoved.

"Bed down, Sheraton," she said flatly.

Hannah took another step. "I told you I just want to check on her. Just let me check on her. I won't talk long."

"And I told you to bed down." The guard stepped out. The door was closing. Hannah was about to call again when the woman in blue with the thick wooden club on her belt decided to give her a piece of advice. "I wouldn't count on any favors, Sheraton. Judge Rayburn was one of us, if you get my meaning. It won't matter if you're here or anywhere else. Everyone will know who you are. Now make your bed up."

The door closed. Hannah hiccoughed a sob as she spread her sheet on the thin mattress. She tucked it under only to pull it out over and over again. Finally satisfied she put the blanket on, lay down and listened. The sound of slow footsteps echoed through the complex. Someone was crying. Another woman shouted. She shouted again and then she screamed. Hannah stayed quiet, barely breathing. They had taken away her clothes. They had touched her where no one had ever touched her before. They had moved her, stopped her, pointed and ordered her, but at this point Hannah couldn't remember who had done any of those things. Everyone who wasn't dressed in orange was dressed in blue. The blue people had guns and belts filled with bullets and clubs that they caressed as if they were treasured pets. These people seemed at once bored with their duty and thrilled with their power. They hated Hannah and she didn't even know their names.

Hannah wanted her mother. She wanted to be in her room. She wanted to be anywhere but here. Hannah even wished Fritz wouldn't be dead if that would get her home. She was going crazy. Maybe she was there already.

Hannah got up. She looked at the floor and made a plan. She would ask to call her mother again. She would ask politely because the way she said it before didn't get her anything. Hannah went to the door of her – *cell.* A hard enough word to think, she doubted she could ever say it. She went to the door and put her hands against it. It was cold, too. Metal. There was a window in the center. Flat white light slid through it. Hannah raised her fist and tapped the glass. *Once, twice, three, ten times.* Someone would hear. *Fifteen. Twenty.* Someone would come and she would tell them she didn't just *want* to check on her mother; she would tell them she *needed* to do that. This time she would say please.

Suddenly something hit up against the glass. Hannah fell back. Stumbling over the cot, she landed near the toilette in the corner. This wasn't her room in the Palisades. This was a small, cramped place. Hannah clutched at the rough blanket and pulled it off the bed as she sank to the floor. Her heart beat wildly. Huddled in the dark corner, she could almost feel her eyes glowing like some nocturnal animal. She was transfixed by what she saw. A man was looking in, staring at her as if she were nothing. Oh God, he could see her even in the dark. Hannah pulled her knees up to her chest and peeked from behind them at the man who watched.

His skin was pasty, his eyes plain. A red birthmark spilled across his right temple and half his eyelid until it seeped into the corner of his nose. He raised his stick, black and blunt, and tapped on the glass. He pointed toward the bed. She would do what he wanted. Hannah opened her mouth to scream at him. Instead, she crawled up on to the cot. Her feet were still on the floor. The blanket was pulled over her chest and up into her chin. The guard looked at her – all of her. He didn't see many like this. So young. So pretty. He stared at Hannah as if he owned her. Voices were raised somewhere else. The man didn't seem to notice. He just looked at Hannah until she yelled 'go away' and threw the small, hard pillow at him.

He didn't even laugh at that ridiculous gesture. He just disappeared. When Hannah was sure he was gone she began to pace. Holding her right hand in her left she walked up and down her cell and counted the minutes until her mother would come to get her.

Counting. Counting. Counting again.

Behind the darkened windows of the Lexus, the woman checked her rearview mirror. Damn freeways. It was nine-friggin'-o'clock at night and she still had to slalom around a steady stream of cars. She stepped on the gas – half out of her mind with worry.

One hundred.

Hannah should be with her.

One hundred and ten.

Hannah must be terrified.

The Lexus shimmied under the strain of the speed.

She let up and dropped to ninety five.

They wouldn't even let her see her daughter. She didn't have a chance to tell Hannah not to talk to anyone. But Hannah was smart. She'd wait for help. Wouldn't she be smart? *Oh, God, Hannah. Please, please be smart.*

Ahead a pod of cars pooled as they approached Martin Luther King Boulevard. Crazily she thought they looked like a pin setup at the bowling alley. Not that she visited bowling alleys anymore but she made the connection. It would be so easy to end it all right here – just keep going like a bowling ball and take 'em all down in one fabulous strike. It sure as hell would solve all her problems. Maybe even Hannah would be better off. Then again, the people in those cars might not want to end theirs so definitely.

Never one to like collateral damage if she could avoid it, the woman went for the gutter, swinging onto the shoulder of the freeway, narrowly missing the concrete divider that kept her from veering into oncoming traffic. She was clear again, leaving terror in her wake, flying toward her destination.

The Lexus transitioned to the 105. It was clear sailing all the way to Imperial Highway where the freeway came to an abrupt end, spitting her out onto a wide intersection before she was ready. The tires squealed amid the acrid smell of burning rubber. The Lexus shivered, the rear end fishtailing as she fought for control. Finally, the car came to a stop, angled across two lanes.

The woman breathed hard. She sniffled and blinked and listened to her heartbeat. She hadn't realized how fast she'd been going until just this minute. Her head whipped around. *No traffic.* A dead spot in the maze of LA freeways, surface streets, transitions and exits. Her hands were fused to the steering wheel. *Thank God. No cops.* Cops were the last thing she wanted to see tonight; the last people she ever wanted to see.

Suddenly her phone rang. She jumped and scrambled, forgetting where she had put it. Her purse? The console? The console. She ripped it open and punched the button to stop the happy little song that usually signaled a call from her hairdresser, an invitation to lunch.

"What?"

"This is Lexus Link checking to see if you need assistance."

"What?"

"Are you all right, ma'am? Our tracking service indicated that you had been in an accident."

Her head fell onto the steering wheel; the phone was still at her ear. She almost laughed. Some minimum wage idiot was worried about her.

"No, I'm fine. Everything's fine," she whispered and turned off the phone. Her arm fell to her side. The phone fell to the floor. A few minutes later she sat up and pushed back her hair. She'd been through tough times before. Everything would be fine if she just kept her wits about her and got where she was going. Taking a deep breath she put both hands back on the wheel. She'd damn well finish what she started the way she always did. As long as Hannah was smart they'd all be okay.

Easing her foot off the brake she pulled the Lexus around until she was in the right lane and started to drive. She had the address, now all she had to do was to find friggin' Hermosa Beach.

"For God's sake, Josie, he's a weenie-wagger and that's all there is to it. I don't know why you keep coming in here with the same old crap for a defense. Want some?"

Judge Crawford pushed the pizza box her way. It was almost nine o'clock and they had managed to work out the details on the judge's sponsorship at the Surf Festival, discuss a moot court for which they had volunteered, polish off most of a large pizza, and now Josie was trying to take advantage of the situation by putting in a pitch for leniency for one of her clients.

She passed on the pizza offer. Judge Crawford took another piece. He was a good guy, a casual guy, a local who never strayed from his beach town roots in his thirty-year legal career. His robes were tossed on the couch behind them. His desk served as a workstation and dining table. In the corner was his first surfboard. New attorneys called to chambers endured forty-five minutes of the judge reliving his moments of glory as one of the best long boarders on the coast. Three years ago, when Josie landed in Hermosa Beach, she got the full two-hour treatment but only because she knew a thing or two about surfing from her days in Hawaii. She'd spent the extra hour with Judge Crawford because he knew a thing or two about volleyball.

Josie Baylor-Bates had been big at USC but when she hit the sand circuit she'd become legendary. Everyone wanted to best the woman who stood six feet if she was an inch, played like a professional, and won like a champion. Few did, but they started trying the minute the summer nets went up. Of course USC and Judge Crawford's surfing days were both more than a few years ago, but still their beach history tied them together, made them friendly colleagues, and gave them license to be a little more informal about certain protocols – including the judge speaking his mind about Josie's current client, Billy Zuni: the surfing-teenage-beach bum with a mischievous smile and penchant for relieving himself in city owned bushes.

"That's a gross term," Josie scoffed as if she'd never heard of a weenie-wagger before. "And it is not appropriate in this instance. I've got documentation from their family doctor that Billy has a physical problem. He's tried to use the bathrooms in the shops off the Strand, but nobody will let him in."

"That's because Billy seems to forget he's supposed to lower his cutoffs *after* he gets into the bathroom, not before," the judge reminded her. "Nope, this time he's got to stay in the pokey. Hey, it's Hermosa Beach's pokey. Five cells and they're all empty. Billy will have the whole place to himself. It's not going to kill him, and it may do him some good. I'm tired of that damn kid's file coming across my desk every three months."

"Your Honor, it's obvious you are prejudiced against my client," Josie objected, pushing aside the pizza box.

"Cool your jets, Josie. What are you going to do, bring me up on charges for name calling?" Judge Crawford laughed heartily. His little belly shook. It was hard to imagine him on a long board or any other kind of board for that matter. "Listen. I understand that kid's got problems. You're in here like clockwork swearing he'll be supervised. I know you check up on him. Everyone at the beach knows that, but you can't do what his own mother can't."

"That's exactly the point. Jail time won't mean a thing. What if I can find someone who'll take him for a week? Will you consider house arrest?"

"With you?" The judge raised a brow.

"Archer," Josie answered without reservation.

Judge Crawford chuckled. "Not a bad idea. Sort of like setting up boot camp in paradise. That would make Billy sit up and take notice. I don't know anybody who wouldn't toe the line just to get Archer off their back."

Josie touched her lips to hide a smile. Judge Crawford steered clear of Archer after a vigorous debate on the unfortunate constitutions of judges facing re-election. As Josie recalled, words such as wimps and sell-outs had been bandied about freely. It wasn't that Archer was wrong, it was just that the opinion was coming from a retired cop who wasn't afraid of anything, who got better looking with age, and could still sit a board while the judge...Well, suffice it to say the judge had been sitting the bench a little too long.

"Archer might do Billy some good," Josie pushed for her plan.

"Or scar him for life." Crawford shook his head and pushed off the desk. "Sorry, Josie. It's going to be forty-eight hours this time and community service. Best I can do."

"I'll appeal. There are a hundred surfers down on the beach changing from their wet suits into dry clothes every morning. Half of them don't even bother to drape a towel over their butts. The only reason you catch Billy is because he's stupid. He thinks everybody ought to just kick back – including the cops."

Crawford stood up, put the rest of the pizza in his little refrigerator, and plucked his windbreaker with the reflective patches off the door hook as he talked.

"That's cute. You still think you're playing with the big boys downtown? Josie, Josie," he chuckled. "What's it been? Three years and you still can't get it through your head that Billy Zuni and his little wooden monkey wouldn't rate the paperwork for an appeal. Let him be. They'll feed him good in Hermosa."

"Okay, so I can't put the fear of God into you." Josie shrugged and got to her feet.

"Only if you're on the other side of volleyball net, Ms. Bates. Only then." Judge Crawford ushered Josie outside with a quick gesture. She waited on the wooden walkway as he locked up.

The Redondo Courts were made up of low-slung, whitewashed, Cape Cod style buildings with marine blue trim. All the beach cities did business here. It was a far cry from downtown's imposing courthouses and city smells. Redondo Beach Court was perched on the outskirts of King Harbor Pier where the air smelled like salt and sun. Downtown attorneys fought holy wars, and life and death battles, while standing on marble floors inside wood paneled courtrooms. Here, court felt like hitting the town barbershop for a chaw with the mayor. Sometimes Josie missed being a crusader. The thought of one more local problem, and one more local client, made her long for what she once had been: a headline grabber, a tough cookie, a lawyer whose ambition and future knew no bounds. But that was just sometimes. Mostly, Josie Baylor-Bates was grateful that she no longer spoke for anyone who had enough money to pay her fee. She had learned that evil had the fattest wallet and most chaste face of all. Josie could not be seduced by either any more.

"You walking?" Judge Crawford called to her from the end of the walk.

"No." Josie ambled toward him.

"Want me to walk you to your car?" the judge offered.

"Don't worry about it. This isn't exactly a tough town, and if another Billy Zuni is hanging around I'll sign him up as a client."

"Okay. Let me know if you and Faye are in on that sponsorship for the Surf Festival."

"Will do," Josie answered and started to walk toward the parking lot. The judge stopped her.

"Hey, Josie, I forgot. Congratulations are in order. It's great that you're signing on as Faye's rainmaker."

Josie laughed, "We're going to be partners, Judge. I don't think there's a lot of rain to be made around here."

"Well, glad to hear it anyway. Baxter & Bates has a nice ring, and Faye's a good woman."

"Don't I know it," Josie said.

Faye Baxter was more than friend or peer; she was a champion, a confessor, a sweetheart who partnered with her husband until his death. Josie was honored that now Faye wanted her, and Josie was going to be the best damn partner she could be.

Waving to the judge, Josie crossed the deserted plaza, took the steps down to the lower level parking and tossed her things in the back of the Jeep. She was about to swing in when she caught the scent of cooking crab, the cacophony of arcade noise, the Friday night frantic fun of Redondo's King Harbor Pier and decided to take a minute. Wandering across the covered parking lot she exited onto the lower level of the two-storied pier complex.

The sun had been down for hours but it was still blister-hot. To her right the picnic tables in the open-air restaurants were filled. People whacked crabs with little silver hammers, sucked the meat from the shells, and made monumental messes. On the left, bells and whistles, and screams of laughter from the arcade. Out of nowhere three kids ran past, jabbering in Spanish, giggling in the universal language. Josie stepped forward but not far enough. A beehive of blue cotton candy caught her hip.

She brushed it away and walked on, drawn, not to the noise, but to the boats below the pier.

These were working craft that took sightseers into the harbor, pulled up the fish late at night; they had seen better days and were named after women and wishes. The boats were tethered to slips that creaked with the water's whim and bobbed above rocks puckered with barnacles. Josie loved the sense of silence, the feeling that each vessel held secrets, the dignity of even the smallest of them. The ropes that held these boats tight could just as easily break in an unexpected storm. They would drift away like people did if there was nothing to tie them down or hold them steady.

Josie leaned on the weather worn railing and lost her thoughts to the heat and the sounds and the look of that cool, dark water. At peace, she wasn't ready when something kicked up – a breeze, a bump of a hull – something familiar that threw her back in time. Emily Baylor-Bates was suddenly there. A vision in the water. The Lady of the Lake. Yet instead of the sacred sword, the image of Josie's mother held out sharp-edged memories. Josie should have walked away, but she never did when Emily came to call.

Even after all these years she could see her mother's face clearly in that water. Emily's eyes were like Josie's but bluer, wider, and clearer. They shared the square-jaw and high cheekbones, but the whole of Emily's face was breathtakingly beautiful, where her daughter's was strikingly handsome. Her mother's hair was black-brown with streaks of red and gold. Josie's was chestnut. Her expression was determined like Josie's but…but what?

What was her mother determined to do? What had been more important than a husband and a daughter *A good daughter, damn it.* What made her mother – even now after all these years she could barely think the word – *abandon* her? Why would a woman cast off a fourteen year old without a word, or a touch? There one night, gone the next morning.

Suddenly the water was disturbed. Emily Baylor-Bates' face disappeared in the rings of ever widening concentric circles. Startled, Josie stood up straight. Above her a group of teenagers hung over the railing dropping things into the water. They laughed cruelly thinking they had frightened Josie, unaware that she was grateful to them. The water was mesmerizing, the memories as dangerous as an undertow. Emily had been gone for twenty-six years. *Twenty-six years*, Josie reminded herself as she strode to the parking lot, swung into her Jeep, turned the key, and backed out. The wheels squealed on the slick concrete. She knew a hundred years wouldn't make her care less. Time wouldn't dull the pain or keep her from wanting to call her mother back. On her deathbed, Josie would still be wondering where her mother was, why she had gone, whether she was dead, or just didn't give a shit about her daughter. But tonight, in the eleven minutes it took to drive from Redondo Beach to Hermosa Beach, Josie put those questions back into that box deep inside her mind. By the time she tossed her keys on the table and ruffled Max-The-Dog's beautiful old face, that box was locked up tight.

The dog rewarded Josie with a sniff and a lick against her cheek. It took five minutes to finish the routine: working clothes gone, sweats and t-shirt on, and her mail checked. Faye had dropped off the partnership papers before leaving for San Diego and a visit with her new grandson. The tile man had piled a ton of Spanish pavers near the backdoor for Josie to lay at her leisure. The house of her dreams – a California bungalow on the Strand – was being renovated at a snail's pace, but Josie was determined to do the work herself. She would make her own home; a place where no one invited in would ever want to leave.

In the kitchen, Josie checked out a nearly empty fridge as she dialed Archer. It was late, but if he were home it wouldn't take much to convince him that he needed to feed her. Josie was punching the final digits of Archer's number when Max rubbed up against her leg, wuffing and pointing his graying snout toward the front door. Josie looked over her shoulder and patted his head, but Max woofed again. She was just about to murmur her assurances when the house seemed to rock. Snarling, Max fell back on his haunches. Josie let out a shout. Someone had thrown themselves against the front door, and whoever was out there wanted in bad. The new door was solid, the deadbolt impossible to break, but the sound scared the shit out of her. The doorknob jiggled frantically for a second before everything fell quiet – everything except Josie's heart and Max's guttural growl.

Bending down, Josie buried one hand in the fur and folds of his head. With the other she picked up the claw hammer from the tool pile. Standing, she smiled at Max. His eyebrows undulated, silently asking if everything was all right now. For an instant Josie thought it might be, until whoever was out there flew at the door with both fists.

"Damn." Josie jumped. Max fell back again, snapping and barking.

Clutching the hammer, Josie sidestepped to the door. She slipped two fingers under the curtain covering the narrow side-window and pulled the fabric back a half an inch. A woman twirled near the hedge. Her head whipped from side to side as she looked for a way into the house. Her white slacks fit like a second skin, and her chiffon blouse crisscrossed over an impressive chest. A butter colored belt draped over her slim hips. Her come-fuck-me sandals had crepe-thin soles and heels as high as a wedding cake. This wasn't a Hermosa Beach babe and Josie had two choices: call the cops or find out what kind of trouble this woman was in. No contest. Josie flipped the lock and threw open the door.

The woman froze; trembling as if surprised to find someone had actually answered. She started forward and raised her hand, took a misstep and crumpled. Instinctively, Josie reached for her. The hammer fell to the floor as the woman clutched at Josie's arm.

"You're here," she breathed.

Close up now, Josie saw her more clearly. The dark hair was longer than she remembered. The heart-shaped face was still perfect save for the tiny scar on the corner of her wide lips. Those long fingered hands that held Josie were as strong as they'd always been. But it was the high arch of the woman's eyebrows and her small, exquisitely green eyes that did more than prick Josie's memory; they shot an arrow clear through it. It had been almost twenty years since Josie had seen those eyes, and the face that looked like a heroine from some Russian revolutionary epic.

"Linda? Linda Sheraton?"
"Oh, God, Josie, please help me."

CHAPTER 2

The last time Josie Baylor-Bates saw Linda Sheraton they were twenty years old and sharing a cheap apartment in downtown Los Angeles. Both were on a USC athletic scholarship, and both were poor as church mice. Josie, for all intents and purposes, was orphaned. Linda hailed from a trailer park, raised by a mother who didn't give a damn if her daughter ended up in poverty or Princeton. That was where the similarities ended.

Josie cleaned fraternity houses to make ends meet; Linda dated the fraternity. Linda would rather dance the night away than crack a book. Josie knew law school wouldn't consider bar hopping a fine arts credit. Linda was hard living, sure of herself, plain talking, and smart as a whip. Unfortunately, her whip didn't crack for academia unless it had to.

She could talk anyone into anything – teachers into grades, boys into adoration, men into gifts, and Josie into setting her up on the volleyball court so that she, Linda, came away looking like a star. It wasn't hard to figure out why men succumbed to Linda's particular brand of charm. There was a strong, sinewy animal beauty about her; a beauty that promised more than she ever intended to deliver. The one thing Josie could never figure out was why she had fallen for the act. Maybe it was because Linda Sheraton made you feel like she deserved the favor, as if she would reward you twofold if you came through for her just once. Josie pulled Linda's ass out of one fire after another, thanking her lucky stars that Linda never asked her to do anything illegal or immoral. Luckily, two things happened before Linda did ask: Josie got a clue and Linda took off.

Three months into their junior year Linda hooked up with a guy from France leaving Josie with an apartment she couldn't afford, a pile of phone bills, and a couple pair of jeans. Josie wore the jeans, got a second job to make the rent, and had the phone disconnected. Sometimes Josie wondered about Linda when she sat at Burt's at the Beach, watching the sweet young things snuggle up to a potential meal ticket. Now Josie didn't have to wonder what happened to Linda Sheraton. Something, or someone, had caught up with her. Despite the clothes, the jewelry and the make-up, she was a mess, and scared to death.

With a snap of her fingers, Josie backed Max off to his rug in the corner. In a jumble of questions and answers she settled Linda on the couch, determined she wasn't hurt or in imminent danger, then left her long enough to grab a bottle of scotch and a glass from the kitchen. She poured two fingers and handed the glass to Linda.

"Thanks."

The glass quivered as Linda knocked back half the drink, sank deeper in the couch and tried to get a grip. Josie sat in the leather chair and put the bottle on the table between them.

"Do you have an ashtray?"

Linda's deep, pebbly voice shook. Her eyes darted around the living room. Spare of furnishing, there were blueprints and books spread over the desk in the corner near the picture window. Linda seemed to see nothing as she fidgeted with the buckle on her belt and the stitching on the couch cushion. Josie got up, found an empty beer can in the trash and put it on the coffee table.

"You don't mind..."

Linda put her drink aside, fumbled in her purse, found her pack, tapped one out, and finally put a cigarette between her lips. Her lipstick had faded, leaving only a faint outline of claret colored pencil. Her hand, and the cigarette in it, trembled as she snapped a silver lighter open. It took three times to catch but finally there was flame. Linda sucked hard and the tip glowed red. She held it away and blew out a plume of smoke while Josie studied her. Three of Linda's knuckles were scraped but they weren't bleeding. Her clothes were messed, but not torn. She seemed to tremble more with outrage than fear.

Finally, Linda tossed the lighter back in her purse, reached for her glass and shot the scotch. One more puff and she dropped the cigarette into the can. It sizzled in the last swallow of beer and died.

"I almost didn't recognize you. It's been awhile," Josie said.

"Yeah, well, you haven't changed." Linda eyed Josie's sweat pants, and the muscle shirt from Gold's Gym that Josie had pulled over her sports bra. "I should have known I'd find you in a place like this. You must still be playing volleyball."

"Pick up games," Josie answered.

She didn't ask if Linda still played. The cut of her clothes, the length of her nails, and the paleness of her skin spoke volumes. Linda wasn't really interested anyway. Her observation was a reaction; Josie was the physical manifestation of word association. Linda licked her lips as if her mouth were dry. Josie nodded toward the glass. Linda pushed it across the table, leaning forward as she did so. Josie did the same.

"Still getting in over your head?" Josie asked while she poured.

"You have no idea," Linda whispered, holding her drink in both hands. She didn't look at Josie when she said: "My kid – my daughter – she's been arrested for murder, Josie."

"Where?"

"In Santa Monica," Linda said.

"Christ."

Josie reached out to touch Linda. Women did that during trying times. But this time the connection wasn't made. Neither of them were that kind of woman. Josie's way was like her father's. Figure out the problem. Deal with it. Linda's way was to stand removed until she figured out who was with her, and who was against her.

"Who do they say she killed?"

"Fritz Rayburn," Linda answered.

"Justice Rayburn? The California Supreme Court Justice?"

There wasn't much that shocked Josie anymore, but this did. There had been no hint that the fire was suspicious much less the jurist's death. Linda poured herself another double. It was gone before Josie could blink. Linda came up for air and looked into the empty glass as if it was a crystal ball.

"The one and only Fritz Rayburn. The governor's buddy. Beloved of all lawyers. Champion of the underling. Soft spoken, confident, fearless, witty, brilliant, perfect California Supreme Court Justice, Fritz Rayburn." Linda raised her glass in a cheerless toast. "That's who the cops say my kid killed."

"Oh, my God," Josie breathed.

"I couldn't have said it better myself." Linda cocked her head and gave Josie a small, wretched smile. "I'm talking mega trouble, Josie. The Goddamn Vice President came to Fritz's funeral. They were talking about nominating him to the real Supreme Court if any of those old shits ever died. The cardinal said the mass. There were a thousand people in that cathedral, and those were only the ones that were invited."

"What's this got to do with your daughter?" Josie got up, grabbed a cold beer and popped it on her way back. Linda hadn't missed a beat.

"Fritz Rayburn was my father-in-law. He was down from San Francisco for the summer break. When he was here he stayed in an apartment at the Palisades house or at the place in Malibu. We were all in the Palisades the night of the fire."

Linda's fingers trailed over the deep cut of her blouse and found their way to the side of her jaw. She leaned into the touch nonchalantly, her posture a strange contrast to the twitching of her eye, the taut cording of her neck muscles.

"Hannah – my daughter – she didn't like it in the Palisades. She's city all the way. Independent. She didn't particularly like Fritz, but to say she killed him is just plain ridiculous."

"When was she arrested?" Josie took a long drink but the beer tasted wrong.

"Just now. Tonight. We got home from the funeral. I changed. My husband and I were going out to dinner to...to talk about something important."

Linda ran the back of her hand under her nose. She shook out her hair. This was the way she used to act when she had to pull herself together for competition. Linda was at her best under pressure. The near-tears were gone; the face she turned toward Josie had fixed to a look of brutal resolve.

"You've got to get her out of this mess, Josie. Hannah is sixteen, she's scared and she's innocent. I want you to get her out of that God damn jail tonight."

Josie rested her arms on her knees, the beer dangling between her legs. She remembered what she hadn't liked about Linda Sheraton-Rayburn. She demanded. She expected. She wanted. Under any other circumstances Josie would have shown her the door. But whether or not her daughter was guilty, Linda was in for a lot of pain. For that Josie was truly sorry and she was sorry she couldn't help.

"There's nothing I can do, Linda. Your daughter's been processed. She is in for the night."

"Don't give me that. I busted my butt tracking you down tonight because I knew if anyone could help, you could."

"This isn't college, Linda. I can't just fast-talk a problem away." Josie put her beer on the side table.

"Besides, I don't work with juveniles. You need some who specializes..."

"Don't tell me what I friggin' need." Linda whacked the coffee table with both hands. The sound cracked through the house. Max's head came up. Linda's face was white with rage.

"Hey," Josie warned, "Take it down some, or take it somewhere else."

Linda may be in trouble, but this was Josie's turf. Maybe not the kind she used to claim, but nobody told her what to do here. Linda, though, didn't give up so easily. She shoved aside the glass, the bottle, and the makeshift ashtray, as if she was clearing the field for battle.

"Okay. Okay. Last I heard you were hot stuff. I mean you got that woman off a couple of years ago and she was guilty as sin. My kid is innocent and I need someone I can trust, damn it. You're not too big to help an old friend who really needs it, are you, Josie?"

"I'm not too big for anything, Linda. I just don't handle the kind of case you're talking about."

Josie looked away. Linda moved her head trying to retain eye contact, doing her best to cajole.

"But you could, couldn't you? I mean, there aren't any rules about that sort of thing, right?"

"No. Nothing like that."

"Then name your price, Josie. Money isn't a problem. I've got enough to buy and sell you. I've got....I've got..."

That was as far as she went. Whatever truth or pity she saw in Josie's eyes it was enough to make Linda stop. Her voice caught. When she spoke again she was begging.

"Please. I've got no one else. My baby didn't do it. I swear. She didn't do it."

CHAPTER 3

Josie's memories spiraled in snippets and snatches.

Big case. Terrified defendant. Protestations of innocence. Josie as champion. Television cameras. Crime scene photos. Interviews. Points of law. Fearful testimony. Children waiting for their mother and the world waiting for the jury.

Worst of all – victory.

Back then Josie believed everyone deserved a defense. Then she met the one woman who didn't. Kristin Davis played Josie like a fine fiddle until every string snapped. Josie who believed that a mother could do no wrong; Josie who looked at Kristin's children and promised to send their mother back home. She should have seen through Kristin Davis. But that was past, and the present had its own set of compelling quick cuts and consequences.

A sixteen-year-old kid in prison for murder. A desperate mother. An old friend. Innocence. Guilt. Who knew? Fire. Fame. Fortune. The eyes of a state – perhaps the country – focused on her through the lens of a television camera. Josie didn't want to be evaluated, critiqued, or judged for standing center stage as crime became entertainment. She did not want to speak for someone who could have, might have, or maybe did the unthinkable. Josie had had enough of that to last a lifetime.

"You're Fritz Rayburn's daughter-in-law, Linda. Call his firm. Talk to your friends. That's the kind of power you need."

"I already did that." She shook her head. "I spoke to Ian Frank, Fritz's old partner. That firm is filled with civil attorneys. They deal in big money. And there are – problems – extenuating circumstances."

"What about Hannah's father?" Josie dared Linda to cut off another avenue of opportunity.

"What about him?"

"He must know good criminal attorneys through his father," Josie insisted.

"Hannah's father took off before I even got the word pregnant out of my mouth. I married Kip Rayburn two years ago. He's Hannah's stepfather. Even I know this isn't the best time to ask him to run interference for Hannah."

Linda's bottom lip disappeared under her top teeth. She put her hand against the wall near the window, looking out as if she was expecting someone. It wasn't a person she was looking for but a decision she had to make. Finally she looked at Josie.

"Okay, I'll be honest. There are business considerations, careers to worry about and Hannah is a small cog in a very big wheel. When Fritz took the bench he had to put his partnership into trust so there wouldn't be any conflict of interest. That didn't keep the firm from trading on Fritz's reputation. It meant high profile clients because an original partner was a California Supreme Court Justice."

Linda put both hands on the back of an overstuffed chair. Her nails poked into the fabric. Her voice dropped another octave.

"Before the funeral we found out that the governor is going to appoint Kip to his father's seat on the California Supreme Court. He was going to announce it in the next few days while emotions still ran high for Fritz. A legacy goes on kind of thing. The firm keeps trading on its association with the highest court in the state, money keeps rolling in, and power is consolidated in their little dynasty. So we go to the funeral. The governor is checking out how Kip handles himself. It goes well. Then Hannah gets arrested and it's everybody for themselves.

"When I asked for help they say they have to think. How is this going to affect Kip's appointment, the firm's bottom line? They distance themselves. Hannah and me are left swinging in the wind. I understand how business works and I love my husband, Josie. I respect the tough spot he's in, but my daughter is a child and she needs help now. So I'm doing what I've got to do."

"And your husband doesn't mind the firm is treating you this way?" Josie asked.

Linda shook her head, exhausted. "Right now I don't know what he thinks. Everything happened so fast. He just kept asking how they knew his father was murdered. How did they know? I mean, he thought the old guy died in an accident. It was like somebody put Kip on a roller coaster and didn't strap him in. He's mourning his father one minute, being tapped for the court the next, and then he finds out the cops think someone deliberately took his dad's life. It's a mess. Everyone's out for themselves. I don't have a whole lot of time to figure out how much a stranger will get behind my kid. You're not a stranger. I want you to help her."

Josie got up and turned toward her bedroom.

"Okay. I've got a couple of favors to call in. I'll get my book."

Linda moved fast, crossing the living room, pulling Josie back.

"No. I want you to do it. I know you. You wouldn't let her suffer. You know what it's like to be a kid who's afraid. You know what it's like to be alone."

"This isn't the same, Linda. You're helping your daughter, not running away from her. Besides, for all I know she could have done it." Josie pulled away. Some part of her was flattered by Linda's confidence, another was wary.

"And what would it matter?" Linda threw her hands up in frustration. "She's still entitled to a defense. That's the law. Isn't that right?"

"It doesn't say she's entitled to me," Josie answered flatly.

"But she didn't do it, Josie. Nobody did. It was an accident. Someone's making a terrible mistake. Josie, you were never mean or cruel. Don't be now. My whole family is in turmoil. Hannah's my baby," Linda cried. She babbled, trying to find the magic that would make Josie change her mind. "She was terrified getting on that bus, being taken away from me. I followed them all the way out to Sybil Brand and they wouldn't let me in. She's alone. Help her. Stop making excuses and help us, damn it."

Linda's fingers dug into Josie's arms again. Her long nails were sharp but the rest of her was losing ground.

Linda's deep voice caught. She whispered frantically, pleading as only a mother can do.

"Do it just this once, Josie. Just go see Hannah. That's all I'm asking. If you saw her, you'd help her. The last thing you'd want is for a kid to be alone and scared."

They stood eye to eye, both of them taller than most men, both of them fascinatingly attractive, and both locked in an emotional tug of war.

"They took her to Sybil Brand?" Josie asked cautiously.

Linda nodded slowly, her face a play of concern and questions.

"They said she couldn't be released until they had a bail hearing because of the charges. That's not going to be 'till Monday. Josie, what is it?"

"Juvenile offenders are taken to East Lake, Linda, not Sybil Brand. Your daughter is in the women's jail. The DA is going to charge her as an adult."

"What does that mean?"

"That means she's looking at hard time if she's convicted. Chowchilla prison, somewhere like that. No sealed records. No short-term juvenile facility." Josie dug deep to find the courage to give Linda the worst-case scenario. "If the DA tacks on special circumstances he could conceivably ask for the death penalty."

❧

Linda was gone by eleven, leaving behind her phone number, her address, and a retainer. Josie put the retainer check in the top drawer of her desk. It could be torn up as easily as cashed, but right now she didn't want to see it. She just wanted to think.

Leashing Max they walked to the Strand, crossing the bike path, wandering on to the sand. Josie headed north, wondering why she'd agreed to see Hannah Sheraton, and knowing it didn't take a rocket scientist to come up with the answer.

Tomorrow a sixteen-year-old kid would wake up scared and stay that way until this thing played out. Hannah Sheraton may never get over what was happening to her, but Josie could at least make sure there was an end to the ordeal. If Linda had needed help Josie would have made that referral. This, though, was a child. This, Josie was drawn to.

Wanting to root around a bit, Max pulled Josie left. The moon was high, the tide low, and the heat heavy. In the distance, party music mixed with the thin wail of sirens. The music belonged to Hermosa, the sirens to some bigger, more impersonal, more challenging place. Thank God she didn't belong to the sirens anymore. Josie looked back at the place that was now her hometown. Hermosa meant beautiful beach. The place used to be a sweep of hills dotted with sheep and barley fields that stretched all the way to the Pacific. Now it was 1.3 miles of small hotels, houses, restaurants, and people who believed in letting everyone be. When it came to crime, Billie Zuni was as bad a dude as the place could come up with. In December there was a sand snowman contest, in August the Surf Festival. In the sixties, the city declared itself a wild bird sanctuary. Little did the founding fathers know that wild birds weren't the only ones who would find sanctuary in this place.

Josie kicked at the sand and gave Max's ancient leash a tug. Hot pink, worn to shreds, it was still clipped to his collar when she found him half starved under the pier. Josie wouldn't buy a new one. That leash might mean something to Max, the same way her mother's hula-girl plates meant something to Josie. She tugged again. It was time to go, just not time to go home. Linda had kicked up a lot of dust, and Josie needed someone to help her clear it. There was only one person she knew who had twenty/twenty vision when it came to navigating the storms of indecision.

She headed to Archer's place.

It took Linda Rayburn forty-seven minutes to get to the Malibu house. She parked the car, retrieved her shoes and purse from the passenger side floor, didn't bother to lock the doors, and didn't care if the hems of her very expensive slacks got dirty.

She walked through the gate, ignoring the impressive entrance. It had grown ordinary like so many things Linda once found intimidating and fascinating about the Rayburn's world. Not that she would trade it. Not that she disliked it. All this stuff was like air: essential and expected, missed only when taken away. She let herself in to the house. Every light was on and the damn thing was quiet as a mausoleum. The shoes and purse were left on the floor for the housekeeper to pick up in the morning.

Linda looked in the kitchen, though she doubted that's where Kip would be. She checked the living room. The glare of the lights made her feel like a walking corpse. She slipped the belt from her hips and tugged her blouse out of her slacks as she went.

The pool lights were on and the floods, too. The dining room with its long glass table and twelve high backed stainless steel and silk chairs shivered with reflected light.

Having searched downstairs there was nowhere to go but up. Resisting the desire to get in bed, close her eyes, and make everything go away, Linda climbed the stairs and walked down the long hall. The gigantic unframed oils that Fritz had been so fond of now looked crass and ridiculous. So much black cut by random slashes of red that looked like open wounds on the dark skin of the canvas. Fritz may have been smart about the law, but his taste in art sucked. What was he thinking hanging those things on the smooth white walls of the Malibu house? Hannah's paintings would have been better. At least she used more than two colors. In fact, right now, Linda would burn all of Fritz's big, ugly, highbrow stuff herself, just to have a little bit of Hannah around.

Linda was at the end of the hall just outside *The Room*. That's what they called it. Not Fritz's room, not the library, just *The Room*. It was where the chronicles of Fritz's life were kept: pictures of Fritz with governors, senators, and even a president or two. Fritz with celebrity lawyers. Fritz with foster children. Fritz, Fritz. Fritz. Pens and plaques, embossed portfolios. Fritz, Fritz, Fritz's place. Little sculptures of judges made of bronze and wood. Gavels sprouted off polished wood surfaces. He hadn't used the room in years and yet it remained untouched. It was a shrine while he lived; God knew what it was supposed to be now that he was dead, now that Kip was in there.

Linda composed herself. There was no door to the room, only a short hall that opened up onto a big space. Linda walked through and hovered at the end. The room was dim, only the desk light was on. Two of the four walls were made of glass. The half moon hung like a piece of artwork in the middle of one of them. Kip sat in Fritz's chair looking as if he'd wandered out of a Norman Rockwell illustration and into a Dali landscape.

Linda shivered. She liked neither Rockwell nor Dali. She liked Kip the way he used to be. Before all this he was his own blank canvas. She liked the Kip who relied on her or Fritz for definition. But Fritz wasn't here anymore, the governor was holding out the things Kip wanted – power, attention, notoriety of his own – and she wasn't the same woman who had left the house earlier that evening. For the first time, the next step in Linda's life wasn't clear.

Kip didn't look at her when she came in. He barely moved as he methodically picked up, looked at, and placed his father's things in a box on the side of the desk. Linda felt him vibrating, radiating frustration and anger. It rolled around the room like a Dervish.

"I don't want to talk, Linda," he said quietly, his voice trembling.

"We have to talk."

"No," Kip held up his hand, "we don't"

"Then what do you want to do? Just sit and wait until we know what ever it is that they know? You want to wait for other people to make their moves before we do? You want to pretend this isn't happening?"

Linda started toward the desk but stopped short. The usual ministrations wouldn't work to soothe him. He didn't want to be touched. She couldn't coax him to bed. He had been changing ever since Fritz died. It hadn't been unattractive or unwanted – until now. Linda backed off, holding herself in check. She would tread carefully until she had the lay of the land. She talked, thinking on her feet.

"You're right. I'm sorry. I'm sorry. I just can't believe this is happening. Everything was going so well," she held out her hands to stop him from interrupting. "But we can control this situation. I spoke to an attorney about Hannah. She's an old friend. She'll get Hannah out of jail. Once that happens we'll send her away to school. Lots of people have problem kids. Everyone will forget about this. My attorney won't bring you, or the firm, into this. She'll deal with this discreetly."

"Discreetly?" In the blink of an eye Kip was up, standing behind the desk, his plain features contorted into disbelief and rage. He picked up a picture of his father and hurled it across the room. Not at her. Luckily, not at her. "How in the hell do you figure the murder of a California Supreme Court Justice can be handled discreetly? When they thought this was an accident nobody was discreet. We won't be able to sneeze without people trying to figure out what goes on in this house. They're going to want a reason Hannah was arrested and if they can't find one they'll make it up. Hannah caused problems from the minute she walked through the door. For my father. For me. Even for you. But now she's going to ruin my life."

"Okay. All right," Linda screamed. She backed up. Afraid of her husband for the first time since she met him, Linda would never let him know. "You've always wanted her gone. Do you want me gone, too? You're such a big man now you don't need me? If that's what you're saying then I'm out of here. I'll take care of myself and I sure as hell won't care who gets taken down if they prosecute my kid."

Kip put his hands on one of Fritz's awards. It was a heavy thing made of crystal and wood. Even in the dim light Linda could see his arms shaking with the tension of his pent up emotions. He fought with himself wanting to lift it, throw it, and cradle it to his breast.

"It was supposed to be my time. I was making it my time. I was standing up…it was all for you and me."

Linda Rayburn watched her husband implode. Slowly he sank back into the chair, his hands still around the hunk of glass and wood. He lowered his head until it rested on the cool wedge of crystal. Linda bowed her own, her hair covering her face, her shoulders slumping. Maybe they were all lost. Finally, Linda raised her head. Her eyes narrowed. Inside there was a sliver of steel left. A little gift from her mother who made Linda what she was –a damn survivor. Linda was going to share that gift with Kip because the last thing she wanted to do was leave.

Slowly she walked toward her husband and wrapped her arms around his head. She pulled him into her. His arms went around her waist as she buried her lips in his hair.

"I know what you did for me. I know what it cost you," she whispered.

"You do?"

"Yes, and I was proud. And now you've got to stay brave and see this through," Linda said.

"I can, but you've got to help me now," Kip mumbled. "You owe me that. After everything I've done. After all the risks I took for you. You owe me, not her. I hate her. It's my turn now."

Linda's heart turned to stone. Just when she thought life was going to be easy it took the cruelest turn of all. She hadn't even wanted one and now she had two children pointing at her, making her part excuse, part reason, part inspiration for the things they did. It wasn't fair.

Linda sighed and caressed Kip's hair. She would do what she could. She'd push Kip to his limit and make him find his courage again. She'd be smart, she'd watch and wait, and move only when it was necessary. But in the end, if Hannah didn't do her part, they were all screwed.

CHAPTER 4

Josie woke up at six with the sun in her eyes, the smell of Archer all around. It was in the sheets, on her body, in the scent of the dark coffee he preferred, the piquant smell of the chemicals he used in his darkroom. The sense of him was everywhere. In the way his clothes were hung precisely in the closet, and in the book of forensic techniques that lay open on the bedside. Once a cop, always a cop. On the bookshelf, a rosary hung over the neck of an empty bottle of tequila. It was a long story. Short version: Archer found religion one night while a buddy lost his. He said he kept the rosary to remind him to play savior only when it was a sure thing. Josie didn't believe him. He could never be so calculating. He had saved her, and she wasn't a sure thing. Josie threw an arm over her eyes for a second, and then rolled onto her side to touch the place where he had slept. The sheets were cold. He'd been gone for a while.

Josie got out of bed and searched for her clothes. She found her muscle shirt and panties but the sweats and sports bra were missing in action. She shimmied into what she had, glanced at the picture of Lexi, Archer's dead wife, and then went looking for the man they shared. She found him on the rooftop balcony, a perk of owning the building.

"Morning," Josie walked up behind him and wound her arms around his waist. He was a big man; made her feel downright dainty. She loved the smell of his shirt. Starched and pressed by the man who wore it.

"Don't move," he commanded.

Josie didn't but only because she didn't want to. She held her breath, loving the feel of him when he was excited by what he saw through his lens. His gut tightened beneath her hands. A solitary muscle rippled. Quick like a snake. A click. He sighed with satisfaction and stood up slowly, surveying the beach once more before turning around to kiss Josie. She kissed him back just long enough for them both to be happy. When she slipped out of his arms, he let her go. No nonsense. No jealousy. No neediness. Respect. Affection. Comfort. Chemistry. It was the kind of relationship people who could take care of themselves did well.

Archer and Josie did it extremely well.

They met a year ago. Archer snapped a picture of her at the pro-am volleyball tournament. She had her hand on her hip, baseball hat on backwards, sunglasses covering her eyes. When the picture was printed, Josie was pleased. She could see her six-pack abs, the ropes of muscles in her legs, and the fine definition of her biceps. Archer said that wasn't what he saw. He saw her glaring at him from behind those glasses, unhappy that she had lost a critical point, determined she wouldn't lose the next one. He knew they would be more than good friends. It took Josie a month longer to figure it out.

"You want more coffee?" Josie picked up the thermal pot to pour herself a cup. He shook his head. Josie and her coffee joined him by the balcony railing.

"I got the sun coming up. I picked up some woman skinny dipping around five." Archer lifted his chin to indicate the surf. Josie looked at him. He had a wonderful profile. He looked like an Irish boxer: strong jawed, short, straight nose, eyes that were dark and close together. Those eyes held a person tight in his line of sight. His was a man's face and a man's body. He didn't own a suit. He was as different from the men Josie used to date as Baxter & Associates was from the kind of law she used to practice. What had she seen in those men in designer suits? Josie leaned into him, playfully banging his shoulder with her own.

"You're going to get sued one of these days when somebody sees themselves on a postcard or in a magazine."

"I know a good lawyer. She wouldn't let me down." He pushed back. Not a hint of a smile. It wasn't his way. He smiled with his eyes, with his touch. Josie knew when Archer was happy. It was the same way he showed hurt and anger and compassion – with his eyes, with his touch.

"I wouldn't count on that," Josie said wryly. "I might decide you're not worth it one of these days."

Archer put a big hand on the back of her neck and followed up with a kiss. He pulled Josie into him, draping his arm over her shoulder.

"This from a woman who lets herself in and has her way with me in the middle of the night? I think I can count on her."

Josie sipped her coffee and stayed nestled against him. He waited just long enough, and then gave her the nudge she seemed to want.

"So? You weren't exactly talkative last night."

Josie chuckled softly. The truth was they hadn't exchanged two words. Archer once told her that he could tell what she needed by the way she came to bed. If Josie wanted to talk she crawled in already debating. When she needed something else – something more personal – she came in quietly, stayed close, he could hear her thinking. He even seemed to know whether it was old troubles, or new, that had to be dealt with.

Then there were the nights like last night. It wasn't sleep she wanted, or talking she needed. Josie needed to clear her mind so she could rest, and Archer had a way of making that happen.

"I had a visitor last night..." Josie began, training her eyes on the runner of sand and the never-ending carpet of blue ocean as she filled him in.

Twenty minutes later they were sitting in the beach chairs on the balcony sharing a bagel, Josie's coffee was cold and her story was over. Archer knew it all: Linda, the history, the girl, the charge, the victim, the retainer – impressive – and the fact that the next move was Josie's.

"You told her you were going to check it out. So check it out."

"Jesus, Archer. You know how I feel about murder – women involved in murder. It's not that easy."

Josie took a bite out of the bagel. She wasn't hungry; she just didn't relish trying to explain again why it wasn't easy. But Archer had made his living investigating criminals, so lawyers were not a great challenge.

"Why not?" He laced his hands behind his head and looked right at her.

Most people found it uncomfortable to look Archer in the eye. They said his eyes were flat, cold and judgmental. Josie always thought of his gaze as a level playing field.

"Because it opens a can of worms. If she's innocent, she's going up against a lot – the press and the DA who really wants a pound of flesh and who knows how the governor's office will play into all this. If she's guilty and I get an acquittal, I don't think I could live with myself. It's sort of like being an ex-nun. I still believe in God, I just don't think He's omnipotent. Besides, it's been a long time since I put together a defense like this." Josie put her fingers to her mouth. She didn't exactly bite her nails but she came close.

"You handled really big cases for sixteen years before you came here," Archer reminded her.

"Linda's a friend," Josie countered.

"She's an acquaintance. If she was a friend I would have heard about her."

"Okay. Okay. Then there's the fact that this is a juvenile matter." Josie held up her hand. "And before you say anything about her being charged as an adult it's still a child we're talking about. I don't know what to do with a kid."

"You know what to do with a client, Josie."

Archer snapped the pedal of his black racing bike he kept on the roof, instead of the garage. The garage was full of files from old cases, keepsakes from the house he shared with Lexi, and a Hummer. That vehicle was a man's hunk of metal that could go anywhere he thought there might be a picture or a perp. Archer watched the pedal twirl for a minute and then looked at her.

"When Lexi died I didn't want to look at another woman. Then you stood right in front of me. I couldn't ignore you and that caused a lot of pain, Jo. I had to figure out if I was happier being with a live woman or living with the memories of a dead one. Do you think you don't miss what you used to do? Maybe this thing is a test. Go see this girl. If you feel hinky, walk away. Just do it because it's the right choice."

"Good job, Archer. Make me feel like two cents. I'm not afraid if that's what you think. I could go down there. I could see this girl and make up my mind."

"Then do it. That's all the mother is asking."

"No. You don't know Linda. She's expecting me to make the trouble go away," Josie objected.

"Who cares what she expects? I'm just saying that if you turn your back now, you'll never look in the mirror the same way again."

"Says you, Archer." Josie pushed herself off the beach chair. She should be on the beach picking up a game, checking on Billy, or laying all that tile. She should be biking to Santa Monica with Archer. She shouldn't even be thinking about dead people and murderers, innocence and guilt, and the thousand ways she knew to spin evidence to make her story sound like God's own truth. And Archer should be a little more helpful. He could at least concede she had a reason to be cautious. When he didn't, Josie bailed.

"I'm going home."

As she walked past, Archer reached up and took her arm.

"You should know what you're made of, Josie. Everybody should know that."

"See you tomorrow." Josie kissed him on top of his head. "Or maybe next week."

She found the rest of her clothes in the bedroom, dressed, and collected Max. If it had just been her, Josie would have hustled down the three flights of stairs. With Max, it took a little longer. On the Strand, Hermosa was coming alive. Rollerbladers, walkers, a mother pushing a stroller, people sipping coffee, reading their paper, and surfers straddling their boards, waiting for the wave they could ride, or the one that would drown them.

Josie didn't bother to watch and see which it would be. She felt her own wave coming and she wasn't ready.

&

From the rooftop balcony Archer leaned on the railing and watched Josie go. He didn't bother to turn the tripod and take a picture of her. He never liked to take pictures of people walking away so he just watched Josie as the early morning people turned to look at her. She was so tall and striking, tanned and confident. He also saw she walked just a little too fast for comfort and not fast enough for exercise, she kept old Max close to her like a friend along to help her find her way in a strange place.

But Hermosa wasn't strange. It was the call of an old, frightening, fascinating place that had Josie Baylor-Bates spooked. Archer could have talked her through it, past it, or out of it, but he didn't. That woman had been fooling herself for a long time. Josie thought she chose to live near the beach in Hermosa and work in a neighborhood law firm because she was disillusioned. That was a lie. Josie had run to Hermosa, hidden her head in the sand of Faye Baxter's little law firm. Now somebody was tugging on her head, and she was trying to keep it stuck in the sand.

Archer took a deep breath and looked away. She was almost out of sight and there was nothing he could do for her now except wait for her to come back. Much as he wanted to go with her, stand guard when she came face to face with that kid, he wouldn't.

Instead, Archer put himself behind the camera and turned it back to the sea. That's how much he loved her.

"Playing devil's advocate." Alex held up his hand. "Can't we pick up those dollars somewhere else? One of the unions maybe? Then we could look for someone with a little more star quality for that slot on the bench."

Davidson himself dismissed that plan.

"It's getting too hot to hit the unions up again. I don't want any more of those 'legislation for dollars' news stories. Kip brings quiet money. Kip's appointment won't look like payback."

"We're dancing around the real benefit. Kip is president of the CLA," Cheryl reminded them.

"He's a hell of an administrator," Alex agreed. "The California Litigator's Association has been real happy with him. Those guys have the bucks and Kip's the main man. He's an easy sell to the public and a moneymaker. There's no downside, so I say we announce tomorrow and minimize coverage of the girl's arrest."

The governor toyed with his glass. His face was long and colorless, his expression unreadable. Finally, he spoke.

"Kip understands we're expecting a lot from him in terms of support during the election and before he takes the bench, right?"

Alex nodded, "Absolutely. Until he takes the oath he raises funds. After that, no impropriety, just association."

"Exactly. Letter of the law is important." the governor mused. "Just to be safe, call Kip. Tell him we'd like a few days before the announcement. Bring me a poll analysis by, say, Monday afternoon. If it's good, I'll announce."

Cheryl and Alex nodded. Cheryl would do a quick and dirty poll, check with Kip, and write a press release to have at the ready. Alex would contact donors and feel them out. If everyone was happy, Kip's appointment would move ahead.

"One more thing." Cheryl hesitated before leaving the hotel room.

"What?" The governor was focused on his ever-present notepad now that breakfast was over.

"The girl. Shouldn't we say something about the girl?"

"The purpose?" the governor asked.

"She's only sixteen. They would expect you to say something about her," Cheryl suggested.

"What's our stand on juvenile offenders in the admission of a felony?" Davidson asked offhandedly.

"It's been a sub-platform to our law and order stance. We've been tough on crime across the board," Alex answered.

"Then we support prosecuting her to the full extent of the law. We have the greatest faith in our justice system and even more faith in those we appoint to uphold the law." Davidson shook his head slightly as if he was disappointed he had to do everything.

"But this is different," Cheryl suggested. "I mean, this girl isn't exactly a hard case, she's Kip Rayburn's stepdaughter."

"She's irrelevant except as a concept," Davidson muttered.

"A concept," Cheryl reiterated as she glanced at Alex who shrugged. A second later Davidson looked up.

"Any more questions?"

"No."

Cheryl and Alex left the governor to his notes and parted ways. Both of them hoped if they ever found themselves on the wrong side of the law, the governor would think of them as something more than a concept. Both of them knew that was a false hope.

CHAPTER 5

"That someone would take the life of a man like Fritz Rayburn…What can I say to that? I can only hope whoever did this feels the full wrath of our justice system – regardless of who they are. I promise, the person I appoint to fill Justice Rayburn's seat will have the same commitment to law and order; perhaps feel even more strongly about it than I do." – Governor Joe Davidson, Good Day LA Interview

"Hannah Sheraton." Josie tattooed her name on the jail log as she stated her business.

"Room three, counselor. It'll be a few minutes."

The officer behind the window flicked her head to the left as she finished searching Josie's portfolio and purse, and then pushed them toward her. Josie nodded her thanks and dodged the guy behind her as she turned to leave.

"Bitch of a place to be on a hot day," he muttered as he pulled the log toward him and signed in.

"Bitch of a place to be any day." Josie answered back, but she was the only one who heard it.

Josie was already standing in front of the door that led to the interview rooms at Sybil Brand. Pushing through the first of two doors when the buzzer sounded she paused, waited for the second buzzer, and then went through. The door locked behind her while she was still wondering if she shouldn't just forget the whole thing. In room number three, Josie tossed her briefcase on the table, sat down, and looked through the glass at the LA County women's jail.

The place was a sprawling complex of old buildings that housed women who committed real crimes: murder, arson, burglary, assault. Hannah Sheraton would be a 'keep away', cut off from the general population for her own protection because of her age. If she were convicted, though, this could be home; this prison with the pastel butterflies painted on the walls to inspire the inmates to come out of the cocoon of Sybil Brand bigger, better, and smarter. But this was also the prison where yellow footprints were stenciled on the floor and each prisoner stepped on them, as if they were balancing on the razor's edge. Forbidden to veer away. Forbidden to look back.

Josie shifted, trying to get comfortable on the wooden chair. It had been a long time since she'd been in this place. It could be twenty minutes before they fetched Hannah. Josie closed her eyes and rested her head against the cold, concrete wall and replayed the conversation with Linda Rayburn.

Linda wove her own story in with her daughter's. Josie had directed, but Linda knew how she wanted the tale to go. One thing was clear; Linda and Hannah did not exist without the other.

Hannah Sheraton. Sixteen. She had been carted around the world with Linda and her lovers, gone through puberty with a bang, and started acting out when she was twelve. Nothing big. Nothing Linda hadn't done. Nothing Linda couldn't handle. Skip classes, smoke a little weed. Try cigarettes. Hang out with guys too old to have good intentions. Chip off the old block. Really a good kid though, just a little wild. Grew up too fast.

Linda went through the scotch like water. She didn't so much as slur a word. She was a hell of a drinker. And always it was back to Hannah.

Smart kid when she was in school. There had been so many schools, but everyone said the same thing. Talented, talented kid. Painter. Oils mostly. Some acrylics. She experimented with other mediums. Hannah had a future if she could just settle down. A big future. Bigger than Picasso.

Josie raised a brow. Linda caught it but didn't back off far.

Okay, maybe not Picasso, but big. Linda took Hannah's paintings to a guy in Beverly Hills. He bought a painting for five hundred bucks. Five hundred was big stuff before Linda met Kip, when Linda was between friends. Hannah was so happy when her painting helped out. That kid was so selfless. But then, it wasn't hard work for her. Hannah was only happy with a brush in her hand.

Josie ran out of scotch. Linda didn't run out of information.

The fire. It started in Hannah's studio. Okay, it wasn't really a studio but Fritz let her use the old west wing to do her painting. She used the bottom floor. When Fritz was in town he stayed in the bedroom suite above. That's where he died. That's where the fire started. Hannah loved that studio. Jesus, if Josie had seen her when they first started living in the big house. It was like being a princess...

Josie put a hand on Linda's arm. Linda refocused. She moved her hands around like she was rearranging a piece of a puzzle.

Hannah got weird. The Rayburns didn't think she was all that endearing, but what could you expect from two men? One had been a widower for ages and the other hadn't married until he was fifty. They were set in their ways. It was hard enough to get used to Linda, much less Hannah. They didn't like the way she looked one bit. But Hannah was beautiful. Linda wanted Josie to know that. Oh, and Fritz took a great interest in Hannah's painting. But the Rayburns also said Hannah needed discipline. Kip was impatient when he paid attention at all. He thought Hannah reflected badly on the family.

Things got worse. Hannah had new tricks. She didn't sleep well. She made everyone crazy with these weird little things she did. Hey, they'd gone from a one-bedroom apartment to a mansion. They'd gone from being two, to being part of a family. That was tough. There would be adjustments. Fritz thought different. He put Hannah into therapy, spent hours talking to her when he was home. He called to check on her. He was a good guy that way. Linda thought, as Hannah's mother, she should make the decisions, but she and Kip weren't married long enough for her to object. Linda didn't want to appear ungrateful and no one had ever been so nice to them before. Damn her acting out like that. Always head games with Hannah. For God's sake, she just didn't know how lucky she was – they were – to be Rayburns.

So Josie was thinking about the dynamic in the Rayburn house when the door opened. There stood the real thing. Hannah Sheraton, drop dead gorgeous and jumpy as a racing pulse.

Even in an orange jumpsuit Josie could see that her body was perfect: slight but full breasted and broad shouldered. Her long black hair hung down her back and framed her face in a riot of tight curls. Her skin was dark, smooth, luminescent, but her eyes were that same spring green of her mother's. She could have stood in front of the Taj Mahal in a gold sari or danced on the beaches of Bali and looked at home. Hannah was an exotic creature, petite and feminine where Linda was tall and feline featured. Hannah was a child of the world and all Josie could think was that the other half of her genetic equation must have been something gorgeous to look at.

The guard, it seemed, was not impressed with Hannah. She put her hand on the girl's shoulder and then gave her a verbal shove.

"Move ahead, Sheraton."

Hannah lifted her foot but before she put it down again, her left hand touched the doorjamb. *Once. Twice. Four. Five times.*

"Come on, Sheraton. I haven't got all day." Startled by the order, Hannah stepped into the room, her face tightening in anger. Before the girl could give the guard any lip, Josie stood up.

"Thanks. We'll call when we're done."

The woman nodded curtly even as her eyes lingered on Josie. Three years had passed but people had long memories. Josie had almost lived at Sybil Brand during the Kristin Davis trial. She had been the poster girl for defense attorneys – get 'em out of jail whether they deserved it or not. Law enforcement didn't care for Josie's brand of lawyering; Josie hadn't cared for it either after Kristin.

"I said I'll call when we're done," Josie reiterated.

The guard left. Hannah didn't move. Her hands were clasped behind her back, her shoulders twitching as if she were pumping those hands up and down.

"Where's my mother?"

Hannah's angry voice wasn't half as attractive as the rest of her. Josie's smile faded. She had worried about calming a frightened girl, not fighting with a pissed off chick.

This was a mistake, Archer.

"Your mother's at home," Josie answered plainly. She motioned to the only other chair in the room. "Sit down."

"Did you check?" Hannah stepped forward then back again, screwing with Josie.

"I saw her night before last night."

"No, I mean did you check this morning? You're sure she's there?" The girl's voice rose with agitation.

"Yes, your mother is at home. She sent me here to help you."

"Are you a doctor? I don't need a doctor." Hannah cut Josie off, her expression a mix of arrogance, anger, and a bit of childish hope. Kids like Hannah never thought anyone saw the hope.

Josie shook her head.

"My name is Josie Baylor-Bates. I'm a lawyer. Now, are you going to sit down or am I going to have to call a guard to put you down." Those green eyes sharpened. Hannah wasn't going to give an inch and the sooner Josie took control the better. She pointed to the chair again. "You've got one minute, or I'm out of here."

Hannah's eyes closed briefly. She squeezed her shoulders back. Those hands were pumping again and then it was over. Her body relaxed, her expression eased into something close to relief. Throwing back her hair she reached for the chair. Josie saw the burn; Hannah saw Josie's look of surprise.

From fingertip to wrist, the skin on Hannah Sheraton's hand was swollen and mottled, red and white. A lacy looking roadmap of darker pigment was the only reminder of what that hand used to look like. It had been over a week since Fritz Rayburn's death. The injury must have been horrible if it still looked that bad.

"Does it still hurt?"

Hannah furrowed her brow and turned her hand to the right and left, right again as she sat down. Putting her injured hand palm down on the table, she gazed at it.

"I don't think so."

"You have to think about it?" Josie sat, too.

Hannah raised her eyes without lifting her head. She was a demonic sprite with those eyes, that skin, her wild hair, and the piercings on her nose and ears. Her full lips curled around her words as if casting a spell.

"Some people can't stand it when the wind blows too hard. There are degrees to everything. I don't recognize pain. I don't even remember it hurting when it happened. I didn't even cry."

Josie pulled a pad of paper from her portfolio.

"I don't know if that's anything to be proud of." Josie noted the date and time on the top of the paper, trying to ignore the warning in her gut.

"I didn't say it was, did I?"

Hannah's burned hand went to her hair, grasped the longest tendril and wrapped it behind her ear. She pulled it forward, wrapped it back and forward and stopped as suddenly as she had begun. She put her hands under the table and looked right at Josie.

"Will you be able to paint?" Josie asked.

"If I can't paint I'll kill myself."

"No you won't. You're in protective custody," Josie muttered, making a point about powerlessness that Hannah seemed to miss. "You can't breathe without someone watching you. But that doesn't answer the question. Your mother told me about your painting, and that the fire that killed your grandfather started in..."

"My *s-t-e-p*." Hannah spelled it out. "Fritz was my step."

Hannah's hostility spike at the mention of Fritz Rayburn wasn't lost on Josie. She tried again.

"The fire that killed Fritz Rayburn started in the place you used as a studio. Do you know anything about that?"

Hannah came right back at her.

"Why don't you ask me if I did it? Why ask me if I know anything about it?"

"Because I want to know what you know about it," Josie reiterated. "If I want to know if you did it, I'll ask you."

"I know that the place was on fire. I know if I wanted to burn down the house I wouldn't have tried to put it out, would I? My paintings were in there." From beneath the table came a light and rhythmic thumping. Hannah leaned close to the wood, her hair spilled onto it, her anger shot toward Josie. "I don't know why you're here. Kip will get me out of jail and take care of everything. He got me back in school when I got kicked out. He fixed it so my mom could get into some fancy club." Hannah's eyes sparkled with challenge, "Kip and Fritz fix everything."

"Not this time, Hannah."

Josie twirled the pen between her fingers as she listened to Hannah's view of her world. The truth was that sometimes saving people wasn't simple, sometimes saviors weren't who you expected them to be, all people don't get saved, and not everyone deserved to be saved. It was time Hannah heard those facts of life.

"Look, Hannah, Fritz is dead, and if Kip were going to help you he would have done it by now. Your mother knows that, so she sent me." Josie leaned forward, crossed her arms on the table and looked right into that gorgeous, defiant face. "You are in a shit load of trouble. Now, if you want to go home to your mother then you look at me, you talk to me, you listen to me, and you cut the crap because, believe me, this is the last place on earth I want to be."

Hannah bit her bottom lip – a gesture so like her mother's. Those broiled fingers were at her hair again. Front. Behind. Front. Behind. Over the ear once, then again. She swished her hair and her lips moved as if she were counting. Her eyes wandered as if Josie was no more interesting than a gnat.

Frustrated, unnerved by her surroundings, sick of this kid's self-absorbed nonsense, Josie shot out of her chair. Her thighs pushed the table as she reached across it and clamped down on Hannah's wrist.

"Stop that," she growled.

Hannah's eyes narrowed. She tried to jerk away. Josie held on tight and Hannah bared her teeth.

"I can't. Do you want to make something of it?"

CHAPTER 6

Josie backed off, slowly releasing Hannah's wrist. She was shaking, stunned at her anger and Hannah's admission.

"No, I don't want to make anything of it."

Josie sank back into her chair. Grown women broke their first hour in this place. Hannah Sheraton was ready to fight. She had guts, Josie would give her that.

"So then don't call me on it."

Hannah slumped in her chair, resentment seeping out of her. Her jumpsuit gaped open. Josie could see one perfectly formed breast sans bra. The nipple was pierced. There was a tattoo staining her shoulder, blue/black and red. Her hand knocked underneath the table in a maddening rhythm. Everything about her said hard as nails but Josie didn't buy it. There was something beyond the anger that intrigued Josie; something in the way Hannah stood up for herself that Josie admired.

"So tell me about what you're doing. There isn't time for me to guess, and you don't want the prosecution to know anything your own attorney doesn't know."

Hannah closed her eyes and kept them closed.

"I do it because that's what I do. I touch things twenty times. It makes me feel safe. I'm obsessive/compulsive. All the doctors say the same thing." Hannah's lashes fluttered. Her lids raised half way in an expression that was weary and guarded. "What a waste of money. What's wrong with liking to know my boundaries? It doesn't hurt anyone. It doesn't even hurt me."

"I think I'll wait for your doctors to tell me if you have severe behavioral problems," Josie said.

"That's rich. They only know what I tell them." Hannah dismissed Josie only to find the ensuing, insistent silence annoying. She filled it. "I'm better with doors than I used to be. I saw you looking at me when I touched the door. That's why I figured you for a doctor. You look like the kind of doctor my mother likes."

"And what kind would that be?"

"My mom likes women doctors. Extreme women."

Hannah put her burned hand to her throat and dropped the fingers down to the opening of her jumpsuit. This was a Linda move. Hannah was a puppy, learning all the wrong things before she was weaned. Sensing Josie's discomfort, Hannah teased.

"The kind of women my mom likes either hate to screw, or they screw too much. That's the kind of extreme they are. She probably likes lawyers like that, too. Which one are you?"

Josie shook her head.

"I've heard that word before, Hannah, so why don't you tell me something I really want to know. Tell me what kind of doctors Fritz liked." When Hannah fell silent Josie pushed on. "Your mother said Fritz Rayburn took an interest in you. She said he paid for some clinics and your doctors."

Josie wasn't playing Hannah's game and Hannah wasn't interested in Josie's.

"They were just places, just people. I don't think he ever met any of the doctors in them. He just sent me there."

"How did you feel about that?"

"Like he was sticking his nose in where it didn't belong; like he was punishing me when I didn't do anything."

The hair was going back and forth again but slower now as if she was seeing Fritz, hearing him, and was pissed at him. Between the words Hannah breathed her numbers. When she reached twenty twirls she stopped and put her burned hand on the table, always in the same place. She was done.

"I'm not going to talk about Fritz. He was just in the house sometimes, that's all. He was a damn hypocrite always talking about the law, and justice, and art, and people falling all over him like he was better than everyone else. Well, he wasn't better, and he wasn't around a lot. So let's not talk about Fritz."

"How did all that make him a hypocrite, Hannah?" Josie pressed for information, looking for the bottom of Hannah's resentment.

She shrugged, "I don't know. He thought he was above everybody. Forget it. Forget him."

"That's all anybody's going to be talking about, so you better get that through your head. You're charged as an adult. You're going to have to start acting like one."

Hannah shifted. She sat up straight, still cautious but suddenly engaged.

"Okay. I'll be an adult. I have some questions. How come my mom sent you and not some guy?"

"We went to school together," Josie answered. "I told her I'd see you through the bail hearing, and then find someone to help if you go to trial."

"Why can't you do it?"

"I haven't done criminal work for a long time," Josie said, averting her eyes. "Not like this anyway."

"How come?"

"Because I haven't," Josie retorted, peeved that this kid should insist on an answer.

"But why?" Hannah persisted.

"Because I was very good at it, and sometimes I got people off who should have gone to jail. Sometimes they hurt more people. That's why."

"Oh, so you're scared," Hannah decided.

"I made a decision not to do major criminal work any more," Josie insisted.

"You didn't choose. You quit. You were scared you'd do it again." Hannah smiled as if they had suddenly found a meeting ground. Now they could be friends. "I'd want you to help me. People who are scared think better. Besides, if you choose not to do something you can choose to do it again – if the person is innocent – right?"

Josie wasn't listening to Hannah. Another voice came out of the walls and wrapped itself around her brain in tantalizing whispers. She had been in this room, in this place, listening to another client say the same words. *Choose me. Help me. I'm innocent. I am.*

"Isn't that right? You can choose, right?" Hannah demanded, and Josie blinked.

"We'll keep our options open," she answered. "Do you have any other questions?"

Hannah eyed Josie, checking out every twitch, every evasion, and every noncommittal statement. Then she started to probe.

"Do you know my mom really well?"

"I did a long time ago."

"Did you know she gave up being a pro volleyball player so she could have me?"

Josie inclined her head. Josie didn't care about that little bit of fiction, but she noted the point of it: Hannah the child wanted to be life-changingly important to her mother. That was something Josie understood better than anyone on earth. In Hannah's case she probably had been, just not the way she thought.

"So, are you sure Kip isn't going to do something for me?" Hannah suddenly demanded.

"Yes, I am."

Hannah nodded. Her fingers were tapping. *Twenty.* Then her left hand covered her right and stroked the mottled skin. *Twenty.* Josie's muscles tightened in annoyance. It was hard to watch, this lack of self-control.

"There's another question." Hannah said finally. "I want to know if you think I'm crazy?"

Josie eyed her coolly and answered honestly.

"I don't know. I haven't talked to your doctor."

"I mean from what you've seen? Counting and touching stuff. Do you think that's crazy?" The tapping began again.

"No, that doesn't fit the legal description of insanity if that's what you're asking."

"Are you sure?" Restless and troubled, Hannah's hands moved a mile a minute.

"Why would you want me to think you're crazy, Hannah? Why would you want anyone to think that?" Josie asked, trying to read between Hannah's lines.

"Because if I was crazy they couldn't say I murdered Fritz, could they?"

Josie finally got it. This girl was thinking ahead, figuring ways to get herself out of this predicament. Her permutations were flawed, but Josie found the exercise to be extraordinarily clear headed for someone so young.

She had done the same thing when her mother disappeared; planned her own destiny, planned how to find Emily. In the end Josie failed to find her mother and learned that destiny had a will of its own. If nothing else, Josie understood and empathized with Hannah Sheraton. When she spoke again, Josie committed herself more deeply than she intended.

"Hannah," Josie said evenly. "I want you to listen to me very carefully. I can review the information the District Attorney has, and try to get the charges dismissed. If I can't make that happen, you will be indicted for murder. Then you'll have a choice: plead guilty, plead to a lesser charge, or we can fight.

"If we fight don't think for me. Don't try to beat this system on your own because it can't be done. Knocking on wood and twirling your hair doesn't constitute an insanity defense. Do you understand that?"

Hannah listened, thinking hard, weighing the worth of Josie's advice against that of other adults she knew. Finally she made a decision. Slowly she brought her hands from under the table, unbuttoned the cuffs on her jumpsuit and deliberately rolled up her sleeves – ten rolls each. Twenty in all.

Hannah held up her arms. At first Josie's eyes were drawn to her hands. Then she saw what Hannah was offering. On the delicate skin of her forearms was a web of scars and welts, red scratches and deep cuts, some viciously fresh. Josie took a deep breath and forced herself not to look away.

"Does this count for crazy?" Hannah asked, holding out what she considered to be her ticket to freedom.

"No, Hannah. It doesn't count for crazy." Josie whispered.

Hannah's expression changed, the hope drained away, the light in her eyes dimmed. She didn't seem as much disappointed as sadly accepting. Lowering her arms Hannah rolled her sleeves down, buttoned the cuffs, buried her hands beneath the table and started knocking the underside again.

One, two, three…ten…twenty.

CHAPTER 7

Archer: "So? How'd it go?"

Josie: "She needs help."

Archer: "And?"

Josie: "Bail hearing's tomorrow."

Archer: "You going to be there?"

Josie: "Yeah."

Archer: "Sounds good, Jo. 'Nite, babe."

Josie: "Nite, Archer."

There were no halls of justice in trailer C, department 32 of the Superior Court, the Honorable Judith Davenport presiding. There were, in fact, no halls at all.

Hannah was scheduled to be arraigned in Santa Monica but the actual courthouse was overcrowded. The proceedings would take place in one of the modular units the state had plopped in the middle of the parking lot in an effort to solve the problem. Unfortunately, while that had been a practical decision it sorely undermined the dignity of the court.

Still, it was what Hannah Sheraton drew. Josie had no doubt that if it came to an actual trial *The People v. Hannah Sheraton* in the matters of arson and murder would be played out on a much finer stage.

It was early. Half a dozen cars were scattered over the asphalt parking lot. Beyond the fence that separated court property from the West LA police station cops were changing the guard. Black and whites pulled in and out. Tired officers went home; fresh ones hit the streets. A roach coach was doing a brisk business in breakfast burritos and bad coffee.

Checking her watch, Josie hurried past a woman dragging a two year old behind her, a couple of attorneys conferring by a green Mercedes, and two marshals before opening the metal door to Department 32. It closed with a thud. The walls wobbled. This was a judicial trailer park hoping for a bureaucratic tornado to wipe it out. Still, there were things that made Department 32 feel just like every other courtroom: a Court TV camera, a jar of candy on the clerk's desk, an empty jury box, and the seal of the state hanging behind the bench. But there was one thing missing: people. Josie thought the place would have been packed. Instead, she tagged only the AP and the LA Times reporters. A young blond man sat in the back. He was too well dressed to be a court watcher, and too relaxed to be the prosecutor. Linda was up front alone. If this was all the public interest the DA could muster, that was a good thing.

Josie shrugged into her jacket then walked down the aisle toward Linda. They had been on the phone for over an hour last night discussing Hannah's history, and what the family was willing to do to secure bail. Josie touched Linda's shoulder and motioned her to move over. Linda looked up, gratitude plastered on her face like an extra layer of make-up.

"I was worried. I thought maybe I was in the wrong place." Linda kept her voice low.

"How long have you been here?" Josie asked.

"Half an hour. Seems like forever." Self-consciously Linda touched her hair. It was pulled straight up and gathered into a sleek knot on top of her head. On her ears were diamond hoops. She was nervous but controlled, a far cry from the woman of a few nights ago. They would have to talk about clothes if this went to trial. The last thing Josie wanted was for Hannah and Linda to look like escapees from Rodeo Drive.

"Is your husband coming?"

"No, he couldn't make it. He had a meeting. But he wanted to. He did."

Josie nodded, understanding it was futile to hope Kip Rayburn would stand by Hannah. Josie shifted closer to Linda.

"There's a camera in the back of the courtroom. Don't react to anything you hear during the proceedings. If you have a question, let me know about it when we're out of here, okay?"

Linda nodded. Josie started to get up. Linda grabbed her.

"What about you? Are you okay? I mean I know you didn't want to do this."

Josie slipped her hand from Linda's.

"Everything is fine. Don't worry," Josie assured her.

Just then the back door opened. Rudy Klein, Deputy District attorney had arrived. It was time to go. Rudy and Josie passed through the bar together.

"It's been a long time, Rudy," she said.

"Not long enough," he muttered.

They took to their respective tables. Things moved quickly after that. The door to chambers opened. Her honor, Judge Judith Davenport, was announced. Everyone stood. The court was called to order. There was a millisecond of silence before Hannah Sheraton, still dressed in orange, was led into the room.

This time she was buttoned up to the chin.

CHAPTER 8

Hannah looked exactly as Josie hoped she would: stunned, vulnerable and innocent. That was good. Fear could be very useful when your client was arrogant, disturbed and young.

Her hands were cuffed making it impossible for her to twirl her hair. The space reserved for the accused was too wide for her to touch a wall. Her hands rose and fell in frustration; she connected with nothing. Panic showed in the way she licked her lips, the way her eyes searched for, and found, her mother.

Josie glanced at Rudy Klein in time to see a shadow of regret pass over his face. Their eyes locked. He was younger than she, but not by much. He had cut his prosecutorial teeth on the Kristin Davis case as a pinch hitter, and Rudy had given Josie a good run. Today he was a surprise, a challenge. She wished the prosecutor had been a stranger.

Josie looked away. Her palms were moist, her heartbeat noticeable. It had been too long since she'd been responsible for someone's whole life. She was afraid. But there was no turning back now so Josie faced the bench. It was time to play.

"Good morning. Call the case of the *People v. Hannah Sheraton.*" Judge Davenport planted her elbows on the desk, clasped her hands and gave them permission to touch gloves. "Counsels?"

Rudy Klein and Josie Baylor-Bates identified themselves. Davenport gave the nod to Josie who waived the reading of the complaint. Everyone knew why they were there. Davenport swiveled toward Hannah. All eyes followed.

"How do you plead?"

"Not guilty."

Hannah looked past Josie to Linda and something passed between mother and daughter. Assurances. Strength. Commitment. Whatever it was, Hannah was overwhelmed by it. She swayed slightly, closed her eyes briefly, and then looked at Josie. She gave Hannah an encouraging nod, knowing whatever she did could never match what a mother had to offer.

Davenport was on to business.

"So recorded. If there are no objections, I'll set a date for a preliminary hearing eight days from today. That will be on–"

"Your Honor," Rudy interrupted, "the prosecution will be proceeding directly to the grand jury for indictment."

Stoned faced, Josie kept her surprise to herself. A grand jury indictment meant that Hannah could be bound over for trial without her defense attorney being privy to the prosecution's case. Not a good thing.

"When is the grand jury scheduled to meet, Mr. Klein?"

"In three days, Judge," Rudy answered. "We're already scheduled."

"Your Honor, I'd like for the D.A. to present any exculpatory evidence to the grand jury and save the defense, this court, and the taxpayers time and money," Josie argued.

"If there were any evidence to exonerate Ms. Sheraton we wouldn't be here."

Rudy smiled brilliantly. Josie ignored him. She'd seen his act before: handsome and boyish, nice suit, charm the pants off everyone within spitting distance. An ex-actor who decided being a lawyer was better than playing one, Rudy Klein had a perfect stage presence, a prosecutor's conviction, and a good mind to boot.

"Very well, then. Notify my clerk immediately if the grand jury indicts. Do either of you have any other business?"

Josie was about to speak when Davenport furrowed her brow and directed her peevishness in the general direction of Josie's camp.

"Bailiff, what is that noise?"

All eyes went to Josie and, not finding the answer to that question, segued toward Hannah. She had closed in on the wood and glass partition, hungry to make contact with something. Her knuckles drummed and knocked against the wood. Her wide lips parted as if she were blowing on a candle as she breathed the count, comforted in her recital, removed from this place and these proceedings.

Embarrassed to be caught napping, the bailiff took Hannah's arm and moved her back. Like an animal disturbed in sleep Hannah bristled but Josie caught her eye. Hannah stepped back but, unable to control herself, she lunged forward again. The bailiff held her tight.

"Apologies, Your Honor," Josie said to the court. "My client suffers from obsessive/compulsive disorder and has been under a psychiatrists care for some time. In order for her to continue her treatment, I would like to arrange for bail at this time."

Rudy was right there.

"Judge this woman set a devastating fire that resulted in Fritz Rayburn's death. This is a woman with a long history of drug and alcohol abuse…"

Josie cut in, demanding the judge's attention.

"This is a young girl who has been under a doctor's care. We will report on her rehabilitation as a condition of her bail. And, I might add, Ms. Sheraton has been wrongly detained. She was, in fact, burned in her attempt to put out the fire that occurred at the Rayburn home. The prosecutor should save his opening statement for the appropriate time, when he has an appreciative audience."

"And Ms. Bates shouldn't jump to conclusions, Your Honor. The defendant is unreliable. She has not been a willing participant in her own rehabilitation. In July of two thousand and two she escaped from the Forman Rehabilitation Center in Oregon."

"If it pleases the court," Josie drawled in disgust. "The Froman Rehabilitation center in Oregon is not a prison facility. She wasn't in custody when she entered, and she was not on the lam when she left."

Rudy was still reciting Hannah's transgressions as if he had Davenport's ear since the first minute he opened his mouth.

"In September of two thousand and three Ms. Sheraton was AWOL from another clinic in Northern California. As recently as six months ago, the defendant was apprehended in San Diego just before reaching the Mexican border. In her company was one Miggy Estrada who had an extensive juvenile record and two arrests since his eighteenth birthday. They had stolen her stepfather's car. In short, Ms. Sheraton is a flight risk, Your Honor."

Josie came back seamlessly into the argument.

"I can bring two thousand files into this court on Los Angeles teenagers who have been joyriding. Ms. Sheraton holds no passport. Her driver's license has been revoked. She is, at worst, high-strung – much like the prosecutor, who seems prone to melodrama."

"And the defense is naïve, taken in by the defendant. She is not giving enough weight to her client's actions," Rudy responded. "Ms. Bates should have learned something from her previous experience."

"That is a cheap shot and irrelevant. We are talking about my client's alleged actions," Josie argued angrily, "there is still the burden of proof, and I don't shoulder that particular burden."

"We are talking about the death of a California Supreme Court justice." Rudy talked over her.

"*Who* died in this tragic fire should be of no consequence to this court's final decision. Determining whether or not my client is eligible for bail is this court's only business."

"There is no need to tell this court its job, Ms. Bates," Judge Davenport snapped. "And both of you seem to prefer arguing at each other rather than convincing me of the matter at hand. I would suggest you behave and get on with it. I have a full calendar."

Josie took a deep breath. This wasn't like her. She felt like a child pointing a finger at a playmate. *He started it.* In years past she had been smoother, more self-assured. In the beach court she was downright laid back. Her nerves were showing. She had reacted badly when she should have steered the argument. That wasn't good. When she spoke again it was with a modulated voice, and eyes that did not dart toward Rudy.

"I'm sorry, Your Honor. But the question of bail is clear. Since the fire at the Pacific Palisades home the defendant's family has moved to Malibu. Flight is more than difficult given the isolation of the property. If Mr. Klein is that skittish, we'll submit to court ordered home monitoring. The Rayburns will pay the fee and allow the prosecution access to the reporting so Mr. Klein can sleep at night."

Josie stepped out from behind the defense table, a confident calm coming over her as the territory became more and more familiar.

"I would further like to make a motion that the court considers a change of venue. The press coverage will be extraordinary in Los Angeles making it difficult to pick a jury. A move to Ventura County might be preferable."

"Oh, please. Your Honor!" Rudy's hands were raised in a gesture of amazement. "This is ridiculous. In this case, *who* the victim is *does* matter. Justice Rayburn served all of California, and all media will give equal weight to covering the story."

Judith Davenport had heard enough. Her clerk handed her a note. She glanced at it, folded it, and wrapped up the matter of *The People v. Hannah Sheraton.*

"You're right, Mr. Klein. The motion to change venue is denied. Deal with the press as you see fit, Ms. Bates. As to the bail request, there is a difference between someone leaving a private institution and fleeing the jurisdiction. Bail is set at a million dollars. I won't require monitoring, but let me be clear. If your client so much as brushes up against the line of the restrictions of her bail she will be back to square one. No second chances. Understand, Ms. Bates?"

"Yes, Your Honor. Her family is willing to take full responsibility."

"I hope they keep their eyes open." Davenport raised a brow as if to say the alternative wasn't pretty. What happened to good old Fritz was top of every judge's mind these days. None of them would want Hannah under their roof.

"One last item, Your Honor." Josie raised her hand. "I would like to request that Mr. Klein bring forward any eyewitnesses he has to the alleged arson."

"So ordered, Mr. Klein." The judge intoned.

"We have no such witnesses, Judge," Rudy responded.

"If that circumstance changes, the order stands. Advise the court and arrange for a line-up. Are we finished?"

They were.

Rudy packed up and walked out without another word to Josie. Hannah disappeared with the bailiff, a young man with long, dark hair stood in her place. Linda stood up and fell in step with Josie.

"I knew you could do it," Linda said under her breath. She clutched Josie's arm, holding her tight. "Didn't I say you could do it?"

"It's only the first step. There's a long way to go. The grand jury..." Josie's eyes stayed on Rudy's back longer than she realized. She was curious about his vehemence. It seemed he was taking Hannah's case personally.

"But I can take her home now, right?"

Linda tugged on Josie's arm. Josie nodded, attentive to Linda as they left the courthouse together.

Josie?" Linda asked as she reached for her sunglasses once they were outside. "Do you think someone saw who set the fire? Is that why you asked about a witness?"

"No. It's a standard question. I didn't really think they had anyone." Josie dug for her keys and kept talking. "But they have something; otherwise they wouldn't be taking this to the grand jury."

"Is that a problem?"

"It means there won't be a pretrial hearing. That mean's the grand jury votes to indict based on what Rudy tells them. There is no chance to present a defense case. I don't like it."

"I didn't think they had an eyewitness," Linda mused, seemingly relieved. "The house is so far off the street. It was so late. Everybody's got security patrols."

"I'd actually prefer an eyewitness. I'd have someone to discredit." Josie took a deep breath. She smiled her reassurance. "Look, I'm not even conceding the fire was deliberately set, but I have to assume the prosecutor's solid on that."

"Hey, Josie." Huddled together, Josie hadn't seen the AP reporter until she was right on top of them. "Nice to see you back in the thick of things, Josie. What's your take on the charges?"

"You mean other than wondering if the District Attorney has lost his mind?" Josie laughed and then gave the reporter something to work with. "Top of my head, I'd say the D.A. has tunnel vision. Hannah Sheraton wasn't alone in the house that night. Mrs. Rayburn and her husband were home. They had entertained that evening and their guests stayed late. The maid was in the house. Her son had been by earlier. The caterer had two employees with him. If the fire was deliberately set – and that's a big if – I could probably make a case against any one of them."

"Who looks good to you?"

Josie wagged a finger.

"I'm not playing that game. I'm only telling you my client had nothing to do with Fritz Rayburn's death."

Ending the interview, Josie took Linda's arm only to stop when the reporter called after them.

"Josie, what do you say to those who might wonder if your opinion is reliable when it comes to your client's innocence? Considering the Davis case, and all."

Josie turned around slowly. Her gaze was steady. The bright morning light caught her hard on one side of her face so that she appeared divided, black and white.

"I say Hannah Sheraton is a young girl who is to be afforded all the protection of the law including a vigorous defense. I intend to make sure she gets it no matter who speaks for her in court."

"Does that mean you won't be–"

Josie turned her back. There would be no more questions from anyone. Rudy Klein hadn't left and Josie wanted to have a few words with him.

"Linda, get Hannah home. Tell her she did good today."

Josie strode across the parking lot. She called to Rudy Klein as he was hanging his jacket in the back of the car, looking for his keys, getting on to the next piece of business. He turned and watched her approach. His handsome face was impassive, his eyes imminently readable. The message was clear. He didn't particularly care for Josie Baylor-Bates, and that surprised her. They hardly knew one another. She hadn't given him a second thought since the Davis trial.

"That was quite a show you put on in there. A little harsh, don't you think?" Josie smiled, knowing the ice needed to be broken. Unfortunately, it was rock solid.

"I would have gone for special circumstances and the death penalty," Rudy said flatly. "But the D.A. didn't want to take a chance there would be any sympathy for this kid."

"That's a little harsh even for John Cooper. If he's trying to curry favor with Governor Davidson by showing he's got balls of steel, he might as well forget it. John Cooper won't get Rayburn's seat even if he burned my client at the stake."

Rudy slammed the back door of his car and opened the front. He hung on it for a minute, shaking his head.

"Boy, you haven't changed a bit. Always looking for the angle, aren't you? John Cooper has been prosecuting juvenile felons as adults since he took office. Cruelty has nothing to do with chronology just the same way chronology doesn't have anything to do with innocence. Or did you miss that during your last trial?"

"Kristin Davis wasn't my last trial."

"Really? I didn't know you were still practicing. I thought you crawled into a hole and stayed there." Rudy put on his sunglasses. "Now that we're clear on the DA's motivation for prosecuting this girl, is there anything else you wanted?"

"A deal," Josie said, surprised he took his failure during the Davis trial so hard.

He had stepped in when the original Deputy D.A. suffered a heart attack. It was late in the game and Josie was in the end zone. Rudy did his best, he had done it brilliantly, but it was too little, too late. Josie won. Six months later Kristin was at her murderous best again and Josie realized she no longer had the stomach for defending those who should have been indefensible. Rudy, it seemed, didn't look at the adversarial system quite so objectively. He carried his disappointment with him like a ball and chain. Victory wasn't exactly an easy burden but it was something Josie dealt with. The chip on his shoulder was beginning to piss her off but it wasn't exactly relevant right now.

"Forget it." He started to get into the car.

"Are you sure you don't want to think about that?" Josie stopped him. "You led with your best shot and I still got her bailed. That should tell you something. If you're going to charge her as an adult, then give her the same break as an adult. You plea people out all the time for worse than this."

Rudy turned around slowly. The car door was between them.

"Fine. Twenty-five to life, no parole before eighteen."

"That's ridiculous," Josie scoffed. "You might as well ask for the max on all counts and make them consecutive."

"That's exactly what I intend to do. The investigators pegged this as arson an hour after they knocked down that blaze. She's guilty."

"That's not enough for murder," Josie argued.

Rudy crossed his arms over the top of the door.

"Then how about this, Bates? Fritz Rayburn sustained a skull fracture. Your girl hit him under the chin hard enough to send him flying. Hit his head on the side of the bed frame and split his skull."

"Did you see my client?" she asked. "Do you think she could hit a grown man hard enough to do that?"

"I've seen women beat up men twice their size and so have you."

"Then I say it's internal bleeding from the fall that killed him. That's not second-degree murder. I might give you assault if you can prove Hannah hit him. But murder? Forget it."

"I could probably make a case for first degree," he said quietly. "Justice Rayburn didn't die from the head injury. He was still alive when the fires were set. Hannah Sheraton killed Fritz Rayburn when she could have helped him. She set those fires knowing he would burn to death. Just one of those special little touches your female clients seem to like."

Josie barely breathed. They stared at one another, Josie silenced for a minute by his rancor. Her throat was dry. The sun seemed to have distorted her vision. Josie swayed ever so slightly but Rudy didn't reach out to steady her. He knew what she was thinking. How could a sixteen year old possibly be so vicious? How could it happen again?

Finding her voice, Josie said:

"Someone killed him Rudy. Don't forget that. There could be someone else."

"Not this time, Josie. That girl assaulted the judge earlier in the evening. There was a witness. Rayburn told the witness he was going to talk to Hannah later."

"And who's the eyewitness to that meeting?" Josie drawled. "You've got nothing but circumstantial evidence."

"And there's a reason circumstantial evidence is admissible, Bates." Rudy pushed away from the door. "I'll send over the discovery. You take a look and see what you think about your client then."

He slid into the driver's seat and was about to close the door. Josie held on to it. She rounded the open door and stood between him and the sun. She was nothing but a silhouette and he looked at her as if he could see through her.

"You still haven't answered the million dollar question, Rudy. Why would she want to hurt that old man?"

"Since when do your clients need a motive, Bates?" he asked, pulling on the door handle. Josie pulled back and kept it open. The metal was hot on her hand.

"Wait a minute. I want to know what this is all about. I want to know if you're going to dump on Hannah Sheraton because you're mad I got Kristin Davis off."

Rudy shook his head.

"No, I'm not mad at you. I think defense attorneys like you are pitiful. You sell out. You create a maze of evidence and argument to help criminals, but you never acknowledge the victims." Rudy looked away. "I'm mad at myself. I should have put Kristin Davis away before it was too late. I'm going to make sure I don't make the same mistake this time."

"It's not the same," Josie insisted.

"How can you be sure, Bates?" He closed the car door with a slam and looked at her through the open window. "How could you live with yourself if you were wrong again?"

❧

Josie peeled off her jacket and slapped it into the backseat of the Jeep. She threw her briefcase in after.

Goddamn Rudy Klein thought he had a lock on conscience? The hell with him. How dare he judge her? Or her motives. Or Hannah's innocence. She pulled herself into the Jeep and snapped on the ignition. The radio blared. Josie flipped it off, threw the car into reverse, and swung out of the parking space. She shifted into drive and curved around to the gate, only to slam on the brakes.

"Jeez!" She slapped the steering wheel.

A truck blocked the exit, the blazing sun was fueling her anger, and all she wanted to do was get back to the office and talk this out with Faye. It was too late to put up the ragtop, so Josie reached in the back seat for her baseball cap.

Her hand was on it but her eyes were on something else. Linda Rayburn was in her car; her head was back. She had loosened her hair so that it fell over her shoulders. Her arm was held out the window and there was a cigarette dangling between her fingers. She was talking to someone sitting beside her.

Josie looked closer, trying to see who it was. Perhaps Kip Rayburn had arrived late but Josie doubted it. This man was too young to be her husband. As Josie watched, Linda sat up. She leaned forward intensely interested in what her companion was saying when she should have been gone long ago, rushing to bring Hannah home.

The passenger door of Linda's car opened.

The man got out.

Josie strained to see.

It was the young, blond man who had been in the back of the courtroom. He was still leaning into the car as Linda turned toward him.

A horn honked. Startled, Josie looked ahead. The truck had moved. There were cars behind her. Josie tore her eyes away from Linda, grabbed her baseball cap, put it on her head, and put her hands on the wheel. Josie Baylor-Bates eased into the left lane and merged onto Santa Monica Boulevard. It wasn't even ten o'clock.

CHAPTER 9

Linda Rayburn shivered, but it had nothing to do with the air-conditioning in the waiting area at Sybil Brand, it had to do with her imagination. She hadn't seen past the steel door that separated the waiting area from the prison but Linda knew what was there and it made her sick. For three days Hannah got up when she was told, went to bed when she was told, ate when and what she was told. She wore that ugly jumpsuit and slept under a coarse blanket. The real world wasn't just far away, it was forbidden.

Linda was imagining herself behind that door when it suddenly opened. She stood up, hands together, sweat beading on her upper lip. What would she say to Hannah? How would they get through the next moments? But the woman who came out wasn't young and beautiful. Her hair was chopped off at the ears, her face pock marked, and her skin leathery. She looked at Linda with flat eyes, unimpressed by the tall lady with the fancy clothes. Linda looked away. She could have been that woman if she hadn't been smart enough, talented enough, and tenacious enough to change everything.

Shaking her head, Linda walked toward the back of the room, then turned on her heel and retraced her steps. The window in the center of the steel door was laced with chicken wire. She paced off the waiting room, empty except for the long row of molded plastic yellow chairs bolted to the floor around the perimeter of the room.

Just when Linda thought she couldn't take another minute, the door opened again and there stood Hannah dressed in the clothes she'd worn when she was arrested. Linda mewled, making a sound that translated into anxiety, relief, and apology.

"Mom?" Hannah's arms pumped. Linda didn't move. Scared now, Hannah's arms went faster. She pleaded, "Mom?"

Hesitantly, Linda stepped forward then rushed across the room, gathering the girl into her arms, nearly crushing her. She held Hannah back, pushed at her hair, and touched her cheek. Then Linda pulled her close again.

Hannah held on tight, her arms wrapped around her mother. Linda felt the patting and counted to twenty. Then it started again, and again Hannah counted to twenty. Linda clung to her daughter and buried her face in the wild frizz of Hannah's hair.

"Oh, baby. You did so good. So good. " Linda whispered her assurances over and over again, but when she looked again she saw the door. It opened two ways. It let women in and it let women out. Quickly Linda Rayburn turned her daughter away from it and headed to the exit. "We're out of here, and we're not coming back."

"Promise?" Hannah asked as they walked free, out into the bright sunlight.

Linda didn't answer. It was hard to talk when she heard the quiver in her daughter's voice, and felt Hannah's hands holding tight to her clothes like she used to when she was small.

Promise?

How could she? No matter how much she wanted to, Linda Rayburn couldn't do that. Not with what she knew.

❧

"That was Alex Schaeffer."

Ian Frank hung up the phone and leaned back in his chair. Kip Rayburn kept looking out the floor to ceiling windows of Ian's office. To the casual viewer he might look pensive. Truth of the matter was he felt sick. He was afraid to hear what Alex Schaeffer wanted. He hated the fact that some kid was the Governor's mouthpiece and another kid, his stepdaughter, might stand between him and an appointment. The last thing he wanted Ian Frank to see was his fear. Finally, he took a deep breath and turned around.

"What? I'm sorry, Ian. What did you say?"

Ian almost smiled. After all these years Kip was still inept at playing his hand. Not that it mattered. Kip had his uses. If the truth be told, Ian almost preferred the son to the father. The son was less complicated, more malleable, smart without being too smart, and Kip was just desirous enough of success to know he would never get it on his own.

"I said that was Alex Schaeffer on the phone. He was at the bail hearing this morning. He talked to Linda after the hearing."

Kip wandered over to a chair and sat down. He crossed his legs. His arms crossed over his chest. He'd stay that way until he was satisfied all was well. It took a lot to make Kip Rayburn relax.

"What did he say?"

"Hannah's bailed. Linda went to get her. They should be home by three. The prosecution is taking it to the grand jury, but Alex is feeling good that there won't be an indictment. He thinks the bail is a good sign."

"Is he a lawyer?" Kip asked.

"Nope, a politician's paid eyes and ears. Those guys understand nuance. That's their job. He's got a good feeling."

Kip sat silently. His arms were no longer crossed over his chest. Instead they rested on the arms of the chair. He was feeling better, but Ian knew he still needed reassurance.

"Kip, it's okay. The governor was very clear that Hannah's problems won't derail the nomination if you handle them the right way."

"I shouldn't have to handle them at all," Kip grumbled. His eyes slid toward Ian. "What would you do? I mean if you were me."

"I guess first thing I'd do is figure out if I thought she was guilty. I'd have a tough time even looking at someone who did that to my father," Ian answered truthfully. His gaze met Kip's head on and he revised that thought. He was, after all, talking about Fritz. "But, that's something you'll have to deal with personally. Next thing I'd do is act judicial."

"Meaning?"

"Think about it. How does a judge comport himself?"

"I don't know, Ian. Why don't you tell me?" Kip snapped.

"Well he doesn't act like a spoiled kid, for one thing. And don't start with me for another," Ian answered coolly. "I'm not your father and all I care about is the health of this firm. If you want my help and support during your confirmation, I would suggest you listen. Be proactive, or Hannah's troubles will overshadow your opportunities."

Kip swung out of the chair and paced. "I don't want anyone looking into my private life, or Fritz's. I don't want them looking into my business."

"Don't worry about it. Business is totally irrelevant to what's going on," Ian insisted. "If you hide away, though, people will ask questions."

"And if I show my face people will ask questions."

Ian threw up his hands, "Kip, come on. Don't think what could happen; decide what you want to happen. If you answer questions then you control the spin. You've got to make a pre-emptive strike because the sooner Hannah is out of the public eye, the sooner she'll be forgotten, your father will be forgotten, and you can get on with your life. Only you can make that happen."

Ian Frank smiled as Kip Rayburn's eyes lit up – finally.

"So you're saying–"

"Have a game plan. Ask yourself what you can do to make this disappear faster. There's no upside to dragging this out like a civil matter."

Kip's fingers drummed on the arms of the chair as he thought.

"If there's a trial?"

"Assist Hannah's attorney. Give her what she needs to wrap it up fast."

"If there's no trial?"

"Send the kid to boarding school. Once she's eighteen she's on her own," Ian said, opening his hands as if he had the world between them. "Unless Linda would object."

"Linda?" Kip cocked his head as if he had just heard something disturbing. "Linda has been very protective."

"Okay, work that out later. For now be supportive, talk about your faith in the law and do what you can to expedite this. The key word is *expedite*. Do that, and Hannah Sheraton is nothing but a memory." Ian rested his cheek on an upturned hand and smiled. "Expedite, expedite. Expedite the matter of Hannah Sheraton."

&

"Hi. Good morning, Ms. Bates."

The new receptionist grinned as Josie came through the door. She was a coat tree of a girl: all skin and bones, hard angles and points. Anorexia would have been the logical assumption if Tiffany wasn't constantly munching, eating, tasting and sipping. Today it was a tall Frappacino and pizza bagel.

"Tiffany, I want you to call me Josie. Got it? Josie." Tiffany grinned and nodded while Josie collected her message slips. There was only one, and Tiffany gave the audio version while Josie read.

"Mr. Fistonich called and said he'd be in the neighborhood and could sign his living will any time. No problem." She stopped for a breath and a bite. "I think he likes you."

"I like him, too," Josie muttered. "Call him back and tell him it's ready. Check with Angie so she can be available as a witness. Whatever time this afternoon is good with me."

"Okay."

Tiffany made a note and took another huge bite of her bagel. Josie crinkled her nose.

"You don't do that when anyone is waiting, do you?" She raised her chin indicating the bagel that had just disappeared into the receptionist's mouth. Tiffany shook her head and put her fingertips over her lips; too polite to speak when it was full.

"Is Faye here?" Tiffany nodded, swallowed hard and said:

"Yes. She wants to see you the min…"

Josie was already gone, stopping in Angie's office to ask her to open a file on Hannah Sheraton, putting her briefcase in her own office, heading down the hall to Faye's, and dropping into one of the client chairs.

"Boy, am I glad you're back. I have had one miserable morning."

"Funny, I heard you had a great morning in Santa Monica." Faye set aside her work and took off her glasses. She looked tired – or worried. "I got a call from Marge Sterling at the AP. Then a man named Wobley from the *Times* got on the horn. They wanted a comment regarding your representation of a girl accused of murdering Fritz Rayburn."

"What did you tell them?" Josie asked.

"I told them the firm had no comment and would issue a statement when it was appropriate. So," Faye opened her hands, inviting Josie to fill her up with information. "What happened between the time I left Friday night to see my grandchild, and this morning? Leaving me a message that you were helping out an old friend whose daughter was in trouble wasn't exactly on target."

"That's what I was doing."

"And you didn't think to mention that this had to do with Justice Rayburn?"

"It was a bail hearing," Josie insisted, knowing she should have given Faye a head's up. There was only one reason she didn't. If she failed, she didn't want Faye to know.

"A bail hearing doesn't take all morning," Faye pointed out.

"I talked to the prosecutor about a deal. I thought I could make it go away."

"And could you?"

"No." Josie shook her head. She looked at her short nails. Her fingertips were calloused from tile work. She dropped her hand, and when she looked at Faye her expression was one of frustration and confusion, anger and concern. "I have a history with the prosecutor. I'm not his favorite person." Josie sat up and forward, resting her elbows on her knees. "He thinks I knew Kristin Davis was guilty when I defended her. He thinks I only cared about winning."

"What's that got to do with this girl?" Faye asked.

Josie's blue eyes rested thoughtfully on a midpoint over Faye's shoulder.

"He wants a pound of flesh to make up for Kristin."

"Is that what you want? To make up for Kristin?"

"Maybe." Josie's gaze met Faye's. "Maybe a little of this is making up because Kristin's kids died because of me. I don't carry it around the way Rudy does, but I think about it. I dream about it. When he laid into me, I wondered what I was doing with Hannah Sheraton. I mean, is she just a challenge? Is the case a challenge? Is that what I was doing there this morning, or was I trying to make amends?"

Faye leaned her cheek on an upturned palm for a second, and then laced her hands in front of her.

"To tell you the truth, Josie, I don't care *why* you were there. I care *that* you were." Faye sighed. She looked disappointed. "Three years ago you swore you just wanted to be part of a quiet, neighborhood law practice and now it seems that's not what you want at all. I've always said you had wide discretion when it came to clients, but I also assumed that you would do me the courtesy of consulting me if what you were doing would impact this firm."

"Everything I do impacts this firm, Faye, and I think all of it has been good. Isn't that why you left me the partnership papers to sign Friday?"

"Don't play games, Josie. You argued for bail, and I had two reporters call for statements. I'm not some yokel. I know this is just the beginning. Thirty years ago I may have enjoyed the attention, but not now."

Faye took a deep breath. She wasn't happy.

"We help real people. Some of them are women running away from bad situations. Some of our clients are old. Most are just plain happy being in this small town. Do you think they'll feel comfortable with the press crawling all over this case? Do you think our clients are going to like it when they see your picture on the five o'clock news, or they can't get hold of you because you're in court for weeks, instead of hours?"

Josie's fingers went to her lips again but she stopped short of biting her nails. She hadn't done that since she was fourteen.

"You're right. Everything happened so fast," Josie mused.

"I understand the lure of old times and old challenges. Look, you're an athlete, Josie. Sport isn't only a physical thing. Once you get wrapped around this you won't quit until you've won."

Josie wriggled her fingers. She made a fist before flexing again. She moved in her chair like a fighter unwilling to admit he was past his prime, but still eager to see if he could survive one more bout in the ring.

"It's the girl who's important." Josie said. "I had a connection with her that I just couldn't ignore."

"That's valid but will you be able to live with whatever you do for her?"

"Rudy is taking this to the grand jury. I've got at least three days to figure that out, I guess."

"Well, then I suppose we'll see what happens in three days, won't we?" Faye picked up her glasses, but when she put them on she didn't seem ready to work. She was looking at Josie as if she wore magnifying glasses.

"I don't want to see you hurt, Josie, and I don't want to see my practice compromised."

Josie tilted back in the chair. She tapped her feet softly. Faye's perspective had put her off her timing and her tenuous commitment. She stood up.

"I'd never do anything to compromise this practice, or you. I'll pass on this if you say so, but Hannah's a step kid stuck in between her mother and Fritz Rayburn's son. Who else is going to defend someone like that?"

"There are plenty who will, Josie," Faye answered truthfully.

"Not the way I will, Faye. I've been on top; I don't care whether I get there again so I don't have an outside agenda. Linda is worried about her marriage; her stepfather wouldn't mind if she disappeared. I'll be there just for Hannah."

Faye knew Josie was walking into a brick wall but she also knew she couldn't do anything about that so she gave neither blessing, nor veto.

"Keep it to a dull roar, Josie, that's all I ask."

Josie stepped away from the desk, a half-smile on her face. This was no resounding cry of support, but it was something. She was almost out the door when Faye called to her.

"Josie, nothing you do for this girl will make up for the past. Not your lawyer past, or your daughter past. You do know that, don't you?"

"Of course," she answered.

It was the first time she had lied to Faye.

CHAPTER 10

"Today, the grand jury indicted Hannah Sheraton on charges of arson and murder. She remains free on bail. No trial date has been set." – Superior Court Press Office

"I am pleased to announce that I will ask the Commission on Judicial Appointments to confirm the nomination of Kip Rayburn to the California Supreme Court. Mr. Rayburn brings a wealth of experience to the bench. On a personal note, Mr. Rayburn's father, Fritz Rayburn, was the victim of a horrible crime. While the Rayburn family has suffered greatly, this experience will set Mr. Rayburn apart in terms of empathy and fortitude. I look forward to Kip Rayburn's confirmation so that he may carry on the excellent work his father began." – Joe Davidson, Governor of California

"I'm honored by the governor's nomination and look forward to the confirmation process. Until then, I will do everything possible to support my wife, and her daughter, during the coming days of Hannah's trial and hope that a judicious solution to this sad problem can be expeditiously found. No, I'm sorry, no more questions." – Kip Rayburn, California Supreme Court Nominee

Archer was in Mexico checking up on a young pup CFO whose board of directors believed he was smuggling drugs in the widgets they manufactured down there in

Baja. He had proved them right in record time, sent a bill from Cabo and was now on a picture safari, incommunicado, camping on some beach, taking his time coming back. He didn't know that Hannah had been indicted, but everyone else in the world did. Nobody could have kept a lid on what was going on. California loved a triangle and, as triangles went, this one was a doozy. Talk radio aficionados were already split with those who figured the stepdaughter was a bitch of the first degree and should fry, those who sympathized with the plight of a stepchild probably pushed to take drastic steps to be noticed, and those who refused to believe a child could possibly have had anything to do with Judge Rayburn's death.

Baxter & Associates was reeling from the impact. Faye wasn't happy. Josie was subdued. Angie, who was used to drawing up standard paperwork, was now organizing the discovery documents: arson reports, timelines, police reports, forensics, autopsy report and interviews with anyone who ever had any contact with Hannah Sheraton. Tiffany barely had time for a snack as reporters called for comments, and new clients with big problems called for consults.

Linda was devastated. She had convinced herself this was all a mistake. When Josie told them about the indictment and what would follow, Hannah touched her mother over and over again trying, perhaps, to comfort them both. Hannah's green eyes never left Josie's face, and Josie did not suggest they think about finding another attorney for the trial. She couldn't in the face of Hannah's silent fear.

On the beach, people who hadn't realized Josie was an attorney suddenly looked at her differently; they had an opinion about Hannah Sheraton. Billy Zuni told Josie to friggin' kick ass. Josie couldn't sleep, so half the patio tiles were laid in the dead of night. When she got the jitters thinking about cross-examination, exhibits, and evidence, she felt suddenly overwhelmed by a task that long ago had been second nature. She wanted Archer back every minute that Hermosa lay under the blanket of dark. But daylight came and there was work to be done and Josie put aside her disquiet.

Four days after the indictment, Linda summoned Josie to Malibu. It was still hot, even though fat, grey clouds hung off the coast adding humidity to the heat equation, as Josie drove Pacific Coast Highway. The Rayburn's beach house was set back two hundred yards off the highway. The closest neighbor was a mile away. The place was lit up like a movie set and might as well have been on its own planet. A giant fingerprint whorl of sand stone served as a driveway; the landscaping was exquisitely sparse: cactus, sea grasses, smooth stones, and jagged boulders. Beyond that there was beach. Prime property. Rayburn had done well for himself before taking the bench.

Twirling the Jeep into the drive, Josie stopped next to a Mercedes. A Lexus and a yellow VW bug shared the space in front of a four-car garage. Josie yanked on the emergency brake, and checked out the VW while she collected her things. The bug needed a wash and there was a boot on the back wheel. Hannah wasn't going anywhere in that thing. Josie got out of the car, tossed her baseball cap in the back, and checked out the amazing piece of architecture the Rayburns now called home.

A seemingly simple construct, closer inspection revealed a marvelous origami box of a home: glass butted stucco, stucco melted into copper, copper ran into tile, and that tile surrounded a pool of water that welcomed visitors with a serenity that masked the problems of the people inside.

A flight of low-rise steps brought Josie to a door as tall as the ten-foot wall that surrounded the house. It had oxidized to the strangely pleasing blue-green of exposed copper. A relief of angles as sharp as a maze of thorns was etched onto its surface.

"Come in, Josie."

Linda's voice, made deeper by the intercom, came through a hidden speaker. Josie scanned for the camera. She should have tagged the security before she was seen.

"What's the trick?" There was no knob or handle on the door.

"Push it."

Josie did as she was told and both sides swung open. Another touch and it revolved. Yet another and it closed again. It was a brilliant collaboration of art and engineering. She pushed again and passed into a courtyard paved in buff colored tile surrounded by walls of smooth stucco. Cut through the middle of this outdoor room was an endless pool. The water seeped under a glass wall that bared the heart of the house.

In front of the glass, in the middle of the pool, stood a bronze statue of a nude woman. She was contorted into a position of perpetual pain, or ecstasy, depending on one's point of view. Josie saw pain of the most humiliating and personal sort. Given what she knew about Hannah, Josie saw…

"Are you coming in?"

Josie tore her eyes from one tortured woman to another. Hannah stood in an opening in the glass wall. Her jeans were cut so low on the hip she could have belted them at her knees. Her white and blue checked long sleeved top was tied under her breasts. Her bellybutton had two piercings. There was a tattoo on her right hip and a streak of dried blood that stuck her shirtsleeve to her arm. Josie's eyes flickered toward that wound only to look away and see the statue.

"Nice place," Josie commented dryly.

"Un-huh." Hannah walked to the pool, hands pumping, counting as she considered the statue.

"What do you think about that?"

"I can't even begin to imagine what's happening to her," Josie said.

"I can." Hannah's voice was flat.

Silently Josie moved away. It would be easy to be drawn into the whirlpool of Hannah's problems, real or imagined. But Josie wasn't her shrink. Josie wasn't her mother. Josie was her attorney and she had to resist Hannah's attempt to make her anything else.

"Your mom's expecting me."

"Kip, too," Hannah said.

"That's half the battle," Josie muttered as she followed Hannah into the house.

"No it isn't," Hannah assured her.

CHAPTER 11

Kip Rayburn was nothing to look at. He wasn't unattractive, simply unmemorable. Light brown hair and not much of it; narrow face and not much to it. He had a slight body that let his clothes hang well but without flair. Yet, Kip Rayburn compensated for his ordinariness. His power was there in the way he stood on the fringe, instead of presenting himself front and center. There was power in his money. There was power now in his nomination.

"Josie, this is my husband, Kip."

Linda touched Josie's arm, then she turned and raised her hand toward her husband. She was a veritable Vanna White in the game of domesticity. Josie had too much to do to play along, so she walked across the huge living room and put out her hand.

"It's good to finally meet you. I'm glad we could all get together," she said.

Kip did a once over and seemed to frankly find her lacking. He didn't like her casualness, her athletic and boyish figure, and her less than classic features. Maybe he didn't like the fact that she wasn't as impressed with him as everyone else seemed to be these days. Still, he hid his feelings under a thin blanket of hospitality, and smiled perfunctorily.

"Some of my colleagues know your work. I understand it was impressive," he said by way of greeting.

"It still is." Without waiting to be asked, she sat in a horseshoe chair and put her portfolio at her feet. "Congratulations on your nomination."

"Thank you. I hope I can live up to the honor." Kip settled on the curved sofa and put both his arms across the back. The pose did nothing for him. "I was going to take over a partnership interest in Rayburn & Frank, but public service is a great opportunity."

"Your father would be proud if you followed either one, I'm sure."

With that, Kip Rayburn changed. One arm came down and rested in his lap, closing him off, the other dropped to the cushion. He crossed his legs. The mention of his father made Kip seem less than master in this house.

"Linda," Kip said. "Will you get us something to drink? Hannah could help you."

"Sure, honey. What do you want?" Linda asked.

"A glass of wine."

"Josie, what can I get you?"

"Nothing, thanks." Josie's eyes flickered to Hannah.

Linda stood up and summoned her daughter. "Hannah?"

"I don't want anything." She crossed her legs and sank to the floor next to Josie, close to Josie.

"Hannah." Linda was sharp. This was no request; it was a command. Hannah stiffened, sitting up straighter. One finger jumped as it tapped frenetically against her knee. Finally, reluctantly, Hannah acquiesced and followed her mother. Josie waited until they were gone before talking to Kip.

"Don't you think keeping liquor here is a little hard for Hannah?" Josie raised a brow.

"The cabinet's locked. We're very clear on the consequences if Hannah steps out of line this time."

"I know the conditions of her bail are very specific," Josie commented, "but it might help her if you simply didn't have alcohol in the house."

"I'm referring to my conditions, Ms. Bates, in my home."

Kip's gaze was steady, his decision final. Josie had underestimated him. Perhaps Davidson had made a good choice in nominating Kip to replace his father. She backed off on Hannah and made small talk instead. She spoke about the house, Fritz's love of art, the huge black canvases slashed with red that were the judge's favorites, Fritz's real estate acumen, Fritz's –

"Here we are."

Linda was back with refreshments, a glass of water for Josie just in case. The only thing missing was Hannah.

"Shouldn't this be a family meeting?" Josie asked.

"It is," Kip answered and Josie understood. Hannah was Cinderella but instead of ashes and stepsisters it was Kip and sand dunes.

Linda settled herself next to her husband. Her long legs were crossed at the ankles, her hand rested on his thigh. Square cut diamond earrings winked brilliantly as she moved and settled and still couldn't seem to find a comfortable place next to Kip.

"Ms. Bates," Kip began. "No matter what the court says, Hannah is still a child and a very disturbed one at that. She is good at letting you see what she wants you to see. The point is, Hannah is ill and she is our responsibility. Her problems are deep, chronic and unresolved. The girl needs intensive therapy, and that's what we intend to see she gets."

"Kip, we shouldn't overstate the situation." Linda broke in but Kip quieted his wife, tightening his grip on her hand. Linda gave no indication that she felt it as she addressed Josie. There was still some of the old Linda left, the woman who had a mind of her own.

"I'm sorry I didn't tell you about Hannah when I first came to see you, Josie. I don't like to admit how disturbed she is. Things have been awful since she found out she has to stand trial. She's cutting herself more often." Linda glanced at Kip and now her hand curled around his. They were together again. "We don't believe she will be able to make it through a trial."

"I've made some inquiries regarding a plea bargain." Kip took over. Josie remained impassive, her heart hardening with each word spoken. "I believe the District Attorney would be open to that. I think a plea bargain would be in everyone's best interest."

The silence was palpable in the glass house with the high ceilings. It wafted upward like heat, leaving the space between Josie and the Rayburns. It was a frigid, unwelcoming place.

"Really? And what are the conditions of your plea?" Josie asked quietly.

"Care, not incarceration, is what we're after," Kip answered.

"That's what you want, Linda?" Josie asked.

Linda got up, unable to look Josie in the eye. She walked toward the tall windows that opened onto the beach. Her reflection in the glass was ephemeral: hands lengthening as they wrung together, face contorting into a rubbery mask of grief, her body a watery column of sky blue silk. Her back was to Josie. That was a dangerous position to be in because Josie's outrage was as sharp as a dagger. But her anger was meant for Kip Rayburn. He was like the kid who plays hide-and-seek, then rats on everyone so he can win the game. When Linda muttered her agreement, Josie turned on Kip.

"Do you believe Hannah killed your father?"

"No. No we don't." Linda was quicker than her husband but he weighed in.

"I didn't say that," Kip insisted.

"Then you have no faith in my ability to defend your daughter," Josie pushed. "Is that it?"

"No." Kip said.

"Of course not..." Linda walked around the couch, trailing the thought into nothingness as she sat down next to her husband. "Josie, our decision has nothing to do with you."

"Well it must if you feel that your husband has to act as counsel and discuss a plea behind my back. I didn't realize you were a criminal attorney, Mr. Rayburn."

"I'm not, but I understand that there are always options in any trial. I believe if you can expedite a matter to the benefit of everyone concerned, then it should be done."

"And that's just going to be a fine attitude on the bench, isn't it?" Josie drawled sarcastically. "Forget justice. Forget the question of innocence or guilt. You'll just make sure everyone's happy by making problems go away."

"Josie, please. This is about what's good for Hannah," Linda cried.

"No it isn't. In fact, I don't exactly know what this is about." Josie leaned on the arm of her chair and pointed with one hand at Kip Rayburn. "And if you're so all fired up and determined to do what's right for Hannah, where were you when she needed your help? The night she was arrested, for instance? The day of the bail hearing when, for your information, I already flew that plea balloon past Rudy Klein. He wouldn't even discuss it. Where were you then?"

"I was mourning my father, Ms. Bates, and I don't appreciate you questioning my motives. My concern is for my wife, myself and, yes, my stepdaughter. If you question that, then why don't you convince me that you can prevail if we go to trial?"

"Why don't you ask me to walk on water?" Josie threw up her hands. "I've had the discovery documents less than a week. If you want me to lay out a defense I can't do it, but I can tell you there are problems with the prosecution. Klein hasn't asked that lesser charges be considered. That means he will have to prove beyond a shadow of a doubt that Hannah intended to kill Fritz, and I'll make that damn near impossible for him."

Kip scoffed, "That's too simplistic. Nothing is ever certain with a jury trial."

"Kip's right. Nearly impossible isn't good enough," Linda murmured. Her green eyes clicked a notch to look past Josie's shoulder. Josie tried to engage her again.

"But, Linda, if we plead out Hannah still goes to jail."

"That's not what we want," Linda said quietly. "We don't want her in jail at all."

Josie pulled back, surprised and curious.

"What do you think could happen? What do you think they would do with her? Slap her wrists and tell her not to play with matches?"

"Hannah can be remanded to a psychiatric facility for treatment. She'll plead no contest to arson and reckless endangerment in the death of my father." Kip was firm. He spoke for both of them yet, unlike Linda, his face was as blank and transparent as the end sheet of a book. "It would be best for everyone. Linda and I both agree."

Josie's elbow was cocked on the arm of the chair. She cradled her chin and looked at the two on the couch. Finally, she shook her head and dropped her hand.

"No. I won't let her plead out to a sentence in a state run psychiatric facility. I'm sorry."

Josie started to get up, but Kip stopped her with a warning.

"You don't have a choice here, Ms. Bates."

"But I do have a voice. Linda gave it to me when she retained me. Listen, if you put Hannah in a place like that she'll never get well. She will be locked up with women who are certifiably insane. Hannah may have problems, but there is no way you can put behavioral difficulties on a par with schizophrenia and homicidal..."

Josie paused and sat up just a little straighter. She'd almost missed it. She slid her eyes Kip's way.

"This isn't about Hannah. It's about you, isn't it? You're worried about your confirmation, so you're going to sacrifice Hannah. Is that it?"

"I resent that." Linda half rose from the sofa but Kip held her back. She shook him off hard. "I'm the one that begged you to take this case, and that should prove I'm worried about my daughter. A trial will jeopardize Hannah's mental health and that's what we're concerned about. Period."

Josie opened her mouth to argue, but before she could Kip asked the million-dollar question.

"How do you know she didn't murder my father?" Kip asked quietly.

"Because she said so in court," Josie pointed out.

"How do you know she didn't set the fire that resulted in my father's death?"

Josie understood the implication. Setting the fire without knowing Fritz was in the house would be a lesser offense and, indeed, Josie could plea bargain down on that. But she knew something they didn't.

"It doesn't matter. Death in the commission of arson doesn't apply here." Josie looked straight at Kip Rayburn. "Your father sustained a head wound before the fire started."

"Hannah hit him? She attacked my father?" Kip stuttered in disbelief.

"We don't know who hit him." Josie answered honestly. "It could have happened in a fall and then we could argue death in the commission of arson. But Rudy Klein believes it was a deliberate assault. That's why a satisfactory plea is going to be nearly impossible. Your only choice is to let me build a defense. Hannah is entitled to that, at least."

"You can take all your entitlement crap and shove it," Kip shot back.

"Kip, please," Linda pleaded, but Kip was on a roll. He ignored her, intent on Josie as if she were responsible for the demon child in their midst.

"From the very beginning we've had to wonder if Hannah set that fire, now we have to think that she may have beaten him? This is too much, Linda. I'm not going to have this woman waltz in here and tell us that we're heartless and self-centered if we don't do what she says. I know Cooper will work with us and that's what I want." Kip paced, so angered he could hardly contain himself.

"But there's a good chance she'll be acquitted," Josie objected as he threw himself onto the sofa, pushing into a corner of the couch.

"Then prove it to me now. Prove that, and we'll go to trial. If you can't, then I have to believe Hannah's a murderer and we are at risk if you get her off. The fact that you're talented enough to do that makes my blood run cold."

Josie was incredulous. What kind of demand was this? *Show me the killer; Hannah can be free.* It was appalling; a black and white demand with no room to maneuver. Even in court Josie would never have to find an alternative perpetrator.

"My job is to prove that Hannah didn't murder your father, not find out who did. You're acting like Hannah is a natural born killer. She's never been violent before, has she?"

"Stop pretending." Kip stood up quickly. His leg hit the coffee table. The glasses shuddered. One fell, spilling the wine over the glass top. "She cuts herself up like a piece of meat. I'd say that's violent."

"Hannah hurts herself, not other people." Josie snapped her head toward Linda. "Linda, for God's sake, there would have been something big before this. Hannah would have killed small animals, torn the wings off butterflies."

Kip whirled and leaned on the empty chair next to Josie's.

"You're not a psychiatrist. We've spoken to her doctor a thousand times. And what does he say? He says 'well, I don't think she's dangerous, but these situations are unpredictable.'" Kip's mimic of the doctor was cruel, and his next words bitter. "If he doesn't know, how in the hell do you?"

His plain face morphed as he pushed away from the chair. He was in charge. He was driven, determined to have his way.

"We're telling you we need this resolved now. We are the ones responsible for her. We're the ones who have to live with her, not you."

Josie stood up. Kip Rayburn didn't have enough game to shut her down. She didn't care whose son he was, or who he was about to become.

"I'm Hannah's attorney and, as such, I am responsible for the welfare of my client. So let me tell you what I know. Hannah won't last a minute if she serves a sentence in a psychiatric facility. You think she's got problems now? Just wait until they release her someday and she shows up on your doorstep. I guarantee you won't turn your lights off at night. Or are you one of those bleeding hearts that think criminals actually go into those places for treatment?"

Josie's hands punctuated every word that came out of her mouth. She whipped toward Linda and back to Kip, trying to find one who would stand with her for Hannah.

"Those places are dark, third rate institutions where overworked doctors make out reports and prescribe electroshock and pills that will keep Hannah so doped up she won't even know when one of the low life orderlies decides she looks like prime pickings. So he'll rape her, and she won't even know it. Or another inmate will..."

"Stop it! Josie, stop it!" Horrified, Linda cried out as she buried her face in her hands. It was Josie who got to her first. She took Linda's hands in her own and forced them down.

"Linda, listen to me."

"Wait just a minute," Kip rushed to the sofa. Josie met him head on, daring him to interfere.

"Back off," she growled, tired of him now. "Linda, look at me. This is your daughter's life. It's not a game. It's deadly serious and what you do now is going to affect her whole life, Linda. You're her mother for God's sake. Do you really think she did something she should go to jail for?"

Linda's bright eyes darted everywhere, searching for the right answer. Her lips parted – pink, pink lips – but it was hard for her to speak. She turned those eyes toward her husband, but Josie put one hand to Linda's cheek and made her focus on the question.

"Do you want Hannah to suffer?" Josie whispered angrily, pushing for a decision.

"I don't want her in jail for something she didn't do," Linda answered back with words that were dry and fragile. Josie chased after them, collecting Linda's wishes like fall leaves and bringing them back to drop in Linda's lap.

"Then don't throw her away. Don't abandon her. A mother can't do anything worse than that."

Linda glanced at Kip. She hung her head and curved toward Josie. They were a conspiracy of two, excluding Kip. This was between them, women who understood a child's life was at stake.

"Can you win?" Linda whispered, and the undercurrent of absolute terror didn't escape Josie's notice. She felt it, too.

"I'll give it everything I've got, Linda. Your gut said to trust me, so trust your gut now." There was a heartbeat of silence, a bubble of apprehension surrounded Josie and Linda. Josie held tighter, whispered more urgently. "Let me try."

Linda slid one hand from Josie's and then the other. She put her fingers to her lips. They trembled. From behind them she called to her husband who stood apart, his eyes shuttered, his body taut.

"Kip?"

"You decide, Linda. She's your daughter."

Josie closed her eyes. Those words were so cruel, so unnecessary. She willed Kip Rayburn to give his wife a sign that he would stand beside her. He didn't. Linda would have to stand on her own. She did it well.

"I want you to try, Josie. I owe Hannah so much."

Josie dropped her head. Linda's pain of indecision was real, but Josie couldn't believe there was even a choice here. If Hannah were her daughter, Kip Rayburn would have eaten their dust.

Exhausted, relieved, Josie stood up. She walked back to her chair and picked up her briefcase. She had to pass Kip Rayburn as she left. She stopped beside him. They would need him.

"It's for the best, Mr. Rayburn. I promise you. No one will think differently."

"We all have to do what we think is right," he said quietly, his back to her. Josie started to leave but he called to her, walked toward her, and spoke to her. "Just so we're clear. I don't like the way you're playing with our lives. My father is dead, and I think Hannah had something to do with it. I don't know what it was, I don't know how she did it, I don't know if she actually lit the match, but I'm telling you she's trouble. So, go ahead and prepare your case. I'll pay your fee. I'll sit in that courtroom and support my wife, but don't you expect me to root for you after what you did to my family tonight. Do you understand?"

"Sure," Josie muttered, knowing she didn't understand anything about this family – especially where Hannah fit in.

CHAPTER 12

Josie breathed deep, filling lungs that seemed to have had all the air sucked out of them. This was not the triumph of architectural living space she originally thought. It was an exquisite tomb, and the time spent in it made her feel intellectually brittle and emotionally dry. Hannah, Kip and Linda, all with their own issues, their own guilt, their own needs, were now going to be locked together through the eternity of this trial because Josie had forced the issue.

The things Josie had known when she arrived – the trial schedule, the essence of her strategy – now seemed less the beginning of a stunningly constructed defense and more a desperate attempt to dazzle a jury that would have the same concerns that Kip had. Worst of all, she hated Kip for making this so damned personal. Josie didn't know if she fought hard because she believed in Hannah, because she wanted to prove that she could win, or because Kip Rayburn's reticence seemed inhuman even under the circumstances.

Still, it bothered Josie that she hadn't acknowledged the fundamental problem. In this family the accused and the victim's survivor were linked together by the tenuous thread of Linda. One of them would lose – or perhaps all of them – and still Josie would be standing. She could retreat to her office at Baxter & Associates when this was all over. She had an escape route. She wasn't in danger of losing a husband, or a daughter. That realization put Linda in a whole new light. She deserved a heck of a lot of respect for what she'd done tonight.

Josie walked back over the flesh colored tiles, past the horridly graphic statue and thought of Hannah, a girl who had no say in her future. Hannah was Fritz Rayburn's charity case; not even a blip on the radar for Kip. Maybe that was what bothered Josie the most. They spoke of Hannah as if she was a leaking faucet that annoyed everyone, but not enough to fix it once and for all.

Josie pushed open the huge copper door and walked back out to the real world.

The stars were brilliant. A near full moon made the white sand sparkle, and spilled a shimmering path of light right down the center of the ocean. Josie lifted her face as a surprisingly cool breeze sifted through her hair. The night was pungent with sea smells, but still she was ill at ease. Something was forgotten. It wasn't until Josie saw Hannah sitting behind the wheel of her Jeep that Josie remembered what it was. She should have said goodbye to her client.

"Hey," Hannah called as Josie ambled toward the Jeep. The floodlights made the black finish look like onyx and Hannah like a vision.

"I thought you were going to leave without saying anything to me." Hannah's lashes covered her eyes in a long, languid motion. Her head swirled and when she looked at Josie again her expression was almost vacant.

"I was," Josie admitted. Whoever said the truth never hurt anyone was wrong. It hurt Josie. She wasn't sure what it did to Hannah. "I'm sorry, I shouldn't have forgotten. I was just thrown off base a little by our meeting."

"Still trying to figure out what happened?"

"I guess so," Josie admitted. She put her hand on Hannah's shoulder and gave her a gentle shove. "Move over."

Hannah crawled over the gearshift into the passenger seat. Her right hand touched the door handle as she settled herself in the new place. Josie waited, forcing herself not to count along. When Hannah was done, she said:

"Kip's jealous, that's what it is. He's supposed to be getting all the attention and everything, but I'm getting it. Plus, he doesn't like things to be complicated. I'm the complication. The trial is a complication and now you are, too."

"What about your mom? She doesn't think you're a complication, does she?"

Hannah whispered. "My mom loves me. Nobody can say different."

"I didn't mean to imply that." Josie put her head back on the seat and looked up at the sky. Hannah's defensiveness was familiar. Josie had been that way about her own mother at Hannah's age. The difference was that Josie wasn't sure if her mother actually did love her.

"She wants to make sure we stay safe," Hannah went on as if she hadn't heard Josie. "She'd do anything to make sure we stay safe. I know she thinks it would be better for both of us if you could just get the District Attorney to send me to a hospital. Kip just thinks it would be easier."

"What do you think?"

"I think it's fucked and so do you," Hannah laughed. It was the first time Josie had heard her do that. It was a beautiful sound and gone too quickly.

"How do you know that's what I think?" Josie laughed, too. It felt good on a night like this when everything else looked so dark and desperate.

"The master control on the intercom is in the kitchen. I heard you fight for me. I didn't hear all of it. I thought mom was coming. She thinks I don't know about the hospital thing."

Josie sat up, retrieved her baseball hat and took her keys out of the console. "So, now that we've got that out of the way, is there something you want to tell me?"

"Yeah, I came out here to check on your car twelve times. Then I sat in it and waited for you," Hannah said.

"And...." Josie prodded, not quite getting the point, anxious to be home.

"Twelve times. Not twenty. Shit, twelve times!" Hannah threw up her hands. She shook her head, angry and frustrated. Her burned hand hit the console hard, keeping double time with her words. "Shit, shit, shit! I thought you'd get it. That's a good thing."

Josie laughed again in spite of herself. She stopped Hannah. Held her hand before the girl reached twenty hits.

"A breakthrough," Josie said softly.

"It's not funny," Hannah jerked away.

"I'm not laughing at you. I'm proud of you. Twelve is better than twenty and two would be better than twelve. Hey, simple arithmetic," Josie assured her.

"Do you think I could do that?" Hannah stared straight ahead, rigid next to Josie, waiting for her to predict failure.

"Sure, why not?" Josie put her key in the ignition. She turned her head and looked at Hannah. "We've got a couple of weeks before things get going, Hannah. If you could get to two that would be good. If you didn't count at all that would be great."

"Maybe. I won't promise."

Sadly Hannah's expression was blank again, the laughter gone. Josie would have given anything to know what was behind that beautiful mask. Some lies, some information withheld, but the bottom line was real; Hannah wanted to be defended and that's all Josie had to know.

"No problem. I know there aren't any promises, so don't worry." They sat in silence. The night was so big Josie felt as if it could swallow up their problems. Hannah had a different thought altogether.

"I'm not an idiot, you know."

"I never said you were," Josie sighed. Children were hard to deal with; children who were on the verge of adulthood must be the hardest of all. Maybe she'd been too difficult for Emily, and that was a sad thought.

"I just want you to know that I'm afraid. I would be a real idiot if I weren't. I can't show it, but for me to know I'm afraid is good. That's a big step."

"Then I'm glad because you should be afraid," Josie said quietly.

"Are you?" Hannah asked.

"Afraid?" Josie kept her eyes on the stars. It wasn't a hard question; it was just hard to answer out loud.

"Yeah," Josie whispered. "I am, but probably not for the reasons you think. You're so young. You have such a long life ahead. There's always a chance I won't win."

"And then there's the thing you told me about that other person you defended, the person who shouldn't have gotten off."

"Sure. There's that. It's history," Josie said quietly. She wouldn't burden Hannah with the story of the crime; she wouldn't scare her with the story of Rudy Klein's desire to avenge that loss.

"Good. You have to think about me as someone who deserves to win, Josie. Someone who is totally, totally innocent. I want you to think about me that way, okay?"

With that, Hannah climbed out of the car. She didn't get far before she turned and came back. She touched the Jeep and left again.

"Goodnight, Hannah," Josie called and started the car.

Once again Hannah ran back toward the Jeep but this time she went to the driver's side. One of Josie's hands was on the gearshift; the other was on the steering wheel. Hannah stood so close Josie couldn't have left without backing over her. Fast as lightening Hannah touched Josie twice, near caresses given with such gentleness, such hope, such raw need and intimacy they unnerved Josie.

"Two times," Hannah whispered and then she was gone.

Kip Rayburn pulled the little chain on the desk lamp and opened the drawer to his right. Inside was his Los

Angeles BAR address book. He took it out and turned the pages, found the number he wanted, and dialed.

He crossed his legs and waited. The phone was answered on the second ring and Kip asked to speak to Rudy Klein. Kip's hand was clammy. His heart beat just a little faster. The things he had done tonight: challenging people, becoming angry, thinking ahead, taking his shot – were so out of character. It felt good; it was frightening. He could still hang up, but then Rudy said hello.

"Yes. Mr. Klein. This is Kip Rayburn."

Rudy Klein didn't seem surprised to hear from him but then that was the sign of a good lawyer. Nothing should surprise a good lawyer – or a good criminal for that matter. Minimal pleasantries were exchanged before Rudy asked what he could do for Kip.

"I received a call from your office some days ago, Mr. Klein," Kip said. "I understand you would like to interview me."

"I'm hoping you'll cooperate. I know it will be difficult given your relationship with Ms. Sheraton. I promise to do everything I can to get information I need from other sources, but…

"That's fine, Mr. Klein. You don't have to worry. You'll have no problem with me. I'll cooperate in any interview and will answer a subpoena if necessary," Kip interrupted. To his credit, Rudy asked no questions. He thanked Kip.

The two men hung up. Kip Rayburn kept his hand on the receiver, thinking he might actually pick it up again and tell Klein that it had all been a mistake. There really wasn't any need to testify. Not yet. Maybe he should have waited to see how things went before putting himself out there. Then he thought again. Ian Frank had been right. Preemptive strikes were weapons of the powerful. Only fools waited until they were on the spot and Kip had been a fool for years, waiting until things with his father got out of hand before trying to put a stop to them. No, he'd done the right thing. Expedite. Expedite.

"Kip? Are you coming to bed?"

Startled, Kip took his hand off the phone. Linda stood in the doorway – tall and gorgeous – looking at him curiously. She was different since Hannah had been arrested; they were different together, too, and not in a bad way. Kip took a deep breath. He would have to tell her. He would have to tell her soon what he was doing.

"Don't you want to come to bed?" She asked and those long fingers of hers trailed across the deep neckline of her negligee.

Yes. He'd have to tell her sooner – or later.

"Was that business, Daddy?"

"Yeah, sport, that was business." Rudy Klein scooped up his son and threw him over his shoulder. Mikey giggled, the way five-year-old boys will, as Rudy twirled him around once for good measure. "Yeah, that was business, and now I'm going to give you the business."

Mikey laughed louder as Rudy carted him down the hall like a sack of potatoes. He sang a song about the wheels on a bus and bounced on his dad's shoulder. Rudy breathed in the scent of his boy as they went. Soap and powder, the smell of a child's soft skin that would disappear in the next few years; there was nothing like it.

Rudy never wanted to forget any of it. The same way he wouldn't forget the sound of Mikey's laughter, the feel of those chubby hands against his back, the voice that was as clear as an angel's, the all too precious moments of childhood that Rudy was allowed to share as his little boy was shuttled between mother and father.

"Here we go!" Rudy whipped him off his shoulder and cradled his back so that Mikey became an upside-down airplane. In a second he landed smack dab in the middle of the little bed. Rudy always kept it made up with fresh sheets in case Pam let him have more than his court ordered visitation.

"Do it again!" Mikey cried, holding out his arms, his little body wiggling with anticipation.

"Nope, it's too late. Time for big boys to be asleep. Mom is coming early in the morning to get you."

"How early?" Mikey asked as Rudy tucked the sheets tight and turned out the bedside light.

"Too, early," Rudy said lightly, trying to keep the sadness out of his voice.

He could put criminals behind bars, he could fight the bad guys on every front, but he couldn't convince the judge who handled his divorce that picking a kid up at five in the morning wasn't good for anyone.

"Daddy, I could stay here 'till you got back from business," Mikey said seriously, willing to forgo the pleasure of putting on his little back pack at five in the morning so mommy could drive him to day care and she could get to her job on time.

"Sorry, sport" Rudy said and ran his hand through Mikey's dark curls, "but mom says she can't stand having you gone one more minute. Not one more."

"Can you stand me gone one minute?" The little boy asked.

Rudy touched his son's face. He smiled and kissed Mikey's cheek.

"No, sport, I can't stand it when you're gone any minutes," Rudy said truthfully. "And that's a good thing. That means that no matter what happens, there are always two people in this whole wide world who want you."

Mikey smiled and turned on his side, settling himself into his little nest, one last thought on his mind.

"I bet some kids don't even have one person who loves them so much," he said with satisfaction.

"I bet you're right, sport," Rudy whispered back.

Standing up, Rudy looked at his boy, still feeling guilty that he didn't have the perfect family. Then he thought of Hannah Sheraton and realized Mikey didn't have it so bad after all. At least he didn't have anyone who was willing to throw him away – or some prosecutor determined to put him away.

Hannah sat on a stool in her room.

It was a very low, very small red lacquer stool. Her knees were drawn up and she leaned over far enough to rest her chest on them. Her arms were wrapped around her legs and her face was turned toward the glass door that opened her room to the beach. Hannah could see out; anyone could see in. But there was no one to see. Kip owned the beach, and the house, now that Fritz was dead.

At her feet was a small black porcelain dish, a delicate silver fish painted in the center. She could see each scale shimmering on its perfect little body. A razor blade lay across the fish's belly. No one could figure out how she managed to cut herself. The cook watched the knives. Kip used an electric razor. Linda rationed disposables so Hannah could shave her legs thinking she couldn't do anything obscene with them. Clever Hannah saved one now and again. She broke open the plastic casing, took the tiny blade and hid it in a pouch in the back of her closet. Hannah still had two blades left in her pouch. The third was on the dish with the fish.

Curled on her stool, Hannah stared at that blade for the longest time. Where, she wondered, did the light come from that caused it to glint in the darkened room? How big was the machine that beveled the edges of that tiny piece of metal? Who invented cutting blades a million, zillion years ago? Hannah wondered if that person had a name, or if they were just like her – just someone.

Time came and went and finally Hannah picked it up. The blade was so small Hannah took some pride in being able to cut just deep enough, just far enough, to draw just enough blood with such a tiny instrument.

She looked over her shoulder on the off chance that her mother might see what was happening and stop her. When the door of her room didn't open Hannah made a parallel cut alongside a long-healed scar. The second cut was short. The third was a series of three cuts all in a line. SOS. Dot. Dash. Dot. Hannah looked at her handiwork, pale in the limited light. There wasn't much blood. She hadn't gone deep. Tomorrow she would go deeper.

Unwinding herself, Hannah stood up and opened the glass door. Leaving her shoes behind, she crossed the patio. The sand was cold; the air was warm. There was a breeze that tousled her hair. Hannah bent down and dug a hole. She worked relentlessly as the dry sand fell in on itself again and again. When it was deep enough, Hannah buried her blade so no child who might stumble upon this private beach would be hurt. Hannah would never want a child to be hurt. Never.

When Hannah was done she prowled the perimeter of the house, holding her cut arm up to the ocean air. The salt stung and the wounds tingled but nothing could really hurt Hannah. Not much, anyway. Not often, anyhow. There had been a time not too long ago, when she was hurt so bad she thought she would die. But that time was almost forgotten. When the trial was done she'd forget it altogether.

Hannah twirled, arms out, her long hair floating in the breeze. Her eyes were closed and every time she peeked Hannah expected to see day. But it was always night. The hours hadn't passed and that's when Hannah got sick.

She stumbled back to her bedroom and sat on her little stool, pulling herself tight in a ball as she rocked. She wished she could paint, but no flammables were allowed around her. That was a no-no. The judge said so. If she could paint, the sickness inside would go away. Hannah made a muffled little mewling sound and rocked her feet heel to toe.

Her chin hurt because it was pushed hard into the knobs of her knees. Her cheekbones felt as if they would crack from the pressure as she clenched her jaw. Hannah closed her eyes and rocked. She thought of Josie. *There's a lesson Hannah. Take a lesson from Josie, Hannah. Life's hard. Deal with it. Fight for it. Stand up, Hannah. Do it for yourself.*

Then it didn't matter whom Hannah thought about. She sprang from her seat, stuck her hand between her mattress and box spring and found the other things she kept hidden. She opened the little box. Three little joints left. Three was her lucky number. Three blades. Three joints. Three people in this house.

The matches were in the bathroom, hidden in the box of tampons. They wouldn't let her have paints but nobody checked for matches. How dumb was that? Outside again, Hannah cupped her hands, bent her head and put a match to the roach. She sucked the smoke in deep and held it. The sick feeling didn't leave. It squeezed her head so she started to walk around the house, ticking and shaking the little box of wooden matches as she went. Shake and shake, counting the times she heard the scratching sound they made. Hannah shook and shook, trying to count the number of matches by the sound. Hannah walked to the back of the house and looked up toward the bedroom her mother shared with Kip. The lights were out. They were asleep. Kip hadn't looked at Hannah yet. All Linda did was look at Kip. All Linda did was say everything would be all right. Hannah just didn't know which of them she was saying it to. Guilt. Guilt. It was the word that connected them all, and kept them all apart.

She walked to her side of the house. Head down and steps measured she paced off her prison. When Hannah had journeyed ten times on that route she detoured inside and walked up the stairs. Hannah was a shadow. No one knew she was there even when it was light. Half the joint was gone; the other half snuffed out and cupped between her hands along with the box of matches. No one would hear them shake as Hannah walked up those stairs and stood outside her mother's bedroom door. She peered through a crack in the door. They were there. Her mother with her long hair and naked shoulders, Kip curled around her in sleep; Kip who would be a judge; Kip who was just like his father. They were there. In bed. Together.

Hannah turned around and walked down the stairs.

Hannah walked up those stairs again and stood outside the bedroom door and looked.

She walked down.

She walked up and stood and looked.

She held the matches and the roach cupped in her hand so no one would hear, no one would smell the smoke, and no one would know she was standing outside the bedroom door looking and thinking and wondering if she had really done the right thing the night of the fire.

Josie sat with her back to the wall, one foot dangling toward the floor, the other propped up on the bar stool next to her. One arm was on the bar, her hand wrapped around a glass of beer. It was still full, but the foam had long since faded. A half eaten burger was on the plate beside her. Eric Clapton was on the jukebox, and a couple of baseball teams silently ran around on the big-screen TV in the corner. A woman nursed a martini at a table near the window. A couple was having a heated disagreement in the hallway that led to the bathrooms.

Other than that, it was a quiet night at Burt's at the Beach.

"Is it my cooking?"

Josie swiveled her head but didn't lift it from the wall behind her. She smiled at Burt. Burt, who was once one of the finest male volleyball players on the circuit, still looked ruggedly handsome despite the crow's feet, and the gray through his long blond hair. He crashed and burned on his motorcycle in ninety-four. Broke about every bone in his body. He still looked damn good, but he lost everything that made him one of the best on the beach: his speed, his agility, and his range of motion. He spent the next two years trying to kill himself with booze and pills. Then he found a good woman and opened Burt's. The good woman wasn't as good as he thought, but Burt's at the Beach was a godsend. He loved his place, and so did people who called Hermosa home. You never had to dress up, the food was basic, good and priced right, every woman was safe, every man who wasn't was asked to leave, and Burt knew everyone's name.

"It's Cordon Bleu as usual, Burt. I'm just not as hungry as I thought I was." Josie pushed the beer mug his way. "Or as thirsty."

"I knew that the second you came through the door. Next time I'll just refuse to serve you. Hate stuff going to waste."

Burt took the plate and put it under the counter. He tossed the beer and put the mug in the sink. He checked out the martini woman and the feuding couple who now seemed to be making up. Then he crossed his arms on the bar and didn't say anything more. He waited for Josie.

"So what do you do when someone mistakes professional help for personal interest, Burt?"

Burt pulled back slightly. "You can't handle some guy? That's a new one."

Josie laughed softly, "Naw, nothing like that."

"Some woman?" Burt raised his brows and wiggled them as he smiled. One of his front teeth was still broken. He didn't want to fix it because it reminded him of how stupid he had been on his bike.

"Some kid," Josie answered. "Some poor messed up kid."

"Bummer," he mumbled as he considered the ramifications of that.

"Yeah. I'm not sure what to do. What do I know about kids?" Josie traced a pattern through the water ring her mug had left on the bar as she lapsed into a thoughtful silence. "Or maybe I'm making too much of it."

Finally Burt sighed real deep. He stood up, took the towel from his waist, and Josie's arm by the wrist. He lifted her hand and wiped the water away. He patted her hand.

"You do what everyone else in the whole world does, Josie. Go home. Get some sleep. Start doing your job in the morning. Everything else will work itself out. It always does. Besides, Archer's due back day after tomorrow, isn't he? That's going to make all right with the world."

"You're right. I'm tired. I'll take Max for a walk and get some sleep."

Josie dropped her foot off the stool, and ten bucks on the bar. Burt swiped it up, watched her go, and wondered if Josie was dumb enough to believe that piece of crap. The truth was, personal stuff like that didn't just hang on, it burrowed like a tick, and that could make you real sick if it was the right kind of tick.

CHAPTER 13

"My client looks forward to getting back to being a child." – *Josie Baylor-Bates*

"I have great faith in the justice system." – *Kip Rayburn*

"I want my daughter home." – *Linda Rayburn*

Linda and Kip dashed up the steps of the courthouse. Josie Baylor-Bates was close behind with Hannah cringing inside her protective arm. Reporters followed, tossing questions and shoving microphones their way. The three adults threw their answers over their shoulders intent only on getting to the quiet of the courtroom.

They had exchanged no more than hellos when they met on the street. Each gave a one-sentence statement. Kip rebuffed Josie's attempts to thank him for coming, for showing support. He was there to show his support for the court, for the system, for a girl who was only accused. It was the line the governor's right hand man, Alex Schaeffer, had suggested he stick with. Kip hated it. Holding Linda's hand was his idea. Linda clung to him. Even when Josie held the door open for them Linda hung back as if afraid something might happen to her if she walked through them. That was understandable. Josie had rushed up these steps with another client three years ago and met her Waterloo. Kip was taut, anxious, and trying to hide at every turn. Understandably so. He wouldn't be able to watch the trial. The prosecution had subpoenaed him. He would wait outside the doors until it was his turn to testify. It was a despicable move by Klein and there was nothing Josie could do about it. Hannah was the only one who remained silent, her eyes downcast, hearing, no doubt, every nuance in the terse exchanges between parents and attorney, attorney and reporters.

Inside, no one spoke. They passed through the metal detectors single file. Purses, briefcases went through the conveyor belt. Arms out. Wands were passed over each of them. They waited for the elevator and entered together. They exited with Linda leading, her arm around Hannah, Kip on the other side of the girl. A tense caravan, they walked into a courtroom filled with curious, respectfully subdued spectators. The clerk was handling last minute housekeeping. The bench rose high off the floor, the seal of the state hung heavy on the wall. Josie and Hannah parted ways with the Rayburns. They went to the seats behind the bar, Josie and Hannah to the table in front of it. Josie put her briefcase on top, pushed the chair aside with her leg. Hannah was already settled, her hands in her lap, looking exactly as Josie had requested. Her wild hair was plaited in a braid down her back, wisps of caramel colored hair curled around her temple, highlighting her eyes. She wore a white sweater set, long sleeved to cover the scars on her arms. Her skirt was flowered in black and navy. It hit below her knees. Her shoes were low heeled; her multiple piercings discarded save for pearls on each earlobe.

Josie leaned down, put her hand on Hannah's shoulder and whispered:

"I'll be right back."

Hannah was quick. Her hand caught Josie's. She held on tight. Without a word she begged Josie with her eyes. *Don't go. Don't leave.* Josie extricated herself. She half-smiled knowing she wouldn't be effective for Hannah if she couldn't banish the ghost of Kristin Davis real fast.

"I'll only be a minute. You can talk to your mom. It's okay."

Josie looked at no one as she pushed through the door, walked halfway down the long hall, went into the ladies room into a stall and closed the door behind her.

Sitting on the toilet fully dressed, Josie cradled her head in her hands. She felt heavy, unworkable, in need of some cosmic grease for joints that hadn't moved in years. She had been so sure the determination, the excitement, the game-day exhilaration would drive away any doubt or fear that still clung to her like a fine sea spray. She was wrong.

"Come on. Come on" Josie gritted her teeth and cheered herself on. This wasn't three years ago. Her client wasn't an evil woman with an increasingly wicked agenda. This was Hannah who called and talked just to make sure Josie was still with her. This was a kid who showed Josie exactly how she tried to put out the fire. This was a case where all the prosecution had was circumstantial evidence. She could do this. She could win, and it would be right.

Sitting up straight, Josie took a deep breath through her nose and held it in her lungs. She put her hands in the pockets of her blazer and squared her shoulder. Her fingers curled around the picture she'd almost forgotten was there. Archer had come early in the morning, missing her as she walked Max. He had taped his favorite picture of her to the door of her house: Six pack abs showing, square jawed face straight on to the camera, hat on backward, and glaring eyes behind the glasses. He had taken it when she lost a point; Archer could see that she meant to win the next one. Now the next one was here. She wanted to do him proud, she wanted everyone to be proud including herself.

Pocketing the picture, Josie got up, washed her hands for good measure, and walked down the center aisle of the courtroom where she sat next to Hannah as the Court TV cameras rolled. Cyrus Norris, the trial judge, took the bench, Kip Rayburn left the courtroom, and Rudy Klein began his case with Chris Keenan, the arson investigator.

Young enough to be the kind of guy every woman would want to have around to put out her fire, old enough to be competent, he was the perfect witness. Blue eyed, black haired and handsomely dressed Mr. Keenan answered clearly and spoke directly to Rudy. They'd run through the preliminaries: when he arrived at the scene, ordering up the dogs, cordoning off the scene, and the suspicious color of the smoke indicating accelerants had been used. Now Rudy propped a board on an easel in front of the jury.

Exhibit one. The crime scene. The handsome Mr. Keenan pointed out where he had found the first indication that accelerants had been used to start the fire. Six feet inside the French doors on the ground level.

Exhibit two. Enlarged photos of the flooring shadowed with burn marks. *Spalling*, he called it. Caused by either high heat or mechanical pressure.

Keenan flashed a bright white, perfect smile at Rudy that radiated right into the jurors' hearts. "The marks were made by high heat. A petroleum-based flammable was spilled on the asphalt tile floor and set afire. When the asphalt curled in the heat the liquid seeped through to the concrete and pooled in cracks. Bottom line, the fire on the first floor was deliberately set using a flammable liquid as an accelerant."

"And could you identify that agent?' Rudy asked.

"Turpentine," the witness answered.

"And the second floor?" Rudy pointed to the exhibit.

"The vapor samples were consistent with a turpentine spill." Keenan answered. "The fire was deliberately set just inside the door of the bedroom where the body of Justice Rayburn was found."

"Is it unusual to find two independent points of origin in the matter of arson?"

"No. It's very common. The arsonist realized she couldn't rely on the first fire to accomplish her objective."

"Your Honor, the use of the pronoun is prejudicial!" Josie was on her feet. Keenan might as well have hung a guilty sign on Hannah with that one.

"Restate, Mr. Keenan," Judge Norris said offhandedly, leaving the outrage for the attorneys.

"In my experience, the first fire is set to destroy something and the second would be started in the hopes of destroying the evidence of the first arson or an additional crime."

"So in this case, the objective of the first fire would be to make sure Fritz Rayburn was killed in that–"

"Your Honor! Speculative and highly prejudicial." This time Josie flew out of her chair. Beside her, Hannah's hands hit the underside of the table in agitation.

Judge Norris shot a finger at the prosecutor. "Mr. Klein that will not be tolerated. The jury is instructed to disregard Mr. Klein's comment. Mr. Klein, you know the boundaries. Don't cross them."

"I was just connecting the dots, Your Honor," Rudy explained, his deceit obvious to his peers. To the jury, that comely face of his wore a look of innocent surprise that he had displeased the judge.

He backed away, smiling apologetically, until the jury could no longer see his face. When he passed Josie, his expression was rock hard. He was happy to have drawn the first blood. They didn't acknowledge one another as Josie stood. Two could play at this game. He nicked a vein; she would go for the witness's jugular. Squaring her shoulders Josie let the jurors get a good look at her. She didn't want them trying to figure out how tall she was when they should be watching as this witness went down in flames.

CHAPTER 14

"Mr. Keenan, you testified that there were pools of flammable liquid found in the crevices of the concrete floor on the ground level. Would you consider that unusual given the inventory you noted in that room?"

"The concentration of the fluid was unusual," the witness answered.

"But the room was used as an art studio. Would it be unusual to find turpentine in a studio?"

"No."

"I wouldn't think so either, Mr. Keenan." Josie smiled, happy that they could instantly agree with one another. "In fact, you referred to the pooling of turpentine as a *spill.* Would you say it was unthinkable for an artist to accidentally spill turpentine in the course of completing a project?"

"No, it's not unthinkable but..."

Josie turned back to him, all business, non-threatening. She was simply intellectually curious, a direct contrast to Rudy's more affable style.

"So it is possible that in a studio, anyone going about the business of creating art could have accidentally *spilled* turpentine in that particular area."

"Yes."

"And even if the artist wiped it up, it would be impossible to see the liquid pooling in the cracks and crevices of the floor. Yes or no."

"Yes," the witness answered, chaffing against the restraint of a one-word answer.

"Thank you, Mr. Keenan. Now, can you tell me what *overlap* is?" Josie changed tracks effortlessly. Let Rudy use the dirty tricks; she would use finesse.

"Overlap is a phenomenon by which a fire burning on one floor licks up to the floor above it and ignites a separate fire."

"During stage two when the fire is free burning, is it possible for a fire to spread by flashover, Mr. Keenan?" Josie asked.

"Yes."

"How about spontaneous ignition?"

"Yes, in certain condit–"

"Convection?"

Josie questioned without defining terms. The rhythm made the words frightening, mysterious and important. She felt swept along with the tempo of the moment. It was a good feeling.

"Yes."

"Pyrolysis?"

"Possible."

"Could a fire spread vertically?"

Keenan raised his hand slightly in exasperation.

"Yes, it could spread up stairwells or pipe shafts. But in this case..."

Josie interrupted, turning toward his sketch of the crime scene.

"What is this area indicated on your sketch of the scene?" Josie pointed to a green box.

"That is a dumb waiter."

"A dumb waiter is a hollow shaft between the first floor and the second floor of that wing, isn't it Mr. Keenan? And the inside of this dumb waiter was charred wasn't it, Mr. Keenan?"

"Yes."

"Consistent with highly accelerated vertical travel of the fire?"

"Yes."

"And this stairwell, Mr. Keenan?" Josie pointed to a rectangular area. "Another vertical path upon which the fire from the first floor could travel?"

"Yes, but that doesn't take into consideration the flash point of the fire upstairs."

Josie lips twitched. She barely took a breath.

"Mr. Keenan, can you tell us when the accelerant was spilled upstairs?"

"Considering the burn patterns, the rate of vaporization of the accelerants, the amount of accelerant left in the carpet samples the spill happened within minutes of being ignited."

"And how was the fire initiated?" Josie asked, leaning toward him as if she was hanging on his every word.

"We found matches on the ground floor. We're still testing debris on the second floor."

Josie walked slowly toward the jury. She stood close as if she was part of them, as if they were a team. Her skepticism radiated outward, engulfing them.

"Mr. Keenan, can you tell us who used that match to set the fire downstairs?"

"No, I cannot."

"Could you tell if the match was dropped by someone? A smoker? Someone lighting a candle?"

"I don't think that is probable."

"But is it possible?" Josie prodded.

"It is possible, but not probable."

"But it is possible," Josie insisted.

"Yes," Keenan acquiesced, his face coloring.

Josie nodded thoughtfully. She began to walk toward Hannah. She was almost at the table, almost by her client's side, when suddenly she looked over her shoulder, held up a finger as if remembering something important.

"Mr. Keenan? How long have you been an arson inspector?"

If looks could kill, Josie would have been incinerated where she stood.

"Six months," he answered.

"That long?" Josie drawled.

"And how many arson investigations have you conducted?"

"Two," he said quietly.

"Including the Rayburn fire?" she asked.

"Objection, Your Honor!" Rudy had finally had enough. "The defense stipulated to his expert status before he took the stand. She has nothing to gain by trying to insult this witness."

"Withdrawn," Josie said quietly, confidently, her point well taken.

Rudy stood up without an invitation to redirect. He didn't button his coat. Instead, he stuffed one hand in his pocket and ran his other through his hair.

"Mr. Keenan, have you completed all the necessary training an arson investigator needs to be qualified in the State of California?"

"I was top of my class."

"And what did you do before you became an arson investigator?"

"I was a firefighter for fifteen years."

"And could you tell the court why you are no longer a firefighter?"

"I lost my leg when I fell through the roof of a burning building while attempting to rescue a woman on the second floor."

Rudy dismissed Chris Keenan, keeping his eyes on Josie as he walked back to his table. Disgust radiated from him. Josie's eyes locked with his. She had nothing to be ashamed of. He would have ripped Chris Keenan to shreds if he'd been in her shoes. He just would have done it with a smile.

"I have no more questions for this very expert witness, Your Honor."

"Then this seems to be a good time to break for lunch."

Judge Norris ended the opening skirmish. Rudy Klein left the courtroom, Linda and Hannah walked out after the spectators. Josie sat for a minute, looking at the bench and the witness stand. The muscles in her body had been locked since the proceedings began and now, suddenly, she realized they had miraculously relaxed. Josie laughed a little and shook her head. She was still standing.

Josie got up and rapped the wooden table for luck and turned around in the silent courtroom, turned around and found that she wasn't quite alone after all. She walked down the center aisle, stopping when she reached the last pew.

CHAPTER 15

"Hey, Faye. Checking up on me so I don't give the firm a bad name?"

Josie slung her purse over her shoulder as she pushed through the swinging gate. Smiling, she joined Faye and together they walked into the hall.

"Just happened to be in the neighborhood."

"Right," Josie laughed and touched Faye's arm, steering her around a knot of attorneys and their clients who had gathered outside department 50. Hannah and Linda were gone. Kip was nowhere to be seen and Josie could only hope that he was with his wife and stepdaughter.

"I met Kip Rayburn. Introduced myself as your partner," Faye said before giving her a sly wink. "I don't think he appreciates your talents."

"There are only twelve people I want to appreciate me," Josie answered. "And I don't want to talk about Kip Rayburn. Come on, I'll buy you lunch. It's the least I can do for the only friendly face in the crowd."

"I tried to get Archer to come but he wouldn't," Faye said as she got into the elevator.

"I wouldn't expect him to."

Josie pushed the button for the ground floor and stood back, a small smile on her face. Faye didn't understand that Archer had been with her since this whole thing started.

Kip Rayburn saw Josie leave the courthouse but gave her no more than a passing thought. Hidden behind the blackout windows of the state owned SUV, Hannah and Linda already sent away in another car to lunch, he concentrated on what Cheryl Winston, the governor's campaign manager was telling him.

"Our polling results indicate there's a fifty two percent approval rating for your appointment. The governor is happy with that."

Kip nodded. *Happy* was not *pleased. Pleased* was not *thrilled.* The governor was simply happy about the results and Kip knew, without a doubt, that two percentage points were all that stood between him and mediocrity. He managed a thin smile while she kept going.

"The focus groups were supportive of you standing by your wife. They split on whether or not you owe Hannah anything. That's to be expected. A criminal case like this engenders strong feelings both ways."

"Did you ask them what they'd think if I testified for the prosecution?" Kip asked.

"Admiration. You score big there. They think you would be courageous. The public doesn't view this as they would a husband testifying against his wife. Remember, half the families in this country are blended. You've got a lot of people who may like their new spouse, but don't care for the kids. Or, they inherited a real bad apple when they got married. No big deal. When it comes to your nomination, they just don't know how you stand on certain issues but they're willing to give you a shot because of your father. Those we polled figured they don't know anything about their local judges either, so what the heck. All in all, Mr. Rayburn, I think we're on target. Just hang in there. Stay cool during the trial."

Cheryl closed her folder and gave Kip a broad smile. She was just a kid. Kip hated being at the mercy of kids. Still, he smiled back. The governor obviously had faith in her, and Kip wouldn't do anything to undermine his standing with the governor.

"I will. It will be tough, but I believe in the system." Cheryl seemed to wince. Kip knew he had to work on his presentation. Sincerity had never been a strong suit.

"That's admirable." Cheryl answered in a way that made Kip feel as if he had shown his teacher a particularly unmemorable piece of artwork. "We're thinking confirmation in about two months. I'll let the governor know everything looks okay down here. If you need us or have any questions, just call me or Alex."

Kip took her card, noted the plethora of numbers – fax, phone, e-mail, and cell – and said: "Thanks."

"Get some lunch." She patted his arm. "It looks like it's going to be a long day. It's great that you're willing to hang out. Makes you look like you're concerned. Oh, you may want to bring something appropriate to read since the press will be seeing you waiting outside the courtroom to testify. *Recent Supreme Court Decisions* might make for a good photo op. I can get you a copy if you want," Cheryl suggested. "And don't worry. Looks like you've got a good lawyer for Hannah. I have a feeling this thing is going to run at record speed. By the time you're confirmed, this trial will be a memory."

With that, the governor's gal took off. Kip didn't take her advice about lunch. He wasn't hungry. Instead, he wandered back into the courtroom wishing he could sit and listen. He wanted to know what the prosecution had. He wanted to know if Hannah was going to be out of his life for good. But he was the one who offered himself as a witness. He couldn't have it both ways. Besides, he really didn't care about the battle; it was the war he wanted to win.

Slowly he walked down the center aisle, his eyes roamed over the jumble of cables and wires that connected the Court TV camera. Everyone was gone. They would be gone for an hour and a half. Kip passed the bar and stood in front of the bench. It wasn't an unfamiliar place but, in his career, his handful of trials had not created a sterling resume of accomplishment. Now, if he were patient, all that would change.

Yes it would.

Without a second thought, Kip Rayburn mounted the steps to the bench and sat in Judge Norris's high-backed chair. Kip leaned back. He swiveled right then left. He looked at everything: the full calendar, the small clock, the state-of-the-art computer, and the gavel.

It was the gavel he found interesting. He picked it up and ran his fingers down the carved handle, over the heavy head with the brass band declaring it a gift of an appreciative staff.

Kip Rayburn sat forward, thinking of nothing and everything all at once. Looking at the gavel he raised the head and brought it down on Judge Cyrus Norris's desk and whispered:

"Guilty."

~

Josie and Faye grabbed a sandwich at the courtyard coffee shop of St. Vibiana's. Los Angeles's new Cathedral had risen like Herod's palace in the desert of downtown. The whole thing had cost good Cardinal Mahoney a bundle of dough and an avalanche of bad press. Some inventive reporter had tagged the thing the Taj Mahoney for all its grandeur in the midst of so much need. Homeless, displaced Hispanic families, the poor of L.A. could be housed and fed forever on half of what it cost to build the thing.

Still, all was not lost. St. Vibiana's served a purpose. It was another stop on the tourist track, a graveyard for those who could afford twenty grand for a prime crypt, the sandwich shop did a brisk business, and the courtyard was an oasis. Statues of Buddy Christ, His sacred thumb raised in a sign of corporal encouragement, were lined up in the gift shop. None of it impressed Josie. She'd seen better churches, and had better sandwiches, but the company was blessed. It was a miracle that Faye had come all this way.

"She's prettier in person. Her pictures don't do her justice. Your client, I mean." Faye pushed aside her sandwich.

"She's a beautiful girl." Josie rose long enough to throw away the paper plates and Styrofoam cups. When she sat down again she asked, "How much did you see?"

"Enough to know you didn't lose any ground," Faye answered. "You should be proud of yourself. You handled that witness well. You're a regular Clarence Darrow."

Josie cocked a grin. "That means a lot coming from you even if it is a line of bull."

"Take it for what it's worth. But when have you known me to lie?' Faye reapplied her lipstick then dropped it in her purse. "Angie put the police reports in order for you. You'll have a summary on your desk tomorrow."

"Good. She's been working hard. I'm sorry I'm taking up so much of her time."

Faye's attention was caught by the Biblical garden; sand and date palms were more interesting than talk of business and Josie took a minute to really look at her. Faye Baxter could have been one of the church ladies whose buses came and went as they checked God's little L.A. acre. Everything about her was perfect – hair, make-up, clothes – but the years and loss of a husband had added weight to both body and soul. When Josie remained silent, Faye took a quick breath and smiled, seemingly embarrassed to be caught daydreaming. She put her elbows on the table, clasping her hands so that she could lean her chin against them.

"The prosecution seems to have dotted all their 'i's. What's your case looking like?"

"I've got my own forensic people and an independent review of the autopsy. It contradicts the prosecution's contention that Fritz Rayburn was alive when the fire started. What it really boils down to is, we say/they say.

Klein's got a lot of circumstantial evidence, and I'm going to have to make sure I knock down the building blocks."

"Are you going to call the girl to the stand?" Faye asked.

"Hannah?" Josie said her name just to hear it. *The girl* label grated on her ears, it made Hannah seem irrelevant. "I hope not, but I won't know until Rudy wraps up. I want something proactive for the defense; something that jury hasn't heard before. Maybe the police reports will have something tight I can use."

"You'll figure it out," Faye assured her.

"You think?" Josie asked.

"I know." Faye stood up and looked over her shoulder. Her nose crinkled. She pushed her glasses up and shook her head at the cathedral. "This place is ugly. It looks like a bunker. I'm not going to make this drive again so I might as well see what all the fuss is about. Come on, I'll help you pray for inspiration."

Faye laced her arm through Josie's, only letting go when they crossed the threshold, walking up a wide, sloped, marble concourse that opened onto a cavernous, cold and calculated place of worship. A couple hundred million bought a hell of a lot of space, some incredible artwork, and a football field of marble that served as an altar. Massive organ pipes ruptured the wall fifty feet above the faithful. Christ was made of bubbled iron, his hands and feet deformed as he hung on a cross, stuck in the floor, earthbound instead of rising miraculously toward heaven. A wood throne was impressive, carved and detailed down to the dimples that would cradle the Cardinal's holy cheeks. The Virgin Mary had been transformed from a veiled, long-suffering, courageous mother to a strange alien-like presence. Her hair was buzz cut, her face a collage of cultures, her gown less a garment and more a suit of armor.

Josie sidestepped into a pew. Faye crossed herself and knelt. Light filtered through paper-thin alabaster panels. There were no windows. Colossal, politically correct tapestries hung on one towering wall; the Stations of the Cross were missing. Pews were lined up stadium style for an unobstructed view of the pageantry du jour.

Today maybe fifty people milled about looking for God. Even Josie was curious. Where was His warmth, the love the faithful sought from the Supreme Being? There were no nooks and crannies for him to nestle in, nor any towering symbol of His might. God was MIA, leaving visitors to be awestruck by man's creativity and cleverness. Not that any of this mattered to Josie. These were observations of an agnostic. Josie was thirty-three the last time she made a simple request of God; send Emily, her mother, home. It didn't work. God didn't listen so she didn't bother trying now. She sat quietly and watched Faye, her eyes closed, her hands folded. Well, maybe He did listen a little. Something had brought Faye downtown, and Josie would be forever grateful. Closing her eyes, Josie took advantage of the quiet and calm while Faye prayed.

When Josie opened them again she was staring at a little girl walking backwards instead of following her teacher down the center aisle. The teacher caught on and hustled the girl back 'round until she was on the right path again. Josie cocked her head. Her eyes wandered to the blood-red marble altar. Faye got off her knees and slid onto the wooden pew next to Josie.

"I said a prayer for you. It is guaranteed you'll come through this unscathed." Faye smoothed her skirt. Josie wasn't listening. Her brain had kicked up a notch. Not quite to miracle status but definitely to an epiphany mode. It wouldn't have surprised her if a chorus of angels started singing and a shaft of heavenly light was surrounding her head. It had nothing to do with Faye's prayers. This was pure inspiration.

I'd die if I couldn't…

Josie sat up straighter and muttered:

"Hannah said she'd die if she couldn't paint."

"What?" Faye asked.

"Hannah said she'd die if she couldn't paint." The tips of Josie's fingers lay lightly on Faye's arm as if that would make her get it. "Faye, look at these people. They're like sheep. They go down the center aisle, to the side, down the steps to the crypt and back up. They don't touch anything. They don't even talk out loud. They're respectful. No, it's more than that. They would die before they did harm to this cathedral."

"And your point is?"

"That's exactly what Hannah does," Josie whispered excitedly, finally facing Faye. "She walks around her house on a specific course because that's the only thing she has faith in, the only place she reveres. Hannah said she checked on her paintings every night. She has shown me that route. The paintings are the last thing she checks. Why? Because the entire house is as precious to her as this church is to these people – her studio is the sacristy."

I tried to save them.

"Faye, I thought it was a figure of speech when she said she tried to save them. You know, like people swearing they'll die if they don't get to the gym."

"But Hannah really meant it, is that what you're saying?"

"Exactly. She would have to feel almost spiritual about her paintings if she was willing to put her hand into a fire. And, if she feels that way, then I bet she couldn't have set that fire because there's a divine significance to the material. There is a meaning attached to those paintings that is greater than the self. That's how Hannah felt about her studio and that is the way these people feel about the house of God."

"That is nice, but what's it suppose to mean to a jury?"

"If Hannah's purpose in life was to paint, if the one place she felt safe and comfortable was her studio, then she couldn't destroy the purpose or the place without destroying her own life." Josie snapped her fingers. "I want Angie to get me as much information as she can on obsessive/compulsives: specifically the extremes of their behaviors regarding their environments. I want to know what kind of reaction they would have if that environment was disturbed, or destroyed."

Faye shook her head. "Forget it. The paintings and studio are gone and Hannah's still kicking. She didn't die because those things were destroyed."

"But," Josie said pointedly, "she didn't destroy them. They were destroyed. That's a whole different thing. She tried to put that fire out because she couldn't be responsible. It's a mental thing, not a physical thing. We call the physical evidence into question – no problem – and with the next punch we establish that Hannah is incapable of destructive behavior regarding her environment."

"That is a stretch, Josie." Faye was guarded but Josie was energized.

"No, it isn't. I can make that jury believe it and understand it. I've done it before. Say it with enough conviction, enough passion, get an expert to back you up, and it becomes real. I need to know how adaptable someone with Hannah's condition really is. That's the key to this whole thing."

Josie checked her watch.

"I've got to run. It's late. Have Angie start checking the literature and the experts the minute you get back. Rudy Klein may not have to prove Hannah had a motive for setting the fire, but I'm going to give them a hell of a reason why she never could have done it."

Josie sidestepped across Faye and was headed out of the Cathedral when she remembered something important. Rushing back to Faye, she leaned down:

"Thank you for coming. You may make me a believer yet."

Faye sat in silence looking at the curious, the sightseers, the true believers, and the bored school children as the sound of Josie's footsteps faded away. It was late. Time to go if she didn't want to hit traffic. Before she did, though, Faye Baxter got on her knees once more. She crossed herself twice. Faye had a terrible, terrible feeling that things weren't going to be as simple as Josie thought.

CHAPTER 16

"I don't know. I figure she did it but she'll probably get off. I mean she's rich, right? If you're rich you get off in Los Angeles." – Steven, 21, man on the street interview regarding Hannah Sheraton

In the four days that followed, the lab technician testified that the charred matches found in the debris of the Rayburn fire were damn near one of a kind or, at least, very unusual. Each matchstick was carved into a tiny octagon, the Chinese symbol for good luck was almost microscopically stamped on each shaft and the sulfur on the head was a neon rainbow of colors. The company that manufactured those matches was in Taiwan. They had a decent foothold on the East Coast but only a handful of customers on the west. The Coffee Haus in the Palisades Village was one of them. Hannah Sheraton was a regular at the Coffee Haus.

Josie asked the lab tech if the charred matches found on the first floor of the Rayburn house came from the box found in Hannah Sheraton's room. He could only be certain that the matches at the scene were exactly the same as those in the box found in Hannah's room. Josie asked if anyone could be sure they came from a particular box.

No, probably not, but…

Josie cut him off but a quick look at the jury told her she'd gained no ground. They liked the connections Rudy had already made with this witness. Rudy called the detective who searched the Rayburn home when it was determined it was a crime scene.

How many boxes of matches from the Coffee Haus had he found in the Rayburn home?

"Two," said the witness. "The Coffee Haus matches logged with my mark and entered as exhibit eleven were found in a foyer table that was situated between the front door and Ms. Sheraton's bedroom. The Coffee Haus matches logged with my mark and entered as exhibit twelve were found in Hannah Sheraton's bedroom, hidden beneath her mattress along with marijuana and a small stash of pills. There were no other matches of that particular brand found in the rest of the house."

"Did you conduct a thorough search of the Rayburn home including the wing that was damaged in the fire?"

"Yes, the house was thoroughly searched and no, I did not find a Coffee Haus box in the wing where the fire occurred."

"So you only found two boxes of those particular matches. One in a hall table near the defendant's room, the other hidden in Hannah Sheraton's room," Rudy asked.

"Yes," came the answer.

Rudy wanted to know about the other things the detective found hidden in Hannah's room. Josie objected. The question was overly broad. Rudy got more specific.

"What kind of pills did you find hidden in the defendant's room?"

"Vicodin. Prescription pain relievers."

"Were the pills in a prescription bottle?"

"No," came the detective's reply

"Did you find a prescription for Vicodin in Hannah Sheraton's name anywhere in the house?"

"No."

"Did you determine what bottle the pills in Hannah Sheraton's room came from?"

"Objection, Your Honor. Speculation. There is no way to know if those pills were taken from a specific bottle," Josie insisted.

"Sustained.

"Didn't you find a prescription bottle on the premises?" Rudy would connect the dots another way. "There was a bottle of the same medication in Justice Rayburn's bathroom."

"Was the bottle damaged?"

"The bottle was dirtied with soot and slightly melted, but the label was intact."

"And what did you conclude?"

"I found that a prescription for Vicodin had been filled for Fritz Rayburn the day before the fire. There were seven pills missing from the Justice Rayburn's bottle; six pills were found in Hannah Sheraton's room. The autopsy showed that Justice Rayburn had ingested one pill approximately five hours before he died."

"Did you find any fingerprints other than those of Justice Rayburn on the pill bottle?"

"We found a partial that matched Hannah Sheraton's right thumb."

"What did you conclude from this?" Rudy asked.

"That Ms. Sheraton had taken pills from that bottle sometime before the fire started."

"Why are you sure she touched that bottle before the fire started?"

"The defendant's right hand was burned in the fire. We could not get a clear thumb print during our booking procedure because of her burn but she had been fingerprinted after an arrest earlier this year."

"I see." Rudy nodded sagely. "It is sad when someone will go to such lengths for drugs."

"Move to strike," Josie called.

"So stricken. Watch it, Mr. Klein."

Rudy barely acknowledged the judge as he went on.

"You also found marijuana cigarettes during your search."

"I did. One was partially smoked."

"Where did you find the marijuana, the Vicodin, and the matches?"

"I found all of these things in a small box. The partially smoked marijuana cigarette was in the matchbox. All these things were hidden in the defendant's bedroom."

"And did the matchbox carry any identification?"

"Yes, it came from the Coffee Haus in the Palisades village."

"The same coffee shop that was referred to by the lab technician?"

"Yes."

"Asked and answered," Josie objected.

"Could you tell if a match from that box had been struck recently?" Rudy moved on.

"Yes. There were marks and sulfur residue on the scratch strip of the box."

"Can you tell when the match or matches had been struck?" Rudy asked.

"Not precisely but the sulfur residue was fresh."

"Was there sulfur residue on the second box?"

"No."

"Were there fingerprints on the first match box found in Ms. Sheraton's room?"

"Yes. They were Hannah Sheraton's fingerprints."

"And on the matchbox found in the hall?"

"There were partials we couldn't match."

Rudy turned to Josie.

"Your witness."

CHAPTER 17

"What pills?" – Note from Josie to Hannah

"Fritz gave them to me. For when I hurt." – Note from Hannah to Josie

Josie took her place in front of the witness. Hannah's explanation sucked so she would have to run around the 'why' of the pills.

"Detective, after you found the box of matches in Hannah Sheraton's bedroom where did you put it?"

"I put the matches in my right pocket," he answered, shifting in the chair. He was an old hand and he did that to be comfortable, not because he was concerned about Josie.

"You put them in your pocket after you tagged them, is that correct, sir?"

The detective blushed. He knew what was coming.

"No, I didn't initially tag the matches."

"Then what did you do with them?" Josie asked, her brow beetling with curiosity.

"I put the box from the bedroom in my right coat pocket. The box from the hall table I carried to the car where I tagged them both."

"Have they changed police procedure, detective?" Josie asked.

"No, ma'am."

"Then correct me if I'm wrong, but aren't you supposed to tag and bag evidence where you find it to protect the integrity of evidence?"

"I ran out of evidence bags."

"So, let me get this straight," Josie said thoughtfully. "Instead of leaving the matches at the scene, going to your car to get the evidence bags and returning, you took this critical evidence with you?"

"Yes."

"And why did you do that?" Josie asked.

"So that the chain of evidence wouldn't be broken. I didn't want anyone else picking up that evidence."

"So you took a chance on contaminating the evidence rather than breaking the chain." Josie nodded as if she understood completely. She asked, "When you reached your car did you immediately mark the box in your hand?"

The detective shook his head. He shifted back to the other side of the chair.

"Not exactly. I put the box from the defendant's room in my right pocket while I unlocked the door to get more evidence bags."

Josie held up two boxes of matches before putting one in each pocket of her jacket. She moved toward the jury, speaking casually as she went.

"Then we can be sure that the box of matches from Hannah Sheraton's room came out of your pocket and was marked and set aside."

"That is correct," the detective replied.

"Just like that?" Josie held up a box of matches. "From your right pocket?"

"Yes," the detective replied.

"Let the record show that the matches I showed the detective were taken out of my left pocket." Josie faced the jury as she held up a small box of matches. "Perhaps the detective had the same problem with left and right on the day he collected and tagged these exhibits."

"Objection, Your Honor," Rudy called, "this is not a made for television movie."

"One more question," Josie said as the judge overruled the prosecutor's objection. "Detective, how do you account for the marijuana cigarette being inside the matchbox and hidden in Ms. Sheraton's room?"

"I don't know what you mean."

"I mean, in your expert opinion, do you think it reasonable that this sixteen year old girl could set a deadly fire in two places, return to her room, have the presence of mind to put her half smoked joint in the same box of matches she used to commit arson and take the time to hide the whole thing neatly under her mattress before running back and sticking her hand in the fire? Do you really think Hannah Sheraton could, or would, do that?"

"Sure, why not?" The detective answered with a shrug.

"Do you know that it takes a minimum of six and a half minutes to run from her room, through the house and to the west wing of the house?"

"I haven't timed it," the detective answered.

"Did you know it took the fire department three and a half minutes to respond to the alarm?" Josie pointed out.

"I read that in their report."

"And did you read that the fire was fully engaged when they arrived?"

"I did."

"And you still believe it is possible that Hannah Sheraton burned her hand, returned to the house, hid the matches without anyone seeing her, and returned to the scene so she could sit behind a fountain and wait for the fire department?"

"Maybe she runs really fast."

"Maybe you need to do the math," Josie snapped.

"Objection." This from Rudy.

"Withdrawn," Josie said with obvious disgust.

Josie took her seat; satisfied she'd given the jury something to think about. She only hoped that Rudy didn't point out there were at least three ways to get from Hannah's room to the scene of the fire and two of them took slightly under three minutes at a full run.

Rudy stood up and buttoned his coat.

"How many matches were there in the box found in Ms. Sheraton's room?"

"Twenty. The other box had twenty-five matches. The boxes are packed with twenty-five matches at the factory. I contacted the manufacturer and confirmed this. I also made notations regarding the count before I left Ms. Sheraton's room. Before I left the hall area I also made a notation of the number of matches in exhibit eleven."

"And would you examine exhibit twelve please?"

Rudy handed the man a clear plastic bag that he opened. He took out the box and opened that, too.

"There are twenty matches plus a partially smoked marijuana cigarette," the detective answered.

"Then I suppose it didn't matter what pocket you put the two pieces of evidence in, did it, detective. It is not as if the content of these two boxes was identical."

Rudy was done.

Josie made a note. She would collect as many Coffee Haus matchboxes as possible and count out every single one. She wanted the detective's history regarding evidence tampering and collection. She wanted it all before the defense had to present its case.

On the third day, court resumed at one thirty. Mr. Hilbrun, proprietor of the Coffee Haus, took the stand. He was short, tanned, uncomfortable in his tie, and unhappy. The Coffee Haus didn't run itself. He should be working.

Of course he knew Hannah Sheraton. She came to the Coffee Haus all the time. Sometimes she was alone, and sometimes she was with a boy with crazy hair. Sometimes she sat in a corner and drew pictures. Mostly she just drank coffee by herself and looked out the window. She fiddled with things. Fiddled and fiddled. Drove him crazy.

Rudy asked. "Is there another reason Hannah Sheraton stuck out in your memory?"

"She ordered a small coffee and took stuff every time she came in."

"What kind of things did she take?" Rudy asked.

"That girl took napkins and those little wooden stir things. She took sugar packets and made piles of them on her table." Mr. Hilburn's face was flushing with the thrill of having a public forum to air his complaints about Hannah.

"What else did she take?" Rudy asked.

"She took matches all the time." Mr. Hilbrun waved his hand and scrunched his nose in disgust at her habit.

"Why do you remember matches in particular?"

"She orders a coffee for a buck fifty and then takes twenty boxes of my matches. Even if I stand there and watch her, she counts out twenty and doesn't get the hint. Kids don't know how much money it costs to run a business. Anyway, she doesn't even smoke."

Rudy crossed his arms.

"What did she do with all those matches?"

"Sometimes she lit them, blew them out, and left them on the table in rows. Like twenty little burned people," He pulled his hands out in front of him like he was pulling taffy.

"Your Honor," Josie groaned.

"Sir, if you would answer the questions simply." Judge Norris waved them on.

"The detective just testified that he only found two boxes of your matches in the Sheraton House. If Ms. Sheraton took twenty each time she came in then why do you think he only found two boxes."

"She didn't take all of them home with her. Sometimes she left them outside. Stacked them up like a little kid."

"Did she leave all of them?"

"Sometimes, and sometimes she took some with her. Kids, they don't know that everything costs. Napkins, matchboxes, lids, toilet paper, wooden stirrers." He ticked the items off his fingers.

"Thank you, Mr. Hilbrun," Rudy interrupted but the witness wanted to say what he had to say.

"...sugar packets, straws..." He shook his finger at Hannah. "If you take all of them, there's nothing left for anyone else. I have a business to run. That's not good. I told you. You should listen, little girl. You should listen."

Hannah stayed attentive to Mr. Hilbrun. She looked as close to beatific as Josie had seen anyone look, but under the table her hands were clasped together in a fist that gently touched the underside of the wood. It took Judge Norris three tries to get the witness quieted down. When he finally managed, Josie was given the nod. She stood up and cross-examined from behind her table.

"How many boxes of matches did people take from your shop last week, Mr. Hilburn?"

"I don't know. Maybe fifty. Maybe a hundred."

"So you had a hundred customers in your shop who smoked?"

"I don't know if they smoked. I just see the matches are gone, so I put more in the basket."

"So you couldn't tell me how many you give out in month or a year?" Josie raised an eyebrow.

"Not this minute," he sniped. "I probably would know if I looked it up and figured out when I order more."

"But it's a lot, isn't it? You reorder quite often."

"Yeah, a lot," he grumbled.

"Do you remember everyone who comes into your coffee place, Mr. Hilbrun?"

"I remember her," he said and pointed at Hannah. He was working himself up again, his cheeks were scarlet and his eyes sparkled as he warmed to his subject. "I remember who comes and goes in my place and who doesn't treat it right."

"Do you know if this lady has come in for coffee?" Josie indicated Linda sitting front row center. He shook his head.

"No, I don't know her." Mr. Hilbrun crossed his arms.

"How about the lady sitting next to her? Do you recognize that lady?"

"No, I don't know her neither." He barely looked but that was okay with Josie. She addressed the court.

"The defense would like to identify Mrs. Peterson, the Rayburn's housekeeper." Josie walked close to Mr. Hilbrun. "Would it surprise you to know that Mrs. Peterson stops at the Coffee Haus at least three times a week?"

"That's good," the witness huffed.

Another giggle from the jury. Josie smiled as if to say this all wasn't so bad, just a misunderstanding. She took her hands out of her pockets and pointed to the housekeeper.

"Would it surprise you to know that Mrs. Peterson has, at one time or another, taken matches from the Coffee Haus?"

"One at a time is okay." He was petulant, tired of being the center of attention. Josie had counted on his waning attention.

"And would it surprise you to know that Mrs. Peterson had a box of Coffee Haus matches in her car the night of the fire?"

"Why should it surprise me?" Mr. Hilbrun shrugged. "I sell good coffee. I should be selling coffee right now and not talking about who comes to buy. So can I go now?"

"Let the record show that the defense has identified Mrs. Linda Rayburn and Mrs. Peterson who lived at the Pacific Palisades home. Both had access to the hall table as well as the defendant's room."

"Hey, can I go now?"

Josie gave Mr. Hilbrun a small, perfunctory smile and excused the witness.

The last witness Rudy called on the end of the third day was the chauffer who had seen Hannah arguing with Fritz. Rudy was to the point. Josie's cross of Theodore

Smith, a large, hulking man with a whispery voice, was short.

"You just testified that the defendant and Justice Rayburn were arguing? Could you hear what they were saying?"

"Nope," the man answered.

"Then how did you know they were arguing?" Josie asked.

"Her hands were going all over the place. I can tell when somebody is pissed, can't you?" He raised a bushy eyebrow. Josie ignored the question and the challenge.

"Did you know that my client suffers from obsessive/compulsive disorder, sir? That she often reaches out to touch something to make herself feel safe?"

"How could I know that?" He dismissed her with a toss of his head.

"Now that you do know, could it be that the defendant was simply trying to find something to touch. Could it be that's why she was waving her arms?"

"Calls for a conclusion, Your Honor," Rudy objected.

Point made. Josie took a tangent.

"Could you see both Justice Rayburn and Ms. Sheraton completely? Their full bodies? Their faces?"

"I could see the old guy's head. I was looking at her back mostly. Sometimes I could see her from the side"

"Then you couldn't always see both of the defendant's hands?"

"No, not always. She moved around a lot," Theodore admitted.

"So you really couldn't tell if the defendant pushed Justice Rayburn or touched him or, perhaps, tried to help him because he lost his balance? He was an old man, after all."

"He wasn't that old." Theodore Smith sized up Josie and nodded a couple of times as if to say no broad was going to trick him up. "That girl pushed the old guy. I saw him fall. I didn't see her try to catch him. That was not the way she was moving." He looked at the jury and warned them: "Don't you believe what she is saying. That girl pushed the old guy."

"Your Honor," Josie snapped. "Instruct the witness to answer my questions and move to strike that last comment."

"So ordered," Norris instructed.

Josie's jaw twitched in annoyance. She began again, drawing up to her full height, clasping her hands behind her back.

"You're a very big man, Mr. Smith. If you believed there was an altercation, why didn't you try to stop it?"

"It happened fast. They were talking, and then he was on the ground. There was no time."

"Talking?" Josie reiterated. "That is a far cry from someone angry enough to assault another person."

"Arguing," the witness corrected. "They were definitely having a strong difference of opinion."

"Did Justice Rayburn call to you for help?"

The man shook his head and his chin dimpled as he drew it up thoughtfully.

"Nope."

"Did he cry out when he fell?" Josie demanded.

"No. But someone needed to help him."

"And why would you draw that conclusion?" Josie pushed. The witness bridled.

"Because he looked afraid," Smith said tightly. "And don't ask me how I know. I know afraid, and that man was afraid of her."

He pointed right at Hannah. He did so with righteous indignation. The rhythm of Hannah's knocking increased. The witness heard it too and his finger wavered the longer Josie remained silent. Finally he lowered his hand then raised it again to wipe his forehead seeming to question his own conclusion. Josie looked at the jury and mused at the witness.

"I guess that little girl scared you, too, since you didn't try to help Justice Rayburn until after she left."

"Objection, Your Honor," Rudy called. "Insulting a witness is not a question."

"Withdrawn." Josie sat down, smiled at Hannah and patted her arm. Hannah's eyes rested on Josie. Judge Norris called it quits for the day and, as soon as the jury was out of the courtroom, Josie asked one more question.

"I want to know about those damn pills."

"One. Two. Three!" Josie and Archer strained to lift the marble fountain and mount it on the side of the patio wall. Josie made the final adjustment. They both stepped back. A flip of the switch and nothing. No water spewed out of the little bird's mouth.

"Forget it. Just forget it. It's too late for this, Archer. Let's call it a day."

Josie sat down on the ground and surveyed the half laid patio tile, and the mounted fountain that wouldn't work. She could see through the open door to the dining room table where papers and files were spread among Chinese take-out containers.

"I can't walk and chew gum at the same time today." She sank to the ground, her back up against the patio wall, one leg up, and one stretched out. Sweeping up the can of beer by her side, Josie tipped it only to find it empty. Archer offered his and then put his hand atop her head. He ruffled her hair as he leaned against the wall and listened to her complain.

"What happened today to set you off?"

"Nothing," she muttered. "Everything, I suppose. I'm missing things, Archer. The cops found Vicodin in Hannah's bedroom along with a roach. Rudy's setting up to say she killed Rayburn for drugs and tried to cover it up with the fire. Hannah says Rayburn gave the pills to help with the pain when she cut herself."

"And what do you say?"

"I say this is beginning to stink. If Rayburn were this saint who sent Hannah away to rehab to get her sober, why in the hell would he give her something as addictive as Vicodin? It makes no sense no matter how much pain Hannah was in. And that's another thing. Hannah doesn't show pain. Not when she cuts herself, not when she burned herself. She made that clear the first time I met her. I spoke to her psychiatrist. Hannah's pain is so internalized she could probably slit her throat and watch it bleed and not blink. So, why would Rayburn be so concerned?"

"Maybe he was the one who had a low threshold for pain. You know how some people are. They nurture, and they worry. Sometimes they don't do it the right way," Archer suggested.

Josie shook her head vehemently. "Nope. He was a judge. Rayburn would be guilty of breaking a dozen laws if he handed out prescription medication to a minor. I don't buy it."

"So Hannah is lying?" Archer asked, taking the beer back.

"I don't want to think so but what other conclusion is there? Especially given her reaction. Hannah was too furious when I suggested she was lying. Way too mad, if you know what I mean. She was trying to make me feel guilty for even suspecting she was untruthful. To make matters worse, I think Linda knew something about it."

"What was the boy wonder doing this whole time?"

"Kip? He was about as interested as a deaf, dumb, and blind man. Once we were behind closed doors it was pretty evident he's barely tolerating Hannah, or me." Josie's fist pounded the ground lightly before she drew her open palm over the tile she had so lovingly laid. "I'm starting to think I made a real bad choice taking this on."

Archer sat down beside her. Josie leaned into him. They sat in silence, shoulder-to-shoulder, hot and tired. Max wandered by. Archer and Josie put out their hands and let them roll across his back as he headed toward the grass. Josie handed the beer back to Archer. When he took it, Josie put her head on his shoulder.

"Are you ever sorry you didn't have kids with Lexi?' she asked.

"Nope."

"Never?"

"I didn't worry about what we couldn't do. It didn't weigh on Lexi." He took another drink, tipping his head back, closing his eyes as if he wanted to savor the moment. The can clattered against the already laid tile as he set it down. "They would have been good kids. Beautiful kids, if Lexi had 'em." He put his hand on Josie's knee. "You'd have beautiful kids, Jo."

"Not me. I wouldn't know how to do it."

"Last I heard it didn't take any practice to do it." Archer's hand traveled up her thigh. His finger caught a thread on her cutoffs.

Josie smiled and turned her head just enough to smell the salt on his bare arm, the leftover sunshine from his day photographing the lifeguards for the city.

"I know *how* to do it; it's the other part that I wouldn't know about; the part about taking care of a kid. I would be so neurotic. I'd be all around, never let him go anywhere. I'd be a hovering mom."

"So? That's good. Just the opposite of what your mother did," Archer said.

Josie disagreed. "No, that's not all there is to it. Look at Linda. She's with her daughter all the time, but there's something wrong there. Linda is still selfish and Hannah is so screwed up it might have been better not to have had a mother at all. Nope, no kids for me. In fact, right now, I'd give anything just to get Hannah out of my head."

"Anything?" Archer asked. Taking a sip of beer then putting his cold lips against her warm neck.

"If it worked, sure," Josie whispered, snuggling into him.

"Tell you what. Why don't we try the cure, and then discuss how much it's worth later."

Josie raised her head, looked into that rugged, wide face of his and then took it between her hands. She kissed him hard. She was going to owe Archer a fortune. Hannah Sheraton was already nothing more than a memory.

✧

"Are you going to be okay, honey?"

Hannah looked up. Linda was put together perfectly: a white dress and jacket, a gold pin on the lapel. Her shoes were bone; her purse so small there was only room for cigarettes and a lipstick. Her hair was down around her shoulders and her make-up was minimal. Though the change had been made for the benefit of the jury, the look had been kept because Kip thought it far more appropriate for a judge's wife. Linda's peach colored smile faded when Hannah's eyes trailed back to the paper.

"What are you working on?" Linda asked even though she knew exactly what Hannah was doing. For the last six hours Hannah painted as if she were sculpting, chipping away at the paper and Linda's nerves. The dining room table was littered with watercolors and brushes, glasses of water and rags. The table was a mess. Hannah had painted without consideration of the furniture, the housekeeper's time, the…

Linda stopped before she said what she was thinking. All she had to do was keep Kip from seeing this and keep Kip from seeing Hannah. A few more weeks – a month at most – and everything would be sorted out. As it stood now she was living with two children: Kip demanding she attend to him and his newfound prominence, Hannah and her constant need for reassurance. Linda knew too much about both of them.

Forcing herself to smile Linda put her hands on Hannah's shoulders, kissed the top of her daughter's head and breathed the scent of shampoo. She let her lips linger in the softness. She almost convinced herself that this was her little girl, her baby, but then Hannah stiffened. The shrug of distaste was slight but imminently insulting. Linda dropped her hands; one look at Hannah's painting the smile followed suit.

Gone were the clear bright colors of oil replaced with opaque grays and blacks, thin blues and sheer browns of watercolor. Night shadows, indistinct figures, and just enough definition so that interpretation could be open for discussion. This painting was damn personal. Linda saw what Hannah wanted her to see: a woman with her back to a girl, a fire behind them both. The woman's hair was long and dark; it streamed out behind her as if she was running away from the girl.

"What do you think?" Hannah asked sharply. Her eyes were down. She pushed the tablet to the side giving Linda a better look.

"Do you think that's funny, Hannah?" Linda fussed over her purse. Hannah pulled the pad back in front of her. The spiral binding scratched the table. Her burned hand held a paintbrush up, its bristles pointing heavenward. Linda pulled out a chair and sat down. "Well, do you?"

The hard end of Hannah's brush clicked against the table. A drip of water squeezed out of the bristles and trailed down the shaft until it fell like a dirty tear onto Hannah's hand. The sound, the movement, the mere idea of this counting was making Linda crazy.

"No," Hannah said, her voice small, the tapping ever more quickly.

"I haven't walked out on you, have I?"

"No." Hannah's voice got smaller but still it slid on a slick of defiance. "They think I'm a drug addict."

"And we know you're not," Linda snapped. "When are you going to get it through your head that all this stuff is just stuff? The thing that matters is whether or not Josie can convince that jury that they can't be totally sure who you are, or what you did. That's what our case rests on – not six Vicodin."

"It's not *our* case, Mom." Hannah slid her eyes toward Linda. "It's mine. I'm the one that everyone is looking at and everyone is talking about? I'm the one they think killed Fritz and the one who does drugs and sets fires. Or have you forgotten?"

"No, I haven't forgotten one damn thing." Linda's voice dropped. "If it hadn't been for me you wouldn't have nice clothes or a big house to live in or a car. You sure wouldn't have the time for all this self-indulgent tapping and walking and checking crap. I haven't forgotten that I'm the one who got you a great attorney, and I really haven't forgotten that I promised you every thing would work out. I always deliver on my promises. Name me one that I haven't."

Hannah's lashes fluttered. The paintbrush tapped, tap, tapped. The gray water wept from the bristles. "Kip's going to testify against me. Josie wanted to know what I thought he was going to say. I don't know what he's going to say, but I'm scared."

"He has to testify, Hannah. They subpoenaed him. There's only an exception for husband and wife. I've talked to Josie about his testimony, too, and I'll tell you what I told her. Kip barely paid attention to you since we've been married. What can he say? What can he know?"

When Hannah remained silent, Linda took a deep breath.

"Look, Hannah, my priority has always been to keep you and me together but I'm in the middle here. I told you when I married Kip keeping him safe would keep us safe. Without him we'd be back in those cheap apartments. Without him we couldn't pay for your defense. You should get down on your knees and thank him for that because he didn't have to…"

"Why should I get on my knees? You're already there," Hannah hissed.

Before the last word was out, Linda grabbed her daughter. Hannah's chair teetered. The paintbrush flew out of her hand; the thick pad of watercolor paper slid across the table and fell to the floor. Linda put her face close to her daughter's. Her make-up had sunk into the lines around her eyes and the small fissures above her lips. Anger aged her; frustration dried her out.

"You listen to me, Hannah. I'm no prostitute. I do what I do so we can both survive. You think there haven't been times when I wanted to just leave you behind and make my life easier? I could have put you in an orphanage. I could have dropped you in a trashcan, but I didn't. I kept you with me, I fed you, and I'm sure as hell not running out on you and you better not run out on me." Linda tried to shake the look of cold fury off Hannah's face. "Do you think this is easy for me knowing what I know? Knowing what went down? Do you think it's easy?"

"No," Hannah mumbled.

Linda's loosened her grip but her voice was no less passionate.

"Without Kip we don't have money. Without money, we don't have a life. Without money, you don't have a defense. Learn that lesson."

"That's not true!" Hannah's anger flared and she struggled to pull away. "Josie would defend me even if we didn't pay her anything."

Linda laughed once as she let go. Hannah might as well have punched her in the gut with that one. The goddess Josie was with them even here. Linda draped her arm over the back of her chair and shook her head sadly.

"I've raised an ungrateful fool." Linda's lip curled in an ugly smile. "How many people have let us down, Hannah?"

Hannah stared at the floor. Linda leaned forward. Her breath, hot and sweet smelling, brushed her daughter's cheek. Linda's perfume surrounded Hannah and Linda's voice was sticky with truth.

"I'll tell you who let us down. Everyone except Kip, so don't kid yourself. Josie cares about this case, but she doesn't care about you more than I do. Nobody cares about you more than I do because I'm your mother."

"I think you care, more than anyone, what happens to me, Mom. I think about it all the time," Hannah said icily. "But Josie cares about all of me."

Mother and daughter's matching eyes met and held.

"You think like a child." Linda reached out to touch Hannah's face but Hannah pulled away just far enough.

Linda smiled tightly. She stood up and stepped toward the door but couldn't leave without getting one more thing off her chest. "Josie's got nothing invested here but time. She doesn't care what's in that sick head of yours. She's not going to go out on a limb for you, especially if she knew the truth. The one thing Josie hates is a liar."

"You're wrong, Mom." Hannah whispered. "She did understand."

Linda's shoulders slumped. It was so hard to be young and optimistic. Maybe it was even harder to be old and know the score.

"No, baby. Nobody does anything just because they like someone."

"They do if they love them," Hannah mumbled.

"Yeah. If you love someone you do anything for them," Linda reiterated almost to herself. She pulled herself out of the reverie. "Just remember that."

"I do," Hannah whispered, reaching out to touch her mother. *Two, three, ten times*. Linda shook her off.

"Josie wouldn't know how to love you, baby. You think a woman who has no husband, no children, and no mother of her own would know how to love a screwed up kid like you? All you are is a challenge, Hannah. Both of us are, and that is why we need to stick together. We're two of a kind honey so don't wish for something that doesn't exist. I know what I'm doing. I always have, haven't I?"

Hannah watched her mother with clear, sad eyes. When the silence became too tedious, Linda wrapped it all up.

"Oh, for God's sake don't look like that. Everything is going to be all right."

Linda needed to go. Kip wasn't happy these days when she spent more time than necessary with Hannah. Still there should be something more, something settling she should say.

"I'm sorry about what I said about Josie. She cares what happens to you. Just don't count on her for too much. Never count on anybody for too much."

Linda was having cocktails with Kip at Shutters in Santa Monica when Hannah closed the door of the Malibu house and ran to the shoulder of Pacific Coast Highway. Her hair was pinned up, hidden under a bandana. She wore a hat pulled low over her eyes even though it was almost dark. Her sweatshirt was old, her jeans baggy. Heavy clothes for a hot night but Hannah didn't want to be recognized. She stuck out her thumb, moving from foot to foot, praying that somebody would stop soon because she didn't have much time. She had to be back before Linda and Kip.

The fourth car on the road swerved sharply and Hannah thanked God for small favors. She ran for the Toyota, hollered 'Huntington Beach' when asked where she was going and climbed in the back even though the guy at the wheel wanted her up front. He let her out in Long Beach. It took her two more rides to make the short hop to Huntington.

Pulling her hat down further, Hannah walked six blocks then circled around the back of Turc's, pulled on the ancient door and slipped inside. No one gave her a second look. The band was playing. People were drunk.

The entire place was sweating pheromones and Hannah needed to find the one man who would understand what she needed; the man she hadn't seen since the night Fritz died.

❧

Josie curled into Archer. He was warm. His arm was heavy across her waist. Taking his hand she put it on her breast as he looked at the clock by the bed. It was two in the morning. It was unlike her to wake in the wee hours of the morning yet here she was with her eyes open, staring at the bedside table. Then she heard it, the sound that had roused her.

On the table, her cell phone vibrated like chattering teeth. She'd forgotten to turn it off and now someone was calling. She inched away from Archer and grabbed it.

"Yeah?" She whispered, her mouth barely working.

A whisper came back.

"One, two, three…"

Josie closed her eyes and listened until Hannah stopped. She closed her eyes, sleep coming over her, Archer reaching out for her again.

"I didn't lie," Hannah said but her voice was far away, the words were lost, Josie was asleep.

CHAPTER 18

"There's no question that Rudy Klein has done a fine job of establishing that the defendant had both the means and the opportunity to commit this crime. Big points are going to be scored today, though. It says something when Kip Rayburn, stepfather of the defendant, is testifying for the prosecution. That really says something, doesn't it?" – Court TV

Eight forty-five. The last day of the prosecution's case. Judge Norris was late taking the bench, and that was just as well because Linda and Hannah were late, too. Josie sat at her table, looked at her watch, then stared at the bench. Finally she checked with the clerk and asked when she thought the judge would be ready. Ten minutes. Not exactly a reprieve, but there was some leeway.

Oblivious to Rudy Klein's curious look and the reporter's more interested ones Josie left the courtroom. The hallway was nearly deserted. Washington's Birthday was just around the corner. Only the courtroom kitty-corner from Norris's was in session. A crying woman sat on the bench outside it sniffling and blotting her nose. Everyone had troubles and Josie's were multiplying by the minute.

She reached into her pocket, got her phone, punched the numbers too hard, missed one and had to start all over. The phone at the Rayburn place rang until the machine picked up. Josie left a short message. She called Linda's cell and did the same.

Where in the hell are you?

Josie dropped her phone in the pocket of her blue blazer. She was halfway to the elevators when one of them opened. No one came out. Josie kept going. Another *ding.* The scraping of the doors. This time Hannah and Linda emerged. Josie covered the next ten yards fast.

"Where have you been?" She grabbed Linda by the arm and twirled her around. The other woman teetered in her heels.

"Traffic. It was down to one lane on Pacific Coast Highway. My cell phone battery was dead so I couldn't call. Hey! Slow down," Linda yanked her arm away. "Are we in trouble or what?"

"Not yet. Judge Norris was delayed. You just cut it damn close. I want us settled at the table before they bring the jury in."

Josie pushed Linda forward while she held the door open. Linda went in but Hannah had fallen behind and veered off toward one of the long benches that lined the hall.

Annoyed, Josie went back for her. Her client had taken a nosedive. Hannah's hair frizzed around her shoulders, her skirt was long and almost transparent. A short-sleeved t-shirt bared her arms. If Josie could make out the tracks of scars and scabs on her arms the jury could too, and that was the last thing Josie wanted the jury to see.

Josie put her hand on the girl's shoulder, angry that all their hard work was going to go up in smoke. "What were you thinking? I told you to keep your arms covered, to keep your hair simple. Those people in there aren't going to like..."

Josie's tirade trailed off. Hannah's head bounced gently like a bobble-head doll, all springs and joints. Unsmiling and bleary-eyed, one thing was clear: Hannah was stoned. So much for Fritz Rayburn's good intentions.

"Hey!" Josie backed Hannah up against the wall. Furious, she still had the presence of mind to keep her voice down. "What's going on? Are you high? You tell me straight up, Hannah, or I've got one foot out the door."

"No. Valium," Hannah whispered. "It's just Valium."

"Oh, Christ. Why would you do something that stupid?" Josie snapped.

"My mom gave it to me so I wouldn't be upset. Kip's going to talk today." Hannah shook her head, trying to find a normal rhythm to her words. "She said it would help. Don't be mad. Please. Please. Don't be mad."

Hannah leaned into Josie. Her limp arms came round Josie. Josie's own hovered and finally wrapped Hannah up and held her close. Hannah relaxed, falling into Josie as if she had found a safe warm place. Taking a breath that started in her gut, Josie tipped her chin up and looked at the ugly fluorescent light fixtures, the long cold halls, the wooden doors that led into courtrooms where any bit of information could be twisted and tied into a package to suit anyone's version of the facts. The prosecution had made a big deal of finding the pills and the joint found in Hannah's possession, and today Linda was pumping her kid full of Valium. Wasn't that a fine visual for the jury? Linda couldn't have screwed up more if she tried. Why in the hell, when mothers screwed up, did it feel like they meant it?

Josie sat Hannah down, ripped off her blazer and draped it over the girl's shoulders. Beneath her own strong fingers Hannah felt birdlike, thin and vulnerable. Josie glanced over her shoulder. Kip Rayburn was watching them. He sat on the bench outside the courtroom waiting to be called. She hadn't noticed him before. The bastard was watching them. Well, Josie would give him something to watch.

Deliberately she got Hannah to her feet.

"Okay, Hannah. It's game time," Josie said quietly. "Keep your arms underneath my jacket. Keep your chin up. Just look at Kip when he talks and remember, when he's done, it's over for the prosecution. I'll be there every minute for you. I promise."

Hannah gave Josie half a smile as Josie laced Hannah's hand under her arm.

"You care what happens to me, don't you?" Hannah asked softly.

"Yes, Hannah, I do," Josie muttered as they walked past Kip Rayburn and into the courtroom.

Rudy was there ready to convict Hannah. Kip was there ready to speak against her. Linda had sabotaged her daughter with her 'good intentions'. This sure wasn't going to be the best day of their lives and Rudy Klein was going to draw it out as long as he possibly could. He was saving Kip for last. Tom Winston, fireman, would kick off the day.

"I found the defendant crouching behind a stone fountain a few feet away from the French doors of the west wing of the Rayburn home."

"What did you do when you found her?" Rudy asked.

"I knelt beside her. The furnace had blown inside the house. I thought I might have to shield her from debris if something else was going to blow. When the danger was past, I saw that she was injured. I escorted her away from the scene and took her for treatment."

"Did you speak to the defendant?" Rudy asked.

"No, I did not."

"Did the defendant speak to you?"

"She said, 'It's all my fault'. She kept repeating that statement. 'It's all my fault'."

Rudy turned away leaving the witness's statement sitting on the jury's doorstep like an abandoned baby.

"Mr. Winston." Josie stepped to the side of the table. "Did you ask the defendant what she meant by the statement?"

"No," Tom Winston answered.

"Thank you."

Josie sat down. Check. *Unclear. Uncertain. That was no confession. Hannah didn't even remember saying it.* Josie would deal with all that in her closing arguments when it would be one of many bits of information woven into the story of the multiple mistakes and misinterpretations made in the case of Hannah Sheraton.

Rudy called the coroner. DNA consistent with Hannah's had been found in various places in Fritz Rayburn's apartments. Hannah's hair was in the bedroom. A drop of her blood in the bathroom. Worst of all, the slightest trace of Hannah's blood was found on Fritz

Rayburn's jaw where a blow had landed before he died. The coroner testified that Rayburn's head trauma also occurred before he died. Actual death was due to smoke inhalation. The body had been partially burned.

Rudy was prepared with show and tell.

One by one he posted pictures of a pitiful, helpless old man sprawled on the floor near his bed.

A close-up. Waist down. Burned to a crispy critter.

The back of Fritz's head. A contusion at the base of the skull, raw and ugly, surrounded by silky, silver hair.

A close-up. Fritz's chin.

Mid-range. Fritz, his hands flung out. One clutching the bedpost as if he was trying to pull himself up, one curled like a child in sleep.

Rudy Klein was building an epic storyboard, making his case about youth and age, limits and a desire for independence, Fritz Rayburn's success and Hannah Sheraton's abject failures. Now he was drawing the lines around Rayburn's vulnerability.

Question: Who could do this to an old man?

Answer: A young, selfish, indulgent, neurotic girl. That's who. Youth gone dangerously awry right here in River City.

The coroner's testimony was destructive; the pictures of Fritz were devastating.

The spotlight turned on Josie.

Rudy looked at her.

Beat that.

Josie did what she could.

The coroner could not tell when Hannah's hair and blood had been left in Fritz Rayburn's apartments. The heat and smoke had dried out the samples.

He had no explanation for the minute trace's of Hannah's blood on Fritz himself unless the defendant had struck the victim, splitting her own skin and leaving blood traces on his chin. Unfortunately there was no way to tell if that was what happened since the defendant's hand was burned, erasing any sign of an injury sustained in an earlier confrontation.

Josie thanked the coroner, wishing they could let the jury go home with nothing more than memories of what had been said here. They were on the edge of a four-day weekend and that could blur even the most prudent juror's impressions. But there was more: the housekeeper. Mrs. Peterson spoke to her hands until Rudy asked her to raise her head and speak clearly.

"I woke up at one forty-five in the morning. I sometimes have a hard time sleeping. I watch television and fall asleep in my chair."

"Did you watch television that night?" Rudy asked.

"Yes, but I heard something outside."

"Outside your window?"

She shook her head. "No, outside – down the drive. It is very quiet at night. You can hear things from blocks away."

"What did you do?" Rudy asked.

"I looked out my window," she responded.

"And what did you see?"

"Hannah running back to the house."

"Did you see where she had run from?"

"From beyond the trees, from the street. I heard a car right after I saw her."

Do you think Hannah had just returned from somewhere?"

"Objection. Speculation," Josie said.

Judge Norris sustained the objection. Josie sent a note to Hannah.

Who were you with?

It was a car on the street.

Josie slid her eyes toward Hannah. They would take up the question again after the day was won. Josie gave Rudy her undivided attention.

"Did Hannah go back into the house?"

"Yes."

"Did she stay in the house?"

"No. I went to her room to see if she was all right. She's a nice girl. Just lonely, you know."

"Your Honor, please," Rudy appealed to the bench.

"The witness is instructed to answer the question."

Mrs. Petersen nodded and chanced a glance at Hannah. She shifted in the witness seat.

"Hannah wasn't there."

"Did you look for her?" Rudy asked.

"No. I knew what she was doing."

"And what was that?"

"Your Honor," Josie said, "calls for a conclusion."

Rudy retraced his steps. "When was the next time you saw the defendant?"

"Ten minutes before the fire started I saw her walking around the back of the house going toward the studio."

"And what time was that?"

"It was about twenty minutes before I heard Mrs. Rayburn call out that the house was on fire."

"And the next time you saw the defendant?" Rudy asked.

"She was near the fire truck. They had bandaged her hand."

"Did the defendant say anything?"

"She said, "why did it have to be like this?" and "it's my fault." She said both things."

"Was she screaming?"

"No. She was very calm." Mrs. Peterson glanced toward the defense table. "I'm sorry, Hannah. I'm really sorry."

Rudy turned the woman over to Josie.

"Mrs. Peterson, did you see Hannah get out of a car?"

"No."

"Had you seen anyone pick Hannah up the night in question?"

"No.

"Mrs. Peterson," Josie asked. "Are you a doctor?"

She shook her head, "No, of course not."

"Then you would have no way of knowing if Hannah Sheraton's reaction to this fire was normal given the circumstances."

"No, I wouldn't know."

"You wouldn't know if she was in shock, would you?"

She shook her head again. "No, I suppose not."

"And Mrs. Peterson, did you actually see Hannah go into the studio?"

"No, I only saw her walking toward the studio."

"Thank you."

Josie sat down. While Mrs. Peterson returned to her seat Josie surreptitiously looked at Hannah. The girl's eyes were sad and blank. Her Valium lethargy was passing, though it was still evident. When Kip Rayburn was called to the stand Hannah stiffened, her eyes sought Josie's.

Then, as Kip swore to tell the truth, Hannah Sheraton's eyes turned downward. She couldn't look.

CHAPTER 19

HOSTILE WITNESS – An adverse witness who is known to offer prejudicial evidence as a result of adverse interest or bias. – Black's Law Dictionary

When Emily Baylor-Bates abandoned her daughter, the marine families closed rank. Josie was transferred to the home of a girl who qualified as her best friend by virtue of the fact that they had arrived in Hawaii at the same time. It took her father three days to get home and, in those three days, Josie imagined her father would blame her for driving Emily away.

But on a warm evening, just around dinnertime, Josie's father appeared. He reached out his hand and with that one gentle gesture he made the world right, made her part of a family again.

That wasn't the way things would play for Hannah. Kip didn't acknowledge her. Hannah listed to the left, her shoulder touching Josie's ever so slightly. She was looking up, right at Kip, telegraphing her anxiety as she knocked the table from underneath. Twenty times. Pause. Knocking again. To Josie it sounded like thunder but no one seemed to notice. Every eye was on the witness

"Mr. Rayburn, what is your relationship to the victim?"

"He was my father."

"And what is your relationship to the defendant."

"She is my wife's daughter."

"Mr. Rayburn, are you testifying of your own free will?"

"Yes, I am."

Josie moved in her seat. This was a powerful salvo. Rudy did not want anyone mistaking Kip Rayburn's testimony as hostile or less truthful because he was connected to the defendant.

"Given your relationship to the defendant, do you feel that you can answer my questions truthfully?"

"I will answer your questions truthfully. My father believed in the sanctity of the law, and so do I."

"Mr. Rayburn, given the circumstances, do you feel animosity toward the defendant?"

"No, sir," Kip answered.

Satisfied, Rudy moved another step closer to the witness.

"Can you describe the relationship your father had with Hannah Sheraton?"

"Objection, Your Honor. The witness cannot attest to such a relationship," Josie objected.

"Mr. Rayburn and his wife and stepdaughter lived in the victim's home, and Justice Rayburn interacted as part of the family. Kip Rayburn can testify to the dynamic of his own household," Rudy argued.

"I'll allow it within reason, Mr. Klein. Your objection is overruled, Ms. Bates."

Rudy gave the bench a perfunctory nod.

"Mr. Rayburn? Can you tell us about the relationship between your father and Hannah Sheraton?"

"Over time, my father became very interested in Hannah's welfare. He believed that Hannah was an extraordinarily talented artist and wanted to see her reach her full potential."

"And how did he show his interest?" Rudy asked.

"My father spent a great deal of time with Hannah when he was home. He talked about art. He explained his collection to her. He bought her gifts to enhance her talent: books and paints, and such. He offered to take her to museums when his schedule allowed."

"And how did the defendant react to this attention?"

"I think Hannah enjoyed being the center of attention at first."

"Objection," Josie called. "The witness cannot know what was in my client's mind."

"Sustained," Judge Norris intoned.

"Mr. Rayburn," Rudy went on. "Isn't it true that the defendant's attitude toward your father was antagonistic?"

"Eventually Hannah became belligerent when my father was in Los Angeles. She would become angry. She told my wife she didn't want him in the house."

"And what did you think about that?"

"I thought it was strange considering it was our home – my father's and mine. She had only been living with us for a short time. Her attitude was appalling given how generous my father had been."

"Did the defendant give you a reason for feeling this way?"

"She said he watched her. He always seemed to be around. She liked her independence. She complained about many things."

"Did Justice Rayburn do those things? I refer to watching Hannah Sheraton."

"I'm ashamed to say he took more of an interest in her than I did. He was very attentive. Perhaps if I realized the depth of her anger toward authority figures my father would still be alive."

"Objection, Your Honor." Josie raised her hand, disgusted with Kip's answer. He was going out of his way to point his finger at Hannah. "The witness is not the jury and can draw no such conclusion. Move to strike."

Judge Norris ordered the strike and Kip cleared his throat. He touched his tie but didn't adjust it. There wasn't a tremor in his voice, and his eyes remained steadily on Rudy.

"Was Justice Rayburn ever concerned for his own safety?" Rudy asked.

Kip shook his head. "No. Never. Even though I think he should have been."

"Why is that?"

"I initially believed a relationship would be good for both of them. I didn't have the artist's eye that my father held in high esteem. I was happy to see he had someone to share his interest." Kip tipped his chin a little higher, his lips turned up in what passed as a smile. "I seldom saw him when he was home anymore. But Hannah was young, she needed his attention. My father understood that Hannah's mother and I were busy."

Rudy let Kip transgress but even he couldn't ignore the sound of a beat that had, by now, become familiar to everyone in the room. The upper part of Hannah's arms rested against the tabletop. Underneath her clasped hands hit up on the wood, working diligently as if she could break through it and find her freedom. Her hair had spilled over her shoulders; her eyes were trained on Kip. Anger radiated off her. Josie could feel it, hoped the jury wouldn't sense it.

Kip ignored Hannah and the sounds but every now and again, a small muscle in Rudy's neck spasmed in sync with the knocking. Judge Norris shifted on the bench, unhappy with the distraction. Josie slipped her hand under the table, putting it between Hannah's fists and the wood. Without missing a beat, Hannah hit Josie and Josie took the blows on her warm, soft palm.

"When did you first notice the relationship between your father and the defendant change?" Rudy filled the silence quickly, unwilling to be distracted.

"Hannah had been with us almost a year. It was summer. She started to be disrespectful to my father. She was rude. She preferred staying in the room she used as her painting studio. Hannah went out and stayed out late if she wasn't painting. There was an older boy who did not go to school. Hannah started seeing him. He was unkempt. He looked like a transient."

"And what was your father's reaction to Hannah's behavior?"

"He told me not to worry. He told me she would settle down."

"Did something happen to change your father's mind?"

He found Hannah and this man in his bedroom. They had been drinking. My father had come back unexpectedly from San Francisco. They had gone through his things. Hannah had an antique pocketknife my father treasured. She held the knife on him long enough for the man to run away. I wanted to call the police but my father didn't want to press charges. He was extremely concerned about her at that point. He took it upon himself to help her. My father cared very deeply what happened to Hannah."

Josie listened carefully, and was suddenly aware that Hannah had stopped knocking. Josie cast a quick glance her way, sensing a rising anxiety in Hannah. She was reassured to see the girl sitting quietly, moving a pencil through her fingers under the table. When she stayed silent, Josie clasped her hands and leaned toward the witness as Rudy continued.

"How did your father help the defendant?"

"He spent even more time with Hannah. My father arranged and paid for treatment. He sent her to some of the finest rehabilitation facilities available. My father was extraordinarily compassionate. I'd never seen him that concerned about a child – any child." Kip's voice caught. It was as if his childhood was suddenly coming into focus. He put his fist to his mouth and cleared his throat. He apologized, "Sorry."

Rudy reassured him with a smile.

"How did the defendant react to Justice Rayburn's attempts to help her?"

"She ran away from the rehabilitation center. Every conversation was an argument. She stole my wife's car. The police found her approaching the Mexican border in San Diego – with that same man. She started smoking marijuana. She began cutting herself. She was always angry. Hannah was either very verbal, or totally withdrawn. It was difficult to know what to do."

"Mr. Rayburn," Rudy stepped forward to wrap things up. "Did you ever see or hear the defendant threaten your father after the incident with the knife?"

Kip's eyes trailed to Hannah and she seemed to shrink, huddling under the blazer like it was a tent. Her head shook in miniature movements, silently denying Kip's testimony or begging him to say nothing more. With no sign that Hannah moved him, Kip Rayburn looked away.

"The defendant screamed at my father that she wished he were dead. She said he would get what was coming someday. That he should just wait." Kip's gaze snapped back to Hannah. He struggled to keep the loathing from his voice. "After all that he had done for her. She wanted him dead. I thought it was a figure of speech. I was wrong."

"Your Honor!"

Josie shot out of her chair ready to object. Rudy looked over his shoulder. Judge Norris swiveled toward the defense. It wasn't Josie they focused on, but Hannah. She was rising from her seat, tears poured from her eyes and down her cheeks. Her body vibrated and shuddered.

"I didn't..." she said sharply, her fury directed toward everyone. "I didn't want him d-dead." She tipped her head back as if she could reverse the flow of her tears. "I just said it. I didn't do anything to him..." A second more ticked away, and then the silence of the courtroom was ripped by gut wrenching sobs. Her teeth gnashed together as if she could bite off her words. Her hair whipped in front of her face, her eyes blazed at the jury, the judge and then at Kip. Her voice rose and she demanded everyone in the room listen "I just wanted...him...to...leave me...alone."

Over and over again she said it, one fist pounding on the table in rhythm. No longer passive and content to have Josie fight for her, Hannah reached for her mother. The blazer fell from her shoulders. Her arm shot out, she pointed at Linda.

"Mom! Tell them now. Don't let him do this. He is lying. You know he's lying."

Paralyzed, Linda stared open mouthed at her daughter. A juror suppressed a cry. Another looked away. Someone gasped. Reporters scribbled trying to describe the bloody mess that was Hannah Sheraton's left arm, trying to explain how a common pencil could become a gruesome weapon of self-mutilation. There was no razor blade but there was no stopping the pain and rage inside Hannah Sheraton from getting out.

Suddenly, the bailiff lunged. Hannah reacted, striking out at him. Off guard, he stumbled back only to come at her again. Linda screamed. Kip shot straight up out of the witness chair but made no move to help.

It was Josie, taller than the bailiff, more determined to do what was right, who pulled a thrashing Hannah to her, felt the blood wet her blouse, and did what had to be done. Stumbling with her client toward the bench, Josie led Hannah past Judge Norris as she said:

"I'd like to request a recess."

CHAPTER 20

"I should have been a mechanic like my father." – Judge Cy Norris to his clerk upon leaving the bench.

Josie once dated an emergency room doctor. She loved his wickedly dark sense of humor, his goatee, and the way he cooked. She didn't like the fact that being near a body of water larger than a bathtub made him seasick, and he wanted to have a house in the suburbs filled with children.

They had parted ways after a year but Josie always remembered something he said. *A great deal of blood could come from just one wound.* Once you found the wound, you could make a decision about what to do: work to save the poor bastard or let God deal with it.

In the windowless holding cell off Norris's courtroom Josie leaned up against the wall and looked for Hannah's wound while someone else cleaned up the blood. The jurors were at lunch, though she doubted they had an appetite. Judge Norris called a doctor, advised he would expect Josie back in the courtroom for her cross, and gave permission for Hannah to be excused in the company of her mother to seek further medical attention – mental or physical. Josie sent back her thanks. He was not only a kind man he was a smart one who wanted to control his courtroom now that the floodgates had been opened: Hannah being half carried away, blood everywhere, Linda barred from the room as Hannah became ever more hysterical, while crying that she was so sorry. So sorry.

For the last ten minutes, though, all had been quiet. The doctor who had responded to Judge Norris's call was an older woman, unfazed by what she found. She spoke little, did her work well, and bandaged Hannah's arm with great care before she left. Hannah's arms were crossed on the tabletop, her head resting on them, and her eyes were closed. It was the first time Josie had seen her completely at rest. No tapping, no counting, worn out, and psychically and emotionally exhausted.

Josie watched her thoughtfully and counted her own failings. She had seen a hundred other clients proclaim their innocence, fall into despair, cry and wail against the system. At one time in her life, Josie had been able to gauge guilt in a split second. It had been a talent left dormant, a dull blade that no longer sliced easily through a client's guile – until now. Now Josie believed what she saw: Hannah was only a poor, confused girl who had sealed her own fate, whether guilty or not. Finally Josie pushed herself away from the wall. It was time to probe for Hannah's real wound.

"We're okay here." Quietly, Josie dismissed the bailiff. He hesitated but eventually left them alone. Josie touched the door as it closed behind him then pulled a chair close to Hannah and laid her hand atop the girl's head.

"Hannah, come on. We've got to talk."

Hannah's lashes fluttered. Her eyes opened. She stared, but saw nothing. It was another minute, maybe two before Hannah found the energy to speak.

"I'm sorry about your shirt. I'm sorry about everything."

"Forget the shirt." Josie petted Hannah, smoothing her hair, talking quietly. "It's the *everything* we need to talk about. Can you sit up? Can you talk to me?"

Hannah's body trembled. She raised her head. It was so hard for her. Finally she sat up. Her hands fell to her sides. She looked at the bandages.

"I don't even remember doing it. I just remember Kip talking and talking."

"Hannah do you want your mother to come in while we get things settled?" Josie asked.

Hannah shook her head. "No. She'll just say she was right all along. I should have done what she said. I should have gone to the hospital but I wanted to show her I was strong, too. I wanted to be strong like her." A pitiful sob bubbled up and escaped. Just one. She put her fingers to her lips. "I just couldn't listen to him anymore."

"Your mom is worried, not upset. We're all worried about you," Josie whispered.

"When you see her, tell her I'll be good from here on. I promise. I don't want to go to jail. I want to go home with my mom."

"That's what we need to decide Hannah." Josie cleared her throat. It was tough to say this. "I think we need to cut our losses here."

Josie fell silent. It was hard to think. If Hannah was unbalanced enough to hurt herself that badly, in such a horrific manner, then what could she have done to Fritz…

"Josie, why haven't you ever asked me if I'm innocent?" Hannah leaned close as if she knew what Josie was thinking.

Josie chuckled darkly. She sat back in her chair and crossed her arms to look at her client. She told her the truth.

"Because I was being a good defense attorney. If I asked you and you told me you were guilty, I couldn't put you on the stand if I had to. If I knew you were going to lie, I'd be suborning perjury. No defense attorney ever asks that question."

"Don't you want to know?"

"I thought I did know, Hannah." Josie held Hannah's gaze.

"Until now, is that it?" The last flicker of hope drained out of Hannah's eyes when Josie didn't answer. "It's okay. I understand."

"No, you don't. I still don't think you deliberately killed Fritz Rayburn. I'll never believe that. But Hannah, nothing is ever black and white. People can look at the same thing and see it differently. You could swear you were innocent and those people in that room would look at the evidence and be sure you're guilty. It's a huge risk we're taking now that this has happened."

"But everything's going to be okay, right?"

Josie lightly touched Hannah's arm. "If you can do this to yourself, then there are really deep problems you have to contend with. I'm going to ask for a continuance. I want you to talk with some doctors. I want the jury to take a breather because what happened just now isn't going to help. Hannah, I couldn't live with myself if I screwed up and put you in jail when your mother was right all along and you need treatment."

Hannah clutched at Josie's hands, missing and trying again until she had them in both her own.

"Please, please don't give up on me. Josie, you can't. I know you don't want to know, but I didn't start the fire. I hit Fritz. Okay? I mean, I think I did. I know I pushed him. I did that. I was in his bedroom. I did scream at him. That's all the truth. I should have told you before, but I didn't think it was important. I thought the fire was important." Hannah pulled on Josie's hands like a child wanting an adult to see things her way. "I didn't see him fall and hit his head. I didn't set the fire. I didn't kill him. I just wanted to get away from him."

"Hannah, stop. Stop." Josie yanked her hands away and fell back in the chair. She put one hand to her temple and closed her eyes. She wanted to close her ears. There it was: the truth. Hannah had been there. Hannah had struck him. Hannah probably set that damn fire and whatever was in her sick mind just wouldn't let her admit it. Josie opened her eyes again, dropped her hand, and leaned forward. "Listen to me, Hannah. I'm your attorney. I have to tell you when it's time to give up."

"But it's not time," Hannah cried. Desperately she tried to control her anger, her good hand scratching at the bandages on her wounded arm. Josie grappled with her until she had Hannah's hand in both of hers. Finally, nose-to-nose, Josie begged:

"Then help me believe that. Did you say you wished Justice Rayburn were dead?" Josie relaxed her grip. She lowered her voice. They were both breathing hard. "Did you?"

Hannah blinked and sat straight up. She clasped her hands and pounded them into her lap as she whispered:

"I didn't mean it. I wanted him to leave me alone. That's what I told him that night. I told him he had to leave me alone. He said he wouldn't and I pushed him. I…I could have hit him. I know I pushed him…I told him…."

Tears came out of her eyes, not in drops but in sheets of moisture that shimmered over her beautiful bronze skin, washed down her cheeks, and fell onto her skirt. Once begun, Hannah couldn't seem to stop crying. It was as if she had saved it up all her life.

"Hannah. What am I suppose to say to that jury? Fritz Rayburn spent time and money trying to get you the help you need. Kip heard you say you wished his father were dead. You were in Rayburn's bedroom. His pills were under your mattress. Now you admit that you hit him, or pushed him, or whatever. How can I convince that jury that you meant anything else except to harm Fritz Rayburn?"

"No. No. No. It wasn't like that. I swear." Hannah sniffed, she sobbed, and she put her hands on Josie's knees. Her eyes were red rimmed and the green iris's sparkled bright. "Fritz was going to hurt me. I had to stop him. Don't you see?"

"Hannah, please." Josie didn't want to hear her fantasies.

"He would sneak up and tell me what he was going to do and then he'd show that little knife to me. He said it was his favorite knife to cut with. That old one. I just wanted to take it away and hide it."

"Hannah, deal in reality."

"Wait, wait," she pleaded, her hands patting Josie's knees, babbling on. "I didn't lie about the pills. He gave them to me because I would need them someday, when he did something that really hurt. And I was afraid. I kept those pills because I never knew when he would come after me, or when I'd start feeling something. He was happy when I was afraid. If I wasn't afraid Fritz wouldn't think it was fun anymore. If he couldn't hurt me, it wouldn't be fun. I practiced cutting on myself so it wouldn't hurt if he did it."

Hannah was crying again and sniffing. The words poured out as she tried to coax a smile of faith out of Josie. Josie took her client's hands and put them together to keep them quiet. She spoke quietly, but firmly. It was time to end all this. Hannah had to admit the truth.

"Hannah, if all this happened why you didn't tell someone?"

"Who was going to believe me? Who was I going to tell?"

"Your mother," Josie answered. "She probably would have killed him."

Hannah bolted upright. She shut her eyes and shook her head violently.

"No. No. No." She said harshly. "Fritz said he knew exactly how to hurt her. He told me that all the time. That's what he said. *I know how to hurt your mother.* I couldn't let him do that." Hannah's eyes searched Josie's face looking for hope, for help. It wasn't there. "You have to believe me. I've never told anyone except for you. Josie, please, please. Look, I'll show you."

Hannah shot up, pushed back her chair and frantically gathered up her long skirt. There was too much fabric and Hannah lost hold. Finally she had pulled it to her waist. Josie saw it all: her agitation, the bandaged arm, the healing hand, the wild eyes that saw something Josie didn't. This child was so near broken Josie wondered if she could ever be put back together.

The plain-faced clock ticked away a minute and a half before Hannah turned back to Josie, a triumphant smile on her tormented face. She tugged at her skirt and stuck out her leg forcing Josie to look.

"Oh, Hannah."

Josie's stomach turned at the sight of the final hurt on Hannah Sheraton's body. Running from thigh to hip was a raised and puckered scar, near white on her beautiful dark skin.

"I just wanted him to leave me alone. That is why I was in his room. That is why I pushed him, that is why that man saw us arguing," Hannah said quietly.

Hannah's young face was bright with hope. Slowly Josie got out of her chair and knelt on the cold hard floor. She reached out but couldn't bear to touch Hannah's skin.

"You want me to believe Fritz Rayburn did this to you? You want me to believe that a California Supreme Court Justice was a sadistic monster?"

Hannah nodded but Josie didn't see. She'd fallen back on her heels, her arms at her side. This changed everything. Hannah was certifiable. She had no grip on reality and Josie's heart broke.

Hannah let her skirt fall over her legs, and then crouched down in front of Josie and changed everything again.

"I can prove it. I know about other people. I know what he did to them. I'm not the first person he hurt, Josie. I'm just the last. Aren't I the last?"

There, on the floor of that cold, small, windowless room Hannah Sheraton told her stories until the bailiff opened the door and told Josie it was time to begin again.

CHAPTER 21

"This one is over." – Maeve Clark, reporter, to herself.

Josie learned how to hold her breath when she was ten. Not just hold it for a minute but hold it as if it was a matter of life or death.

The first morning they were in Hawaii, before the boxes were unpacked, Emily Baylor-Bates bundled her daughter into their old car and drove off the base to find an adventure.

Two hours later, Emily and Josie picked their way down a bluff through a light tropical rain toward a stretch of white beach, blue water, and waves that curled on to each other. Laughing, meeting the waves head on, Emily ran into the water. Josie went after, apprehensive, but so anxious to be her mother's daughter. Emily turned her back. A wave caught her and lifted her up. She reached out her hands calling to Josie over the roar, moving further into the bright blue water, moving away from Josie.

Josie, smaller and more vulnerable than Emily, was buffeted by the waves. It took all her might to stand her ground. One hit her. Another came. A third slapped her down, dragging her into a whirlpool of sand and water. Josie was twisted head over heels, her small arms flailing, until she didn't know which way was up, or where down was. She hit the sand hard. Salt stung her shoulder where it was scraped bloody by shell and rock. Over and over again Josie was tumbled and dragged on the rocky bottom only to be sucked back up into the churning, crystalline bubble of water. She was suffocating. Death was around the corner. There was no savior in sight. She wanted her mother. Where was her mother, Josie wondered, as Hannah fought for her life?

Just when Josie was sure she couldn't hold her breath one minute longer, just when she was sure she was going to die, the ocean threw her up on shore. Lying on the sand, gasping for air, Josie looked up. Emily was dancing in the waves, oblivious to everything but her own pleasure.

Hannah Sheraton had been like Josie. She had held her breath as she tumbled through the beautiful treacherous waters of the Rayburn house while Linda and Kip danced outside the surf and Fritz dragged her under the tide of his sickness. Linda hadn't saved her, but Josie would. She was convinced that Hannah's story was not a fantasy. The girl knew too much, gave too many names, and was too specific as to Fritz Rayburn's particular habits. By the time the court reconvened Josie knew what she had to do. She had to believe in Hannah unconditionally.

Mired in her outrage, guarding against the slippery slope of skepticism, Josie stood rigidly behind the defense table; eyes forward as she controlled her breathing and planned her attack. Josie didn't realize Linda was near until she heard her voice.

"You can't keep me out of that room," Linda hissed. "I'm her mother."

Josie looked at Linda, unmoved by such outrage. It was too little too late. Josie stepped to the bar, close enough to smell Linda's expensive perfume, to see the little scar on the side of her lip twitch.

"I can do what I damn well please," Josie assured her coldly.

"You're going to kill her. I told you that in the beginning. It was just a matter of time before she went nuts. Tell the judge now. Tell him you want to talk to the prosecutor about a plea."

Josie looked at the empty jury box. She could hear Linda's voice but Josie's mind was elsewhere. Her entire defense would have to change now and she wasn't clear what direction it would take. Self-defense? Battered woman's syndrome? All Josie knew was that Linda hadn't just ignored her daughter's pain; she had inflicted it on Hannah with her selfishness. Finally, she looked at Linda.

"You are disgusting. Did you think I wouldn't find out what Rayburn was doing? Why didn't you tell me up front? What was there to protect? Your husband? Your reputation? It would have all been so different if you just told me."

"I don't know what you're talking about," Linda snapped, but she'd gone pale. She took hold of Josie's arm. "What are you going to do? What did Hannah tell you?"

"You'll know when everyone else does," Josie growled. "Now let go of me and sit down, or I swear I'll make this worse for you than it needs to be."

"Josie, I don't know what Hannah told you…"

But Josie had turned her back. People were watching. Linda sat down, pulling herself tall, squaring her shoulders. Behind her, spectators were filing in, wondering about Hannah and judging Linda. Linda hated judgment. How could they know anything about her life? How could these people – the press, the spectators, the vacant faced bailiff and clerk, the jury and even the judge himself – presume to think they knew anything about Linda, or the way she had raised her daughter, or the things she had to do to survive? It sickened Linda Rayburn to think that anyone felt superior to her – even if it was only their perception.

Linda threw back her head, turning just as Rudy Klein walked past. He fixed his eyes on her until he pushed through the swinging gate of the bar. Unnerved, Linda's chin dropped and her hand went to her throat. There was something in those eyes of his that put her off as sharply as if he had poked her with a stick; as if she was a rock he was trying to turn to see what crawling things were underneath.

Then the judge was seated, the court reporter's hands were poised above her machine, and Kip was being called back to the stand for Josie's cross. Kip stopped to touch Linda's hand. That was all it took to put her on the right track again. The end was too close to let anything knock them off course. Finally Kip seemed to understand that.

Judge Norris instructed the jury to attend to the matters at hand and gave Josie the nod. Standing in front of Kip Rayburn, Josie clasped her hands low, planted her feet and led with her strength.

"Mr. Rayburn, isn't it true that your father, Justice Fritz Rayburn, abused you?"

The silence lasted exactly five seconds before the buzz started.

What did she say? Did I hear that right?

"Objection, Your Honor!" Rudy called out, on his feet, as pale as his witness. "This is outrageous and beyond the scope."

Josie was quick and fierce. Her head snapped toward the bench for only as long as it took to explain herself.

"Goes to credibility, Judge."

"Request a sidebar, Your Honor," Rudy demanded.

Norris crooked a finger, simultaneously calling for quiet, threatening to clear the courtroom if he didn't get what he wanted. Josie went reluctantly, unwilling to take her eyes off Kip Rayburn. She wanted him to feel the depth of her disdain. Norris covered the microphone on the bench and leaned forward. Rudy went first. He was so incensed Josie feared he would combust.

"Your Honor, this is outrageous. Ms. Bates will have a chance to present her case but to abuse this witness with histrionics is blatant sensationalism and demeans this court."

"Oh please," Josie shot back in disgust. "You opened the door. This witness has testified to the kind nature of Justice Rayburn. He has painted a picture of a selfless man bent only on helping my client and that is, quite simply, untrue according to my client. I should be allowed to explore the character of the victim since the prosecutor is holding that character up to scrutiny."

"She is right counselor," Norris ruled.

"Then limit the scope, Your Honor," Rudy pleaded. "Allow Mr. Rayburn to testify only to what he experienced in regard to the defendant."

"Your witness is already on the record regarding his insights into Justice Rayburn's treatment of my client. If you limit me, I will have no way of discrediting his testimony without him admitting to perjury. Please, Your Honor. This girl deserves every opportunity to prove her truthfulness."

Norris hesitated. This case had taken a turn that would whip public interest to a frenzy and that worried him. He was already hearing the sound bites, the debates, and the speculation that would erupt on talk shows and in the press. A California Supreme Court Justice had gone from saint to sinner and it was clear Josie Baylor-Bates was going to milk this for all it was worth. Still, he had a job to do. Much as he hated to, Norris would let this play out.

"Overruled, Mr. Klein. Step back."

Rudy went back to his corner, unnerved by the ruling. He was barely seated when Josie closed in on Kip Rayburn. The man looked gray. His hair seemed to have thinned. He seemed to have wilted inside his suit. Then she saw a spark deep in his eyes. Kip wasn't afraid. He was examining the predator and the nature of her attack in order to protect himself. That meant only one thing. Hannah hadn't lied.

"Mr. Rayburn. I ask you again, when did your father, Fritz Rayburn, start abusing you?"

"I am not going to answer that."

"Your Honor, permission to treat as hostile." Josie never took her eyes off Kip Rayburn as she circled and left him open to the jury's scrutiny.

"So directed." Norris instructed.

Josie inclined her head in thanks. She could now demand his answers, insist on the truth, pound at his responses until she was satisfied her client had been well served.

"Do you need the question read back, Mr. Rayburn?" Josie asked.

Kip let his eyes linger on Josie for a minute. His expression was condescending. His gaze wandered to Linda. Josie could feel the minute their eyes locked. Methodically he surveyed the spectators and the jury. Finally, disdainfully, Kip Rayburn answered the question.

"My father never abused me, Ms. Bates."

"Did Justice Rayburn use a wooden paddle on you when you were eight?"

"Yes."

"When you were twelve did your father cut your right index finger so deep that it exposed the bone and took twenty-seven stitches to close it up?"

"That was an accident. He was trying to show me how to whittle," Kip said.

"With a carving knife, Mr. Rayburn?" Josie asked disdainfully.

"You had to be there, Ms. Bates," he answered.

"And on your ninth birthday did your father lock you in the closet with a..."

"This is ridiculous." Kip Rayburn muttered. One hand went to his mouth; the other was cocked back on the arm of the witness chair.

"Mr. Rayburn, you are directed–" Judge Norris began but Kip had other ideas.

"No. I will not be directed to talk about things that are personal. The way my father and I dealt with one another is no one's business. This isn't about me. It's about her." Kip tossed his head toward the empty defense table.

"Fine," Josie stepped forward. "Then tell us this, Mr. Rayburn, did your father abuse Hannah Sheraton?"

"Of course not," Kip snorted.

"Verbally?"

"No."

"Emotionally?"

"No."

"Did he touch her, Mr. Rayburn?"

"Only in the way a concerned old man would touch a child he cared about."

"Did he physically discipline her?" Josie snapped.

"He disciplined her within reason," Kip shot back.

"Did that include burning her with wax from a candle, Mr. Rayburn?"

"I beg your pardon."

"Wax. Hot wax on her thigh. Hot enough to burn through a summer skirt. Did your father do that?"

"No! I mean, how would I know? I didn't monitor my father's behavior."

"Considering the way your father *disciplined* you, don't you think you should have watched how the great Justice Rayburn interacted with the defendant?"

"Hannah was a big girl..."

"So you're saying that your father only abused small children. Is that what you're saying?"

"No, that's not what I'm saying. Do not twist my words. You cannot twist them to suit you. Hannah was the one who abused my father. Hannah was the one..."

Josie threw herself back into the courtroom, her arms raised in disbelief.

"Hannah was fourteen when she came to live in your home and barely fifteen when your father first took an interest in her. We've all seen her. She weighs one hundred pounds, and you want to tell this court that she was the one who abused..."

"Objection," Rudy roared. "Counsel is blatantly badgering this witness."

Forgetting Kip Rayburn Josie turned on Rudy.

"What is outrageous is that my client is on trial when it is the Rayburn family that should be held accountable for what they have done to her. How far did you look for a perpetrator, Mr. Klein? How far were you willing to go to sacrifice a child so that you could make a name for yourself – or was it to protect the reputation of a dead judge?" Josie's eyes slid to Kip. "Or is your office protecting the next Justice Rayburn, Mr. Klein?"

"Ms. Bates, that is enough," Judge Norris warned.

"No, I want to know. Were you afraid if you tried to find the real criminal someone might have dug up the fact that Fritz Rayburn wasn't such a good guy after all?"

"That's ridiculous. Your client had the means and the opportunity. Your client set that fire." Rudy was half out of his seat, outraged at the turn of events.

"That is enough!" Norris roared and his gavel crashed onto his desk.

Josie took too many steps back, moving so close to Kip that she could almost touch the wooden railing between them. She rerouted herself again. It was wrong to be so aggressive, so outraged. Righteous indignation would help her client, not an attack. The silence was deafening. Rudy Klein sat down. Josie pulled herself together.

"Continue with this witness in an appropriate manner, Ms. Bates or you will be sanctioned."

She turned toward the jury then back again, her head bowed in thought. Rudy fumed in his chair. Josie was composed once more.

"Is it true your father was abusive to you, yes or no?"

"No."

"Mr. Rayburn isn't it true that in the two days before his death you and your father fought violently."

"I wouldn't characterize it that way," Kip answered.

"Did you argue?"

"Yes."

"What did you argue about?"

"A business matter."

"During that business *disagreement*, were you so outraged that you threw a glass decanter at your father?"

"Yes. It was a mistake."

"Did you resolve the matter?"

"We would have," Kip replied.

"So at the time of his death, you still harbored ill will toward your father for a current transgression. Yes or no."

"No."

Josie didn't give him time to breathe.

"Did you harbor ill will toward him for his treatment of you as a child?"

Kip swallowed hard and answered, "No."

"Were you upset that your father paid so much attention to the defendant."

"I didn't think it was healthy."

"You didn't think it was healthy," Josie reiterated. "That's an interesting choice of words, Mr. Rayburn. For whom was it unhealthy? For Hannah Sheraton?"

Kip ignored the question and answered as he liked. "There was an unhealthy concern on my father's part for a girl who didn't know the value of his attention."

"Are you still contending that your father only had Hannah Sheraton's best interests at heart?"

"Yes." Kip leaned forward in his chair, daring her to take this further. Josie pulled herself to her full height, a small smile on her lips.

"Mr. Rayburn, do you know the penalty for perjury?"

"Yes, I do."

"Then answer this question truthfully. Was your stepdaughter abused by Justice Fritz Rayburn?"

Kip couldn't contain himself any longer. He stood up and leaned over the railing of the witness box. His tone was cruel, and his plain eyes seemed dead.

"If I had any knowledge of abuse in my home I would gladly tell you because then everyone would see that Hannah is a murderer. If my father did such a despicable thing, if any of what you said was true, at least that little shit would have a decent motive for killing my father. Or didn't that occur to you, you bitch?"

Time stopped. The courtroom reverberated with the echoes of Kip Rayburn's fury. His face, so ordinary in repose, took on angles and shadows carved by the twin blades of raw emotion and brutal honesty. He trembled as he stood looking down on Josie Baylor-Bates. His hatred of her was palpable. She took a step forward, holding out her right hand as if to ask the judge to give her a moment. It was Josie and Kip in that instant. Everyone else faded to black and the camera captured them in close-up.

"If everything I said is true," Josie said firmly, "then Hannah isn't the only one with a motive to kill your father is she, Mr. Rayburn?"

CHAPTER 22

"In my chambers!" – Judge Cy Norris

"Sit down!"

Judge Norris bellowed as he swept into his chambers. He yanked at the zipper on his robes and fought his way out of them. Behind him Linda and Kip, Rudy and Josie scattered. Linda took a chair, as did Rudy. Josie and Kip stood on opposite sides of the room.

"Your Honor," Josie began.

"Not yet. Not yet, Ms. Bates. You just give me a minute here to cool my jets." Norris huffed. Adrenalin kept him from his seat. Behind the desk he paced like a caged animal; long strides in a short space. His hands were on the side of his head before they landed on his hips. The temperate looking man who had initially taken the bench had a formidable temper.

Finally he stopped, grasped the back of his chair, and hung his head. In the silence that ensued he finally sat down, tented his fingers and looked at them. He was, in a word, appalled.

"Mr. Rayburn. I will not accept that kind of behavior in my courtroom. Period. And I am disturbed to think that your behavior might be repeated in your own courtroom were the governor to allow you to take the bench."

"It isn't my courtroom I'd worry about, it is your own."

"Mr. Rayburn," Norris snapped.

"This entire trial is a farce." Kip sounded off. "You've enabled that woman to degrade these proceedings by attacking me and my father in public when she had every opportunity to ask me those same questions before this trial began. This is a calculated attack."

"You will show this court respect, sir," Judge Norris intoned, "because you have no standing except as a witness here."

"It doesn't matter *when* I ask a question," Josie insisted, ready to fight with Kip. "I expect a truthful answer. If you were going to turn a blind eye to what was happening in your own home then I had no choice but to bring it to the court's attention." Josie whipped her head toward Judge Norris. "Your Honor, I request a continuance. I need more time to fully prepare now that I have this information. I need to see what bearing the victim's behavior, this witnesses' behavior, has on my case."

"Your Honor," Rudy jumped in. "There is no need to put the court out because Ms. Bates' client has been less than forthcoming. The defense has had ample time to uncover and investigate all aspects of this matter. We aren't talking about forensics that need additional testing, or an eye witness that needs to be located."

"I should say not," Kip drawled. "There couldn't be a witness, or evidence, because nothing happened to that girl. Ask my wife. Ask her."

All eyes turned toward Linda. She sat with her knees together, her hands fisted in her lap. Her face was the color of chalk, her eyes cold as ice as she stared at Josie.

"Why are you doing this to us?" Linda lifted her hands slightly.

"Did you know, Linda? Did you?" Josie asked quietly. But Linda didn't answer. She turned to Judge Norris.

"Your Honor, my daughter is ill. She lives in a world of fantasy. Hannah lives in her own mind. She paints pictures; she makes up lives for herself. She smokes marijuana. She reinvents herself every…"

"Linda!" Josie cried. "What are you saying? Hannah has been abused, and she has the scars to prove it."

Linda dropped her head before swinging it toward Josie, glaring at her from beneath her long lashes.

"Don't you dare tell me about my daughter, Josie."

"I'm not. I'm asking you to look at her objectively. Look at what that man did to her," Josie pleaded.

"And I'm telling you to look again." Linda shook back her hair and sat up straighter. "You always could tell a fake when we played ball, Josie. You should be able to tell one now."

Josie's eyes narrowed. Something was wrong. It was there in Linda's tone, the shadow behind the eyes.

"This isn't sport, and Hannah isn't my opponent, Linda," Josie said cautiously.

"No, this isn't sport," Linda whispered before finding some strength and starting again. "Hannah is a sick girl who has taken up every minute of my life with worry. I don't mind for myself, but she can ruin my husband's career, and the reputation of a fine man who died a tragic death." She turned toward Rudy then to Judge Norris.

"How can you let this happen? How can you let her insinuate these things? Whatever Ms. Bates believes she saw, Hannah probably did it to herself; whatever she told you are the imagining of a lonely teenager who has never fit in anywhere." She turned her gaze back to Josie. "This isn't helping Hannah, Josie. This isn't helping any of us."

Kip stepped in.

"If you stay this course, Ms. Bates, you will be on the wrong side of a slander suit. We want Hannah to plead no contest to all charges. Mr. Klein, I'd like you to negotiate a plea bargain. We will advise you of new counsel."

Josie scoffed.

"You know counsel can't be replaced without good cause, and I haven't done anything but act in the best interest of my client."

"That's a laugh," Kip snorted. "I can replace you this minute. I won't pay one more cent for this kind of representation."

"So this is all about money and appearances." Josie nodded, resigned to what she had to do next. "Fine. Let's remove her from you – not me from her. Judge, Ms. Sheraton is being prosecuted as an adult. She should make her own decisions and, if there is a question as to the legality of that, Your Honor, then I'd like to go on record with my intent to file for emancipation of the minor Hannah Sheraton to sever all legal ties with Linda Rayburn."

"You can't do that," Linda cried half standing. Kip grabbed her shoulders and settled her again.

"Your Honor, this is a mockery of the system," Rudy argued. "Emancipation was never meant to be used this way."

"Then leave me alone to defend that girl!" Josie pushed the envelope without a thought to the consequences.

"Quiet. All of you." Norris cut the air with his hand and looked at each one in turn. Josie infuriated and determined, Linda stiff with rage, Rudy anxious to get this proceeding back on track, and Kip Rayburn hurt, angry and dangerous. There was something else in Kip Rayburn, too, but it took Norris a minute to identify it. Then he had a word for it. Shame. Shame could be a powerful motivator.

He gave his order.

"I'll talk to the defendant. Alone."

CHAPTER 23

Josie knew one thing: all problems could be solved.

Fritz Rayburn was a problem. Someone solved it by eliminating the source. Josie's father solved his problems by the book. Emily Baylor-Bates ran away. Linda turned a blind eye, some people ignored their troubles, and some created bigger ones to take their place. Then there were people who solved their problems the good old-fashioned way – they worked at it. Ask the right questions, determine if answers were truthful, make a plan, follow through and regroup if necessary.

Now they were waiting to see how Judge Norris would solve the problem of Hannah Sheraton.

Linda and Kip sat in the empty jury box, isolated, huddled together, and holding hands. Kip didn't move; Linda couldn't sit still. She leaned into her husband, put her hand on his knee, draped her arm over his shoulders, dropped her head so that it nestled against his jaw, and spoke to him in whispers. The only thing Linda Rayburn didn't do was look at Josie pacing in the back of the courtroom.

Josie checked her watch incessantly, and wished a thousand times that Norris would have let her stay in chambers while he spoke to Hannah. She promised silence. He had dismissed her, and now time wasn't going any faster because Josie was up and moving. She sank onto the back pew, put her knees together, and splayed her feet outwards considering the fine point on the toe of her high-heeled boots.

"Bates?"

Josie started and sat up straighter, instantly on her guard. Rudy Klein swung himself onto the pew in front of her.

"What's going on out there?" Josie cocked her head toward the door, keeping her voice low.

"The press is getting ready for a feeding frenzy. You're headlines again. That's quite a talent."

"Anything else?" Josie had no patience for him and this little game of dredging up the past.

"No. I guess not. Just thought you might like some company. I suppose I was wrong."

Rudy started to get up. Josie stopped him.

"Sorry. Sorry. I'm a little sensitive at the moment."

Rudy sat down again. He hung one hand over the back of the pew. He spoke quietly, thoughtfully.

"You're not the only one. And you're not the only one who feels bad about all this." Rudy sighed. His fingers drummed lightly on the back of the bench. "I've got to tell you it makes me feel terrible. I admired Judge Rayburn. I don't want to think he could do what you're saying he did. Not to a kid. Not his son or that girl."

Josie looked at Rudy as his voice trailed off. He was a truly handsome man. His hair waved back from a broad, intelligent brow. The eyes that looked so lazy were actually bright and telling. He had probably been a hell of an actor but he wasn't acting now. Rudy was disturbed and fighting to stay true to his own charge.

"I don't think anyone wants to believe it, but that is what we've got," Josie said.

"Maybe. Maybe not," Rudy sighed and rubbed his hand over his eyes. "I just wonder if you really know what you're doing. I mean the press is going to run with this, a lot of things are going to be called into question: Rayburn's judgments, the governors, your own part in this."

"Are you concerned for my professional reputation?" She slid her eyes toward him, wary of the opponent at rest.

"I wouldn't like to see you go down the tubes and I think you might. You're running with a ball but you didn't consider who made the pass." Rudy rested his chin on his hand. "Maybe asking for a continuance and checking out the kid's story before you came out with all guns blazing might have made a little more sense"

"It's nice of you to worry about me. I think my reputation will survive," Josie drawled.

"Hey, come on. I'm not rooting for you to go down, this is just some advice. Whatever is between you and the girl's mother is between the two of you. But what she has to say about this girl being delusional, or self destructive, or whatever, may be right."

"And I believe my client," Josie answered. "That's enough."

He shook his head, sliding his arm off the back of the bench in dismay, genuinely distressed.

"Then you're going to be the only one. Fritz Rayburn was a California Supreme Court Justice. I can recite his resume chapter and verse. There has never, ever been a hint of scandal and now a girl with mega problems is crying foul. You've got to see the downside of all this."

Josie pulled her feet together and leaned forward. She kept her voice low.

"Rudy, why does age and accomplishment count for more than youth and fear? I think telling me about this was a pretty gutsy thing for Hannah to do. I wish she'd done it earlier. She knew people would react the way you are. Nobody wants to scrutinize Fritz Rayburn, or call him to account. Do you think Kip would have stood up for Hannah if she told him? Do you think her mother would?"

"I would, had there been credible evidence," Rudy insisted.

"Right. The same way you're willing to believe her now," Josie scoffed. "Give me a break, Rudy."

She turned her head. Kip was watching them, and when Josie caught his eye she was overwhelmed with sadness for everyone: Kip, Linda, and especially Hannah. Then she looked around the courtroom and the feeling passed. No one in here did anything because they felt sorry for a fellow human being. Here everyone was driven by a higher purpose, and Josie's was justice for a girl who had no power.

"You said you and the DA want to hold kids who kill accountable." She sat up straighter but still spoke quietly. "Why shouldn't accountability work both ways? I'd like to think you'd prosecute Fritz Rayburn if he were accused. I'd like to think I would defend him because everyone is innocent until proven guilty. But Fritz Rayburn isn't my client. Hannah is. She deserves everything I've got to give including laying the truth out like a bed of nails and making you lay down on it. I expect you to fight back hard, but what I really expect, Rudy, is that we'll just get to the truth. Most often this is where the truth finally comes out if you dig deep enough."

Rudy Klein pulled his lips together. Josie Baylor-Bates believed in her client as much as he believed Hannah Sheraton was responsible for Justice Rayburn's death.

"I can bury you with this abuse thing if you pursue it, Bates. It's motive pure and simple," he said bluntly. "I'll talk to the District Attorney about a deal. Let's make this go away before it goes any further."

Josie looked over at Kip Rayburn then back at Rudy. "No, Rudy. This time I'm right. It's a reason for Hannah to have defended herself not the other way around. No deal."

With that, Josie stood up. The door of chambers had opened. Judge Norris had Hannah by the arm and was escorting her into the courtroom.

Linda rushed out of the jury box, hands out to her daughter. Hannah looked away and stayed close to Judge Norris. Kip stood behind Linda. Rudy followed Josie until they had all congregated behind the bar. Judge Norris and Hannah were in front of it. Norris spoke quietly and firmly.

"I have decided to grant a continuation per Ms. Bates' request. This trial will resume on Tuesday the sixteenth. This court will recognize Ms. Sheraton's adult status without emancipation proceedings. She has chosen to have Ms. Bates continue as her defense attorney. She has also decided there will be no further discussion of plea bargain unless the attorneys are present, and the defendant agrees."

"Oh, God." Linda uttered a cry under her breath and turned into her husband.

"I am, however, in a quandary regarding where Ms. Sheraton will live for the duration of these proceedings."

"I don't understand. She'll come home with me," Linda said. "Didn't she say she wanted to come home with me? Hannah?"

"After today the court will decide where Hannah lives. It is clear to me that the emotional wounds in this matter run deep and cut two ways. The court is sympathetic to both parties, but" he held up one hand, a finger toward heaven, "I will not have this defendant intimidated or subjected to undue influence during the course of this trial. Because of what happened here today, I am reluctant to release Ms. Sheraton to the custody of her mother while she resides with Mr. Rayburn."

The judge looked over Linda's shoulder to her husband.

"I understand how difficult this must be for you, Mr. Rayburn. I know that the choice to testify for the prosecution must have been a very difficult one. However, that choice will not soon be forgotten in the same way that your suspicions will not be put to rest easily. There will be no magic once you walk out of this courtroom that will allow you and Ms. Sheraton to reside civilly under the same roof for the duration."

"Judge," Josie stepped forward, "the ramifications would be even worse if Hannah was remanded to county care. I know the court wouldn't want to see any more harm come to her."

Norris smiled sadly, "No, this court does not. But harm comes in many guises. While I don't want her in physical distress, I also don't want to see any deterioration of her mental state. If the hostility exhibited today continues because she is confined to her home I'm afraid that's what I see in her future."

"But..." Josie began to argue. It was Kip who ended the discussion.

"I won't be going back to the Malibu house," he said. Linda gasped and turned toward her husband, forgetting Hannah.

"Kip, there's no reason to do this. I'm sure we can work this out," Linda insisted but Kip ignored her.

"I won't be going back, Judge." Kip's voice was flat, his expression determined. He seemed unmoved by Linda's touch, her panic, and her need.

"Ever? Kip, you don't mean you're never coming home, do you?" Linda whispered softly.

"Mrs. Rayburn?"

Judge Norris called. Linda blinked. She hesitated, reluctant to take her eyes off Kip. Her skin was pale. Her hands were trembling as they grasped her purse. She looked stunned.

"Mrs. Rayburn, I will need your assurance that your priority will be your daughter. From now until the end of this trial you will be responsible for your daughter's whereabouts twenty-four hours a day. Is that clear? Mr. Rayburn will not be in the Malibu residence. If you see him, you will take steps to ensure that your daughter is monitored and safe."

Linda looked from Kip to the judge and back again. Linda was being called upon to divide the baby and Josie held her breath, wondering which she would choose. Finally, her voice low, her eyes unable to meet Norris's, Linda nodded.

"Yes. I understand."

"Fine. Mr. Rayburn will advise this court of his residence."

"The house in the Palisades." Kip's gaze leveled first at Hannah, and then at Josie.

"My clerk will need the full address and phone number," the judge instructed. "Mrs. Rayburn and Ms. Sheraton will continue to reside in Malibu. If there is a problem with this, other living arrangements will be made for the defendant. I would prefer that doesn't happen. In fact, I hope I have made clear how very much I don't want that to happen."

"Can I take Hannah home now?" Linda asked.

"Yes. I won't change the provisions of bail as long as Ms. Sheraton abides by them. Is that understood?"

"Yes, sir," Hannah whispered, her eyes darting to her mother, her right hand moving against her thigh in measured beats.

"Good. Then I suggest you all go home. Mrs. Rayburn is to leave every possible channel of communication open for Ms. Bates and her client. Is that understood?"

"Yes," Linda murmured.

Josie stepped forward to offer her support but Linda was quick. She wanted nothing to do with Josie. Linda bundled Hannah up and pulled her away from Josie, the court, the judge, and Rudy Klein. Josie followed, catching up with Linda at the door.

"Hannah. Linda. Wait," Josie called.

Linda's head whipped around. She pulled Hannah closer.

"Haven't you done enough today?" Linda sneered.

"Mom, please," Hannah begged. "I did it. I told her."

"Shut up, Hannah. Don't make it worse." Linda's eyes blazed as she stepped forward so the judge wouldn't hear them. "Just stay away from us. You've ruined everything. You've ruined my marriage. You've made my daughter crazy."

"Mom," Hannah cried. "Please, it isn't her fault. I only told her about what Fritz did to–"

"Shut up, Hannah. Don't say anything else." Linda tightened her hold, claiming Hannah.

"You can't keep her away from me, Linda," Josie warned quietly.

"I'll do what the judge says, but it doesn't mean I'm going to let you destroy everything either. I earned this family. It is mine and I'll figure out a way to keep it together." Linda hitched her purse and tightened her grip on Hannah. "Now, I think my daughter has had enough for one day. I know I certainly have."

"Hannah, are you all right?" Josie asked, bypassing Linda.

Hannah nodded.

"Okay. I'll call later."

"You will not," Linda snapped before remembering the judge's order. "At least give us a little time."

Josie stepped away, hands up as she backed off.

"Okay. Okay. Just listen. The press is set up at the main entrance. It's a zoo out there. Take Hannah down the freight elevator to the left."

Josie held Linda's gaze. Hatred in Linda's eyes; resolve in Josie's. Without another word Linda put her hand on the side of her daughter's head, steered it onto her shoulder, and hustled her out the door.

Josie turned back to retrieve her jacket and briefcase. Kip Rayburn was deep in conversation with Rudy. Judge Norris had returned to chambers and Josie had eleven days to find out exactly what kind of man Fritz Rayburn was, and who else might have wanted him dead.

❧

Linda started drinking at six. She smoked half a pack of cigarettes while she listened to Hannah tear up her room. Hannah's rampage lasted forty-five minutes. The silence stretched into two hours as Linda waited for Kip to walk through the door. She was positive he would defy the court order and come to her.

At nine Linda figured she was on her own. Putting aside her drink and her cigarettes, Linda walked to the back of the house. Hannah was sitting on her stool, rocking and counting. The bedding was in a pile, the pillows tossed toward the bathroom. Hannah's clothes were ripped from their hangers, grabbed from the drawers and dumped on the floor. A razor blade was in a small dish at Hannah's feet. It hadn't been used, thank God. Linda closed her eyes, breathed in through her nose and said:

"You don't have to worry. Kip isn't coming home." Hannah kept rocking. Linda tried again. "He'll come around. When this is all over, we'll still be here." Linda eased into the room. She stopped with her back against the wall when she was within Hannah's range of vision. "Did Fritz do what Josie says he did?"

"Yes," Hannah whispered.

"Why didn't you tell me, baby?"

Linda choked on the words. She sniffled and put her hands to her lips. Just the thought of what Hannah had been through brought back bad memories of Hannah's father. His dark eyes and thick lashes, the way his hands felt on her, the way he made love – the way he hit her, twisted arms, broke bones. He had been gorgeous to look at and deadly to live with. Linda hadn't told anyone about the abuse because there was no one to tell in a country where beating your woman was a sign of manliness. Eventually Linda walked away because she could. It was different with Hannah. She was a kid. She had tried to run and Fritz had always brought her back. Still, Hannah could have said something. If she had, everything would have been different. Everything.

"Why didn't you tell me?" Linda asked again. She swayed against the wall and put out her hands to steady herself. She had drunk too much, thought too much, and lay awake too many hours over the last weeks trying to figure out what to do. "Why didn't you tell me, Hannah?"

"Because you didn't want me to."

Slowly Hannah turned to look at Linda. Her hair fell across one side of her face, her green eyes sparkled. The energy it took to destroy her room, the futility of all this, had left her exhausted.

"That's not true, Hannah. If I had known it would have changed everything. It…"

Linda was on the floor, her arms around Hannah before she knew what had happened. Her hands were in

Hannah's hair, holding her face, her tears falling on Hannah's shoulders.

"You're drunk, mom. You're drunk." Hannah pushed Linda away but her mother held on tight.

"No. I just feel so sad. If I had known what he was doing I could have bested the old bastard. Everything would have been so simple. So different." Linda sobbed and clutched at her daughter but Hannah pushed her hard. Linda fell back, splayed on the floor. "You must have been so scared. If you told me I could have stopped him from hurting either one of us. It would have been so simple."

Hannah sat on her stool and listened to her mother's protestations. There had been no comfort in Linda's embrace. The sound of her mother's voice didn't soothe her. The promise that it would have been different didn't mean shit because Fritz was dead. It was done. All of it.

Kip Rayburn let himself into the Palisades house and did everything he always did when he got home. He walked up stairs to his bedroom and put his wallet and his key on the bureau in the dressing room. He flipped on the bathroom light and the lamp at the bedside. He sat on the bed and took his watch off.

The place was as it always was: spotlessly clean, perfectly appointed. He should have come home weeks ago when the police released the property. He wandered through the house, touching the elegant, traditional furniture, looking at the classic artwork. Fritz had done well with this house. Anyone would have believed he had come from money, grown up with the finest things. He was a master of disguise, that old man.

Kip went down to the kitchen but he wasn't hungry. He poured himself a drink but didn't taste it. Finally, he did what he knew he was going to do all along: he opened the front door and walked the grounds.

Kip passed the fountain where the fireman had found Hannah. The little stone peeing boy atop it was dry for the time being; the water cut off while the wreckage was cleared. Part of the staircase still stood. One of Hannah's paintings had only been partially destroyed. A workman had propped it near the fountain as if he had found something precious. Kip kicked at it as he walked, resisting the temptation to stomp it into the ground. This wasn't the time to lose control. He'd never done it as a kid – he'd only done it once as an adult – and look what happened.

His shoes scraped on the bare foundation. Funny how the smell of fire lingered, clung to nothing but concrete, how it felt hotter the minute he stepped onto the slab, how the tinkle of the ice in his drink seemed to echo off the nonexistent walls.

Sinking onto the bottom step of the staircase Kip Rayburn looked up into the night sky, then out toward the gardens. He looked at the hills and canyons of the Palisades and then he started to laugh. Anyone listening might have mistaken it for crying. It struck him funny that he was sitting in the ruins of his home, facing the ruin of his life, the loss of his father and the estrangement of his wife. In the final analysis, Fritz Rayburn was the only thing that had ever, really, truly belonged to Kip Rayburn and Hannah Sheraton had taken that away.

Wouldn't Fritz get a kick out of this mess?

Wouldn't he love to see how miserable everyone was?

Kip Rayburn thought about all this as he put his head against the wall and laughed and laughed until he cried.

⁂

Rudy Klein got home just before the late news began. He stripped down to his t-shirt and boxers. Dinner was a box of crackers and a hunk of cheese, a glass of milk, and a Ding-Dong. A Rudy dinner; a Mikey dessert. Rudy picked up the Ding-Dong and started taking off the silver wrapper just as a commercial came on.

Keeping an eye on the television he dialed his ex-wife.

"Hey," he said. "It's late. I'm sorry. I just wanted to ask a favor. Go in and kiss Mikey once more for me."

"He's asleep, Rudy," Pam grumbled. "And I was almost asleep."

"I know. But what's it going to hurt? Come on."

Suddenly, thoughts of Mikey and his ex-wife flew out of his head. Rudy Klein hung up the phone while Pam was still complaining. The news had started and the headline was the Rayburn trial.

⁂

Josie and Archer sat near the window at Burt's at the Beach so they could keep an eye on Max who was fast asleep on the still warm sidewalk. The burger platters were on order, a pitcher of beer sweated between them, and Archer's contact sheets were spread over the table. Before he could hand Josie the loop, before Josie could tell him what had happened in court, Burt called:

"Hey, Josie. They're talking about you on TV."

Everyone in the place fell silent. All eyes turned upward as Burt adjusted the sound on the set.

"Oh, my God," Josie breathed.

Archer tipped back in his chair and whistled softly. Josie looked back at him. He raised an eyebrow.

"Had a tough day, did you, Jo?"

<\/>

Alex Schaeffer and Cheryl Winston were dressed to the nines. Governor Davidson hadn't bothered with black-tie, but then he seldom did. In another part of the Bel Air mansion, two hundred people dined on game hens, heart of palm salad, lobster bisque, and crème fraiche atop apple tartlets. They would raise an easy half a million for the governor's coffers this evening, as long as no one saw what the three of them were seeing now.

Lead story on the news was Linda Rayburn and her daughter surrounded by a crowd of reporters jostling for position. CBS had done a fabulous job. Their cameraman got a clear shot of Linda's beautiful, angry face, and their reporter managed to stick a microphone right under her nose to catch every vitriolic word.

"What about my rights as a parent? That's what I want to know. The judge says that Josie Bates has rights, and my daughter has rights, but I have none. I'm disgusted. My daughter needs help. She doesn't need to be pulled in six different directions by the court. Where are the people in this world who believe that a parent has the best interest of their child at heart? Where are the people who will stand up for the family? I can't believe any of this is happening. Josie Baylor-Bates should be shot for what she's done today."

Alex turned off the television. The skirt on Cheryl's dress rustled as she turned toward the governor. The governor stared at the blank screen for a minute then stood up, buttoned his coat and said:

"Find out what happened in court, and why the wife of our Supreme Court nominee is acting out in front of everyone in the whole damned state."

CHAPTER 24

"Who does this lawyer think she is? God?"

"Those parents are financially and morally responsible for their daughter. If that lawyer wants to be responsible for a child, then let her have one of her own and take all the responsibility."

"This is like a really late term abortion. That girl is being ripped from her mother and somebody should do something about it."

"Maybe something weird is going on here. Maybe something did happen to that girl. Shouldn't someone find out about that?" – Callers to KFI Talk Radio

"Come on in." Faye opened the door of her home wide and gave Max a pat as she motioned Josie toward the sunroom.

"Thanks. Sorry I didn't get the message until now. I was at Archer's last night." Josie said. "I feel like I've been run over by a truck."

Josie veered off to the kitchen, settled Max, and poured herself some coffee. In the sunroom she sank onto a chair, tucked her legs beneath her, and wrapped her hands around her mug. Faye was already settled. A teacup was on the table at her elbow. The weather had cooled and she wore a sweater to keep out the cold but the look of consternation on her face sent that chill right to Josie.

The *Los Angeles Times* was on the table with the tea. The front page carried a picture of Linda Rayburn holding onto Hannah for dear life. Faye had the Valley paper and the *Daily Breeze*. Each one was opened to that picture of Linda and Hannah outside the courthouse.

"The *Times* has an old picture of you on the inside page." Faye tossed it toward Josie. "You looked good with long hair."

Josie shifted. One foot hit the ground just as the *LA Times* fluttered to the floor. She reached down, picked it up, and snapped it open. Josie bit her bottom lip as she scanned the story, then looked with disgust at the picture on the front page.

"Linda deliberately put herself in this situation," Josie muttered. Then to Faye: "I told her to go down the freight elevator. I don't think she cares about Hannah at all."

"Did you threaten to file for emancipation?" Faye asked, not bothering to respond to Josie's observation.

"Yes, I did," Josie answered. "They were trying to railroad Hannah. They were dismissing her accusations. Linda was ready to give her up. Everyone in that courtroom had an agenda that didn't include what was in Hannah's best interests."

Faye shook her head in disbelief.

"What you did was drastic and uncalled for, Josie. Your client had enough problems without alienating her mother and half the people in this city. There is a serious question that you overstepped your bounds as an attorney. Threatening emancipation was emotional blackmail."

"Oh come on, Faye." Josie tossed the paper onto the floor. "Everyone in that room was ready to go to bat for a dead judge. Without me, Hannah wouldn't have had a voice at all. Linda and Kip Rayburn would have sold her out for an insanity plea just to keep this quiet."

"Did you ask Hannah what kind of representation she wanted, or whether she wanted to be legally and irrevocably severed from her parent?"

"Since when does a client dictate strategy?"

"Since her life is at stake on so many levels. I would think her input would be invaluable – at least to an attorney who honestly cares about what is best for her client," Faye shot back.

"That's all I care about, and all I think about, Faye. Hannah was in no condition to think about anything, much less make decisions. It's all there." Josie indicated the newspapers. They hadn't missed a thing, not Hannah's self mutilation, not Kip's outburst, Linda's outrage, or Josie's accusations

"I think that was the point Linda Rayburn was trying to make," Faye said. "Hannah is a disturbed kid, and you've put yourself in an untenable position. You're a lawyer, Josie. You can advise. You can suggest. You can't change legal relationships – especially that of a parent and a child – at your whim. You didn't confer with your client, or her mother, before you made that threat. Why are you being so bullheaded about this?"

"Because it is unfair. Because if I don't fight hard, Hannah will end up in a mental facility and she doesn't belong there. And she sure doesn't belong in prison. Not knowing what we know now." Josie untucked her other leg. She thought Faye was going to help her, stand by her. Now it felt like Faye was lined up against her. "Look, I spoke to Doctor McGrath late last night. He's one of the country's foremost experts on obsessive/compulsive disorder. He's sending me a complete report on the ability of a person who suffers from this disorder to affect their chosen environment. For some people it's wiping up the kitchen, for others it's locking the doors. They couldn't do anything to alter that environment. It would be akin to them cutting off their nose to spite their face, literally. When they are threatened by outside influences – like Rayburn's abuse – they work harder than ever to protect the things and places that make them feel safe and secure."

"That's what you're relying on? Josie, for goodness sake, you've lost your perspective," Faye cried.

"That's compelling stuff when you add it to the questions about the physical evidence and how the fire started. This will explain Hannah's DNA on Rayburn, but exonerate her of the act that actually killed him. I know that when I wrap it up in closing and tie it all together, they won't have any choice but to acquit."

"I'm sorry Josie, but the prosecution has a leg up. A girl killing an abusive man is a whole lot easier to swallow than a girl being unable to light a match because she doesn't like to upset the balance of nature. To argue that Fritz's abuse made her compulsion worse sounds like hocus-pocus. It's dangerous what you're doing. You say you want to help, and yet you don't see that you might be solidifying a more acceptable motive."

"Okay. Fine." Josie was peeved. She put her hands on her thighs. "Look, Faye. You haven't been behind this from the beginning. And I don't want to be rude, but this is a little out of your league. I promise I know what I'm doing. I have options, so let's drop it."

Her nerves frayed, Josie started to get out of her chair but Faye stopped her.

"It's not going to be that simple, Josie. I hadn't quite decided what to do, but you just helped me make up my mind." Faye's eyes never left Josie's. There was no hesitation. Indeed, Faye suddenly seemed to harbor a smoldering anger. "I don't want this case in-house one more minute."

There was a beat of silence, a pause in which Josie and Faye squared off. Faye had the advantage of surprise.

"I've called Sandra Johns. She's sharp, quick on the uptake. Hannah would do well with her and you've got ten days to bring her up to speed. I want you to recuse yourself and pass this along."

"Don't you think we should ask Hannah how she feels about new counsel? Or maybe we should just let Sandra show up when court resumes and surprise her?"

Josie's voice was dry with sarcasm.

"You didn't ask her about emancipation, did you? What you should do is tell Mrs. Rayburn so she has a chance to meet Sandra... What you should do is show some respect, Josie."

"I am showing respect to my client by doing my damndest for her. I won't let this go because I hurt your feelings by pointing out the obvious. You've never been in this arena, and you have no experience with which to judge."

"Stop treating this like a personal challenge. Hannah is sixteen years old, Josie," Faye cried. "Do what is best for that girl and get her someone who is more objective. Bring her mother back into the picture or you're going to destroy Hannah, the relationship with her mother, and yourself."

Josie shook her head hard. Ruining a mother's relationship with her daughter was the last thing she wanted.

"You're wrong. There are priorities. The first is to win this trial. Once that's done we can worry about relationships. Besides, Norris would have to approve new counsel. He's not going to do that after today. This thing is already too hot to handle. If you've got a problem, let's talk about it. Don't go behind my back and talk to Sandra Johns. If you don't have that respect for Hannah, at least have it for me."

"Okay, let's talk about professional respect," Faye agreed. "Let's talk about Helen Sterling. You were supposed to talk to her about her property settlement. You never called. Billy Zuni was released and has been trying to see you for the last three days. Not even a phone call. Let's talk about your time sheet. You haven't done one, and the billing cycle is already over. Let's talk about Angie who's been working overtime for you every night and not a word of thanks, just more directions and demands. Where do you want to start, Josie? What do you want to discuss when it comes to your professional behavior?"

Agitated, Josie waved her hands.

"I'm sorry, okay? I've let a few things slip, but now I have some breathing room. I'll get all that done in the next few days. I'll have the time sheet on your desk Monday morning. But you're forgetting that this isn't just about the next few weeks. This is about an opportunity for this firm," Josie insisted, hoping Faye would look at the big picture. "The fee we're getting for this is big and we can use it to upgrade. We can afford another paralegal. The notoriety will bring in bigger and better clients, Faye. This case could put this firm on the map."

Faye got up but she didn't go far. She turned away from Josie for a second and collected her thoughts. When she was ready to talk again Faye was a calm, controlled, and committed woman.

"Charlie and I founded this firm, Josie. I nurtured it. I kept it small and quiet because the people who need me are small and quiet. I told you when you started this thing with Hannah that I didn't want it to impact my business, but that's what's happening. I don't want Angie's time monopolized. I don't want reporters on my doorstep. I don't want my clients to worry that we're going to take anything away from them the way you have taken Hannah away from Linda Rayburn."

"That's unfair," Josie argued. "This is a unique situation."

"Josie, you know exactly what I mean and I resent you thinking you can out maneuver or shame me on this. I won't allow it."

Josie dropped her chin. She looked at her hands, spread her fingers, and checked out her short nails. Quickly she pulled those fingers in, making two fists. Her hands were shaking.

"You said there were options. I only heard one. Referral."

There was a heartbeat and then another. Faye was rock solid. There wasn't a shadow of doubt or regret on her face. There wasn't a tremor of indecision when she said:

"You can take care of this on your own, Josie."

"Faye," Josie breathed in disbelief. "You'd cut me loose?"

"I don't agree with your tactics. I resent the fact that you think I don't understand them. The publicity is going to do my firm more harm than good. Tiffany took a phone call late last night threatening us because of what you did to Linda. Your troubles haven't begun and already I've had enough." Faye was exasperated. She moved closer to Josie and sat on the edge of the coffee table. Her voice was reasonable and sad. "What am I supposed to do? Spend my day worrying about how Hannah Sheraton is going to affect me, and my business, instead of serving the people I care about?"

Josie could feel that chill starting deep in her gut. She had that same feeling the morning her mother disappeared, a deserter from the family post. She felt it when she learned Kristin Davis's children were dead. Josie wrapped her arms around her body but raised her head high. She had learned something during those long ago tests. Fear was one thing, showing it quite another.

"This isn't just your firm anymore, Faye. We're partners, or have you forgotten?" Faye's expression melted into genuine sadness. "You never signed those papers, Josie. You have no legal standing in my firm."

Josie was out of her chair, agitated, frightened, disbelieving, and still wanting to fight.

"Faye, I can't believe you'd do this…"

Don't send me away. Don't leave me alone.

"You've left me no choice," Faye answered.

"Why is it that someone like Hannah doesn't need as much help as somebody down the block? Because she's pretty? Young? Because she has big problems? You haven't even talked to her, Faye. You don't know her at all. She couldn't have done what she's accused of, and I know it in here."

Josie put her fist to her chest. It was a ridiculous, melodramatic gesture of solidarity, but that was what she felt for Hannah Sheraton. Everyone was willing to walk out on this kid or throw her away, and that made Josie's heart hurt.

"I don't want to talk to her," Faye cried in frustration. "I want you to forget about her, come back to work, and deal with the people you told me you wanted to represent when I hired you."

"You are so full of it. You're not even listening to yourself. You want us to help people but only certain people."

Josie planted her hands on her hips and turned her head toward the window. Her back was to Faye. Clouds hung over the horizon. Josie wanted the sun to come back so she could go outside and pick up a game of volleyball, sit on the beach with a beer, and get her work done between nine and five. She didn't want to feel this kind of passion again, yet there it was. Her gut burned with it. Whatever had driven Josie all those years ago was driving her again. But this time it was fine-tuned. This case was more than a challenge to Josie's intellect; it was a challenge to her emotional well being. Faye had drawn the line. Josie would have to step over it.

"You're not putting limits on what we do as lawyers, or how we do it, but on who we do it for. I wouldn't have expected it from you, Faye."

"I wouldn't have either, Josie. I just know this isn't what I want for my firm and, bottom line, this is still my firm."

"You're not giving me any real options here, Faye," Josie whispered.

"Refer her, or take her out on your own," Faye said plainly.

Josie didn't move. She couldn't move. Something inside her said that she was the only one who could help Hannah. The arrogance of that was ridiculous, but there it was.

"Josie?" Faye's voice surrounded her, challenged her.

"I heard you." Josie faced Faye. "Those are ultimatums, not options."

"I'm not going to defend my decision," Faye answered. "Even if you win, there isn't going to be a happy ending, Josie. Sad thing is that I think you're the one who is going to be hurt when this is over. You make a commitment as a lawyer to be a clear-eyed, clear-headed advocate. You are supposed to be unmoved by the mitigating circumstances, and able to put aside your experiences and emotions as a woman in order to do your job. You're not doing any of that. This is just too personal for you. Step away now and take a real good look at yourself, Josie, before you go any further."

"I'm doing the right thing. I may be the only one who is. Bottom line, Hannah deserves her day in court. That's the business we're in."

"I agree, just let her have that day with another attorney." A flush crept along Faye's jaw line, and regret in her eyes, but she didn't back down.

"I hate all this, Faye," Josie said.

"So do I," she answered.

"Then hang in there with me. Get back to where you were thirty years ago when you promised to be a lawyer, not just someone who steps in when Mr. Jones down the street gets a DUI."

"That's low, Josie. I won't have you talk to me that way."

"And I'm hurt," Josie answered. "I've got to believe there is a reason Linda came looking for me. Maybe we're supposed to help this girl just to prove our brains work and our hearts aren't all closed off. Maybe you need to care about something since your husband died, and maybe I need to learn to live because I checked out of the real world three years ago. Did you ever think of that?"

"Don't go there, Josie. You don't have any right to talk about Charlie. As for you, I don't know anything about you. You've been protecting yourself ever since you walked through my door. All I did was give you a place to hide."

"Then maybe that's what I'm supposed to find out. Not just what kind of attorney I am but what kind of woman I am." There was a heartbeat of silence. Josie took a deep breath. "I can't go back to the office and pretend this doesn't matter. I need to take a leap of faith in Hannah's innocence and my own worth. I'm asking you to stand with me, Faye."

"And I'm telling you I won't," Faye answered without hesitation.

"Then do it for friendship."

When Faye didn't answer, Josie nodded. With a snap of her fingers she called Max from the corner, clipped his leash and said:

"Screw you, Faye."

CHAPTER 25

"A cold front is moving in. Expect temperatures in the sixties through Thursday." – Johnny Mountain, Channel 7 Weather

There is an impressive vein of concrete that winds from the hills of Palos Verdes and ends in Malibu. It ribbons through all the beach cities in between and plays host to anyone who is drawn to the ocean. Josie and Max ambled down Hermosa's portion of that mile-long bike path after they left Faye's place. A quarter of a mile from her own house, Josie stopped. A guy on a fifteen hundred dollar bike whizzed by her, intent on breaking the land speed record to Malibu. The smell of grilling onions filled the air. Lunch was being served up at The Strand Café. Four men with gorgeous bodies played volleyball with a vengeance, yet somehow unable to get their game into a rhythm. Josie could have shown them how it was done, but even a pick up game wouldn't cure what ailed her.

An ancient woman in baby-blue warm-ups and rhinestone glasses held hands with a man in purple pants and a checked shirt. Families walked together, dogs pulled their owners on roller skates, and no one minded that the weak sun left the water looking gray and uninviting – no one except Josie. Faye had knocked the air out of Josie's world, flattening it so there was no place to maneuver.

Behind her, Josie heard the scrape of skates and a chorus of giggles. She pulled Max close as a group of teenage girls went by. They had poured their overactive glands into swimsuits the size of postage stamps and laced their feet into roller blades as big as Nevada. They were oblivious to the chill, unaware that the earth was out of kilter, but they looked damn cute with their Frankenstein feet, their big tits and tiny butts.

To her left was Archer's building. His very own. It was purchased long ago when Lexi was alive and Archer thought he had the world on a string. It was one of the original three-story apartment buildings that graced Hermosa Beach before the money came in and people who could afford to tear down a bit of California history did just that. But this one still stood. The paint on the wood framed windows was peeling. Rust streaked from the metal balcony and spilled over the rose-colored stucco like mascara tears rolling down old rouged cheeks. The salt air was a landlord's bane, but there were flowers in the little bed, and tenants to Archer's liking in each apartment.

Josie looked up. She could just make out Archer's camera pointed out to sea. Hitching Max close, Josie climbed the stairs slowly letting the old dog rest at each landing. At the top she didn't bother to knock.

"Archer?"

Josie walked around a brown tweed sofa, wide enough for two to snooze comfortably on a lazy Sunday. The back was dimpled with three giant buttons covered in the same fabric. Josie's mother had a coat with buttons that big when she was young and Josie was a baby. She saw a picture once. It was the only picture she could remember where her mother was dressed up. Josie wondered about that coat. It was too frumpy for the days of hip huggers and peasant blouses; too old for someone so young and beautiful.

Archer's papa-san chair was in one corner. There was a La*Z*Boy and a low coffee table strewn with travel magazines. She looked toward the balcony. It was empty.

"Jo?" Archer stood in the bedroom, a towel around his waist another in his hands, ready to dry his hair.

"Hey." Josie stood her ground but let Max go. Archer ruffled the dog's ears and kept his eyes on Josie.

"What happened?" Archer pushed Max aside and took a few steps.

"Faye just booted me out, Archer. I'm on my own with Hannah."

Archer wrapped the smaller towel around his neck. Josie walked toward him. He held out a hand and drew her close. He was dewy from his shower; water droplets were still nestled in the hair on his chest. Josie put her head on his shoulder; her arms were caught beneath his. He had wrapped her up like a treasured possession.

"Want some help?"

"Got any problems helping me prove Rayburn was one sick son of a bitch?" She asked forlornly.

"Not a one, Jo. Not a one."

CHAPTER 26

"Even if there's an ounce of truth to what they're saying about that judge, then that girl had a right to do what she did – if she did it. Well? Need I say more? Ever hear of the movie The Burning Bed, for God's sake?" – Talk radio/Inland Valley

"So, like, here's the question. Did Governor Davidson know this guy was a sicko when he appointed him? If he did, then I'm voting Republican. Hey, what about the guy's son? Maybe he's a weirdo, too. Politics. Davidson can go pound sand." – Talk Radio/Sacramento

"Hey, have you seen that chick? Sixteen ain't sixteen anymore. She probably loved it." – Talk radio/Hollywood

"If they just would put prayer back in the schools..."– Talk radio/San Diego

Josie walked out of terminal three and dropped her duffle bag at her feet. She dialed Archer's cell. He was where he said he would be: Starbucks just off Sepulveda, nursing a coffee, waiting for her call. Ten minutes later he maneuvered around LAX and pulled his Hummer up to the curb. Josie threw her bag in the back seat and settled herself in the front.

They met in the middle and kissed one another. Archer checked his side mirror and was back in the flow of traffic before he heard the click of her seat belt. He skipped the turnoff to Sepulveda south that would take them home, and instead rolled down Century Boulevard at a decent clip for that time of day.

"Where are we going?" Josie asked, disappointed she wasn't headed home.

"Dinner." he answered.

"It's three o'clock," Josie pointed out.

"Yeah, well, it will take us awhile to get there."

"Okay." She sighed and rolled down her window. It had been bone-chilling cold in San Francisco. Los Angeles was cloudy, but still warm enough for Josie to be comfortable in her shirtsleeves. She cocked her elbow in the open window, and laid her left arm over the back of the bench seat.

"Hannah's story checks out," Josie said. "I found Lyn Chandler. The woman clerked for Rayburn for six months third year of law school. Now she's on the partnership track at Monikar & Finacker. Smart lady. Good looking. Petite. Light-skinned African-American."

"Interesting," Archer commented. He changed lanes, moving the tank of a car through traffic like he was slaloming on razor-sharp skis.

"So, Lyn Chandler was working for Rayburn for three months when he puts his hand on her shoulder and squeezes hard. You know, he hits that little nerve right here." Josie dropped her hand to the base of Archer's neck for a second. "She says she didn't think anything of it at first. He'd touched her before. There was nothing sexual about it. Usually the contact was brief and in context of him looking at her work. But that time he hurt her. She said something, but Rayburn made light of it.

Told her if she wanted to be a player she was going to have to toughen up. That's what the law is about."

"Lay it on her. Nice touch," Archer muttered with a dispassionate approval. He had a great appreciation for those who performed well, whether they be cop or criminal.

Josie adjusted her sunglasses as he stopped at a light. The neighborhood had changed. Warehouses and airport hangers gave way to one of those nondescript arteries that connected the vital parts of LA. This one was peppered with small houses and smaller businesses. Every window was barred, every flat surface graffitied. The billboards were in Spanish. Instead of touting sleeper seats to the Orient, they advertised family planning and beer. Josie leaned her head back and closed her eyes, as if trying to remember the sequence of her interview. Archer hit the gas, Josie picked up the story.

"It gets better. Rayburn left an open knife in the top drawer of his desk. Newly sharpened. She had reached in that drawer a thousand times to get his calendar, but this time there's a knife sticking out the side of the book. She cut her hand and wanted to use his bathroom to get a towel to stop the bleeding, but Rayburn wouldn't let her. He didn't offer to help, and suggested she use the bathroom down the hall for the clerks. Rayburn let her clean up the blood in there, and told her she could see a doctor on her lunch hour if she thought the cut needed attention. In his opinion though, it looked like a clean slice."

"Nice of him." The Humvee slid forward as smoothly as Archer's next question. "How'd he explain the knife?"

"He didn't. Lyn said he never explained anything. Not when he dropped Blacks Law Dictionary on her hand. Not when he grabbed her arm hard enough to leave a bruise. He would just keep talking as if nothing had happened. She said it was spooky. At the end of the day she'd always wonder if these things were accidents. She wondered if she was nuts."

"Sounds like he enjoyed the head games as much as he liked the physical stuff. That's why nobody ever caught on. Rayburn had no nerves, I swear," Archer said. "What's the upshot?"

"I asked her to testify. She said no. The bastard was dead but there were just too many people who still thought Rayburn was God's gift. She figures it is in her best interest to have clerked for a respected justice for six months, than to be the one who levels accusations against him."

Josie slid her arm off the back of the seat and opened her purse. It had been dry in San Francisco. Her skin felt tight but she didn't have any cream, nothing to soothe that feeling that she was going to crackle like old glass. She flipped her bag shut.

"I could subpoena her, but she'd put such a spin on her testimony it would end up looking like she was grateful to Rayburn for keeping her on her toes. What did you pick up?"

"Rayburn had two disciplinary actions against him when he was with the LAPD."

"That was a lifetime ago."

"Still of interest for our purposes. Shows a pattern. He picked on hookers. One was beat up pretty good. Cut and burned. Another tripped, and Rayburn dislocated her shoulder and broke some teeth when he helped her up. It's ancient history. Got it from a couple of retired cops. They figured the hookers got what they deserved."

"Any chance of finding those women?" Josie asked without much enthusiasm.

"Nope." Archer tapped the brakes. A woman was trying to navigate a stroller and three small kids across the middle of the street even though a crosswalk was half a block away. "But I got a good lead on something more current. And this is where we find out if my source is any good."

Archer drove another half block, made a sharp left, and cut off conversation with a pull of the emergency brake. He sat for a second before getting out of the car. Josie did the same and met him half way. Leaning against the hood she pulled her shoulders back. Josie tightened the muscles in her butt to work out the kinks from her flight, and used the time to get the lay of the land.

The strip mall had seen better days. The parking lot needed to be resurfaced. White stall lines had faded to perforation marks. Vandals had scored the glass of the phone booth; the phone itself was missing a receiver. A liquor store anchored one end, a dry cleaner the other. The liquor store did the better business. In between were a pet store that specialized in snakes, a Japanese Anime video shop, and Marguerite's – tamales, burritos, and check cashing.

"Rosa Cortanza is who we're looking for." Archer took a few steps toward Marguerite's and opened the door. "Come on. I'll buy you a taco and won't even put it on my expense account."

Josie pushed off her perch and took him up on his offer. She walked into a place that was just like a little slice of heaven.

In Los Angeles there are restaurants that served Mexican food, and Mexican restaurants. This was the latter, the real deal: fresh salsa, tortillas made by hand, meat roasted until it fell off the bone, shells deep-fried in lard. Dark, rich mole. *Carne asada.* Chilis. Frijoles. Marguerite's restaurants wore those smells like a coat of wet paint but it was empty except for a young woman sitting at one of the tables flipping through a magazine.

Her black hair was short at the crown and waved long at the nape of her neck. Razor cut bangs fell over eyes outlined in kohl, and shaded in gray. Her nails were long and purple. Rhinestones winked from the tip of each one. Her jeans were tight; her shirt was big and loose. The sleeves were rolled up just enough that Josie could see that the tattoo on her forearm was homemade. She closed the magazine when Josie and Archer took a table by the wall. A picture of Our Lady of Guadalupe blessed their choice. A red neon Coors sign hung along side like the Virgin's nightlight.

The woman came at them with a basket of chips and a tub of salsa. She slapped both on the table. From under her arm she whipped out two menus featuring a matador and bull on the front. The matador was poised on his toes, his cape a flourish at his feet, his body angled forward as he stabbed the bull with a massive sword. It was an appetizing image.

"Rosa Cortanza?" Josie asked the minute the woman disappeared.

"Fits the description," he answered as his eyes ran down the menu. He closed it, set it aside and dug into the salsa. "Wish I had my camera. I like her look."

Rosa was back. They ordered: number 8 combo with enchiladas, tacos and tamales, beans, rice and a side of corn tortillas for Archer, two tacos for Josie. The waitress didn't say a word as she took their order, and their menus. Far from surly, she wasn't exactly worried about their dining pleasure either.

Rosa Cortanza brought Archer's combination on a platter and Josie's tacos on a small plate. It took them seventeen minutes to eat and they waited on Rosa five more before the check arrived. They were still the only ones in the place. Josie checked out Rosa, letting her mind linger on the woman a little longer each time she came to the table.

Rosa was a young woman who had nowhere to go and nothing much to do. She kept body and soul together, pampering the body with fake nails and makeup while ignoring the soul. Maybe she had a kid waiting at home. Maybe she lived in a two-bedroom house with a dozen family members. Maybe she had a man. It was a no-brainer she'd hung with the gangs; all Josie had to do was look at her tattoos to know that. What wasn't so easily divined was whether or not Rosa would want to talk to them – much less to a jury – or whether a jury would give credence to anything she said.

Rosa put the check down with the same flair she had delivered the salsa. Archer held up a twenty. She reached for it. They were both holding onto the greenback when he said:

"I wonder if we could talk to you about Fritz Rayburn."

The bill quivered, pulled taut between her and Archer. Rosa's eyes narrowed for a split second, and then she laughed. It was the sweetest sound. Rosa whipped the bill out of Archer's fingers and laughed all the way to the register. When she came back with the change she brought a chair with her. Rosa put the change on the table and straddled the chair. Resting her arms on the high back, Rosa Cortanza looked at the both of them and said:

"What the hell. Let's talk."

CHAPTER 27

"My mom's husband was gone, so when the job came at the Rayburn house she grabbed it. Worked like a slave, but what was she going to do? She had me and my brother to feed, put clothes on us. My brother, he was older than me. I was ten. Hell, I thought I'd died and gone to heaven living in that big house."

Rosa snorted at her ridiculous fantasy. She unrolled the fingers of one hand, poking holes in the sky with her rhinestone tipped nails.

"Why is it poor people are so friggin' stupid, huh? We think if we live between the walls and climb under those pretty white sheets in our little rooms in the back that we've made it to the big time. We're so damn grateful. I hate that shit. I look back, and I can't believe we ever fell for all his crap."

"Do you mind if we start at the beginning before we get to the crap part, Rosa?" Josie tossed back the drink their hostess had offered when it was clear they were going to be at this for a while.

Rosa had locked the door and flipped the open sign around. Marguerite's was closed. Not that anyone, as Rosa pointed out, would really care. The place was about to go belly up and she was just sticking around because that's what she did. She stuck around people and places and things until they broke down on her, shit on her, or just went away.

Josie could get behind that. When Rosa brought out the shot glasses, the salt, the limes, and the tequila, Josie was proud to drink with her. She saluted Rosa on the first two shots. They both sucked the salt from their hands, their dark heads tipping back, their long throats opening up to let the burning liquor slide down into their bellies. They sucked on the lime to cool their lips and Rosa refilled the tiny glasses. Josie nodded her thanks but kept this one in front of her, fingers lightly on the sides of the shot glass. Her eyes were trained on Rosa as she did her math. Rosa was twenty, maybe twenty-two at most but she seemed older by at least a decade. It was in the way she sat talking with them so casually, the way she drank so indifferently, and the way she let them know in the smallest ways that she was never relaxed enough not to be on her guard.

"Okay. You got the time; I'll give you the whole story."

She shot her liquor and pushed away the glass. Rosa spread her fingers to check out her nails. They were an expensive set, but she wasn't admiring her manicurist's handiwork. Rosa Cortanza was either thinking how far she'd come, or trying hard to remember way far back. She gave her head a little jerk, one of those very nifty gestures that street kids seemed to learn before they can walk. She wondered where Rosa had picked it up. Not living at Fritz Rayburn's house as the maid's kid.

"I was born here, in the U.S. My parents were wetbacks. I have a brother in Mexico somewhere. He went back home one Christmas before we started living at the Rayburn place. He couldn't get back into this country. My mom always meant to send money to get him but it never worked out. There was a sister after me. She died when she was little. Needed a heart or something. She died and then a little while later my brother went back to Mexico. My mother starts getting weird. She figures she's a failure because I was the only one left. You know all that shit about children being blessings from God. My mom really believed it. She figured she was cursed because she couldn't take care of her blessings. So that woman loved me to death. Like if she couldn't take care of me it meant that God was pissed at her and she'd go to hell."

"That's a lot to lay on a kid," Archer muttered.

"Tell me," Rosa laughed. "When my dad left for a better piece of ass I was really in for a treat. You'd think I'd been the Virgin birth. God was telling my mother that she had one more chance to get into heaven. Hey, either of you smoke?"

Archer and Josie shook their heads. Rosa shrugged. She was used to not getting what she asked for.

"It's okay. So, anyway, my mom couldn't keep the apartment without my dad's paycheck. She was cleaning houses. Forty bucks a pop. I used to think we were rich because she kept all that cash in a little box. I didn't know that's all we had. Most of it was ones and fives so it just looked like a lot of bucks." Her nails clicked against the chair back. "Hey, doesn't matter. Anyway, somehow she finds out about the job at the Rayburn place. It was a live-in gig. No more rent. I'd get to go to the Palisades' schools. God had dropped a damn plum in her lap. She spent all night on her knees giving thanks when she got that job."

The door rattled. Two men in work clothes were hungry. Rosa turned around to look, but ignored them. When they wouldn't give up she yelled at them in Spanish in a tone that didn't sound like she was too concerned about losing their business.

"Was Rayburn living in the house fulltime?" Archer wanted to know.

"The old judge? Well, I guess he wasn't so old, but he seemed that way to me. Old and kindly." Rosa chuckled wryly. "But what did I know? I was a kid. Anyway, yeah, it was the old man and the son living there."

"And life wasn't so good?" Josie asked.

"For a while it was. I went to school and I came home on the bus. It was a hike back to the house because the bus didn't go on that street. Palisades didn't like their streets mucked up with buses. So that brings us to the good stuff. The old man kind of came and went. He was traveling a lot."

Rosa's chin fell onto her crossed arms. There was a tear tattooed next to her right eye. She'd lost at least one homeboy. There were probably a hundred thousand tears tattooed on her soul if she was anything like Hannah.

"It was raining one day when I got off the bus. Rayburn pulls into the neighborhood at the same time. I don't know if it was planned or if it was just fate. You know. Whatever, he was there. He picked me up and took me home. Man, he was something. Big car. Big house. A judge. I was safe in Rayburn's house. Nobody messed with me." Rosa snorted a laugh. "What an idiot I was.

"The guy was sick. It started out with little stuff. You know. A pinch. A push. I had a splinter. He used a pocketknife to get it out. But it was the rainy day when I knew I was in big trouble. He picked me up when I was half way back to the house. I was all wet. Rayburn took me inside. Took me up to his private bathroom and dried me off. Told me he wanted to help out my mom because she worked so hard. We would surprise her and get me all cleaned up.

"Rayburn got a towel. He dried me off. My shoulders. My legs. Nothing weird about it. Then he got another towel and he started drying my hair. You know how you do?" Rosa lifted her chin and checked out her audience to make sure they were attentive. She put her hands up and pantomimed. "He threw the towel over my head and started to rub, but it was really hard. I guess I hollered or pulled away or something. He stopped. He kept the towel over my head for a minute then dragged it real slow off of me. I looked up and could see him in the mirror. I'll never forget the way he looked at me."

Rosa's expression changed. Her features snapped tight, muscle-by-muscle, like shutters in a house closing against a big wind.

"He was thinking real hard, like he was looking for something he couldn't find. You know how something changes and you can't put your finger on it? That's what happened to him. He sort of melted. I don't know how to explain it. His eyes weren't nice anymore. They were dead. His face kind of lost all its muscles. His skin was hanging off his cheekbones. It was like some kind of horror movie. There was something wrong."

Rosa lapsed into silence. It lasted just long enough for her to be in that room again, looking up at Fritz Rayburn with her big, dark, innocent eyes. When she started again Rosa talked slow, her voice was sad.

"So, anyway, he's mad. He tells me he didn't hurt me. So I figure I'm an ungrateful little slut and better get out because I don't know how to take a favor nicely. But he grabs my arm when I try to leave. Rayburn says you have to finish what you start. You always have to do that. So I figure, okay. I mean, who am I to say no to him? I'm standing there in this big marble bathroom. I'm in all these mirrors and he's in all these mirrors. I look like a rat and he's dressed in a really nice gray suit and a shiny blue tie. His shirt was really white. My mother ironed those shirts. She starched the heck out of them and they could stand up by themselves when she was done. He looked perfect and I looked like what I was – a piece of shit."

Rosa breathed deep. She looked at Archer then spoke to Josie.

"So I'm looking at him in the mirror. He walks around me, standing kind of in front of me but facing the mirror. I'm like this little soldier standing really straight with my arms down by my sides. I remember shaking but thinking I better not let him see that I'm shaking or he'll get mad. He picks up the blow dryer and holds it near him. I remember thinking it looked like he was loading a gun. He held it down at his middle and checked it out, looked at the settings. Finally he turns around and points the thing at me. Not at my hair but at my face. He doesn't turn it on, just points it at me then he walks real slow until he's standing right behind me. The thing was always pointing at my head like he was holding me hostage.

"He looks at us in the mirror. He put one hand on the side of my head, the hair dryer is pointing at the other side of my head. He pushes my hair to the side so that my neck is bare. It was cold there because my wet hair had been all stuck against my skin.

"Rayburn puts the blow dryer in his other hand so the cord is around my neck." Rosa's hands were going through the motions. "I put my hands up, you know, to push the cord over my head. He told me to leave it. He said it real quiet, just like he's telling me to go back to sleep. So I didn't touch the cord even though I could feel it pulling against my throat. I was shaking, man. Nothing bad had ever happened to me before, but I knew something bad was happening right then."

Rosa smiled wryly as if having some sick appreciation for the moment now that she could look back on it.

"But he was so smooth. It was so slow. Rayburn turned on the dryer. He turned it on hot. First he put it so that my hair blew out around my face. He ran his fingers through it. His fingers got caught in the tangles. He yanked through them and tears were coming to my eyes because it hurt so much. Once I could see that a whole bunch of hair came out when he pulled. I think he could feel me shaking because the side of his body was touching my back. He smiled a little. Just a little bit. Then he started drying the hair down here, at the neck. It was getting hot. I moved my head. It hurt so bad. He...."

Rosa put a hand over her mouth. Then she reached over and pushed her shot glass to the middle of the table. Archer poured. Rosa drank it fast, not bothering with the salt or the lime.

"Shit, I haven't thought about this for a long time," she muttered. "So, okay. Rayburn takes his free hand and he holds my head and he puts that damned hair dryer on my neck. Right on it. Man, I could smell my skin burning and then I screamed. That bastard kept it on me like a second more and then he takes it away. It burned me bad. I'm telling you, it was like a hot iron"

Rosa lifted the back of her hair and turned so that Archer and Josie could see the raised white scar just behind her ear.

"That bastard branded me."

They sat in silence. Archer and Josie watching; Rosa with her head down, her lashes lowered. Finally she looked at them again, tears in her eyes. She wiped them hard; she was ashamed they were there.

"Then?" Josie asked.

"Then he was normal again. He told me that the burn looked bad. He knew I wouldn't want to bother my mother so I should stop crying. Then he said didn't I feel better now that I was all dry, and didn't I love the rain."

"And that was it?" Josie pushed, wanting every damning detail.

"No. He gave me a tube of something. Told me it would help with the pain where I accidentally got burned. Man, that was the weirdest part, you know. To do something like that and then pretend like it was an accident. I'll never forget it. Never."

The afternoon came and went, the dark descending early now. Rosa got up a couple of times. She turned on the lights including the Coors sign hanging near the picture of the Virgin Mary. She told her stories as she put the frijoles over a low flame. Josie helped set out the silverware for the customers Rosa said would come after they got off work in the factories, and the airport, and made their way home to tiny houses and dilapidated apartments.

Rosa talked about a reign of terror that lasted until she was fourteen.

Rayburn came at her when she least expected it. She stayed at school as late as she could. She dodged her mother's questions, endured her mother's laments that she was going bad because she stayed away from home, because she stopped going to church. God was going to send Rosa's mother to hell because she had failed the jobs of a woman – wife and mother.

"I got so damned sick of hearing all that crap."

"But you never said anything." Josie spoke quietly as she centered the fork and knife on a small table. Rosa leaned over to arrange the salt and pepper at the same time. They didn't look at one another. Rosa said:

"He would have sent my mother away. She would have been deported. You can deal with a lot when your mother's there, you know? I was protecting her. I was brave for her. I wanted my mom to go to heaven." Josie flinched. Rosa saw it. They had something in common after all, the lawyer and the woman who served beer and beans. Rosa whispered. "Yeah, you know."

Josie stood back. She said: "It didn't go on forever. You survived. Did Rayburn lose interest?"

Rosa shook her head. "He never lost interest. He hurt me wherever he found me alone. The principal told me I was a lucky girl that such a great man took an interest in me. Mostly he talked. He told me what he was planning.

He whispered it because he liked the fear. Naw, he loved the fear. Then one day he did the worst."

Rosa was having trouble talking. She paled. Those black-rimmed eyes darkened until they looked like holes. Josie could almost reach through them and touch the pain that had left Rosa's body and lived in her brain.

"Rosa," Josie said quietly. Archer picked up the bottle on the table. He lifted it her way. Rosa put out her hand as if to say it didn't really help.

"It was just before Christmas. The INS came. Rayburn told me later he had my mother deported. They didn't take me because I was a citizen. Great country, huh?"

"What happened to your mom?" Archer asked.

"I don't know." Rosa smiled weakly, as though she had lost emotional blood and desperately needed a transfusion. "She never came back for me. Hell, she probably figured I was going to be well taken care of."

"What did you do then?"

Archer was still leaning in the corner of the booth, one leg half up, one arm on the table. She gave Archer a small smile with her answer.

"I went to a friend's house that night. There weren't many Latinas in Palisades High School. We stuck together. When my friend's parents tossed me out, I found myself some new friends on the street.

"When the governor appointed Rayburn, I laughed so hard. I remember because I was in jail for assaulting a guy who tried to do me when I didn't want it. I nearly killed the dude. I guess it was just a delayed reaction, you know. He hurt me. I hurt back this time. I get popped, and he walks. So when I see a guy like Rayburn getting in charge of the law I figure everyone's screwed. I felt safe locked up and I was there long enough to get my GED. I had a teacher who cared. She made sure I knew how to talk right in case I wanted to get a real job when I got out."

Rosa filled the last saltshaker, screwed on the top and took care to center it just so with the pepper. Her fingers lingered on the cheap glass.

"I think my mom's dead. I just have that feeling. But you know what?" She didn't bother to look at Archer or Josie. "I think she's in heaven. She didn't know about Rayburn. She did her best."

They didn't have long to consider the state of Rosa's mother's soul. Rosa had unlocked the door and now it opened. A mean looking man came in holding a tiny baby in his arms. A woman with beautiful long black hair followed. They sat in the far corner, probably tagging Archer for a cop.

Rosa did her thing. Salsa and chips slammed on the table, menus handed out. Water glasses filled. No ice. She made her rounds and ended up back with Josie and Archer. She swiped the bottle of tequila off the table.

"Not like it hasn't been fun, but it is rush hour," she said flatly.

Josie put her hand out. She took hold of Rosa's sleeve.

"Would you testify for us? My client is sixteen. Rayburn did her, too."

"Yeah, I know. I read the papers. I've got nothing to lose, but I don't think it's a good call. The prosecutor will pull my record."

"But you won't say no?" Josie asked.

Rosa shook her head, "Naw. I'll even wear a dress if you want. You know, cover up." She shook back her sleeves and showed her tattoos.

"Thanks." Josie held out her card. Rosa looked at it. Finally she took it.

"If you think of anything else, you call me. Okay?"

"I have a feeling I'll be thinking of a lot about Rayburn."

Archer left a big tip. Josie shook Rosa's hand. Archer had the door open; Rosa was taking the big man's order. Josie was about to leave when she remembered something. When Rosa went back to the kitchen, Josie followed.

Rosa was tossing peppers and onions into a hot pan. She looked over her shoulder. Josie stepped to the side. It was hot in the little kitchen.

"Rosa, you never really talked about Kip Rayburn. He was living in the house, right?"

She shrugged, "If you call it that. I doubt he's ever lived."

"But he was in the house so didn't he know what his father was doing to you?"

She threw a handful of shredded chicken into the pan then reached for a huge jar of cumin.

"He didn't pay attention. I could have been the dog for all he knew. I stayed out of his way and he stayed out of his father's way much as he could. Those two were a mess," she said as she stirred the peppers. "If the old man liked it, Kip hated it. If Kip loved it, the old man hated it. It didn't matter what it was. Me, a piece of meat, the color of the wallpaper," she shrugged. "The only difference between those two was that Kip just hated what his father loved. The old man destroyed whatever his son loved."

Rosa heaped the chicken and peppers onto tortillas, folded them and doused them with green sauce. She looked at Josie and gave her a lopsided grin.

"It's a good thing Kip didn't love me, huh?"

CHAPTER 28

It was dark, not late, when Archer pulled up to Josie's place. Josie's head was back, her eyes closed. It looked like she was asleep, but she was thinking about Rayburn's M.O. His preference was clear. Dependent girls. Women of color. Young. Each of them accepting Fritz as just a scummy part of life. All of them had a lot to lose: mothers, careers. All of them assumed they couldn't fight back. All except Hannah who was just that much more flawed than the rest, and that made her even less believable.

"We're home, Jo." Archer said.

"Thanks, babe," Josie whispered. "We did good today."

Archer took Josie's duffle out of the back.

"You coming in?" she asked.

"Am I still on the clock?"

Josie shrugged. "What if I said no?"

"Then I'm coming in."

Archer carried her bag, one arm slung over her shoulder. Josie picked up the mail, opened the door, and flipped on a light. Max ambled out of the back room. Archer petted him and let him out into the backyard, leaving the French doors open.

Josie filled his dish with food, replaced the dog's water. It was good to be home. She put the coffee on. Archer had wandered into the dining room and was looking at her mother's plates.

"I like these." He pointed to the wall.

"You say that every time you look at them," Josie laughed.

Josie liked them, too. Her mother's hula girl plates were her prized possession, two intact and one broken. Years ago Josie's father had dropped the plate while packing away Emily's things. When he was asleep, Josie opened the packing boxes and took the two plates. She retrieved the broken one from the trashcan and hid all three in her room. They were the first things Josie hung in her home. She could still see the crack that dissected one of the hula girls. Josie once thought she kept those kitschy plates because one day her mother would come back and be grateful. Now Josie knew she kept them to remind her that broken things can be mended, but there is always a scar.

Archer moseyed toward the living room; Max wandered back in. All was right with the world for now. Josie poured two cups of coffee, handing one off as she passed Archer.

"What are you going to do, Jo?" Archer asked.

"I'm thinking about breaking this down into two phases. First one is the assault on Rayburn. I'd put Rosa on the stand in a heartbeat. She's sympathetic. Rudy won't break her down. I'd like to find someone else who would corroborate in court." Josie took a drink, staring at the floor while she thought. "On the arson, I'm going to go with the doctors. Hannah couldn't have burned her studio. The defense is clear, and understandable, if I break it down that way."

"That jury is going to want another option on the arson."

"Then we go after Kip. He's the likely option. Something Rosa said puts me in the right frame of mind to look more closely at him. He's not the passive fool I thought he was. He proved it in court. There's a lot of anger there. I want to know what Kip and his father fought about. If it was Linda, Hannah, or business like he said."

Josie's words trailed off as she noticed the blinking light on her answering machine. She pressed play out of habit and took a minute to collect her thoughts. The first message was Ian Frank's secretary. Yes, Mr. Frank would meet with Josie in the morning, nine sharp.

"Want me to go with you?" Archer asked. "Might be good to have someone else listen in on what Rayburn's old partner has to say."

"No. I'll see him on my own. You check out..."

The machine was talking again. It was Hannah asking if Josie was okay. Counting. Counting softly but Josie could hear it. Asking Josie to call when she could. Then something muffled. The phone clattered and the line went dead.

Josie stopped the machine and picked up the phone. She dialed the Malibu house.

"She doesn't sound good," Archer muttered and then fell silent. "Nothing?"

Josie shook her head. She disconnected.

Archer checked his watch, "She's probably on her walk."

"Probably," she mumbled but Josie was unsettled. Josie punched the answering machine again hoping the next message was Hannah calling back, surprised to find it was Linda. She had tired of waiting at the house and was at Borelli's restaurant. She wanted to see Josie. Please.

"Please?" Archer looked surprised.

"Please," Josie reiterated with a grin.

"Want me to go with you, Jo?"

"Sure." Josie disappeared into the bedroom. She tossed her duffle on the bed and came back to the living room with her leather jacket on. "I guess Hannah must be with her."

"Suppose so," Archer answered as they parted on the doorstep. Josie wanted to walk and clear the tequila out of her head. Archer garaged the Hummer. They met at Borrelli's front door within a minute of each other.

Linda was waiting in the bar at a table for two, dressed all in black from the tips of her Italian boots to the last coat of mascara on her lashes. She started to smile when she saw Josie but lost it when she figured out the man who opened the door was part of the package.

"Linda?" Josie greeted her.

"Who's this?" Linda eyed Archer.

"Archer. Linda Rayburn. He's working with me on Hannah's case."

Linda nodded. Archer checked her out then made his excuses. He would wait at the bar; the two women would talk.

"Do you want something?" Linda lifted her cocktail when they were alone.

"Yeah. I'd like to know where Hannah is." Josie took a seat.

"She's at home," Linda said, peeved that she wasn't directing the conversation. "I meant did you want something to drink?"

"No, thanks and I'm not sure Hannah is at home. I just called. There was no answer."

Linda waved away the concern.

"She's probably out doing her walking thing. You know how it goes. Couple times around the house. Some weird dancing on the sand. Back in the house. Back outside again. I wouldn't worry about it."

Josie took a deep breath. She put her elbows on the table and raised her hands, clasping them under her chin.

"But I do worry, Linda. If you're not with Hannah, and I can't reach her, you are defying a court order. Judge Norris didn't say to take Hannah home and lock her in. He said that you were supposed to supervise her."

"He didn't mean twenty-four hours a day." Linda complained.

"Yes, he did."

"Well, that's ridiculous. She's in the middle of nowhere without a car. You know, there are things I absolutely have to do and that's just the way it is."

"Like what? Sneaking out to see your husband?"

Linda stiffened and grabbed her glass. She drank deep and then hesitated. Slowly the glass came down. She put it on the table and kept her eyes on it for a minute as if suddenly realizing it wasn't the answer to anything.

"No. Like walking away to see a friend," Linda said quietly.

"Christ, Linda," Josie breathed.

"No. I mean it. Don't sound like that. This isn't some kind of game," Linda insisted, uncomfortable with her confession. "Look, I don't know about you but not a lot has changed since college. We were never very good at making friends."

"I was too busy studying," Josie reminded her.

"I was too busy chasing after the next guy," Linda said. "Now I'm alone. I've never been alone before. Kip hasn't called. He won't come to see me. All the women I used to know are steering clear until they see how this plays out. Jesus, Josie, I'm not made of stone. I needed someone to talk to."

"It's not like you to feel sorry for yourself," Josie said.

"I'm not. I'm lonely, Josie, and I've been that way for a long time."

"Then just imagine how Hannah feels."

Linda sighed and closed her eyes; her free hand went to her forehead.

"I've spent a lifetime imagining how Hannah feels." The hand came down. Linda looked bleary eyed and sad, but Josie imagined it was the liquor. This may be the first time she had ever seen Linda Rayburn drunk. "Don't you think I know exactly what kind of mother I've been? I was too young to have a baby and I made Hannah grow up too fast. Maybe I thought she was going to be my built in friend. I didn't know how to be a mother. You were the smart one. You never had a kid. Women like us shouldn't have children."

The glass was up again. Josie watched her drink, unsure of what to say. She had been ready for a fight, ready to defend her strategy. She was off her stride now that Linda had asked for her friendship.

"You want to know something?" Linda leaned across the table. "I thought raising Hannah was about feeding her and putting clothes on her back until she was eighteen. But it's more than that. It wasn't until this happened that I realized I really loved my girl. I really, really do and that's the real hard part."

"Then why are you fighting to sell her out, Linda?" Josie interrupted. "Why are you taking chances with her freedom now? You're not stupid. You know Norris wanted you with Hannah twenty-four seven. Do you want her to go back in prison?"

"Who's going to tell Norris that I took a little R & R? You? I don't think so." Linda sighed. "See, that is the funny thing. You like Hannah better than you like me, so you're willing to protect her more than me. That's not right. You were my friend first. Maybe I need you now."

"Don't do that, Linda. Don't use people, especially not Hannah," Josie said wearily. "It isn't about who I like or don't like, it's about the rules."

"I'm tired of rules," Linda cried, her eyes filling up again. "You don't know what it's been like. Every time I try to play by rules I get smashed into the ground. You know, I really loved Hannah's father and I tried to be good for him. Where did it get me? Beaten up and kicked around. So then I started sleeping around and having some fun and you know what it got me? Good times, nice things, money, beaten up, and kicked around. Then I met Kip and you know what that got me? Every damn thing I ever wanted: someone who needed me, nice things, and a good home for me and my kid. He loved me back. He needed me."

Linda motioned for another drink. The bartender nodded. Josie caught Archer's eye for an instant, and Josie knew how lucky she was. They were silent as Linda was served, the empty glass taken away. Linda held onto it.

"Now it's all going away. Kip doesn't live with me. The Governor isn't sure if he wants to appoint him to the bench. You're running around trying to prove Fritz was a sick son of a bitch. And he was. I don't doubt he was. But Jesus, Josie, it's over. He's dead. He's dead and everything was going to be okay until you did that to Kip. God, Josie, don't you see. What you do to him, or to Hannah, you do to me. I thought we were friends. I really need you to be my friend."

"I am your friend. I'm trying to save your daughter."

"How? By sacrificing my husband?"

"If that's what it takes. If that's where the truth is."

"You don't care what the truth is." Linda's fist pounded lightly on the table. The little candle flickered and jumped. "You just want to prove you can get Hannah off the way you got that other woman off. You didn't care what the truth was then either."

Linda turned her head but Archer was right there, boxing her in. She didn't like the direct hit of his gaze so she swung her head back in time to see a shadow cross Josie's face.

Linda picked up her cigarettes and tapped one out. She tried her lighter but it wouldn't catch. Opening her purse she pulled out a box of matches. The flame flared, illuminating the middle of her face. She blew out the flame, tossed the match into the ashtray and pulled in the smoke hard, letting it out at her leisure. Her head was back, her hair hung past her shoulders. The smoke wafted toward the ceiling. She watched the smoke, Josie watched her. It was illegal to smoke in a restaurant in Los Angeles

County. No one stopped her. No one ever stopped a beautiful woman from doing anything.

"You're not sure about Hannah, are you?" Linda chuckled, but it was an ugly sound. "Oh, God, all this time I'm thinking I'm a little off here, but it's you. You started something you're going to finish, no matter who you hurt, and still you're not sure that Hannah didn't do it."

"Don't be ridiculous."

"No, no," Linda insisted, pushing across the table, her cigarette held high. "You've been thinking what I've been thinking. What if you're wrong about Hannah and she's like that woman you got off. The one who killed her kids after you defended her."

"This is nothing like that. Nothing," Josie insisted.

Linda ground out her cigarette.

"Maybe it is. Maybe Hannah's got you fooled the same way that lady did. Maybe you're going to screw up Kip's life and mine and send Hannah home and..."

Josie got up. Her chair toppled. She reached back to get it. Linda's eyes narrowed. Her jaw tightened. She grabbed for Josie. Her face tipped up, her long neck looked like alabaster in the dim light, her eyes like jewels. "For once in your life, think about other people instead of what you want."

"No one else matters but Hannah," Josie said in a whisper. "Why isn't that crystal clear to you?"

"Because life is more complicated than that, and you know it better than anyone." Linda pushed her case, her fingers digging into Josie's arm. Linda was a strong woman. "You had tunnel vision with that Davis woman, too. That woman wasn't what she said she was. You got her off, and then she turned around and killed her children. I saw some pictures. Those children looked like sleeping angels, didn't they? All covered up with white sheets, their arms crossed over their chests. Their hair so light against the pillows"

Josie yanked away but Linda spoke in a frantic whisper. Her voice mesmerized Josie.

"And when they pulled those sheets back those little children had no bodies, did they Josie? Their mother had slit them open and taken everything out just to see if she could. No other reason."

"I don't need to hear this. It has nothing to do with Hannah," Josie shot back.

"It has everything to do with Hannah, and me, and Kip," Linda growled, half rising. "Only this time it could be the daughter doing it to the mother. That woman used a knife to do her dirty work. Hannah lit a fire. In the end it's all the same, though, isn't it? People die horrible, gruesome deaths because there are horribly, sick people out there who aren't held accountable."

Josie was listening but all she could see was Linda's lips curling around words she couldn't understand.

"I guess what I want to know is why haven't you learned anything, Josie? Why don't you err on the side of caution? Do you want to see me like Fritz? Do you want to see my legs burned black and know my lungs were seared..."

"It would never happen."

Josie straightened. She could feel Archer watching her, ready to come to her rescue. But who could rescue her from memories, possibilities, and visions?

"Don't ruin me, Josie. Don't ruin my family. Don't make a mistake that might harm all of us. Send Hannah where she belongs. Get her help, Josie. Help me."

Josie closed her eyes, trying to banish the thought that Linda could be right. Her knees were weak, her breathing shallow. Maybe it wasn't Hannah who needed defending, but those around her. Josie opened her eyes, suddenly exhausted. Her lips parted but no sound came out. Linda, was looking at her, purse in hand, ready to leave, but needing to share one last thought.

"None of us really knows what the right thing to do is, Josie. I just came here tonight because I needed a friend. I guess I didn't find one. If you get Hannah off you're playing with my life. If you keep pointing at Kip you're playing with his, and still you don't know if Hannah is really innocent. Could you live with yourself if you bet wrong twice, and you were responsible for letting another killer go?"

"This isn't the same, Linda. This isn't the same at all."

Josie put her fingertips to her temple. Her head hurt. It was the tequila. Or maybe it was the worry over Hannah. No, it was Linda. Linda was conjuring up ghosts that did more than haunt Josie. They feasted on her heart and soul; they made her question her motives and her judgment.

"Sure it's the same," Linda whispered urgently. "Maybe you can't see it, but I can because I'm the one that has to sleep in that house and now I'm alone there with Hannah. I have to wonder every night when I go to bed if I'm going to wake up. I'm scared, Josie. I'm not asking you to throw the trial. I'm not asking you to forgive my mistakes as a mother, but I shouldn't have to wonder if I'm going to die because of them."

"Stop it, Linda." Josie dropped her hand. She wasn't going to be seduced by this woman's speculations or threats. "You're not afraid of anything. You never have been."

"Okay, Josie." Linda was resigned. "Think what you want. If anything happens, you won't have anyone to blame but yourself. And when it does, you won't have anyone to live with but yourself. Maybe that's the saddest thing of all."

Linda left Josie standing alone at the table. Archer pulled out her chair. She sat down.

"Take a minute, Jo." He slid into the chair Linda had just left. "She doesn't leave it very warm."

Josie's eyes flickered up and then away. Finally she leveled her gaze and looked right into Archer's eyes.

"Could I be wrong about Hannah?" she asked.

"Yeah. You could be."

"Do you think I am?"

He shook his head. "Rayburn hurt her bad. Maybe she snapped. I don't know. I guess it's a matter of faith."

"I don't have any of that, Archer."

"It's okay. I do," he answered.

He reached in his own pocket, pulled out a couple of bills and put them in the little black folder the bartender had left. Taking a deep breath, Josie reached for her phone. She dialed Hannah once more. Once again the phone rang and rang.

"I've got to go home, Archer."

"She's still not answering?" Josie shook her head.

"Don't worry about it, babe. Her mom will be home soon enough. If there's something wrong, she'll call. She's not that stupid."

Josie got up. Archer did the same. Josie was half way to the door when Archer called to her. She looked back. He reached to the floor and ambled over to her.

"I've got a present. Linda Rayburn left it."

Archer lifted her hand, put something inside and closed her fingers over it. When Josie opened it she found a box of matches that had come from Linda Rayburn's purse; matches that stood in when her fancy silver lighter couldn't manage a flame.

"Coffee Haus," Archer said.

"She stops there sometimes," Josie said wearily, twisting the box between her fingers with little interest.

"It's not exactly around the corner from Malibu so either she's been up that way to see her husband or…" Archer hesitated.

"Or?"

"Or, Linda Rayburn had them in that purse all this time. The cops searched the house, but I'll bet they didn't search the people who lived in the house."

Josie's hands closed over the matches.

"You'll check it out?"

"First thing in the morning, babe." Archer put his arm over her shoulder and steered her out the door. "I'll swing down Malibu way while I'm at it. Just a little drive by to make sure Hannah is doing okay?"

"Thanks, Archer. Want to come home with me?"

He shook his head. "Not tonight. You're tired. Get some rest."

Josie kissed him. Her arms went around his waist. He felt good but he was right. She needed to be alone. There was a lot to think about. Flipping up the collar of her jacket she walked home.

Josie lay down on the couch with the phone in one hand, her other buried in Max's fur. Her eyes were on the picture window even though she couldn't see the ocean. Not meaning to sleep without talking to Hannah, sure that Linda's accusations and protestations would keep her awake all night, Josie somehow drifted off. She dreamed of dead children and childless women.

CHAPTER 29

Hannah sat on her little stool in the sand. She had a joint but it was untouched. She had spent the night pacing the beach, the house, her room, measuring off space to pass the time until her mother came home. Josie was gone. Hannah had left a message and Josie would call. She was sure of that. Once Hannah thought she heard the phone ringing and she ran fast into the house, but it must have been her imagination. No one was on the line. She went back to the beach, and her stool, and the cold, wet night until it got too cold, and too wet. Finally she went inside, wishing she wasn't alone – until her wish came true.

Kip had come in so quietly, so unexpectedly that Hannah almost died of fright. It had been days since she'd seen him and nothing had changed: not his long face, his thinning brown hair, his white shirt and beige coat, his khaki slacks. He looked the same yet there was something different. Kip was looking right at her. He actually saw her. He had never done that before.

"Where's your mother?"

Hannah shook her head. She tried to answer and couldn't. The second time she managed a whisper.

"I don't know."

Kip didn't move. He didn't seem to be breathing but his eyes trailed over Hannah. He took in the twists and turns of her hair, the slope of her cheekbones, her lips, the cut of her t-shirt, the cleft of her breasts. Hannah's skin jumped with the prickle of nerves. Her heart beat faster even though she breathed more slowly. Maybe everything hadn't ended with Fritz's death. Maybe…

Kip took a step. He was leaving. No. He changed his mind. Hannah could see the vent on his coat, the flash of a heel on his shoe. She could feel him thinking. His hatred seeped through the wall. His heel was raised as if he might go forward, but then again he might fall back. She prayed for him to disappear. Instead Kip Rayburn walked right into her room. She cringed on her stool. One more step. He was standing over her, so close she could smell him. The smell of fear was on him. Hannah knew it well.

"You are a stupid little bitch. Everything would have been fine without you. Everything." Kip lowered himself, hunkering down so he could look straight at her. "The mere fact that you exist is abhorrent to me. What you did to my father turns my stomach."

"I didn't–" Hannah said.

"You didn't what? Hit him? Push him? Seduce him? Make him so much less than he was? Well," he sighed, "I think you did. But what's really sad is that, in the end, it's all my fault. I brought you into this house. I knew he was weak, and I brought you here to tempt him. You and me, we're guilty as sin. But he was my father, Hannah. Mine. And you took him away from me when he didn't really want you." Kip pointed a finger at her. His entire body vibrated with his desire to hurt her. "In fact, no one has ever wanted you, have they?"

"My mother did. My mother does," Hannah whispered.

"Really?" Kip stood up and looked around at the room. "Then where is your mother? She's not here. If she wanted you so much then why isn't she here?"

Hannah shook her head. Her lips moved with the counting. But Kip had had enough. He reached out and clamped his hands on the side of her head to stop her. He pulled her close, half off her little stool.

"Stop it. Stop it or I'll...."

Just when Hannah thought he would squeeze hard enough to crush her skull they heard sounds. A door closing. Footsteps. They were paralyzed, linked together in their private little power struggle only to be suddenly reminded there was another world. Slowly Kip released her. He was pale, shaking as if surprised to find he could be so vicious, yet not really surprised at all. It ran in the family.

"Kip?"

Linda Rayburn stood framed in the doorway looking at everything. Hannah. Her legs pulled up to her chest, arms wrapped around them, trembling as if she was chilled to the bone. Against the wall was Kip, his arms hanging slack by his side, his expression melting with his anger and grief and, above all, hatred.

No one spoke. Finally, Kip threw himself toward the door and pushed past his wife. Panicked, Linda screamed at Hannah.

"What have you done? What?"

"Mom, I–" Hannah said, but Linda didn't wait for an answer. She darted after her husband.

"Kip, wait. Wait." She caught up with him in the dining room, unable to make him stop until she sprinted ahead.

"Get out of my way, Linda. It's all over. My life is over. Everything is over. And it's her fault. I don't want to look at her. I don't want her in my house."

"What about me? Do you want me? Isn't that why you came? To get me? I can make it better. I always have. I always will." Linda hustled in front of him, her hands out, touching his chest, his shoulders.

"Just get out of my way," he slapped at her hands but she persisted.

"No, answer me. Kip for once in your life say what you want. What do you want?"

Kip grabbed her hands and shook them.

"I want people to stop talking about us. I'm sick of it. I can't go anywhere. People ask me if my father really did those things to me. At the club they make jokes about the women and girls and my father. They look at me and wonder if I ever did what he did. The governor called. He is withdrawing the nomination. Can you change that?"

"Yes. Yes. I promise. I'll talk to him. We'll figure something out. It will be all right," Linda insisted, frantic to calm him. It was an impossible task.

"Don't be stupid. Nothing will be all right. Not until she is gone." He whipped his head around to glare at Hannah. She had followed cautiously, hugging the walls, the furniture, watching to see where the danger was coming from. But Kip's eyes were blurred. He saw nothing, and he could do nothing. He dropped his head and shook it. "Everything was fine when it was just him and me. No one knew. I could take anything if nobody knew."

Linda pulled him to her. When he resisted, she moved into him, forcing herself on him, angry and determined to stop the hemorrhaging emotions that would kill reason.

"I know. I do know. I swear. I've been there. But I can make it right."

She soothed him with the truth. It was an awful, ugly truth that weakness was better stomached in private, behind the doors, in the dark. Fritz knew that. Kip knew that and, most of all, Linda knew. The weak were bound together. Maybe that was why Fritz and Kip and Linda had coexisted as easily as they had. Maybe that was why Hannah never found her place in the Rayburn mix. Her weakness was open. It didn't shape her heart and soul; it only touched the delicate tissues of the mind.

"Mom?"

Instinctively Linda pulled Kip closer as if to protect him from her daughter. Kip twisted out of her grasp and stepped behind his wife. He ran a hand through his hair. His plain face was mottled with the color of emotions long held private.

"Leave him alone." Linda closed in on Hannah and lowered her voice. "Haven't you done enough?"

Hannah's eyes flicked to Kip and back to her mother. Her hand reached out. She touched Linda's arm. Once, twice, three times and Linda slapped her away.

"Mom, please. I didn't do anything. He came here. He scared me. I thought it was going to be like Fritz."

"Stop it." Linda grabbed Hannah's arm and railroaded her back into her room. She whipped Hannah against the wall, out of Kip's sight. "It's not going to be like that. Don't even think it. Kip's not like that, but don't push him, that's all I'm saying."

"But..." Hannah grappled to get a hold on her mother. Linda gathered Hannah's hands together and held them tight.

"I'm telling you to trust me. I've got to take care of Kip so I can take care of us – of you."

"No, I'm not going to do it anymore. I'm not going to take care of her," Kip screamed.

Linda let go of Hannah's hands. Kip wasn't finished with them.

"Kip, calm down. We'll work this out."

"You work it out. You take care of it." Kip turned to leave. "But not with my money. Not in my house. Not for that little bitch."

"Christ," Linda muttered, watching his back as he stormed away. "Kip, wait. I'm coming with you."

"Mom!" Hannah screamed, choking back her sobs. "Don't leave me. Please, Mom. Don't leave. Don't."

Linda bared her teeth and her eyes flashed as she turned on her daughter. Everything was walking out that door, and she'd be damned if she'd let it go without a fight.

"We need him you little bitch," Linda hissed, turning again to rush after her husband.

It was then Hannah changed the trajectory of the night. With a scream she flew past her mother and lunged at Kip Rayburn. She was crazed with the fear of being left alone, out of her mind with the thought that her mother – her mother who she loved beyond reason, who she would do anything for and had done anything for – would leave her for this person.

"You can't take her away. She's supposed to be here. I'm not supposed to be alone," Hannah screamed.

Tripping on the slick floor, Hannah's knees hit hard but she was close enough to take hold of Kip's legs. She grappled. She pulled hard. Kip fell forward, smashing his shoulder against the wall. Fritz's black and red canvas shivered above as he steadied himself. Hannah grunted, crawling up his leg, snatching at his clothes and screaming, but he was quick. One leg was free. Kip kicked hard catching the side of Hannah's head. She reeled back and rolled into the opposite wall. Linda screamed. Hannah's arm flew across her brow, her other hand went to her lips to stifle the cry. She would not cry. Never again. Never in front of him.

"Kip stop!" Linda joined the fray, yelling again and again.

Hannah heard him coming. She heard Linda's high heels click on the floor and Kip's grunts as he struggled with his wife. Then it was over. Only the sound of breathing could be heard in the big, high-ceilinged house. Hannah felt Kip standing over her. Her eyes flew open. She would not close them. She would watch whatever was coming. This time Hannah Sheraton was determined to watch it happen.

But Kip Rayburn did nothing. He just stood there, his fists balled as he looked at her.

Slowly Hannah struggled to stand up. Kip stepped back. She leaned against the table, pained to see that Linda was waiting to see what would happen, and who would win. Kip stepped back again and again until he was at the door. Hannah matched him. Her head hurt. She put out a hand to steady herself. She took one step forward, and then another. Her lips moved with counting.

"Two," she whispered. "Three. Four..."

"You're a lunatic," Kip said coldly.

Hannah stopped moving, counting, thinking. Linda was immobile even when Kip walked past her, heading out the door to his car. Mother and daughter looked at one another: One pleading for help, the other steeling herself with determination. Linda rushed to Hannah and took her by the shoulders. She shook her hard.

"Don't you call anyone; don't you answer the phone. They'll take you away if you do. I swear they will. They'll take you away Hannah. Do you understand? Don't do anything until I get back. I'll fix it, if you don't screw it up now."

Those were the last words Linda Rayburn spoke before she ran after her husband. Hannah stumbled after her mother, stopping before she reached the thorn gate. She heard two car doors slam and the squeal of tires on the drive. In the ensuing silence, for just a moment, Hannah Sheraton crumpled onto the tiled patio. Her only company was a tortured woman of bronze forever standing alone in the still pond waters of Fritz Rayburn's home.

Hannah dressed fast. A coat. A hat. A scarf. She looked at the phone once more, wanting to call Josie.

Don't talk to anyone.

Don't screw up.

They'll take you away.

Hannah buttoned her coat as she ran through the house and opened the door to the outside. The Volkswagen was there, still booted. The old Mercedes was in the garage. Hannah ran for the kitchen and rummaged through the drawer where they kept extra keys. Nothing. She pulled the drawer further out to search in the back but she pulled too far and the drawer fell with a clatter to the floor.

Jumping back, Hannah cursed and ignored the mess. If the key to the Mercedes was there she didn't have time to look. She needed to figure this out and there was only one place she could go.

Seconds later Hannah was running through the house, past Fritz's paintings, out the front door, and past the statue. She burst out of the thorn gate and didn't bother to close it. Hannah ran all the way to the highway. The sound of the ocean drove her on. The sound of cars pulled her forward. Someone would stop for her. They had to. She would make them. Someone needed to get her where she was going before she did something she shouldn't do.

Linda Rayburn stood naked at the long windows that overlooked the grounds of the Palisades house. One arm was crossed under her heavy breasts, the other was crooked, a cigarette held between her fingers. Thoughtlessly she brought the cigarette to her lips, pulled the smoke deep into her lungs, and held it there before letting it seep out through her lips.

Behind her Kip slept in the big bed, curled like a child into a tight ball, one hand under his cheek, exhausted from his meltdown. In front of her, Linda could see the west wing of the house. The charred wood had been removed, new wood rose in its place, framing the room just as it had been before the fire. The yellow crime scene streamers were long gone. The little stone boy peed into the fountain. The gardens were manicured. The stars twinkled. The Palisades slept and Linda Rayburn wanted to lay her head down on her pillow and do the same, but there were too many things to think about.

Hannah. Number one. Always Hannah. That had been an ugly scene. Kip had been wrong to kick her, Linda wrong to leave her, but what was done was done. Linda should feel guilty for following Kip, but she didn't. A genetic flaw. Her perpetual failing. She wouldn't apologize for it even to herself. You worked with what you had, you did what you could, and you made choices based on need. Kip needed Linda more than Hannah did, and Linda needed Kip. Hannah was strong and always had been. She would survive the night. Linda wasn't sure Kip would have if he'd been left alone.

Josie. She was in the mental mix. Funny how, in the dark, Linda could see so clearly. Her path had crossed Josie's so long ago and only for a short time. Yet it was as if Josie had been with her every damn day of her life since college, looking over her shoulder, passing judgment. She put her back against the wall and watched the cigarette smoke wend its way toward the ceiling. She admitted it was all in her mind – this thing with Josie. That sense of competition, of being not quite as good as Josie Bates. Or at least it had been. Now it was real. There was a tug of war for Hannah's future, and that's not what Linda had anticipated at all when she sought Josie out. This was supposed to be a win-win situation, but Linda was losing.

The cigarette came to her lips. The smoke filled her lungs.

No, this wasn't what she had anticipated at all.

Her eyes roamed the room. It was more beautiful than any she could have imagined in all of her years before she met Kip. She let her gaze rest on her husband.

Kip. Kip. Linda would like to think that she loved him, but the bottom line was she didn't know how to do that. He made her the center of his universe, which was better than Linda had ever had, so she was grateful. He'd had it tough with Fritz. Linda understood. She was sympathetic. She even liked Kip because he didn't demand a whole lot. But love him? No. She was broken somewhere inside. She couldn't love like other people. But for Kip she came close. For Hannah she came even closer. For herself?

Well....

Linda stubbed out her cigarette and crawled into bed with her husband. He uncurled himself. She put her arms around him and lay with her face against his back. She could have done worse. She had done worse than Kip Rayburn. In the end, it was really Hannah, Linda worried about. Poor, sad, sick, dangerous Hannah. Only Linda knew how dangerous Hannah could be, and it scared her to death.

CHAPTER 30

"405 North is packed and the transition to the 10 toward downtown is backing up. Rush hour has started early. Expect more delays than divorce court." – KFWB traffic report

"I'm sorry to have kept you waiting, Ms. Bates. The freeways get worse everyday."

Josie ended her call to Archer. He was headed to Malibu just as Ian Frank walked into his office. He didn't waste a lot of time on the niceties, but wasn't one to disregard them either. He was pleasant, focused, and comfortable in his domain. And a nice domain it was.

This man, worth millions, lived his professional life in a room that, at first glance, was less than impressive. It was the second glance that did the trick. The desk was simple with clean lines, as was the chair, but the wood quality and leather grade was exquisite. Instead of the artwork and honors Rayburn favored, Frank's walls were noticeably bare save for his Harvard Law School diploma and that was hung on a slice of wall near the door as if, once earned, it was of little consequence. Large plants in full foliage brightened the corners. Floor to ceiling windows afforded a spectacular view of the Hollywood hills behind Ian Frank. At Josie's back the view was equally rich. The eye bumped over the stair-steps of the downtown skyline before skimming over the cities that paved the way to the coastline. On a clear summer day Ian Frank could see the ocean but Josie doubted he was ever tempted to play hooky. There was a bit of the farmer in him; he looked up to check the way the wind blew. From his greeting Josie imagined she was just a breeze in Ian Frank's world.

"So what can I do for you?"

"I want to talk about Fritz Rayburn," Josie said, telling him something he already knew.

"What can I tell you? I didn't much care about Fritz's personal life while he was alive, and I don't much care about it now."

"Don't you think you should, Mr. Frank?" Josie asked.

"And why should I, Ms. Bates?" Ian Frank seemed amused.

"Because a law firm is reliant on its goodwill, and the firestorm surrounding the Rayburns could affect that. Telling me about them might keep damage to a minimum."

Ian laughed. He had a wonderful face, a beautiful head of dark gray hair. Trim and handsome, he was a man that would set widows and divorcees scheming.

"Fritz Rayburn's interest in this firm was put into a trust when he took the bench. He wasn't a practicing partner. Whatever you're digging up may impact your client, but the goodwill on my balance sheet is going to be worth exactly what it was worth yesterday, or the day before."

"You seem to be the only one who isn't concerned about the impact of Fritz Rayburn's habits. The governor is worried. The family is worried. The DA is worried," Josie pointed out.

"The governor has reason to worry. Fritz was his prized appointee. No one will believe that Fritz's shortcomings weren't discovered in a background check. So, if Fritz was a bit off, and the governor's office covered up, that will be a public relations nightmare. You can't put the horse back in the barn, you know. " Ian shook his head with certainty. "As to Kip, he'll be disappointed and embarrassed when the appointment doesn't go through, but he'll still be a partner in this firm. Money soothes a great many hurts. But all that aside, gossip or fact, none of this affects me."

"Your clients might not feel the same way." Josie pointed at him as if he kept those precious people nestled in his breast pocket.

"Hell, half my clients are worried about their own skeletons, Ms. Bates. In fact…"

He was interrupted when the door opened. Standing just outside of Josie's line of sight was a woman who was dutifully giving Ian Frank a reason to curtail this meeting.

"John Blosser is on his way," she said with all the interest of someone who had done this a thousand times over the course of as many days.

"Thanks, May. Ms. Bates and I will be wrapping up soon." Ian Frank gave Josie his full attention and a ridiculously patronizing look that was meant to hurry her on. She, in turn, didn't give him an inch.

"Mr. Frank, I'm not intimidated by you, and I am not impressed by your clinical analysis of Fritz Rayburn's conduct. I used to live in a place like this. I used to sit in a chair just like yours. I know, in these surroundings, that nothing is sacred – not even the idea that business exists in a vacuum. I am living proof that it doesn't."

"I know your history, Ms. Bates, but this is very different. We deal in numbers, in mergers, in huge estates, and corporate entities," Ian Frank countered easily. "That kind of business doesn't titillate the public interest.

"Unless someone tells the tale correctly and I can tell it in a way that will make people sit up and take notice. Do you think the mothers and fathers in California would take kindly to knowing that the man who was legal counsel to Comfy Toys also terrorized young girls? Do you think the very vocal black coalition in this state is going to turn the other cheek when they find out that Rayburn's taste ran to women of color? "

"And I would be curious to see who the mothers and fathers of California have more loathing for: an attorney who uses her power to isolate a young woman from her mother or an old, dead man who hasn't been affiliated with this firm for over seven years. And, if Kip Rayburn were to admit his father was overzealous in his discipline, there would be a great deal of sympathy for him, don't you think? Oh, Ms. Bates, we can all spin and in the end, when all is said and done, neither of us will win but I'll come out on top. I know my clients. Their attention span is even shorter than mine."

Josie sat forward in her chair, too. She tried another tack; one that she had no doubt would fail, but, when desperate, desperate measures are called for.

"Then tell me about Fritz Rayburn and his son because you're a good man, Mr. Frank. Tell me because it might help Hannah Sheraton."

A flicker of interest ran across Ian Frank's face. For the first time he was truly engaged in the conversation.

"It isn't as though I don't have sympathy for your client, Ms. Bates. My sister has a daughter that girl's age. It's hard to know what's true and what isn't even when it is your own child, so I will be truthful. I don't know anything for sure that will help you. If I don't know it to be fact, then it doesn't exist and that's really all there is to it. I give you credit for sticking your neck out but, then, you don't have all that much to lose, do you? I'm not in the same position."

Josie jumped on the opening. It wasn't more than a hairline crack in his demeanor but it was enough to tell her that he had a conscience.

"You're right. I don't have anything to lose so that means I can fight tooth and nail. Just tell me what you suspect. Give me access to your personnel files. Let me talk to the women in this firm. Tell me if you know anything about the fight between Fritz and Kip Rayburn. All I need is your permission. I'll be discreet. All you have to do is give me the sword. I'll slay the dragon and you keep the castle."

Ian Frank put his elbows on top of his well-kept desk and clasped his hands. He let them fall back against his lips once and then he put them in front of him. He didn't think longer than a second.

"There isn't a businessman on this earth who would believe what you just said. No. I won't open this firm up to you. Though I have a great deal of faith in the practical mindset of our clients, I won't help you tip the balance. Now, I know you're a fine attorney, but I'm probably better. If you try to get a court order to go into my records, I will stop you." Ian opened his hands as if in apology. "Eventually you may get what you want but I'll keep you tied up until this trial is over. I'll protect what's mine and that, as they say, is that."

"I thought this firm belonged to Kip now, too," Josie reminded him.

"You think he's going to give you permission to go after his father on his own turf?" Ian laughed.

"No, I was just curious to find out if he understood he'd be second fiddle around here. That you're the one who will be making all the big decisions."

"That's exactly how it is, Ms. Bates, and I don't think Kip will mind. I've done well at the helm of this firm. I will continue to do my job well and make him rich. I will support him if he is on the bench. I have a great deal of respect for Kip."

"Did Justice Rayburn have the same respect for his son?"

"I have no idea," Ian laughed. "Fritz and I weren't friends. We were business partners. We made business decisions."

That was it. The moment Josie was waiting for. Ian Frank was lying. Josie had cross examined too many witnesses, completed too many interviews, represented too many defendants not to know that lies weren't always dotted with beads of sweat and didn't always quiver with the telling. Sometimes lies came as they did with Ian Frank; behind an expression so controlled it was unnatural. He looked straight at her. There was just the hint of a smile on his lips. It had been there before she asked the question and it remained after. He didn't react to the ridiculousness of the query by waving it off or throwing himself back in the chair as if she was wasting too much of his time.

"You liar. A law partnership is closer than most marriages. You know everything." Josie put her hand on the top of his desk; she made sure she didn't look away. "You're not concerned about the emotional value of Fritz Rayburn's legacy so what's the deal you made? Was Kip going to be an active member of the firm? Was he just going to collect the partner's share? There had to be documents that were signed, discussions held, decisions made. Were you and Fritz on the opposite sides of the fence when it came to good old Kip?"

Ian Frank's eyes clouded. He was wary, on his guard. Sexual aberrations were something to pass off but now Josie was treading on sacred ground – the firm's.

"Fritz didn't know he was going to die, Ms. Bates, so passing on his interest in the firm wasn't exactly top of mind."

"Fritz Rayburn was a lawyer, Mr. Frank, and so are you," Josie drawled. "Lawyers don't leave anything to chance where their firms are concerned. Was Kip the beloved son, trusted with the legacy over your objections? Did you welcome him, but Fritz wanted him controlled? What was the deal? You might as well tell me because I swear I am going to kick up a ruckus until I find out."

"Mr. Frank?"

Ian Frank's eyes snapped to the doorway. May was back.

"Yes, what is it?"

The woman's expression changed from bland to startled. It was tough to be snapped at when you were just following orders.

"Mr. Blosser is on his way up."

Ian Frank dismissed her by looking back at Josie. She pressed her case.

"I know that Kip and Fritz had a huge argument just before he died. I want to know if it was about business. I know that you..."

Ian Frank stood up abruptly. He put out his hand and said:

"This interview is over, Ms. Bates. I have an appointment."

Josie hesitated. She stood up too but ignored the hand he held out to her.

"I'll be calling you to court, Mr. Frank, so clear your calendar."

Ian Frank lowered his outstretched arm. He was not insulted, and he wasn't stupid enough to dismiss the message.

"That is your prerogative, Ms. Bates. In fact, if time permits, I might even show up. It could be fun to see what would happen between us in a courtroom."

"I assume you wouldn't ignore a subpoena?" Josie raised a brow.

"I've always found sympathetic consideration given to the schedules of busy attorneys. Even the court knows its only business at the end of the day," Ian reminded her.

"No, Mr. Frank, at the end of this day we're talking about a young girl's life and I'll bet the system will see it my way. If I want you on that stand, that is where you'll be."

Josie made her statement and her exit. Ian Frank let her go without another word. By the time she made it to the elevator he was dictating a memo. When the elevator came, Josie had to step back for a man who was in a hurry. The receptionist greeted him as Mr. Blosser, the man Ian Frank was waiting for. In the minutes it took the elevator to whisk Josie down fifty-four floors Ian Frank and his client had probably slapped one another on the back a few times and were sitting down to business. Ian Frank probably hadn't given Josie Baylor-Bates another thought, but someone else had.

"Excuse me."

Fingers touched Josie's arm. The touch was light and surprising. Josie's mind had been on the rich possibilities opened up by Kip's fight with Fritz, and now a woman she didn't know was railroading her. The woman's body pulled in tight against Josie, steering her to a corner of the lobby before Josie reached the door to the valet parking. Josie looked down to see who was insisting on a moment of her time. It was May, the one whose job it was to interrupt Ian Frank.

"I have to talk to you," she said, her voice quiet, her eyes lowering as she linked arms with Josie. Deftly the short woman herded the tall one into an alcove. She backed Josie up until they were well hidden behind a wall of black marble and a bank of telephones.

"I don't want to testify in court, okay. I don't want to lose my job, okay. But somebody needs to tell you about him." May laid out the ground rules before Josie even knew what the game was.

"You mean Fritz Rayburn?"

"No, no. Not the old man. The young one. Kip. Stupid name for a grown man. Kip is the one you need to know about."

She squinted up at Josie but it was her tone of voice that was telling. May hoped she wasn't talking to an idiot.

CHAPTER 31

The conversation lasted no longer than five minutes. May was her last name; she didn't offer a first. Easy enough to find out, but Josie wouldn't unless it was absolutely necessary. May lived up to Josie's initial impressions. She was exacting, professional and got to the point.

She heard what Josie had asked. About Kip Rayburn. About Fritz Rayburn. She had worked for the firm for fifteen years. She'd seen a lot. She wouldn't lie. If it was anything else except this, she would have kept her mouth shut, but she'd been following this case. May had read about it in the papers, heard about it on the news, and discussed it with people in the firm. Oh yes, despite what Mr. Frank thought, people in the firm were talking about Fritz like crazy, and that included some clients. May thought it was awful that they had brought charges against Hannah as an adult. She wasn't convinced that the girl had killed her grandfather. Why? Because May knew that other people were really upset with Justice Rayburn. Not that she liked what Josie had done. She thought the emancipation deal was a raw one. There had to be another way. But there it was. The ball had bounced. Still, at the end of the day, May figured Josie's instincts were right.

"Specifically?" Josie wanted to know everything May did.

"Kip Rayburn," May answered. "He and his father had been fighting for six months and it was getting ugly."

"Because?" Josie prodded though May seemed less in need of encouragement than waiting for Josie to ask a question. May had been around lawyers too long.

"Justice Rayburn was going to assign his share of the partnership to Mr. Frank unless his son – "May paused and shook her head. She made a face as if there was something distasteful in her mouth "Unless he divorced his wife. I'd never heard anything like it. That old man wanted his son to trade his wife for money. I heard them arguing. I typed the codicil to his will."

May had heard at least three fights about the matter. Mr. Frank wasn't in favor of it. Kip had worked with the firm. He was an asset. Justice Rayburn was unmoved. He hated Linda and her 'half breed' daughter. May heard Mr. Frank accuse Justice Rayburn of playing dirty, just doing it to make Kip miserable, just doing it because he could. He was angry because Justice Rayburn was using the firm badly. Mr. Frank hadn't liked Mr. Rayburn for a long while. She could tell by the way Mr. Frank answered the phone when the judge called, and the way Mr. Frank ran the firm like it was his own without consulting Justice Rayburn on important matters.

"So, what happened?" Josie asked.

"I don't know," May shrugged. "I don't know what Kip Rayburn decided to do but his father was bringing it to a head. For some reason he wanted Kip to make a decision fast. Now that I've heard about what he did to that girl, maybe he wanted to get rid of the evidence. Get the mother out of the house and the girl goes too. Maybe that is why he offered Kip that weird deal."

"Did Mrs. Rayburn know about this?" Josie asked.

"I never saw her. I don't know. But I do know that Kip was going to fight tooth and nail. He didn't want a divorce. He said she loved him and nobody ever had. It was sad. I heard him crying once. The old judge was laughing at him."

"Do you think he was mad enough to do something desperate? Do you think he was angry enough to kill his own father?"

Josie looked over May's head. A man had stopped in the entry to the alcove. May looked over her shoulder and eased herself away. The man changed his mind and went on to the parking structure. May lowered her voice and talked faster.

"I don't know. I saw bits and pieces. They were really angry. I heard raised voices, and you didn't hear that when it was only Mr. Frank running the place. Even he got crazy when the other two men went at it. What was sad is that Justice Rayburn seemed to be having such a good time. I think he liked sticking it to his son – maybe even to Mr. Frank. I think he'd been doing it so long it was second nature. I felt sorry for Kip Rayburn. Grown man being treated like that just isn't right."

"What about Mr. Frank?" Josie's eyes scanned the comings and goings outside the alcove. No one was interested in them.

"What about him?" May followed Josie's lead and checked over her shoulder now and again.

"Maybe it was in his best interest that Kip didn't divorce. Then he wouldn't answer to anybody if Rayburn died. Maybe he wanted to hurry along the process so he could have the firm to himself."

May rolled her eyes. She knew two things better than most people: the law wasn't always about justice and that lawyers sometimes weren't very practical.

"If Mr. Frank killed Justice Rayburn he would still have had Kip for a partner. The codicil hadn't been filed. Nope, if you have to look at anyone, look at the son. He was between a rock and a hard place and he was in agony. The girl he didn't care about, but the wife was a different matter altogether."

Archer didn't have to look far to know that there was a problem at the Malibu house. The huge copper gate stood open, twisted to three quarters as if someone had slipped out in a hurry. He pushed it all the way open with a fisted hand and walked in, calling for someone – anyone. The place was silent as a tomb.

Careful not to touch anything, Archer checked it out. Front door: open. Entry rug: off center, one corner flipped back. Dining room: two chairs down. He moved slowly. Warily. Silent now. Ready to run into a living, breathing human being, or step over a body.

Nothing in the hall.

Hannah's room. A mess. Little stool tipped over. Little dish with a blade. Archer peered closely. No blood. Good sign. French doors that led to the beach. Open. A closer look. Sand at the entry. Feathered. There was no wind now so it had to have been open all night.

Archer moved upstairs, staying close to the wall, watching the doors. All were open. All was silent. The master bedroom was pristine. The bed hadn't been slept in. Downstairs again he wrapped his finger in the tail of his shirt and activated the answering machine. Last thing he wanted was his prints in this place. There were two messages from Josie asking Hannah to call. The kitchen: crap all over the floor. A junk drawer ripped out and spilled. No cocktail glasses, no dishes, no food, nothing normal. Whatever had gone down had happened fast and furious and followed a path – Hannah's bedroom, through the dining room and living room, out the front door, and through the gate.

Poof.

All gone.

He walked the perimeter looking for anything that would give him a clue as to where gone was. Linda's car was in the driveway unlocked. Hannah's bug was still booted. Someone had come to get Linda, or Hannah, or both. Archer guessed Kip, but Kip wouldn't take Hannah to the corner if she begged on her knees.

Archer planted his feet in the white sand and looked out to sea. If Linda was taken away and Hannah left behind, then where was she? He hoped to God she wasn't out there, under the deep blue sea. There was only one way to find out, and it wasn't by making a phone call and asking politely. He'd have to find the gruesome twosome – Kip and Linda – and look them in the eye to find the truth. Archer trudged back around the house just as an old Valiant pulled into the drive. A woman dressed in white got out, a sweater over her arm, and a shopping bag in her hand.

The maid.

"*Hola*," Archer called and went to meet her.

It took less than two minutes to find out she came every other day. She would be no help to Archer. He thanked her, told her the place was a mess and heard her mumble 'so what else is new' in Spanish before he got in his car and set his sights on the Palisades to check out the Coffee Haus, and track down the elusive Rayburns.

Josie inched along the freeway, got through the tight patch, and took off as soon as she passed the Century turnoff. The ragtop rattled, she could hear the engine purring under the hood, and her brain was hanging right in there with the car. She wanted to call Archer but knew there would be no way to hear him over the freeway noise, so Josie made mental memos as she wove into the fast lane and out again to pass a tractor-trailer.

Archer was top of the list. Josie would have him running for the next three days, checking out every bit of the Rayburn's lives: the women Linda hung with at the gym, the few she drank with, the ones she served with on those charitable committees where someone named Rayburn would be welcome. Josie would have him talk to the partner's wives at Rayburn & Frank. Archer would go to Kip's club, talk to those who knew him well. Purpose: find out who knew about Fritz's 'deal' with his son.

Josie changed lanes again taking cursory note of the mobile impressions: a man on a cell phone, a gray Mercedes, a girl singing at the top of her lungs in a white Toyota. Billboards went by in a rush of color and light. The electronic message board warned of a slow down at the next turnoff but Josie flew past – no traffic jam in sight. She exited the freeway at Rosecrans. Thirty minutes later she'd navigated the surface streets and was home. Gathering her purse Josie walked down the driveway snapped the remote over her shoulder and closed the garage door. She dug in her purse for her keys and hurried around the corner of the garage only to slow her step, stunned to see who was waiting on her doorstep.

❧

"Hey."

"Hey," Archer called back, raising a hand as he hiked across the impeccable lawn that swept up to the Rayburn's Palisades estate. The kid who called to him was short, tanned, and buff. His shirt was off and he was surrounded by a couple thousand dollars' worth of flowers and plants.

"Did you bring the mulch?"

"Nope. Sorry. Wrong guy."

"Damn. I need that mulch. These beds are like totally dead after that fire. I need to work in some mulch here. I called the company two hours ago."

"Sorry," Archer shrugged, "can't help you. I'm looking for the Rayburns. Are they here?"

"I got here about six. I haven't seen anybody." The kid squinted toward the main house. "I seen the cars, just haven't seen them."

"Archer."

He put out his hand, shook the kid's

"Rene," the young man filled in the blank.

"Nice to meet you. I'm actually looking for the daughter."

"Hannah?" Rene nodded. "I haven't seen her either."

"What about before the fire? Did you see anything then? Anything out of the ordinary?" Rene squinted into the sun as he thought.

"I'm here one day a week. I don't know what's ordinary. They walk right by me. Except Hannah. She said hi when she saw me. The old man didn't like it."

"Was he mad?"

"Naw. Only heard him mad once. I was here late because the sprinklers weren't working just right. So I'm over there," he chucked his chin toward a bank of leaded glass windows. "And I'm fiddling with the timer trying to get it reset and I hear the old man and his son going at it. I never heard a peep out of that house before and then it sounds like World War three going on."

"What did you do?" Archer walked over to the fountain and ran his hand through the clear, cool water. Rene followed.

"I listened," Rene laughed again. "It's not like gardening is real exciting."

"Did you hear what they were saying?"

"You a cop?" Rene asked.

"Just a friend of the girl."

"I didn't hear much. I..." Rene hesitated. "Hey, you're not going to tell them I was listening are you? I don't want to get fired."

Archer shook his head and flicked the water off his finger. "I'm the last person you have to worry about. Just curious, that's all."

"Mostly I just heard the yelling not all the words. Then the young guy comes close to the window and he screams at the judge and I hear him say, "she's your problem, not mine" and "what's there to be afraid of?

"Then he moves away and I can't hear what he's saying, just the yelling. I almost have the sprinklers fixed when I hear this big crash. I dived onto the grass because I thought it was a gunshot. It wasn't. Somebody threw something and it hit the window frame just where I was standing." Rene shook his head remembering the day. "I would have been in big trouble if that thing hit the window because I was just underneath it."

"What happened then?"

"Nothing," Rene answered matter-of-factly. "They said a few more things I couldn't hear, and then I was done and I left."

"When was this?" Archer asked.

"One, maybe two days before the fire."

"Anything after that?"

"Not that I know. Nobody was living here after the fire. I just kept the grounds." Rene's eyes narrowed and he nodded toward the circular drive. "They're back now."

Archer followed Rene's gaze. Linda Rayburn had come out the door. She was dressed in a long, filmy gown the color of cantaloupe. It didn't leave much to the imagination.

"What a babe," Rene sighed.

"Yeah," Archer answered, "A real sweetheart."

&

"Faye?" Josie jogged the last few steps, hugging Faye Baxter with her free arm, pulling away long enough to grab her keys and rush to the front door. "My God, I can't believe you're here. I'm so happy to see you. I'll say it. I missed..."

"Josie, I'm sorry. I couldn't get you on the phone," Faye talked fast but Josie was talking over her. Faye tried again, louder to make herself heard. "I tried your cell but couldn't get through."

Josie pushed open the door and motioned Faye in with a nod of her head.

"I was downtown. Probably out of range. Come on in. How long have you been here?"

"About twenty minutes. Josie, I've got..." Faye inched closer.

"Just a sec. I've got to let Max out." Josie was a step inside the door when Faye clamped her hand on Josie's shoulder.

"Josie, stop," Faye cried. Then more softly, "Stop."

"What? What is it?" Josie dropped her briefcase. Faye had her attention.

"It's Hannah. She's been hurt."

"Where? Where is she?" The blood rushed to Josie's cheeks.

"She's in Long Beach Memorial Hospital."

"Long Beach? What in the hell is she doing there?"

"I don't know. I only know she's hurt pretty badly."

"Please tell me she didn't try to kill herself?" Josie pleaded.

Faye shook her head. "No. Nothing like that. It was an accident. She was hitchhiking. A truck swerved to miss a car on Pacific Coast Highway and hit her. She was in Huntington Beach and the paramedics took her to Long Beach Memorial. Hannah had your card with the office number in her pocket. The nurse in ICU didn't go through her clothes until this morning. Hannah's been there since late last night."

"Does Linda know?"

"Not from me. I told the police who Linda was so I'm sure they've contacted her by now."

"Maybe, maybe not." Josie balled her fists on her hips. "I swear, I don't know what Linda was thinking leaving Hannah alone. What a mess. Hannah running away is unbelievable. I told her..." Suddenly Josie stopped. She put a hand to her brow. "Oh God, then Hannah's alone at the hospital."

"I just don't know anything else, Josie." Faye clasped her hands in apology.

"I know. It's okay. I appreciate you going out of your way, Faye. I really do." Josie walked a circle. She slapped the wall with her open palm and stormed across the room. She ripped the receiver off her cradle. "Linda wants the mother of the year award and then leaves Hannah alone to do whatever she wants. God, she's stupid. Norris will have Hannah back in jail before Linda can blink and it will be her fault."

"Norris may not have time to revoke Hannah's bail, Josie. From the little I know, Hannah may not live that long."

Josie held the receiver away from her ear. Faye could hear the ringing of Linda Rayburn's cell phone go unanswered and then Linda Rayburn's voice came over the line. She wasn't home but if the caller would leave a message she could get back to them.

Faye picked up the receiver and listened just as Josie ran out the door.

CHAPTER 32

"*Are you family?*" – *Nurse/Intensive Care*

"*Yes.*" – *Josie*

Hannah wasn't beautiful anymore.

She was swollen, raw, shaved, bruised and broken.

Her face was red and black on one side, her skin shredded where she hit the pavement; microscopic flecks of blacktop were still embedded in her skin. A patch of hair had been shaved from the top of her head to her right temple. A long, ugly line of stitches ran from the edge of her eyebrow into the bald patch. A monstrous bit of machinery had her head locked steady, bolting her into a box that would keep her from moving if she ever woke up. One arm was bandaged from fingertip to shoulder. The other was in a splint. Josie could see the outline of Hannah's legs and breathed a sigh of relief when she counted two. Without her make-up, her piercings, without being able to see those green eyes, Hannah suddenly became what Josie had always argued she was – a hurt child.

Josie touched the sheets that were so tightly tucked around Hannah. Her fingertips quivered. Her arm felt heavy. The memory of the Davis children, dead under pristine white sheets, flashed into Josie's head. She snatched her hand back. Instead of looking under the sheet, Josie leaned forward and touched what was left of Hannah's hair and whispered.

"Hannah, what have you done to yourself? Hannah?"

Hannah didn't answer but someone else asked:

"Who are you?"

A small woman in big green scrubs walked into the room like she owned it. A surgical mask and stethoscope dangled around her neck. She glanced at Josie, grabbed Hannah's chart, spent some time with it, looked at the monitors and finally at Hannah, yet it was clear she was waiting for an answer.

"Josie Baylor-Bates." Josie slid her hand away from Hannah.

"You don't exactly look like a relative? Only relatives are supposed to be in here." The woman in scrubs hung the chart back on the end of the bed.

"I'm her attorney. The cops called my office. I just got the message."

"Attorney, huh?" The woman actually smiled. "Guess in some cases that might qualify as family. You must have got here before he did."

"Who?" Josie looked over her shoulder.

"There's a cop outside," the woman said matter-of-factly. "He's not supposed to let anyone in or out. I told him it's not like this baby is going anywhere any time soon, poor thing. I told him he might as well go home, but he looks like he's digging in."

The woman adjusted the drip tube on Hannah's IV. She looked at a monitor above the bed once more.

"I'm Fran Taglia. I caught her in emergency." Doctor Taglia stepped back, her expression one of compassionate detachment. "She doesn't look like a murderer."

"This one isn't even close," Josie muttered. "Do you know what happened?"

"Not the details, just that it was a car accident. They must have hit her hard." Taglia sighed and crossed her arms. "I'd like to say she's a lucky girl, but I don't think this kid has had a stroke of luck in her life. I was following her trial. I figured you worked things out, because I haven't heard a peep lately."

"We've had a recess. Unfortunately, we'll be back on the front pages when the press gets wind of this. She was supposed to be monitored twenty-four/seven."

"You don't have to worry about that now. We're a twenty-four/seven kind of place."

Doctor Taglia put her hand out and held onto the IV stand like she was leaning on a fence post. From across the hall came the sounds of *Jeopardy*. A muted call bell rang. Dinner trays clanged while they were collected. The scents of alcohol and medicine, bodies long unwashed, salves and creams overwhelmed Josie. Taglia was immune to it all.

"We're going to keep Hannah heavily sedated so she won't move her head," she said. "There's some swelling on the brain. Her neck's bad. There's a hairline crack at the base of her skull and a big one on the right side of her head. We've already been inside to take care of the internal bleeding. She had a ruptured spleen, and a collapsed lung. Taken together it seems overwhelming, but Hannah is young, she's in good shape. She'll get over everything if she wants to." Doctor Taglia straightened up. "I saw her arms. She's a cutter. There's a lot of hurt with cutters. Maybe she'll just lie there and wish herself away."

"No," Josie answered positively, "she won't do that. We've come too far for her to do that."

"Unless she didn't want to go as far as you did," Taglia mused.

"I guess we won't know until she wakes up, will we?" Josie raised her brows.

"Guess not." Doctor Taglia checked her watch. She had better things to do than debate a lawyer. "There's a call button right behind her head. If she moves, ring."

"If anyone calls you it will be me, not her." Linda Rayburn filled the doorway for an instant then stormed into the room. "I want that woman out of here now, and I want to know who let her in. Only family is supposed to be in here and I sure as hell don't count her as family. Now get her out."

"Hey," Doctor Taglia stopped Linda with a word and a hand on her shoulder. "I think you better keep your voice down."

"And you better keep out of my way." Linda ripped Taglia's hand off her shoulder. "I'm Hannah's mother and I want to be alone with my daughter until the doctor who treated her can find some time to come up and talk to me."

Linda tried to push her way past Taglia but the doctor wasn't easily moved. This time she had Linda's arm and she gave it a yank, keeping her tone friendly and concerned.

"Well that's just fine because I'm the doctor in charge. Now let's calm down or that man outside this door will help you into the waiting room so you can cool off."

Doctor Taglia cocked an eyebrow, silenced Linda, and took her hand.

"Good girl. I'm glad you're here. Hannah needs a reason to come back to the land of the living. What she doesn't need is a knock down drag out at her bedside. She's drugged up pretty good but that doesn't mean she can't hear and feel. So, are we on the same page?"

Linda drew herself to her full height and pulled her hand away from Taglia.

"Yes. Now, may I please request that only the family be allowed in this room?"

"Linda," Josie said, "Give me a few minutes. That's all I want."

The look Linda shot Josie was loathsome.

"It's your fault she's hurt, Josie. She was running away. She couldn't take this fighting and bickering any more. She didn't want you to..."

Josie moved away from Hannah's bed, mindful that the sleeping girl might hear her. Instinctively, Linda shadowed Josie.

"Linda I need to know where you were last night before I talk to Rudy Klein and Judge Norris. I need to know, now."

"You're going to lay this on me? That is rich." Josie turned her head away from Linda's venomous whispers. Linda ducked hers to make sure Josie looked at her. "What do you know about being a mother? You never even had one. You don't know about the choices you have to make to protect your kid. Last night I was damned no matter what I did. You don't think this is going to make me feel like shit for the rest of my life?"

A deep fury exploded inside Josie, but she lowered her voice even further so Linda would be the only one to hear what she had to say.

"You were doing what you wanted to do last night; I just don't know where you were doing it. I swear, when I find out where you were I'm going to recommend Norris charge you with contempt and child endangerment. That means jail time, Linda."

"You want to have it both ways, Josie? You want Hannah to be an adult until she screws up, and then you want it to be my fault because I didn't babysit her. Screw you, Josie."

Josie backed off, reading Linda's danger signals. This wasn't going to do Hannah any good.

"Okay, you're right. I'm sorry. It's time for us to be adults and let Hannah be the kid. But when she's better, Norris is going to want her in a monitored place."

"We'll cross that bridge when we come to it." Linda had had enough, but Josie was insistent. As much as it tore at her to see Hannah hurt, Josie was a lawyer and knew that contingency plans had to be made.

"Linda, mistakes have been made on both sides. I apologize for mine, but the fact of the matter is we need to be together on a plan for the court." Josie paused almost convincing herself that leaving Hannah alone was a mistake and not a selfish indulgence. "I want Norris to release Hannah to me instead of putting her through the system. That way you can have access to her and...."

Linda grabbed Josie's arm and spoke through clenched teeth.

"What is wrong with you? My marriage is ruined, Hannah's lying there unconscious, and you're worried about who the judge is going to let her live with? How about just worrying whether or not she is going to live? How about that, Josie?"

"Mrs. Rayburn. Mrs. Rayburn." Doctor Taglia called to Linda as she pried her fingers loose. "Stop now. This isn't doing anyone any good."

Linda blinked, looking at the doctor as if surprised to find her so close.

"She wants my daughter to live with her. How can she ask me to make that kind of decision?" Linda asked quietly, as if Doctor Taglia had the answer.

"You don't have to make any decisions right now," Taglia assured her as she walked Linda to the bed and settled her. Linda seemed as weak as her daughter, the fight gone out of her. When she spoke, it was as if she were only a curious observer in all this.

"Does she hurt? If she's going to die, will she hurt?"

Taglia caught Josie's eye as she put her hand on Linda's shoulder.

"She's not in any pain. I promise we haven't missed anything on your girl. Hang in there for seventy-two hours, okay? I promise she won't die."

"Are you sure? You're really sure?"

Doctor Taglia hesitated. It wasn't the question that was odd, only the way it was asked, as if Linda wanted Taglia to look again.

"Yes, I'm sure," Taglia answered, patting Linda's shoulder. "If Hannah knows you're here everything will be fine. Okay?"

Linda's shoulders were hunched; her head was bent. Doctor Taglia eased away but not quickly enough to miss the next question.

"Did she say anything about me?" Linda whispered.

Josie moved forward, curious to hear the answer.

"Hannah couldn't ask for you, but I know she would want you here," The doctor answered. "Maybe she said something to the people who transported her."

"Who did that?" Linda's eyes were still on her daughter.

"The paramedics? Their names will be on the report. I'll make sure you get it. Right now just stay with your daughter."

Doctor Taglia shrugged and melted away. There were other patients, other people to be cared for. Josie moved to the foot of the bed.

"Linda, I'd like to stay with you."

"Don't talk, Josie. Just go away," Linda muttered.

"Hannah needs both of us now," Josie insisted quietly.

"Go away Josie or I swear, I'll kill you. Linda's voice was dull and dark. It made the threat seem terrifyingly real.

"I care about her, too," Josie breathed, stunned to find out how much truth there was in that, but Linda was unmoved.

Linda's head swiveled toward Josie. Her green eyes were so much like Hannah's and yet so different: harder, worn, and unforgiving.

"I never asked you to care about my daughter. She was your client. That's all, Josie. Hannah was just your client. Now go on. Get out."

Josie opened her mouth and then thought better of speaking. Without another word Josie walked out of the hospital past the uniformed officer and knew Linda was wrong. Hannah didn't belong to either of them now. Rudy Klein had claimed her as a ward of the court.

CHAPTER 33

"Stop," Josie whispered, pushing Archer's hands away.

Archer rolled onto his back amid the tangle of blankets and sheets. Minutes ago they had been a tangle of arms and legs, lips and hands. They tried too hard to find love and found only sex and not very good sex at that.

Now they looked at the ceiling, seeing nothing through the darkness, overly aware of each other's disappointment, disenchantment, and disillusionment. Archer because he could do nothing to help Josie; Josie because she could do nothing to help Hannah.

"It wasn't your fault," he finally said.

"Exactly what isn't my fault, Archer?" Josie asked. "That Hannah ran away, or that she got hurt? Or that there's a guard on her, or that she's going back to jail? Or that Linda and I are in this bizarre tug of war over what's best for her?"

Archer stayed silent, unmoving, knowing the only way to heal her soul was to let her talk.

"Maybe the police are at fault? Her mother? Her father – whoever he is. Her stepfather? Rudy? Maybe it's Hannah's own fault, Archer. I really haven't ruled out that possibility. You know, maybe she's just a murdering, sociopathic kid who thought she knew how to work the system, got caught in the wheels and panicked." Josie turned onto her side, her back to Archer. "Maybe she was running out on me. It has happened before; people leaving me without a word."

Archer's jaw tightened. That was it. He swung his legs over the side of the bed. He loved Josie but he'd heard this song before, this self-pity, this little girl lament. People got over shit. It was her time.

"She wasn't running out on you – she was just running. The weird thing was that she was going north on Pacific Coast Highway. I took pictures when I checked it out."

"Well, aren't you just so damn efficient, Archer? Besides, which side of the road she was on doesn't mean anything. Rudy will argue she was fleeing. You should know that."

"Hey, Jo, I'm not the enemy and this isn't like you."

Archer walked toward the bathroom. In the dark Josie could just see his silhouette: big, filling her bedroom, taking up her space when she wanted to be left alone.

"Oh, Christ," Josie muttered before hollering at him as he started to close the bathroom door. "You don't know a damn thing about me."

Archer threw open the door. His arms held either side of it as if he was trying to restrain himself.

"I know what it's like to have a tough case. I know what it's like when you feel like your client royally screwed you."

"Hannah didn't screw me up. I screwed myself when I started caring about her instead of just working like a lawyer should." Josie sat up fast and reached for her t-shirt. She didn't want to be naked around Archer. She didn't want a shred of intimacy in a life that was feeling so cold and out of control. "You've only known me for a year, Archer. It's all been so good for us. You've never seen me when things aren't good. Now you are. I'm pissed and I'm sad and I'm torn up inside because something happened, and I wasn't there for Hannah. Her mother wasn't there. She's just a kid and she was trying..."

Archer threw up his hands in frustration.

"Jo, stop qualifying this thing. You couldn't have done anything about this. Hannah was bolting God damn it!" He walked toward the bed. He put out his hand and smoothed Josie's hair that had spiked where it rubbed against the pillow. He put his hands on her bare thighs and hunkered down, speaking softly. "I'm sorry she's hurt and I'm sorry she's going back to prison but shit happens, Jo. You can't make the world right, you can only try to make some things okay."

"I only had one case, Archer. I used to juggle ten. If only I had called Hannah once more last night. If I'd sent Linda home right away..." her voice trailed off. "But I didn't, did I?"

"Hannah made her choices. You didn't push her. You can't defend someone who doesn't want to be defended," he pointed out.

"Or someone who is guilty? Is that the next part of your little sermon, Archer?"

"Jo. Please. Don't do this."

Josie pushed his hands away. He retreated but didn't back down.

"Look," he said, "I gave you what I had and we both know what the prosecution's going to do with it. The fight between the Rayburns was about Hannah. It looks like Hannah was running. She admits to being in Rayburn's rooms, she admits hitting him. Call Klein. See if you can work a plea. The DA can't be too happy about the way things are going. It could be in everyone's best interest to make this go away."

"What do you want, Archer? Why are you here? I don't need anyone to tell me to throw in the towel. I already thought about it." Josie dug her hands into the pillow. "But that would make me a quitter, or a fool, because I believed Hannah. Isn't that just the way I want to think of myself, as a loser and a fool."

Archer found his pants and whipped them off the chair. He was an easy-going guy but even he had his limits.

"I'm saying you need to shake it off like a pro. Your job is to make the call, take care of your client."

"I'm going to take care of her. I'm going to defend her."

"You'll lose."

"You haven't even heard the defense. How can you condemn her, and me, at the same time, Archer? You of all people."

"I don't want her to go down for life, Jo, but I don't want you dreaming about that kid for the rest of yours."

Archer pulled his shirt on and sat on the edge of the bed with his shoes in his hands. He turned around so he could look at her. Even in the dark Archer knew that all Josie wore were a t-shirt and a look of despair.

"Once the prosecutor finds the gardener you won't be able to argue self defense. He was clear that Kip was aware his father was afraid of Hannah. The accident investigation shows that Hannah was in Huntington to meet Miggy Estrada, the man she was arrested with last year, the man who broke into Fritz Rayburn's apartments with her. Estrada has disappeared. Nobody is going to believe she's just a poor, sick kid anymore."

Josie raised her head defiantly. "I'm not going to do anything until I talk to Hannah. I want to hear it from her."

"You can't even talk to her! She is unconscious." Archer threw up his hands, exasperation getting the best of him.

"God, Archer, I thought I could count on you. I thought you told me to go for it, to find out what I was made of. Guess we're both finding out what we're made of. You can give up, Archer, but I sure as hell won't."

"Time for us to get on with our lives, Jo." He pulled on his shoes. He was ready to go. "That's all I'm saying. I already lived with one woman who suffered; I don't want to do it again. Cut your losses."

"I'm not throwing Hannah away," Josie insisted. "I'm not abandoning her, and I'm sure as hell not going to pass judgment when she hasn't had her God damn day in court."

"It's going to be worse for her if she does have it." Archer stood up, he towered over her. "You've proved you can get back in and fight, now prove you can do it right."

"That's what I'm doing. There are a million reasons to run. Maybe she was just scared. I'll work my butt off to prove she's innocent until she tells me different. I don't care about Rudy's circumstantial evidence or what somebody told you today. She's hurt, and someone's got to help..."

Josie's voice was lost inside her somewhere. Sentences weren't finished. Tears were lurking. She was a little girl again; fighting to stay strong while her world was falling apart for no reason. When Josie turned her back on him, curled up and left no room for him in her bed, in her life, in this case, Archer did the only thing he could do.

He left.

CHAPTER 34

"Guaranteed to slim your thighs, your butt, your abs in three weeks or double your money…" – Infomercial 2:30am Monday

Josie woke with a start and sent a cascade of papers over the side of the bed as she did. It was less than two full days after Hannah's accident, and less than seven hours until she was due in court to present defense arguments. She'd fallen asleep with her case files spread out over the blanket and the television on. Archer's report was among them. Not that it mattered. What Hannah had done since the fire would not be raised by the defense, what happened before it would be. Archer didn't agree with the strategy; Josie was going it alone. They'd work on what was between them when this was done. She didn't think about missing Archer; she just did.

Josie's neck was crooked on the stack of pillows and her glasses were still perched on her nose. Groaning, she shook her head to clear it and pressed on her neck to work out the knot. She felt the stirrings of a second wind, snapped off the television, and tossed the remote at the foot of the bed. TV may suck, but everything else was looking good. Hannah was stable. There was no permanent spinal damage; the swelling on the brain had been reduced significantly. Her arm would heal. The internal injuries were being monitored. Hannah wouldn't walk out of the hospital tomorrow but she would walk out. In another day or two Josie would be able to talk to her.

Josie rolled off the bed and picked up the mess of papers on the floor, and put them in her briefcase. The bedside light cast a bright circle on the rumpled spread. The rest of the room was gray with middle-of-the-night light. Max slept.

In the bathroom she threw some water on her face, ran her hands through her short, short hair, and mentally checked off the witness list. Doctor Choi, an independent coroner would dispute the prosecution's time of death. There would be exhibits to chart the progress of Hannah's path as she checked her surroundings, mathematical calculations that would prove it impossible for her to light two fires and then hide the matches. Doctor McGrath would spend quality time going over the meticulous behavioral attributes of an obsessive/compulsive. Rosa's testimony would make a big splash. A subpoena had been served on Lyn Chandler. Worried about being disbarred, Lyn would never commit perjury. Doctor Ritchland, an expert on child abuse, would testify that abuse victims seldom attacked, much less killed, their abuser.

Josie flipped off the bathroom light, picked up her briefcase, and shuffled through the bedroom to the hall. Dropping her briefcase by the front door Josie turned to go back to bed, but stopped. Every nerve tingled, sleep was forgotten as she narrowed her eyes and checked out the doors that led to her half finished patio. A butterfly fluttered up in her stomach. Someone was moving out there and they wanted in.

Josie slid into the corner.

Okay.

She was scared.

Okay.

But not that scared.

Slowly, keeping flat to the walls, Josie backed out of the living room just as she heard a muffled crack of glass and the click of the lock. In her bedroom, she eased the dresser drawer open and wrapped her hand around the heavy, cold metal of her father's gun. Stepping away, her eyes toward the bedroom door, Josie released the safety. With both hands on the grip she pointed it out and away as she retraced her steps.

She paused in the shadows. She could feel him in the house. Pulling the gun into her chest, the barrel now pointed up and out, Josie stole a look around the corner. His back was to her as he bent over her dining room table. So casual. So sure of himself.

Josie pulled her head back, laid her body tight against the wall. She closed her eyes, slowed her breathing the way her father showed her – the way a soldier did – and ignored the pounding of her heart. Committing her first impressions to memory – the exact time, the mode of entry, the stance of her intruder – Josie moved out from her corner, planted her feet wide, raised the gun stiff-armed and took aim.

"Stand up slow and make like Christ unless you want your head blown off."

CHAPTER 35

He moved like a dancer, each vertebra rolling into place as he obliged her. His arms floated up and were held out to the side. He wiggled his fingers and rotated his hands to show his palms. Nothing up his sleeve. He shook out one foot and then the other. A real funny guy but Josie wasn't laughing.

She took long measured steps toward him and short cautious ones to maneuver around the broken glass and the open door. She closed it with her foot. He was a good boy and didn't move. Her back was to the wall, the hula girl plates were above her and beneath those plates was the dimmer switch for the lights. Josie turned it on high. The man at her table closed his eyes and turned his head against the sudden brilliance. Josie squinted but didn't look away.

He was young, black, and well fed but skinnier than she first thought. From the back, all she had seen was his big jacket and baggy pants; the pant hems were frayed from dragging on the ground, the jacket was army surplus, not service issue. He wore a heavy sweater that was striped in dark colors. There was a diamond in his ear. His skin was smooth, his nose small, and his eyes glittered with amusement. He sported a small goatee and an impressive mass of dreadlocks that cascaded over his shoulders and dangled over his brow.

"Hold up, mama." A gold tooth glinted as he smiled, trying to appease her. "I ain't gonna hurt one hair on your head, and I sure as hell don't want none of my hairs to be hurt neither."

"No problem. Nobody will get hurt because we're just going to wait right here until the police come." Josie reached for the phone on the kitchen counter and lifted the receiver.

"Aw, you didn't do that, baby." He started to lower his arms but Josie notched the muzzle up an inch. "Come on, mama. I'm gonna drop 'em right here. Right here, okay?" He lowered his arms inch by inch, testing her. The barrel of the gun kept pace.

"Keep them where I can see them," Josie warned.

"Call the man and I don' tell you what I got for you," he warned, agitated now. Cautiously he picked up a spiral bound book that lay on the table and held it close. "You want to help Hannah, then you be smart about the cops."

Josie's heart skipped at Hannah's name. The hand with the receiver quivered. She narrowed her eyes, trying to read this man, trying to find that edge in her gut that would give her a heads up to be cautious. It wasn't there.

"One time offer, baby. For Hannah," the man sing-songed.

Slowly Josie put the receiver back in its cradle, never taking her eyes off him. The gun was getting heavy. She held it with both hands and waved him toward the hall. Josie opened the door to the closet.

"Get in," she said.

"What? You crazy? I won' be going in there," he cried backing up and waving his hands.

"Yes, you will. Now get in until I let you out."

Complaining, muttering, the man walked past her and into the hall closet. He crossed his arms over his chest. Josie held the gun at the ready.

"What's your name?" she asked.

"Miggy," he answered.

Josie nodded, shut the door and braced it with a chair. Miggy Estrada. *How about that?* Josie headed for the kitchen and the phone once more. She dialed fast. One ring and it was answered. Josie leaned on the counter and said:

"Archer. I need you."

~

"'Bout time. You better be believin' you're gonna be sorry for treatin' me so bad."

"I've heard it before you little piece of shit." Archer took him by the arm and sat him down at the dining room table. Josie settled herself at the other end, and Archer took the chair next to her.

"Oh, big man. Big old man," Miggy shot back.

"Big enough," Archer said smoothly. "Now, where've you been? What do you want? And why'd you have to break in here to get it?"

"I be at another club, man. I didn' know you was lookin' and I didn' know Hannah was hurt 'till this mornin', man. And even if I knowed you was lookin', you think I'm stupid enough to come straight to you? All that'd get me is time, man. I know 'bout court. I know 'bout lawyers."

"Yeah? Like what do you know?" Josie asked.

"Like if I tol' you I've been with Hannah, I tol' you I been at the big house before the fire, you be pointin' at me and sayin' I done the crime. I like Hannah, I don' like her 'nough to go to the big house for. Unh-huh, mama."

"I don't work that way," Josie answered knowing any number of lawyers would lay blame on someone like him just to get their client acquitted. "Look, I just want to know what you've got. I want to know why Hannah was willing to risk going to jail just to see you. Are you lovers?"

Miggy snorted and smiled, his gold tooth showing, "I don' go with babies. She's a beauty, but a baby. Hannah just need me to talk to. She don' think about jail. She just scared. You was gone, her mama was gone. Her mama's man come into the house and scare her, so she run to me."

"Kip Rayburn was at the Malibu house with Hannah?" Josie asked.

Miggy's head went up and down solemnly, his locks bouncing like springs.

"He tol' her she was a lunatic, man. He kicked her. He made her afraid. So when she saw him drive away, and her mama go with her man, Hannah got scared and come to me. It's always safe with me. I don' want nothin' from her and she can talk."

"Were you going to take her to Mexico?"

Miggy shook his head.

"Naw, that don' work. Hannah and me tried before but she couldn' do it. Couldn' leave her mama. Hannah love her mama too much." He looked from Josie to Archer, his long lashed eyes looked pained. "She hurt bad? I'd hate it if Hannah is hurt bad."

"She'll be okay," Josie assured him and left it at that. The minutes were ticking by. "But it's going to be bad for her if she has to go to jail, Miggy. If you've got something for her, if you can help, then I need to know right now."

"Hannah brought this. She says anything happen to her, she wants the book safe."

Miggy pulled the spiral bound book from inside his jacket. For a split second he held it and then, with a flick of his wrist, he sent it sliding toward Josie. Archer intercepted it. He put it between the two of them. Josie flipped open the cover. Here was Hannah's soul, and the talent Linda had sold for five hundred dollars.

Sketches. Watercolors. Ink and pencil.

Her own burned hand. Red watercolor and ink. The fingers were elongated and the injury magnified. The work spared the viewer nothing.

Ruins of the house painted in pastel; Fritz Rayburn's face exquisitely etched into the strokes that formed the remains. Archer saw it and traced the outline until Josie saw it too.

Josie turned the page. Here was the sucker punch. The dark haired woman was running away from the girl and the burning house was in the background. This was a picture of Linda turning her back in horror. Hannah was left behind.

"That girl's got it goin' on and she don' know it," Miggy said sadly.

Josie shut the sketchbook.

"She's talented, Miggy, but this isn't evidence. You didn't need to break in to give me this. It won't help Hannah."

"Wasn't the pictures I wanted to give you," Miggy laughed. He got up again and took the book away from Archer. This time Miggy opened it to the back pages. "Was the writing. Here."

He pointed to a garden of scribbles. Bubble printing that spelled her name. The word mom in all its incarnations. Bits and pieces of sentences. Broken hearts sketched and snakes wound 'round columns of words. Josie held it away so she could read without her glasses. Poetry.

"Listen to this," Josie murmured.

Cut off from help
In my heart, my head
Cut down to the quick
By the person I loved
Now dread
So loyal, loving
Deep in trust
Given away for lust and lust and lust

"She didn't exactly feel like part of the family, did she?" Archer noted and pointed to another note. "It's dated July 31. 'Which Will He Choose'. She knew Fritz wanted Kip to divorce Linda."

Josie lifted her eyes.

"Did Hannah know that Kip might divorce her mother, Miggy?"

"For sure. Thought it was all her fault. Hannah thought every bad thing ever happen was her fault."

Josie crossed her arms, "Archer, that's what she meant. The divorce, the problems between Kip and Fritz. She thought they were all her fault for just existing. The fire was just another bit of bad luck."

"Rudy will say Hannah was trying to protect her mother by killing Rayburn," Archer pointed out.

Josie buried her face in her hands. When she dropped them, she talked to the table.

"I need something real."

"I got somethin' more," Miggy dug in his pocket and handed Josie a piece of paper. "I was gonna be leavin' that. That's what you need to know."

Josie read the note then shook her head as she looked quizzically at Miggy. "Ask who was in the bedroom? Do you mean Fritz's bedroom?"

"Naw," Miggy whispered dramatically. "Her mama's bedroom. You know how Hannah's always touchin' and checkin' everything in the whole wide world?"

"Yeah," Archer said.

"So, man, she checks everythin' important but nobody ask what's most important of all?" Miggy leaned back in his chair and grinned, that gold tooth glinting. He held up a hand in a papal gesture. "Her mama's most important. She look in on her mama every night. Las' thing. Anybody ask what Hannah seen when she checked in that room the night the old judge died?

"Well, did you?"

CHAPTER 36

"Hannah? Hannah? Was Kip in bed when you checked on your mother the night of the fire? Hannah? Can you wake up enough to tell me about Kip?" – Josie Baylor-Bates Long Beach Memorial Hospital, 6:15 AM

"Ask her..." – Hannah Sheraton, Long Beach Memorial Hospital, 6:16 AM

"Ms. Bates, you've kept this court waiting."

"I'm sorry, Your Honor." Josie pushed through the bar. The jury wasn't seated but the press was ready. Judge Norris wasn't peeved, just curious.

"Do you want to offer the court an excuse?" he asked.

"No, Your Honor, only an apology."

Josie put her briefcase on the defense table then stood at ease behind it. Norris was bouncing slightly in his chair, thinking. He sat up slowly and put his elbows on top of the desk. A moment later he raised one hand and crooked his finger. Josie stepped around the table. Norris's eyes flickered toward the prosecutor.

"You, too, Mr. Klein, if you like."

Rudy joined Josie. Together they looked up and leaned forward. Norris covered the microphone.

"Your client, Ms. Bates, how is she?" Judge Norris asked.

"Still sedated, but healing. They expect to transfer her to the prison ward in another week, perhaps sooner."

Norris nodded solemnly. "You understand that I can't allow another delay?"

"Yes, Your Honor. I'm ready to move forward," Josie answered.

"Mr. Klein?"

"The people are ready, Your Honor."

Judge Norris motioned them back. Rudy glanced at Josie. She walked past him. Both stood while the jury filed into the box then took their chairs when Judge Norris called the court to order. For the record, he reminded them of the matter at hand and then he was ready.

"Ms. Bates."

Josie stood. Her fingertips rested lightly on the table. There were pages of notes for each doctor she had meant to call, doctors whose testimony would seem almost inconsequential if her gamble paid off. She moved those notes to the side and looked instead at the ones she had frantically scribbled after seeing Hannah, ideas that she had relayed to Archer who, in turn, was searching for corroboration of the information Miggy had given them. In this minute, as the courtroom waited, Josie agonized about her choice: build the case, or go for the jugular. Finally she looked at Norris. It would be the jugular.

"The defense would like to call Linda Rayburn to the stand."

Josie turned around and watched the old Linda walk down the aisle. If she was surprised to be called she didn't show it. She was a woman above the fray, a lady who wore her money well. Her dark hair was pulled into a low chignon once again. On her ears were moons of Mabe pearls. Her make-up was exquisite, her suit worth more than the jurors made collectively in a month. Gone was the pretense that she was just a regular mom standing by her wronged daughter. From the set of her shoulders, to the look in her eye, Linda wanted everyone in that courtroom to know that she was a Rayburn. No one would compromise her or her family – especially Josie.

Linda took the oath. Josie waited. She could feel her heart in her chest. She could hear every beat. She was afraid that what she was about to do was motivated not by the quest for justice, but by her hatred of Linda who had committed a heinous crime against her daughter by leaving her. If that's what she was about, then Josie knew this would be the last time she stood as an officer of the court. Taking a deep breath, she put the question of her personal intent out of her mind. She would look into her heart later; decide what her own truth was later. Now the yellow legal pad was in her hands. The notes were there to guide her, but they had been hastily written before dawn and they were inadequate in the face of Hannah's directive.

Ask her.

Question: Was your husband in bed with you the night of the fire that killed Fritz Rayburn?

It was a good question but one that would do no good without a properly laid foundation. That was the way the law worked. A trial was a building. Josie had blocks, Rudy had blocks and the jury was watching each of them build their case like a house. Rudy's foundation was built on opportunity, forensic evidence; Josie's would be built on emotions, motives, and the consequences of personal failure. The stronger foundation would win the day.

Leaving her notes behind, Josie walked toward the jury, turned and presented herself to Linda. Before Josie could begin, the door in the back of the courtroom opened. Everyone looked; only Josie knew enough to be relieved. She asked the court's indulgence.

"A minute, if it please the court."

With a flutter of his fingertips Judge Norris gave his permission for her to talk to Archer. Archer looked Josie in the eye. His were as she expected: a level playing field. She could only imagine what he saw in hers. He handed her a manila envelope. Nothing more passed between them. Archer took a front row seat. Josie pulled out the contents. She read quickly, digesting the information, understanding instantly that Archer had brought her the concrete she needed to convince the jury her foundation was strong.

"Ms. Bates?"

"I'm sorry, Your Honor," Josie mumbled and looked up.

It was Norris who had called but Linda who caught her attention. In that moment Josie was blessed with the gift of absolute clarity. She and Linda were not friends and never had been. They had lived together as girls, parting just on the verge of womanhood. What Josie had found amusing, exciting and exotic as a girl, she now recognized as nothing more than the underpinnings of Linda's selfishness, arrogance and greed. Linda had burst into Josie's life again, and pulled her into this rollercoaster of a ride. She had been stronger then Josie that night. Now Josie had stepped out of the car and onto the platform. She could see the trajectory of that rollercoaster and knew where it had to stop. With the information Archer had brought, it would roll right up to Kip Rayburn's doorstep.

"Mrs. Rayburn," Josie began. "What kind of relationship do you have with the defendant?"

"Hannah is my daughter," Linda answered.

"Would you describe your relationship as close?"

"Extremely. Hannah and I have been through a lot together."

"Mrs. Rayburn, were you married to Hannah's father?" Josie asked.

"No, I was not. Last I heard that wasn't a crime."

Josie ignored the editorial.

"So you raised Hannah without family support? No grandmother? No siblings?"

"No. No one."

"Do you believe you were successful as a single mother?"

"I think I did a good job. We never went hungry. We were always clothed. There was always a roof over our heads."

"Did you and Hannah live alone?" Josie's expression remained neutral but Linda caught wind of something. Perhaps it was just a slight flicker of Josie's eyes narrowing, perhaps it was the way Josie rushed the question, eager to get to the answer that set her off. Whatever it was, Linda was on her guard.

"Sometimes we lived alone," Linda answered cautiously.

"When you didn't live alone, who were you living with?"

"I dated while I was single. Some relationships were more serious than others."

"How many serious relationships resulted in new homes for you and your daughter? The daughter you were so devoted to." Josie asked.

"Objection, Your Honor," Rudy called. "Ms. Bates' attitude is judgmental and she is trying to influence the jury."

"Mrs. Rayburn may answer the question, but let's not communicate personal views by word or tone, Ms. Bates." Judge Norris nodded toward Linda directing her to answer.

"I don't know exactly how many serious relationships I had," Linda answered tightly.

"Two?" Josie suggested.

"More than two, I suppose. I was single quite a long time."

"More than five?" Josie gave her another option.

"There were a few," Linda snapped. "Some were personal relationships; others were just people who became roommates."

"How many female roommates did you have?"

Linda hesitated. That lip was disappearing under her top teeth. It was a gesture that made her appear thoughtful. The spark in her eyes made her seem dangerous. To her credit, Linda kept herself in check when she answered.

"None were women. I found men more suitable roommates. They were more reliable. You could always count on them for – friendship. Men know the meaning of that word, unlike some women I know." Linda leaned forward slightly. "But if you're trying to imply that I slept around, I resent the implication. I would like to point out it has nothing to do with the matter at hand."

Judge Norris listened. Rudy did not object. They were as curious as everyone else where Josie was headed.

"I'm trying to determine how often you and Hannah moved between the time Hannah was born, and your marriage to Kip Rayburn," Josie assured her casually. "I'd like to know how many places you lived in those fourteen years."

"I don't remember. I moved for better jobs, for opportunities. I moved sometimes because I was seeing someone special. I was looking for a safe place for Hannah and me to live and a good man to settle down with. It took me awhile to find that."

"How many times did you move, Mrs. Rayburn?" Josie pressed, unwilling to be led down another path.

"I don't remember," Linda barked.

"I just want to be clear," Josie suggested, unfazed by Linda's tone. "Each time you moved you were looking for the best situation for both yourself and your daughter, is that correct?"

"Yes, that's right." Linda relaxed.

"And no one was acceptable until you met Kip Rayburn, is that correct?"

"I wouldn't say acceptable. I didn't fall in love until I met Kip," Linda explained. "That's the point, isn't it? Love."

"Yes, Mrs. Rayburn. That is exactly the point," Josie agreed quietly. A heartbeat later Josie was on track. "Did the fact that Kip Rayburn was very rich, that he lived in a very big house, that he had a prominent name influence your decision to fall in love?"

"I didn't decide to fall in love. It happened and, yes, I was glad he was stable and financially secure."

"So you married Kip Rayburn for love and because he could provide you and your daughter with a good home?" Josie asked.

"Yes, that's right."

"And concern for your daughter's future was a large part of your decision, is that correct?" Josie prodded.

"Yes, of course," Linda answered.

"So you chose a man who testified in this court that he took no interest in Hannah. Who, in fact, had washed his hands of her?"

"Objection, Your Honor," Rudy called. "Mr. Rayburn's testimony is part of the record, and I believe it is qualified by the fact that he regrets that he took little interest in the defendant."

"Sustained. If you have a question, Ms. Bates, ask it or move on," Judge Norris directed.

Josie walked a few steps toward Linda. Her chin was down; her eyes were on the ground. When she stopped, Josie raised her head and looked toward the jury box, but at no one in particular.

"Mrs. Rayburn, was there ever a time you considered yourself a bad mother?"

The only sounds heard in the courtroom were the staccato touch of the court reporter typing and the incredulous laugh that came from the witness stand.

Josie let her eyes slide past Linda toward Judge Norris.

"Your Honor, I would like this witness to be considered hostile to the defense. I do not believe she has my client's best interests in mind despite the fact she is the defendant's mother."

"How dare you," Linda breathed.

"So directed," Norris responded.

With that Josie gave her full attention to Linda Rayburn. The gloves were off.

"Isn't it true, Mrs. Rayburn, that you have not been the perfect mother?"

"At least I am a mother, Ms. Bates. I don't have to steal someone else's child to feel like a woman," Linda answered coldly.

Josie's jaw tightened, her chin jerked slightly as if she'd taken a well-landed blow. Not that it mattered. She was still standing and would be at the end of this.

"Your Honor, direct the witness–"

"All right." Linda gave in quickly. "No, I'm not the perfect mother. I don't think anyone is the perfect parent or the perfect person. We all do what we can to get by – including you."

"Mrs. Rayburn, isn't it true that you often based your selection of gentlemen friends on their ability to take care of you financially, as opposed to a decision based on their character?"

"No, that is not true. I was not kept."

Josie opened the envelope and pulled out a sheet of paper.

"In the last sixteen years your IRS returns show ten different residences. Of those residences, you have lived with Kip Rayburn for two years. That leaves nine residences since your daughter was born. By tracking those addresses we find that, of those nine, your name only appeared on two leases. Do you remember whose names were on either the leases or mortgages of those remaining seven residences?"

"Not all of them, no," Linda answered, touching those big, expensive earrings. Her neck muscles corded. She chanced a glance at the jury. Josie didn't bother. She knew exactly how interested they were.

"Let me refresh your memory, Mrs. Rayburn. Dan Burdon of New York. An investment banker. Steve Witsick, New Jersey. A gentleman who seems to have a rather large income from a trust fund, as well as two convictions for assault on women. How about Dominic Cort–"

Linda interrupted. She lifted her chin.

"Yes, I remember them."

"All of them, Mrs. Rayburn?"

"Yes," she answered coldly, "all of them. Do you want me to list them? Do you want me to give you a list of all the men I slept with even if I didn't live with them? If that is what it is going to take to help my daughter, then I will do that."

"Your Honor." Rudy raised his hand. "Counsel is badgering the witness."

"Overruled," Norris intoned. "The witness will confine her remarks to answering the question."

Josie's lips twitched. She was pleased that the judge saw it her way, but she took no pleasure in doing what she had to do.

"Then, when you took the important step of moving in with these men, you believed those relationships would lead to a stable home for your daughter, Hannah?"

"No. I mean, yes. I…"

Linda's fingers went to her throat before trailing down the open neck of her blouse. To her credit, her voice was controlled and unapologetic when she spoke again. Linda was good under pressure and she had figured out where this was going.

"I am not a saint, Ms. Bates, and I'm not the best judge of character. I've often asked my daughter's forgiveness for making choices that weren't appropriate. I was young and stupid. That's not a crime. None of that is a crime."

Josie stepped forward crossed her arms on the wooden railing that separated her from Linda. She could smell Linda's perfume, and see the outline of her lipstick, and the shine of her gloss. Josie studied her face then looked her in the eye. Linda had finally made the wrong move.

"How about abandonment, Mrs. Rayburn?" Josie asked clearly. "Would you consider abandonment a crime?"

"I imagine it would depend on whom one was abandoning," Linda answered carefully.

Pushing away, Josie pulled another sheet of paper out of the envelope. She walked a half circle in front of the witness stand.

"Your daughter, Hannah, for instance." Josie looked up from her papers. She inclined her head like a relative concerned for Linda's health. "Would you consider it a crime to abandon a nine year old girl for, say, three days?"

Linda blanched. She turned her head toward the bench. There was no help from the judge. The jury strained to see, but could not. Linda offered her profile to Josie. Her expression was one of pure, controlled hatred. Josie let the question hang, and it was Rudy who broke the silence. His timing was off; his objection lacked the right level of passion to be effective.

"Assumes facts not in evidence."

"Sustained," Norris directed solemnly.

Josie held a sheet of paper toward the bench. The judge took it, looked at it and handed it to the clerk.

"Your Honor," she said. "I would like to submit a report from the Chicago Police Department as defense exhibit twenty-two. Mrs. Rayburn, were you arrested in July of nineteen ninety-four for abandoning your daughter in a hotel room in downtown Chicago?"

Linda was still as a statue, pale as a ghost.

"Mrs. Rayburn," Josie demanded, "did you pay a fine and did you serve four months in jail beginning in July of nineteen ninety-four because you were convicted of abandoning your daughter, Hannah Sheraton, and endangering her life by leaving her with no money, food or supervision?"

Slowly Linda swung her head back to Josie. The two women stared at one another.

"Yes," Linda said evenly. "All that is true."

"And where had you been, Mrs. Rayburn?"

"I was..." Linda hesitated. A lie was in the making. Josie could see it.

"What, Mrs. Rayburn?" Josie pressed, moving one step closer, daring Linda to tell it. "What could possibly have kept you from returning to your daughter? It must have been something dire. An emergency? A matter of life and death? What was it, Mrs. Rayburn, that kept you from this daughter you loved so much?"

"I had been with a friend and lost track..."

Linda hung her head. If it had been anyone else, if it had been any other circumstance, Josie would have backed off. But this was Hannah's life that hung in the balance and the woman who held the key to exoneration had never once told the whole truth in her life.

"Lost track of what, Mrs. Rayburn? Time? You actually forgot about your nine year old daughter because you were…"

"I was partying," Linda growled defiantly. Her shoulders were squared. She raised her voice and threw her head back. She would not be cowed by this proceeding or shamed by Josie. Josie, whom she hated for making Hannah believe in fairytales. "I partied a lot back then. I'm not proud of it. I was very young when I had Hannah, and it took me a long time to grow up. In some ways she grew up faster than I did. Are you satisfied?"

"I simply want to be clear, Mrs. Rayburn. You lived with a variety of men. At one time you abandoned your daughter and were arrested for endangering–"

"Your Honor, Mrs. Rayburn's past is her past. She is not on trial here."

"Ms. Bates, enough. Move on with this witness."

Norris was peeved, Rudy confused, and Linda raging, but Josie was going to do this by the numbers because the only people that counted were in the jury box.

"Your Honor, Mrs. Rayburn's past behavior goes to establishing a pattern regarding how Mrs. Rayburn's parenting habits affected the defendant's attempt to control her environment," Josie argued.

"Then make it clear where you're going, Ms. Bates, or drop this line of questioning."

"Thank you, Judge." Josie discarded the manila envelope and went back to Linda. "Let's talk about Hannah growing up. Did she ever complain about your lifestyle? Moving often, changing schools?"

"No. She never did," Linda replied.

"Did you ever ask her if she minded moving?"

"The subject never came up. Hannah was a good girl. She is still a good girl."

"Did Hannah exhibit any displeasure or anxiety over the way you were living?"

"You mean like give me trouble? Run away? Things like that?"

"Yes, exactly," Josie answered.

Linda shook her head, and the pearl earrings looked too heavy now.

"No. She never did anything to cause trouble. She always came right home from school. Always did things around the house. She was hardly ever gone."

"Would you say she seemed obsessed with being home? Or at least obsessed with being in a place that was familiar because of your frequent moves?"

Linda hesitated, "She stayed very close to home. She sometimes became insistent that I stay close to home."

"Was it about the time of your abandonment that Hannah started exhibiting the symptoms of her obsessive/compulsive disorder?"

"Yes," Linda answered quietly. "She started counting then."

"Did she do anything else?"

"She began to touch things, especially in the house. Doorways. Windows."

"Hannah was particularly attentive to ways to get out of whatever place you were living in, is that correct?" Josie asked.

"Yes," Linda answered.

"And was it about that time that Hannah started checking on other things."

"Yes," Linda answered, clearly relieved that the spotlight had turned to Hannah. "She would often check the locks on the doors before she went to sleep. Sometimes she would check on toys, or clothes in the closet."

"Would she follow the same path every night?"

"Yes."

"No matter where you were living?"

"It didn't matter if we were in a hotel room."

"Would it ever change?"

"Only in terms of how long it took her," Linda said, cooperating, anxious to have this done. "It all depended on how big the house or apartment was."

"And where was the last place Hannah checked every night before she could sleep?"

"I don't know what you mean? I mean the last place she checked was the last place," Linda said, exasperated.

"Isn't it true, Mrs. Rayburn, that the last place Hannah checks every night is wherever you are sleeping? Isn't it true that Hannah cannot go to sleep unless she is sure that you are in bed and asleep first?"

Josie walked slowly toward her. Linda's worst nightmare was unfolding under the glaring lights of the court. Josie could feel people investing in it, understanding it, waiting for Josie to ask that final question that would change the course of this trial barely moments after the defense had begun its case.

"Isn't it true, Mrs. Rayburn, that Hannah would look into your room four, five, sometimes six times a night to make sure you were there? To make sure that she hadn't been abandoned once again?"

Josie was one step closer to Linda then two. With the third she stopped and Linda still remained quiet. Josie raised her voice.

"Isn't it true, Mrs. Rayburn, that Hannah checked the room you shared with your husband, Kip, on the night of the fire that killed Justice Rayburn?"

Josie had Linda now. Norris stopped bouncing in his chair. Rudy had leaned forward and crossed his arms on the table.

"Mrs. Rayburn," Josie demanded. "Did Fritz Rayburn threaten to ruin your husband professionally if he did not divorce you?"

"Oh, my God," Linda breathed, her fingers shaking as they covered her mouth.

"Is it, or isn't it true, Mrs. Rayburn?" Josie turned toward the bench. "Your Honor, direct the witness to answer the question."

"Objection, Your Honor. Hearsay. Mrs. Rayburn could not have first hand knowledge of what was between her husband and his father."

"That's not true, Your Honor," Josie said quickly. "Hannah knew about the ultimatum. I would like to mark her journal as exhibit twenty-three. You'll see that it indicates that she knew there was every possibility her mother and Kip Rayburn might divorce. If my client knew of this arrangement, then it can be concluded that Mrs. Rayburn also knew."

"I'll allow this line of questioning." The judge waved her on. Josie ran for the finish line.

"Did you know about that threat, Mrs. Rayburn?"

"Yes, I did," Linda answered.

"And do you know what your husband's decision was regarding this ultimatum?"

"He would never divorce me," Linda whispered. "Never."

"So Kip Rayburn was willing to lose his inheritance, willing to endure the public humiliation his father was going to visit on him, all for you?"

"Fritz never would have followed through. He loved Kip."

"He loved him so much he locked him in closets and he almost cut his finger off. Fritz Rayburn loved his son so much that he enjoyed threatening him and controlling him even as an adult. Fritz cared so much about his son that he wanted him to destroy the only thing he held dear – his marriage?"

"Fritz played games. That was all. He never would have done it," Linda insisted.

"And you were sure of that, Mrs. Rayburn?"

"Yes."

"Was your husband sure of that, Mrs. Rayburn? Was Kip Rayburn positive that his father was going to back away from that threat, or was Kip Rayburn driven to find a way to stop his father, Fritz Rayburn, from destroying his life?"

Linda hesitated. She looked at the judge. Her eyes shifted to Rudy then darted frantically to the spectators, looking for someone who would save her from this. That hand was back at her throat only this time the gesture was not alluring. Her nails scratched a long red welt down her neck before she realized what she was doing.

"Objection, Your Honor. Calls for a conclusion. If Ms. Bates wants to know what Mr. Rayburn thought–"

"Withdrawn. Withdrawn." Josie waved her hands as if she could erase that question. She closed the gap between her and Linda.

"Mrs. Rayburn, do you know if Hannah looked into your room the night of the fire? Less than 48 hours after your husband had words with his father regarding your marital status. After your husband violently attacked his father by throwing a heavy vase at Justice Rayburn. Did your daughter check your bedroom that night?"

"Yes, she did." Linda's voice quavered.

"And was your husband in bed with you, Mrs. Rayburn?"

The silence was full to bursting as the two women looked at one another.

"Mrs. Rayburn, your husband was angry with his father. Your husband testified that he had a heated argument with his father and had thrown a heavy object at him. Mrs. Rayburn, was your husband in bed with you when the fire started?"

Linda leaned forward. Her voice was low, her words for Josie only. Her eyes were full of fearful tears and her lips trembled.

"Don't go there, Josie," she begged.

"Answer the question, please. When Hannah did her nightly rounds and looked into your bedroom to make sure you had not abandoned her, did she see both you and your husband in bed?"

"I'm begging you," Linda whispered, but her voice was harsh. There was no pleading only a warning. "Don't do this."

Josie put her hands on the wooden railing that surrounded Linda.

"Is your husband more important than your child, Mrs. Rayburn, the same way every man you've ever been with has been more important than your child?"

"Argumentative, Your Honor," Rudy called.

"She is a hostile witness, Judge," Josie shot back, her eyes never leaving Linda's. "She is hostile to this court, and to her child, and to anyone who might stand in the way of Linda Rayburn getting – and keeping – exactly what she wants."

"Ms. Bates, ask the question," Norris snapped.

"I have, Your Honor and I will keep asking it until I get an answer."

"Don't bother. I'll do it." Judge Norris took the matter out of Josie's hands.

"No," Josie roared. "She is my witness."

"Ms. Bates!" Norris was equally adamant. "Step back."

Reluctantly, Josie did as she was told.

"Mrs. Rayburn, was your husband in bed with you the night the fire started? If you do not answer, or you do not answer truthfully, I will hold you in contempt of court and you will go to jail. Now, was he, or was he not, with you?"

The courtroom itself seemed alive. The collective breath of all those present was held so that it seemed the walls heaved in anticipation.

"No." Linda choked on the word. Her head fell back, and her long and beautiful neck arched toward the ceiling as she gave up, gave in and told the court what it needed to know.

"Did he go to bed with you?" Josie took over the questioning once more.

"No," Linda admitted.

"Did he ever come to bed that evening?"

"No."

"How do you know that?"

"I know because I was awake. I was waiting. He was upset that night."

"With his father?"

"Yes, with his father," Linda shot back. "Because his father had treated me badly in front of our guests."

"Mrs. Rayburn, were you worried that your husband would give in and save his inheritance by divorcing you?"

Linda shook her head, "Never. Never. If my husband was going to do that he would already have filed the papers."

"So he was willing to give up his relationship with his father, his father's partnership interest in the firm, and everything else to stay with you?"

"I didn't say that," Linda answered coldly. "He said he would work it out."

"And exactly how was he going to work that out, Mrs. Rayburn?" Josie demanded. "How was he going to do that?"

"He wasn't going to do it by killing his father, if that's what you're implying."

Linda's shoulders began to shake. It was just a small tremor at first but Josie was close enough to see it begin. This was not a manifestation of anger but of something else entirely: Linda Rayburn was breaking down. The pressure of having to choose between truth and a lie was bringing her to the breaking point. When she turned back to Josie, her shoulders had slumped in defeat, her face was pale, those green eyes that turned up so exotically were seeing the future, and it wasn't pretty, or safe, or filled with promise.

"Then tell this court, do you know where he was when the fire started?"

"No, I do not."

"Mrs. Rayburn," Josie began.

"Josie, please. Don't ask any more," Linda begged. "Kip didn't do anything. I swear he didn't."

Josie refused to listen. She was overwhelmed by outrage on behalf of Hannah, the girl who had always paid the price for Linda's cowardice and greed, the daughter who protected her mother at every turn, only to take second place to the men in Linda's life. Josie's fist hit the railing, underscoring her next words.

"Do you know where your husband was, Mrs. Rayburn?"

"No, I don't. I imagine he was sleeping in the guestroom. He did that when…"

Josie twirled away and took two strides toward the jury box. Every eye was on her, and every mind was following her lead.

"Maybe we should all imagine. Maybe we should imagine that your husband was at the west wing of your home fighting with his father. Maybe we should imagine that in his rage he pushed his father and the old man fell and hit his head." Josie whirled back toward Linda but went no closer. "Maybe we could imagine that it was Kip Rayburn spilling turpentine on the floor and lighting a match so that he could protect his interest in Fritz

Rayburn's law firm and remain married to you. Maybe we should imagine that!"

Rudy was on his feet hollering. "Ms. Bates is making up a story. This is not evidence. This is fiction and conjecture."

"This is a witness hostile to the defense, Judge." Josie stormed toward the bench, putting her hands on top of it as if she could force Judge Norris to validate her questioning. "You designated her hostile and her refusal to..."

"No. No," Linda cried. Nearly hysterical, she grasped the wooden railing, shaking it as if she might escape by tearing it down. "No. Don't even say that. Kip didn't set that fire. He didn't hurt his father. He couldn't–"

"He couldn't what, Linda?"

Josie whipped around. She could feel the fire in her cheeks, she was caught up in the fight for Hannah, and she would not lose. Josie was feverish with the infectious sense of victory. This time she would win. She would save the right person.

"Why not? Is it any more outrageous than imagining Hannah, that poor, confused girl could have set that fire? That girl who was so terrified of losing you, and her home, that she checked on you every night? Why is that any more reasonable?"

"Because it's just not right. It's not right."

Linda's bristled with anger, but behind her eyes there was true pain. If Josie had not been caught up, if the end of her quest had not seemed so near, she might have been touched by that pain and loosened the tension on the lasso that was her questions. But the momentum was too great. She walked. She pointed. She raised her voice, and with her height she swooped toward the witness stand and tightened the rope around Linda, choking the answer out of her.

"Why couldn't he have done it? Why isn't it right to ask that question? He wasn't there with you in bed. He did not come to the scene of the fire until it was put down. He didn't call for help, you did. You gave him time to get away. You were protecting him all this time weren't you, Mrs. Rayburn? Protecting your husband over your own child. Isn't that the case, Mrs. Rayburn?"

Josie's voice rose to a sharp note that cut through the tension in the courtroom and divided the onlookers into those who couldn't wait to hear the truth, and those who were afraid to. With gargantuan effort Josie pulled back. Her voice dropped. She was exhausted. Her hands fell to her sides and she pulled herself to her full height.

"He wasn't in the bedroom when Hannah checked your room. He hadn't come to bed that night. He was fighting with his father over matters that concerned his life, and yours. There is no reason your husband couldn't have set that fire, is there, Mrs. Rayburn?" Josie took a few steps forward. "Is there, Linda?"

Linda was crying hard. Mascara seeped around the corners of her eyes. The small scar at the side of her mouth looked ugly and raw; Linda looked old and tired.

"Yes, yes there is," Linda whispered.

"Then tell us," Josie asked. "Give us one good reason not to imagine Kip Rayburn setting the fire that killed his father."

Linda raised her head slowly. She no longer cared how she looked, or whom she spoke to. She had made her decision.

"He couldn't have done it because I saw who did."

Each word was hyphenated with a sobbing breath. Josie pulled away, as stunned as anyone in the courtroom. She turned to the bench but there was nothing to say, no objection she could make. Linda was confessing to the last thing Josie wanted to hear.

"I don't know where Kip was. He wasn't even in the house. It was Hannah. I saw Hannah do it."

"What?" Josie gasped.

She looked for the lie in Linda's face but couldn't find it. All she saw was Linda's struggle, her pain, her choice. Linda was choosing to give Hannah up.

"Mrs. Rayburn, do you know what you're saying?" Judge Norris asked but Linda ignored him. She wanted to talk to Josie.

"If you'd just stopped when you should have," Linda whispered miserably. "If only you had done what I asked you to do and sent Hannah away this wouldn't be happening."

"You saw her?" Josie choked on her own words.

"What kind of woman makes a mother do this to her own child, Josie? What kind of woman are you?"

With that, Linda buried her face in her hands and still everyone could hear her asking:

"How could you make me do that? How could you?"

CHAPTER 37

There were things missing in Hannah Sheraton's hospital room. The contraption that held her head steady was gone. The IV that had fed her was gone. The pallor was almost gone. Linda was gone.

Josie was there.

The television on the wall opposite Hannah's bed flickered. The sound was mute so Josie watched the closed captioning run across the programs as they changed. She had made the news. Cameras caught her leaving the courtroom pushing through reporters and family rights activists as Archer, huge and calm, cleared the way. It was a frantic mime on TV but Josie's brain rang with the memories of the sound. The reporters: *How do you feel, Josie? Are you giving up? Were you surprised?* Enraged Family First activists: *How could you push a mother that far? You accused Kip Rayburn. Destroyed a family.*

The world was furious with Josie but no angrier, no more disappointed than she was with herself. She had broken the first rule of examining a witness: don't ask the question if you don't know the answer.

For two hours and fifteen minutes, as Hannah slept, Josie had sat in this room trying to figure out why she had done it. Was she simply caught up in the drama of it all?

The late night meeting of Miggy, the tantalizing information he had given her. The possibility that Josie could not only exonerate Hannah, but also offer lady justice the real perpetrator in her place had proved to be a powerful draw. Had she craved the headlines that would declare her to be a heroine who stood by Hannah when no one – not even her own mother – would?

Josie put her head in her hands. Who knew what her motivation was for running headlong into such a disaster? And who could tell why she needed to hear from Hannah herself that what Linda said was true? But there it was. Josie would not leave until Hannah had admitted to this crime.

And even then…

Even then Josie was not ready to give up. Josie knew that she could still defend Hannah and let the girl walk free. She was sure of it. Josie would call Ian Frank and May to the stand to corroborate Fritz's threat against Kip. She would call Rosa and the subpoenaed Lyn Chandler. Josie would follow through with her plans to bring medical experts to testify. She would grill Linda Rayburn and find out the last detail of what she *thought* she saw. Josie would call Kip Rayburn and rip him to shreds in front of that jury.

Closing arguments would sound like a soap opera: Was it Kip? Was Linda protecting her husband by trading on her daughter? Was it Hannah who was lying and Linda who was telling the truth? Who knew? How could they find out? What evidence, she would ask, did the prosecution have that would convince them beyond a shadow of a doubt that Hannah was guilty? Certainly it wouldn't be Linda's testimony, not when Josie was finished with her. The jury would be exhausted, and Josie would offer them reasonable doubt like a soft bed. All they had to do was fall into it.

Unfortunately, Josie couldn't exhaust her own mind. She planted her elbows on her knees and clasped her hands high enough that she could rest her chin on them. She looked at Hannah Sheraton.

Are you guilty? Could you be?

And if she was – and if Josie convinced the jury that Hannah was innocent – and if Hannah was freed–

Josie's ghosts were raising their heads just as Hannah Sheraton woke up and asked for water.

Josie stumbled as she got up. She managed the water and Hannah managed a smile.

"Here. Oh, God. I'm sorry. I'm not very good at this," Josie said quietly. She kept her fingers on the straw and guided it to Hannah's lips. When she'd had enough, Josie stepped back. "Want me to sit you up a little higher?"

Hannah nodded. Josie pushed the button. The bed whirred. The guard outside the door looked in more from curiosity than concern.

"You look better," Josie said.

Hannah blinked, still caught in the twilight sleep of her medication. She was getting better every day, but the process was slow and painful. Josie pulled at the sheet and the thin blanket that covered Hannah. The girl's eyes fluttered closed. She sighed. Josie waited, looking around, noting the other things that weren't in Hannah's room. No flowers, no cards, no one to wish Hannah well, or offer hope that her troubles would end. No one except Josie and Hannah knew it. Josie felt Hannah's fingertips touch the top of her hand. Startled, she almost drew back. Instead she took the girl's hand in her own.

"I'm so tired all the time," Hannah whispered.

"I know," Josie said quietly. "You're healing."

"Where's mom?" Hannah asked. "I need to tell her something. I need for her not to worry."

Josie's lashes fluttered, almost closing over her eyes. She wouldn't tell Hannah the whole truth right away. Instead, she said:

"You mom went home. It was a hard day in court."

Hannah moved. She winced. She resettled, still unsure of what her body could do without causing pain. Hannah lay back again, exhausted.

"I'm sorry about the accident. I wanted to tell you especially," Hannah whispered.

"It doesn't matter now, Hannah. Really, it doesn't." Josie's thumb petted the soft skin on the back of the girl's hand. Hannah's fingers were tapping Josie's palm and under her breath, Hannah was counting as if reciting a nursery rhyme. Josie couldn't listen anymore.

"Miggy came to see me, Hannah." The counting stopped. Hannah's eyes closed but her chest rose and fell more quickly than it had when she was sleeping. She was listening. "He told me that you checked your mother's room the night of the fire. I asked your mother about that night. I asked her if Kip was in the room with her. She told me he wasn't. I thought he set the fire."

Hannah's closed her eyes tight; her hand went slack in Josie's grip. She took a deep breath.

"Did she tell you what did happen?"

Did she tell on me?

Josie swung her head away. She couldn't look at this child. She still wasn't looking when Hannah opened her eyes. Hannah tapped Josie's hand – but just once.

"She told you something else, didn't she?" Hannah's throat was dry again. Josie moved to get the water but Hannah clasped her hand. "Didn't she?"

"She told me she followed you that night. She told me she saw you light the fire." Josie looked into Hannah's green eyes. They were Linda's eyes. *Truth teller or liar?* How could Josie ever know?

"She told you that?" Hannah whispered, tears springing to those eyes, shock reflected in them. "My mom told you…"

"She told the court, Hannah. The jury heard it."

Josie moved her chair closer to the bed and hesitated. The muscles in her jaw were tight to the point of pain. The next words she spoke would seal their fate and tie them together for eternity. If Josie were wrong, she would spend every night of her life waiting to hear that Hannah Sheraton had killed again. But if she were right, Hannah wouldn't go to jail.

"Don't worry. I've laid the groundwork. The court knows that your mother abandoned you. They know that she had more loyalty to Kip than to you. I have witnesses that will testify that Fritz was abusive. The jury will have no choice but to acquit. You were only defending yourself when no one – not even your mother – tried to help you. Do you hear me? I am going to win for you."

Hannah convulsed. Her chest seemed suddenly concave with the intake of breath. Her hand tightened as she gripped Josie for one moment of grief and then she lay silent. Finally, Hannah's head turned on the pillow.

She looked right at Josie and in her eyes was the purest pain Josie had ever seen.

"I want to quit now, Josie," Hannah said softly.

"No, no, Hannah." Josie held the girl's hand tighter. "I can discredit your mother's testimony. I can…"

Hannah shook her head. Tears came out of the corners of her eyes. Her voice quivered but her message was clear.

"Just tell the judge I want to stop now. I know you wanted to believe. I did, too. But now let's stop. I'm just tired, Josie, so let's stop." Hannah looked at the ceiling. "Tell him for me."

Josie started to protest.

Hannah closed her eyes. She didn't want to hear anymore. Deliberately Hannah took her hand away from Josie's.

It was over.

CHAPTER 38

"What do you want me to do with these?"

Archer held up the stack of exhibits that Josie had planned to use in her defense of Hannah Sheraton. She looked up from the files she was sorting. She held out her hands. Archer brought them over and stacked them against a chair so she could look.

"I don't believe it, Archer. I don't believe she did it. At least not the way Rudy made it sound. If Hannah set that fire it wasn't cold blooded murder," Josie muttered, looking at one exhibit and then another.

"You don't want to believe it, Jo," Archer answered. "I don't either, but there was nothing else you could do after her mother testified."

"I couldn't be that wrong twice." Josie went on as if she hadn't heard him. Sitting cross-legged on the floor, she held up a piece of paper as if it would prove something. "Look, here's the timetable of her walk every night. Hannah couldn't have looked into that bedroom, made it to the west wing, set those fires, run back to her bedroom to stash the joint and matches under the mattress, and then go back and stick her hand in that fire. The walk to the bedroom would just add too much time."

Archer stayed silent. He petted Max while he waited for Josie to run out of steam.

"And there's something else. Think about it," Josie dropped the photo to her lap and looked at Archer as if he were a member of the jury. "If you were Linda and you saw your child committing arson – whether or not you knew Fritz was upstairs – would you just stand there without screaming at her or trying to stop her? No," Josie scoffed. "You would try to stop her. And if you did that, there would have been some physical evidence. Extra matches dropped at the scene, marks on the ground, and maybe scratches on Linda. And even if she didn't fight to get Hannah to stop lighting the fire, Linda wouldn't have just stood around and watched her kid stick her hand in the fire."

"Maybe Linda stuck it in for her. Maybe Linda was glad that Hannah was doing what she was doing," Archer suggested.

"What? You mean she didn't stop Hannah because the outcome suited her? Possible, but not probable." Josie tossed the timetable back into the file, and the file onto the floor. "I don't know. The more I think about this, the less sense it makes."

"You're making it too complicated, Jo," Archer said. "You're assuming that the matches under her mattress were the ones used to set the fire. You're assuming Hannah ran back to the house. They didn't search Hannah that night. She could have had a pack of those matches on her and tossed 'em later. Everybody was too busy with her hand, putting out that fire and finding the old man, to think about that."

"Yeah, yeah, yeah." Josie leaned over and looked at another piece of paper. "But the doctors. What about them? They were positive that Hannah couldn't have set that fire and destroyed her paintings. I'll never buy..."

"Jo. Enough." Archer pushed Max's snout out of the way and half rose from his chair. He took the exhibits. "It's over. It's done. Hannah's sentenced. And I'm storing this stuff so you can sleep at night."

"No." She grabbed them back, glaring at Archer. "It's only been a week. Hannah may change her mind. She may want to appeal."

"Don't hold your breath." He got up and went to the kitchen to grab a cup of coffee. The pot was empty. He talked to her from the doorway. "She isn't saying boo to anyone, or anything. She's done with it, Jo. You should be, too."

"I have to do something. I'm going to try to get her a transfer to a psych ward. It will be better than being a 'keep away' or transitioning to the general population when she's eighteen."

Archer wandered back into the dining room. He picked up a box and packed some of the exhibits. Listening to her go on – again – as she got this out of her system.

"Did you see this?" Josie held a black and white picture toward him.

"I've seen everything six times, babe." Archer pulled a length of tape and cut it with his teeth. He switched it away from his lips and looked over his shoulder to glance quickly at the picture.

"Well, what did you make of it? I mean look at those indentations under the ash." Josie was peevish, like a single mother coming home after work to find the kids had trashed the place.

Archer hunkered down next to her, abandoning his chore. He put his hand on her shoulder and looked at the picture.

"Those are Hannah's footprints. They matched 'em to the shoes she was wearing. There's no question on that one."

"I know that. But her footprints are on top of the ash. I didn't think about that before."

"Meaning?" Archer asked.

"Meaning by the time Hannah got there the fire had burned long enough to create a thin coat of ash on the ground. Hannah stepped on top of it. That means she was there after the fire started, doesn't it?"

"And she was probably there before the fire started. Then she changed her mind and came back to try to put it out. Hannah's thought process isn't exactly linear, Jo," Archer said.

"But it's just a thin coat of ash. Her footprints are on top but look underneath. Look." Josie rummaged under a pile of papers and came up with a magnifier. "Look. See those evenly spaced indentations. Whatever those marks are, they were made before the fire started. The fire had been burning long enough to create that thin coat of ash and Hannah stepped on that. The lab tested her shoes. There was ash on them but very little dirt. If she had walked into that room to set the fire her footprints would be on top of those indentations. Right? Her footprints wouldn't have been on top of the ash. Right? I don't know why I didn't see that before."

Archer chuckled but never cracked a smile. Instead he squeezed her shoulder. "Maybe the fire was started by a crazed golfer."

"No, the indentations are too wide and shallow for golf cleats," Josie mused.

Archer slid the picture from her fingers, picked up the file, and put it inside the box he was about to seal. Josie watched him as he stacked three files together and put them in too. Finally he taped it up, walked over to Josie, took her face in his hands, and kissed her forehead.

"Salt in the wound, Jo. The gardeners probably made those marks. Hannah said she tried to put out the fire. That means the fire was burning. If the fire was burning there would have been ash on the ground outside the door. Come on. Ash, no ash, little holes in the ground. It doesn't mean a thing. Hannah copped to the deed."

"She told me to stop, that's different than saying she did it," Josie said evenly. Archer dropped his hands. Only time would make this better. He couldn't kiss this and make it go away. If he could take a picture and steal her hurting soul he would.

"Put it aside, Jo. Go talk with Faye. Come with me to Baja but whatever you do forget about this one."

Josie hit the table leg with one hand and pushed off the floor only to plop herself in a chair.

"I just don't want to believe it. Everything was circumstantial about this case until we found out about the divorce thing. You saw Kip, he is one cold son of a bitch. He had every reason to..."

Archer put his hands on her shoulders and kneaded the tight muscles there. Josie rotated her neck but nothing helped. Archer bent down, kissed the back of her neck, the little naked part behind her ear where her hair had been razored. He put his fingertips on the same spot.

"I can't listen anymore, and if I'm not here you'll stop talking." Archer picked up his jacket. He opened the door and poked his head out. "Least it's stopped raining. You should go for a walk."

"Sure," Josie muttered, but she was the only one who heard it.

Archer was gone. Josie balanced on the back legs of the chair, still looking at the evidence photograph. It was dark and grainy, hardly the kind of thing that would make a photographer's career. She counted the indentations across and down. Josie looked at it until she was cross-eyed. The photos of the fire scene, the photos of Fritz Rayburn, the photos of Hannah's injuries, the photos of Linda standing next to Hannah by the fire truck, all those had been committed to memory. But this one had been set aside, ignored, and now it seemed so damn important – now when everything was over and she had failed.

Josie sighed and let the chair fall back to the ground. She tossed the picture on the table. It was just another one out of a hundred photographs taken that night. There were too many maybes, too much of a chance Hannah was guilty and a small chance she wasn't. Either way, Hannah had pled guilty in front of Judge Norris. It was enough for the court. That should be enough for Josie. Hannah was gone, sentenced to life without the possibility of parole. There was nothing more definitive than that.

Josie put all the files, the loose papers, the photos and charts into the case boxes and lugged them to the spare room. She closed the door and hoped that in a week she'd forget all that stuff was in there. In the kitchen she rinsed out the coffee pot, she touched the message Archer had taken from Rudy Klein and thought about returning the call. Instead, she picked up Max's old pink leash.

"Hey, big boy," she whispered as she crouched down beside him. He raised his face as if he was going to kiss her. Josie took his ears in her hands and nuzzled her cheek against his fur. Max's tongue flicked out and missed her. She pulled back. "It's okay. I appreciate the effort."

Josie turned his collar, clipped on his leash, and went out the front door. The night was moist and fresh, dark and deserted. Josie and Max were halfway down the walk when Max fell onto his haunches, pulling Josie back. He growled, his eyes glowing orange as a turn of his head caught the porch light just right. Attuned to his instincts, Josie stopped short and planted herself. She was ready for whatever, or whoever, was behind the overgrown bougainvillea bush. Josie relaxed. There was nothing to fear back there, only someone to loathe.

"What do you want?"

Josie pulled Max close to calm him even though she'd rather let him loose on Linda Rayburn. Not that it would do any good. The woman was like a cat with nine lives – always landed on her feet – and always seemed to land unexpectedly on Josie's doorstep.

"I want to talk. I think we need to talk."

"When you want to talk, call. This is my home. You're not welcome here."

Turning on her heel, Josie went toward the beach but Linda darted at an angle to intercept her. Josie sidestepped. Linda followed.

"I need to talk to you about Hannah," Linda insisted.

"Maybe you should talk to Hannah. She's been hoping for a little conversation from you all her life."

"That's what I want to do, but she won't see me." Josie pulled on Max's leash. They went around Linda. It didn't help. Linda followed, raising her voice, unwilling to give up. "You think you're the only one that feels bad? Do you think you've got some lock on feelings, Josie? Josie? Come on. Hannah is in jail. I don't want her to die in there without talking to me."

"Then you should have thought about that before you did what you did." Josie threw that suggestion over her shoulder.

"You mean tell the truth? You mean I should have committed perjury?" Linda yelled. "Is that what you mean Ms. Bates, attorney at law?"

Josie stopped again. She was on the bike path, almost at the beach. She could outrun Linda in a flash. She could leave her behind. The problem was that Josie knew she wasn't ready to leave Hannah behind, and Linda was the link.

"I'm taking the dog for a walk," she said tersely. "Come if you want."

Josie set a brisk pace but Linda wasn't deterred. She was shoulder to shoulder with Josie; the dog was between them. Josie slid a look toward Linda. She looked different, but still beautiful. Tonight she was in jeans, a turtleneck and a windbreaker. Her hair was pulled back into a ponytail. Josie's sense of déjà vu – of Linda as a co-ed – was unsettling. How often they had walked back to their horrid little apartment, tired from a workout, disappointed from a loss, or exulted by a win. They had been so young, so able to bounce back from bad news and run with the good. It was such a long time ago. Now it took longer to reconcile disappointments. Their losses weren't measured in points, but lives and confidence and affection. Those feelings of camaraderie that Josie had once shared with Linda were gone for good.

They reached the pier. Josie and Max turned left. Linda might as well have been on a leash, too. All three walked to the end, passing under the high lights, their illumination ghostly and flattened by the sea mist. The last vestiges of rain hung in the air. Their shoes were soft. They were shadows gliding soundlessly over the weather worn wooden planks.

"I'll have the files packed up by the end of the week. Let me know who is going to be handling the appeal and I'll send them along," Josie said just to hear herself talk. She was unable to walk with this woman in comfortable silence. Suddenly Josie stopped, unable to keep what she was thinking inside any longer. "I think you lied, Linda. Or at best, I think you weren't sure what you saw that night, and I hope another lawyer can get you to tell the goddamn truth during an appeal."

Linda's head cocked to the side as she listened. She lowered her eyes then wandered to the railing that ran the length of the pier. Her shoulders rose and fell as she breathed in the salty ocean air. Josie looked at her back, knowing that there wasn't much to see below but dark.

"And what's that truth, Josie?" Linda asked.

Josie took a step forward and then another. Her voice was low, her words were sure.

"I think the truth is that you would have said anything to protect your husband. Or maybe you just wanted all this to be over and pointing the finger at Hannah was the way to make that happen."

Linda raised her head. Josie could see the lovely curve of her cheek, her thick, dark hair, and those long lashes that shaded her exquisite green eyes.

"What you're saying is that it never was, never could have been, Hannah." Linda sighed. "Why is it you're the only one who sees clearly, Josie? I've always wondered that? Why are you the final word?"

"I'm not. I only ask the questions until I'm convinced I have the final answer. In this case, I don't think I've got that."

Linda lifted her face to the ocean breeze. She inhaled. Josie could hear the breath come out of her mouth for a long time as she exhaled. Finally Linda turned around and rested her elbows on the railing. She crossed her feet at the ankles.

"It's kind of moot, Josie. There won't be an appeal if Hannah doesn't want one, and how am I going to know if Hannah won't talk to me? Hannah won't talk, period."

Just then a huge wave cracked against the pilings. Max skittered behind her at the sound. Josie pulled him close then stuck her hands in the pockets of her jacket. It was a nesting night, the kind of weather that inspired beach people to light wood in fireplaces long unused, the kind of night that made Californians think they were actually having a season, the kind of night that Josie treasured when she shared her bed with Archer. Josie's soul was tired. Her mind was tired. She didn't want to fight with Linda anymore.

"What do you really want, Linda? Do you want to be friends? If that's it, then you can just turn around right now. We never really were friends, and we sure as hell aren't going to be now."

"No, I'm not here for me. It's Hannah," Linda admitted. "I was hoping you would try to convince her that she needs to see me. It shouldn't end like this between a mother and daughter."

"Shit happens between mothers and daughters, Linda. Get used to it. Leave it alone for awhile," Josie said, offering the best advice she had.

"Easy for you to say, she's not your daughter. But you tried to make her feel like she was. You tried to take her away from me with all that understanding crap you fed her," Linda said peevishly. "Now I want Hannah back. I want you to go ask her to talk to me. You owe it to me to at least to try, Josie. I mean after everything you did."

"You know what, Linda? I think we all screwed up big time. So if you want to talk about debt, if I owe anyone, it's Hannah. And pay back isn't getting you a face to face so you can get under that kid's skin again. That's about where I'm willing to leave things. I'm sick and tired of the both of us."

"Don't give me that. I did what I could," Linda snapped.

"Yeah, you were real helpful when you testified. There's nothing like an eyewitness account from the defendant's mother."

"What choice did I have?" Linda cried as Josie started to walk back down the pier. When Josie didn't stop, Linda hurried after her. "Tell me, what choice?"

Josie laughed softly and shook her head. She stopped walking.

"You're forgetting one thing, Linda. I didn't ask you if you saw *who* set the fire, I asked where your husband was when the fire was set. If you'd answered the question I asked, Hannah wouldn't be in prison right now."

"Yeah," Linda shot back, "and Kip would be there for something he didn't do. That's a choice?"

Josie started on again. This argument was accomplishing nothing.

"Give me a break. You put Hannah in prison, not me, and I'm not going to try to get you off the hook."

"Jesus, don't say that," Linda breathed, "I swear, it just came out when you were pounding on me about Kip. It wasn't fair. It just made me so mad that Hannah would tell you that Kip wasn't in bed. After everything he did for her. I couldn't believe she would be that ungrateful. She's the one that made all this happen."

Josie threw up her hands and wiggled Max's leash. He started to walk a little faster. She went with him and Linda followed. Angrily, Josie kept talking.

"Hannah never said a word against you, or Kip. Not one. It was her friend from rehab who told me. Miggy Estrada came to my house and gave me Hannah's sketchbook. He told me Hannah checked on you every night. He told me about Chicago."

"That loser? He's the one that did this?" Linda cried in disbelief.

"If Miggy's such a loser, and he's who Hannah went to for help, what does that make you?"

At the end of the pier Josie jumped the few feet to the still wet sand and helped Max. When Max hit the ground they both headed toward the water, the night air did nothing to cool Josie's frustration.

Linda jumped down too and jogged to Josie's side. The breeze kicked up. The fog had come in. Linda's hair had frizzed around her face. She pushed the stray hairs back behind her ear and followed when Josie took a sharp left to dodge the wash of a wave. Linda grabbed Josie and twirled her around.

"Listen. I did what I could do ever since that kid was born. Maybe I didn't ask Hannah all the right questions because I didn't want to hear the answers, okay? I was afraid to hear them. You did what you could do to save her, but the fact of the matter is Hannah finished this whole thing by pleading guilty."

"So leave me out of whatever else goes down now, Linda."

Another wave was coming in. It broke a few feet away and skittered up the sand. Josie stepped back. Linda did the same but not fast enough. They both looked down just as the water pooled around Linda's shoes.

"Damn." Angrily Linda lifted her foot to shake off the seawater then stepped back when another wave followed close behind.

Josie stayed put. The water ran over the top of her shoes and Max's paws and rushed back out to sea. It left the sand glistening with wet, smooth again as it waited for the next wave – or the next footstep that would leave an imprint.

Oh my God.

Josie's psyche doubled over with the brutal blow that had just been delivered. There in the shimmering sand was a pattern Josie had seen before. They were shallow indentations at the heel and toe; the same pattern that had been left at the door of Hannah's studio. It was a pattern that belonged to the person who walked into the west wing before the fire started, the person who left before Hannah's paintings fueled the fire that killed Fritz Rayburn. Those marks were made by a murderer; those marks were made by Linda Rayburn.

"Josie. Jesus, you're going to get soaked."

Startled, Josie looked up. The water came again but Josie was rooted to the ground. She looked at Linda's feet then back at the sand until finally she caught Linda's curious gaze.

"Oh, Christ."

Josie pulled Max close. He stumbled with her, away from the water. She stumbled in the sand, lurching backwards, knowing one thing and one thing only. She needed to get away from Linda Rayburn.

"Look, it's late. I've got a lot to do, Linda. I can't help you anymore. I can't. I just can't."

Josie started toward home but Linda took her arm. Max's tail went down and a growl came up. Josie looked at the hand that held her and then up into Linda Rayburn's face. The breeze blew Linda's ponytail over her shoulder and nipped at the back of Josie's bare neck but it was the look in Linda's eyes that raised the goose bumps on Josie's skin.

"I want to go home, Linda," Josie said quietly.

"Okay. I just want to make sure we understand each other." Linda put her free hand in her pocket. Josie tensed. Her eyes darted over the deserted beach. If Linda had a knife or a gun in that pocket Josie needed a plan but Linda had neither. She had an envelope. "I have your check."

Josie looked at it and tried not to shrink away. She couldn't touch this blood money; she couldn't bear the touch of this woman who had given up her only child to save herself. Josie's brain pounded with that knowledge. She had been so blind; ignoring Linda's questions about eyewitnesses and Hannah's survival.

"We're square, Linda."

Josie shook off Linda Rayburn's hand and backed away. She kept her eye on Linda Rayburn a minute longer, then turned and trudged across the sand, careful to walk even though she wanted to run. Gulping air in an attempt to calm the beating of her heart and clear a mind that was racing with the implications of what she had just seen Josie tried not to arouse Linda's interest. Her back burned where she was sure Linda was watching, her interest sharp and keen. At the bike path, Josie chanced a glance over her shoulder. Linda was standing where Josie had left her but she was looking out to sea, not at Josie after all.

Linda's hands were in the pockets of her jacket. Her feet were wide apart and her head was up. She should have looked lonely standing there on that stretch of beach; instead Linda Rayburn looked as if she was an army of one and was stronger than the invading force.

Josie jogged the rest of the way home.

CHAPTER 39

"Archer. It's Jo. Call me back ASAP. Sooner than that. Call me." – Josie Baylor-Bates, 10:34 PM

"Hi there, Josie. What are you doing?"

Linda Rayburn's voice was so sweet she could have been greeting a lover. That lilt might have called him back to her bed or teased him into a favor or put him on notice that she was on to his game, but Linda Rayburn wasn't talking to a lover. She was calling to Josie who knelt on the floor of the spare room in a puddle of light from the lamp on the small table.

Josie stiffened when she heard that sultry, peppery voice. Her hands trembled and her stomach turned with a sudden sickness. Bad times were coming. The landlord was there, and the rent was due. Frozen in mid-air, Josie's hands hovered over the array of photographs she had ripped out of their file jackets and spread on the floor. Slowly, she sank back on her heels as Linda Rayburn circled around, towering over her, confident as could be.

"Did I leave the door open?"

Josie's eyes were steady as they met Linda's. There was no flicker of surprise, no current of fear to betray her astonishment at finding Linda standing in her home – uninvited, unexpected, and unwanted.

Linda's shoulders raised playfully, a coquette's apology. Her smile was charming and edgy.

"Nope. Front door's closed up tight," she said.

"I didn't know you could pick locks, Linda."

"Didn't have to, Josie. This isn't the most secure place in the world. You should have had someone take care of that broken pane on the back door. Easy as pie to get in."

Josie was lulled by the shadows in the room, Linda's casualness. Her jacket was zipped up so that the collar framed her face. Her cheeks were rosy red from the cold. She was wearing gloves. Josie didn't remember her wearing gloves while they walked. There was sand on the carpet. Linda's shoes had tracked sand into the house. Her shoes. Josie was looking at them – staring at them – when Linda laughed.

"Your game face isn't so good anymore, Josie," Linda chided. "There's something on your mind, and I have a feeling it just might have something to do with me."

"Not everything revolves around you, Linda." Josie tried to fake. Linda wasn't fooled. She chuckled.

"Oh, I think you're fibbing. I saw something change out there. You didn't think I noticed that? It was like a friggin' light bulb going on over your head." Linda leaned forward and pantomimed. The smile faded, her eyes hardened. "Why don't you just tell me what got your short hairs up? Does it have something to do with what you're looking at, Josie? What's that? There." Linda nudged the photographs with her toe. "That one. What's that one?"

Josie picked it up and held it out to Linda. It was self-explanatory but Josie said:

"You and Hannah by the fire truck." Linda took it. Her brow furrowed. "It was two o'clock in the morning when the fire broke out."

"I didn't exactly look my best." Linda let the photo flutter to the floor.

"You were dressed," Josie pointed out. "You were fully dressed, Linda."

"I threw some clothes on when I saw the fire. It's just a top and slacks, my shoes. It took a few seconds."

"But you saw Hannah start the fire," Josie reminded her. "That's what you testified to. You saw her. If you saw her, then you had to be dressed before the fire started. Then you had to be outside when the fire started. Why were you outside?"

Linda checked out her nails. She looked around and found little to interest her.

"Hannah looked in my room. I knew she did it every night. I followed her when she left."

"Did you stay dressed every night just so you could follow her?"

"No. Just that night. I did it that night," Linda said, wary now but still in control. "She was having problems with Fritz, Josie. She wasn't in her right mind. A good mother looks out for her child. I wanted to make sure she didn't get into any trouble."

"If you were following her, Linda, why didn't you stop her before she set the fire?" Josie moved slowly as if her position was uncomfortable and she wanted to settle in while they talked. She put her hands on the ground, a runner's stance. She tried to get up but Linda raised her foot, put it against Josie's shoulder and eased her down.

"I like it this way. Why don't you just stay there," Linda suggested.

Josie sat down again. This time her legs were to her side, her hands on the floor next to her. Her eyes were sharp, trained on Linda's face but also her hands. Above all, Josie wanted to keep Linda's hands in sight. She knew how quick Linda could be.

"What was the question, Josie? I forgot. It's so different when you're sitting in front of everyone in a courtroom. Then you remember every question. You have to really be sharp in a courtroom. It's different here. All cozy. I just forgot what you asked."

"I want to know why you didn't stop Hannah if you saw what she was doing. There were two flash points. You could have seen the first one in Fritz's room through the window. Hannah would have had to take time to spill the turpentine, to light the match on the second. You're strong. Even if you weren't, you could have stopped her just by calling her name. Hannah would do anything for you. But I guess you know that."

"No," she sighed, "I don't think I could have stopped her. I was too far behind. I wasn't sure which route she took. It was a huge home. A perfect home, Josie. It was a perfect life."

"Hannah took the same route every night, Linda. Mrs. Peterson testified to that."

"Maybe she didn't that night. Things can always change," Linda said. "But, with all these questions, it seems you think something else happened."

"Maybe you were there before Hannah. Maybe Kip wasn't the only one missing when Hannah looked into your room. I mean, if you lied about Hannah setting the fire maybe you lied about you being in bed. In fact, I never asked you if you were there, did I?"

"Ooh." Linda pursed her lips. "That's a good one, Josie."

"Maybe you weren't so sure about Kip's undying devotion after all. Could that be it?" Josie baited her.

"That's a lot of maybes, Josie."

"That's my job, but sometimes I'm not so quick. But look…"

Josie reached for the box next to her. Linda's foot shot out. She stepped hard on Josie's hand. Josie crumbled and gasped, gritting her teeth against the pain as Linda brought the full force of her weight down on her.

"There's nothing in there but pictures, Linda. I promise." Linda eased up. Josie slid her hand from underneath Linda's foot. "Look, I just want to show you Hannah's sketchbook."

Linda stayed close enough to control Josie if she had to. Cautiously, Josie reached inside the box. Carefully she opened the book.

"I thought this was a picture of you leaving Hannah behind. But this is Hannah watching you run from the fire you set. She was confused and scared, and her beautiful paintings were in that downstairs room." Josie raised her eyes. "Hannah didn't lie. She did try to put out the fire, and she didn't even know Fritz was lying upstairs. She didn't know because she lied about that, too, didn't she?"

"Fritz was abusing her. She didn't lie about that," Linda said lazily. "I can't believe that bastard did that to Hannah."

"No, I mean the other thing. Hannah had been in his bedroom. She didn't hit Fritz, you did. That first night I saw you there was a scrape healing on your knuckles. It could have been a week old. Your DNA and Hannah's would be virtually identical."

Josie pushed the sketchbook toward Linda. She pushed it as far as she could so that she had to lean forward and balance on her knees. Josie raised her eyes, still talking, tensing her muscles and gauging Linda's balance.

"Hannah was willing to take the rap for you, wasn't she, Linda?"

Linda walked to the far corner of the room, moving as if choreographing a war dance. Six steps and then a turn. Her head was in profile and her neck was taut. She was out of range. Josie relaxed and watched for the next opportunity.

"It wasn't supposed to be like that. Everybody was supposed to bend over backwards to make this go away because Hannah was a minor, because she was Fritz Rayburn's granddaughter. It was a great plan considering how fast I had to come up with it when they figured out the fire wasn't an accident." Linda threw her head back and raised her eyes heavenward as if to ask for answers not forgiveness. "Who would have thought they could make a case out of all those little, idiotic things: matches and hair in his bedroom and everything? I almost died when you asked Klein to name eyewitnesses during the bail hearing. Remember that? I figured I was dead right there."

Linda turned again. She was staring at Josie with such intense hatred Josie felt it searing into her.

"And then you made it all so much worse. A plea, Josie. That was all I wanted. Just plead her out, send her to a hospital. She was sick, anyway. A couple of years wouldn't have made a difference. But no, you had to go for it. You had to win. Do you know how hard it was to face my kid everyday knowing that all the promises I'd made her were shit?"

Linda sniffed and turned up her nose.

"And she just stood there and took it. Hannah reeked with that damned sanctimonious silence, her unadulterated love, that whole mother/daughter thing. You don't think there was a shit load of guilt there for me?" Linda touched the table, the wall.

"Then there was you and Hannah. She trusted you, not me. That really hurt, Josie. It truly pissed me off. More than that, it worried me. I thought she'd tell you the truth. I knew you'd come after me if she did that."

"Then why didn't you tell me the truth? I could have helped you."

Linda took a deep breath and let it out. She splayed her legs. Josie's eyes went to the shoes. Linda didn't notice.

"That is a stupid question. Fritz wanted me gone. Hannah thought it was her fault that Fritz was making Kip divorce me, and all the time it was just another little fun activity for Fritz to enjoy. Kip had no patience with Hannah. He resented her. Do you think if I was indicted Kip would hang around? I explained all this to Hannah. She understood."

"Oh my God. You blamed her for ruining your perfect gig?" Josie managed to sit back on her heels again, ready once more to sprint if she had to.

"No, dammit!" Linda struck the wall with her fist. "I was telling her the facts of life. The fact is there wouldn't have been any problems in my life if I didn't have her. It took me years to find someone suitable, someone who loved me enough to take me with that kid in tow. I did what I had to do to protect us. I got rid of that damn freak of an old man. I saved myself. I saved Kip. I saved her. I saved all of us. When she was arrested, it was her turn to do what she had to. That's just the way things shook out."

Linda twirled toward Josie. She fell to the ground, right onto her knees so that they were close enough to feel one another's breath.

"Hannah was screwed without me and she knew it. If Kip divorced me we'd be back on the street, me sleeping with anything that had enough money to feed us. If Kip stayed with me, and Fritz cut him off, we'd still be back to square one. No money. No prestige. Nothing."

"Linda, listen to what you're saying," Josie said quietly. "Kip is a lawyer. You wouldn't have been destitute. It never would have come to that."

Linda's eyes blazed as her face came closer still. She tipped her head as if she might kiss Josie. Instead she pointed out Josie's stupidity slowly, almost sensually.

"And we wouldn't have been rich." She pulled away. "Kip wouldn't have lasted a minute in a two-bedroom track house with me and Hannah while he got himself situated."

Josie shook her head, trying to understand what Linda was telling her.

"Did you ever once think about Hannah?"

"That's all I did, you bitch," Linda hissed. She threw herself away from Josie and curled up against the wall. "I didn't mean to kill Fritz. I just wanted him to be reasonable. But he laughed at me. He called me names. He told me I was trash. I hit him. He fell. There was blood. After that, I knew it would be more than a divorce if Fritz had his way. He'd prosecute me, and he'd enjoy it. So I tried to cover it up." Linda chuckled a little. She pulled her ponytail over her shoulder and brushed at it. "I guess it didn't surprise me when the cops figured out Fritz hadn't exactly died a natural death, but what did surprise me was Hannah. I thought after a few nights in jail she'd give me up. The stupid little piece of useless baggage loves me. Don't get me wrong I love her, too. I'm not saying the choice was easy. But the closer you got to trying to put this off on Kip, the more I knew it was her or me. That's what it really boiled down to. Just survival. It's always been about that."

Linda's voice trailed off. She blinked as if she couldn't see clearly any longer.

"You know, when Hannah was in the hospital I prayed that she would die. Not just for me, but for her, too. She wouldn't have to worry anymore. She wouldn't have to be afraid anymore. Hannah could go to heaven and count angels with God."

"No, Linda. You wanted Hannah to die because it would be easier for you. She's not the bitch, Linda, but then you've known that all along."

Before she got the last word out Linda flew forward, hand raised, and slapped Josie, catching her behind the ear. Josie fell to the side, her head hitting a chest of drawers. There was a taste of blood but it was inside her mouth, somewhere she couldn't quite locate. She righted herself. On all fours, Josie let her head hang as she tried to keep still until the room stopped spinning, praying Linda wouldn't hit her again. Her prayers were answered. Linda stood up and walked circles around Josie.

"You're just as bad as she is. Always passing judgment. Oh, you never said anything when we were in college but that judgmental thing was always there. Just like Hannah. It was in your eyes. In the way you did just the opposite of what I would do. It was always there in the way you wouldn't say things, Josie. Jesus, you two are like nuns. Like martyrs. I hate martyrs."

Linda was breathing hard. It took a lot of energy to tell her version of the truth. Josie raised her head. The pain behind her eyes was excruciating, the ringing in her ears agonizing, the story fascinating. She closed her eyes and waited, opening them when she felt a touch. Linda had hunkered down and put her fingers under Josie's chin. She was lifting it. Josie saw stars when she tried to yank her face away.

"Josie," Linda said conversationally, "there just wasn't any choice. What would happen to Hannah if I went to jail? Who would take care of a crazy, half-breed kid like her better than I did? Do you think Kip was going to step up to the plate?"

"There were other choices, Linda," Josie said. "You could have left Kip."

Linda barked a laugh. She poked at Josie's shoulder.

"Oh right, like I was going to leave Kip? I'm forty years old. My looks aren't going to last forever. I'm not a lawyer. How would I have supported Hannah? How would I have paid for all those doctors?"

"Maybe if you just made a living and loved your kid, she wouldn't need all those doctors," Josie answered back.

Linda shook her head; her hand was swift, moving in a knife-like, manic gesture, "Still telling me what's best for me and mine. God, do you ever stop?"

She grew quiet and thoughtful as she fooled with the fingers of her glove. Her brow furrowed.

"The only thing I feel bad about is Fritz hurting Hannah." She looked up; her gaze seemed sharper than usual. "The funny thing is, if I had known about it Fritz would still be alive. I could have threatened to tell about the abuse; he'd have to stop messing with Hannah and back off the divorce thing. It would have been a damn simple Mexican standoff." Linda pushed Josie, clipping her shoulder. She was so angry. "What in the hell are you looking at? What have you been looking at all this time?"

Josie's head lolled from side to side. She looked disoriented, confused. She slurred her speech.

"Your shoes," she managed to say.

"What about them?"

Carefully Josie sat back, feigning confusion. Her head still hurt but the nausea caused by Linda's blow was almost gone. Josie reached for the photos, finally finding the one she wanted. Sitting on her heels, Josie handed it to Linda.

"What is this?"

"Hannah's footprints outside the door where the fire started," Josie whispered.

"So?"

"Her footprints are on top of the ash," Josie said.

"So?" Linda drew the word out until it sounded like an obscenity.

"Underneath the ash are indentations." Josie took a deep breath trying to clear her head, disgusted at the simplicity of it all. "Just like the soles of those driving shoes you're wearing. Tod's. Shallow, rounded cleats." Josie swung her head up. She felt a hell of a lot better now. "You walked into the west wing before the fire started and you walked out before there was ash on the ground. Hannah saw what you did. She walked through the ash into a burning house to save her paintings. You ran away. Hannah could have died in there. You…are…such….a bitch."

With that, Josie lunged for Linda's leg and swiped it from beneath her, chopping to the back of her knee. Linda's leg buckled and she let out a cry of surprise and grasped at the side table. The table toppled: the lamp fell. Caught up in it, Linda tried to throw it away but succeeded only in pulling the plug out of the socket.

In the dark Josie scrambled up, balancing herself on the tips of her fingers. She took the first step in a sprint for the door but the glossy photographs were like black ice. Her front foot slid out from beneath her. Josie landed in a split that sent her sprawling before she tucked into a roll, protecting her head as she hit the doorjamb. A second later she scrambled up, grabbed for the door and pulled herself forward. Behind her, Linda swallowed a bellow of rage.

Just as determined, Linda charged. A bigger woman, she hit the wall hard with her shoulder but Josie was faster. She threw herself into the living room, lost her balance then righted herself. The sense of triumph didn't last long. Linda was on her, clutching at Josie's leg, pulling hard enough to lay Josie face down and flat. In a second, Linda had Josie's left arm in a lock behind her back. Straddling her, Linda Rayburn leaned over until she was lying on top of Josie, pushing the breath out of her. Linda's cheek was against Josie's hair, her lips near Josie's ear.

"What are we going to do now, Josie?" Linda pulled harder, wrenching Josie's arm until it felt like it was being pulled from its socket.

"Don't be stupid, Linda." Josie huffed, barely able to breathe much less speak. "You've left enough trace evidence in this place to make a case."

"And so has that idiot, Miggy. He'll be the first one they go after if I kill you. Your friend Archer will back me up, won't he? Bet he knows Miggy was here. My fingerprints aren't on anything but I'd bet a million that his are. I'd bet..."

Josie heard it before Linda did. Max's growl. Josie strained to see him but her face was pressed hard into the floor. She caught a glimpse of him struggling to his feet. He barked loud and long.

"Shut up!" Linda screamed and yanked harder on Josie's arm. "Shut him up!"

Josie cried out in pain. Max lunged but he was old and didn't get very far. He growled and snapped as Linda fought him off, scuttling off Josie long enough to kick the animal in the chest. Max yelped, and then the yelp turned to a whimper. Josie looked back in time to see him stumble and Linda go after him in a blind fury. Linda screamed and kicked him again and again. She picked up a lamp and clubbed him. Max went down, his legs giving out as he backed away.

It was all the time Josie needed. She ran to the hall and into the dining room heading for the back door. Linda was on her in a second but Josie twisted away and reeled into the dining room wall. Above her, her mother's plates shook loose. One hit Josie's shoulder, and the other hit the floor with the crack of gunfire as it shattered.

Linda whirled toward the sound. Locked in on Josie, Linda hurtled across the room, tossing chairs out of her way. Her hip hit the table and threw it off center. Josie pushed back against the wall and sank to the floor, steeling herself for the assault. Linda would be on her before Josie knew it. She watched. She waited. Linda drove forward, thinking of nothing but keeping Josie from telling her secrets, thinking only of herself, and that was Linda Rayburn's downfall.

No strategy.

No patience.

No game.

She lunged.

Terrified, Josie still held her ground, judged Linda's trajectory and moved at the last possible moment. Gripping a shard of pottery Josie raised her hand and slashed. She felt the give as the sharp edge of the plate fragment hit skin and tore through veins; Josie prayed she could hold on long enough for it to work through an artery. Instantly, Josie's hand was covered in blood. It spurted onto her face and into her hair.

Josie turned her face away but it was too late. The blood was in her mouth, her eyes, on Linda Rayburn as she fell into Josie Baylor-Bates' arms. The impact sent them both skidding across the wooden floor, crashing into the corner of the room.

Josie's hand was still on the shard of porcelain and that shard was still buried in Linda Rayburn's throat when the outside door was kicked open. The last thing Josie saw was a gun, a man in blue and Linda Rayburn's bloody neck as she was lifted off her.

CHAPTER 40

"In a stunning turn of events, Linda Rayburn was indicted for the murder of California State Supreme Court Justice, Fritz Rayburn. She is being held without bail pending her trial. You may recall that her daughter, Hannah Sheraton, pled guilty to the crime but new evidence showed that..." ABC News

Josie turned off the ignition. She knew the story by heart. Newspapers, radio, television, there wasn't a reporter in the country who hadn't called her for a comment. She had declined them all.

The sun had come back with a vengeance and October was looking like a record setter. Taking off her baseball cap Josie tossed it in the back seat, slid her sunglasses down her nose and checked out her black eye in the rear-view mirror. It wasn't looking too bad. More green than purple, the bruise should be gone in another week. Her left arm was in a sling but she cheated and opened the door with her left hand anyway. After all, her arm wasn't broken, just a good old-fashioned dislocation.

She took a deep breath and stepped down from the Jeep. It seemed a lifetime ago since she'd been here to meet Hannah. Thanks to Archer she was alive to remember the first time. Surprised by Linda, Josie hadn't hung up the phone just right. When Archer got back from Burt's his answering machine was still recording the sounds of a struggle. He led the charge. He brought the cavalry. Archer wrapped Josie up in his arms and carried her to the ambulance. Not a word was said. What he felt was in his touch, and in his eyes. That was Archer's way. He found Max and got him to the vet. Since then he had nursed them both with such tenderness, in such watchful silence, that Josie wept with gratitude when she was alone. No one had ever treated her as if they were afraid to lose her. But now she was well and Archer had kissed her goodbye, knowing what was being done today had to be done alone.

Josie crossed the parking lot, opened the door to Sybil Brand prison, checked with the officer in charge and waited for Hannah Sheraton to be released.

Ten minutes later, Hannah stood in the doorway and for the hundredth time Josie Baylor-Bates was struck by her beauty. That skin was still the color of milk chocolate; her green eyes were still as clear and bright as an emerald. The only thing that was different was Hannah Sheraton walked toward Josie Baylor-Bates and stopped only twice to step back and begin again.

Hannah smiled softly, sadly. She put out her hand. It was completely healed but still carried the scars of the fire. Josie nodded. She smiled. She touched Hannah's hand and then her hair.

"I think you're going to start a trend."

Hannah's hand went to the tight curls of the new hair that was growing in over her scar. Broken, mended, always a scar. Just like the hula girl plate. The tongue and nose studs were gone. The heavy bandages on her arm were gone. The make-up was gone. Everything about her was bare and fragile as if she was rice paper waiting for the gentle stroke of a brush to define her.

"Maybe," Hannah said shyly. Awkwardly, she pointed to Josie's eye. "You're hurt, too."

"So, I guess we've got something in common," Josie said. She put her hand on Hannah's shoulder. Come on. Let's get out of here."

Together they walked out the door. The prison was behind them, the Jeep in front. Josie rounded to the driver's side. She took her time getting in and winced when she reached in the back for her hat. Hannah stopped her. She was the one who got the baseball cap and put it on Josie. Hannah leaned back and made sure it was straight.

"Okay?" Josie asked, touched by the gesture. Hannah nodded and both of them sat in silence, looking at the prison.

"Josie?"

"Yep."

"I'm sorry for my mom. I'm sorry for everything."

"It's all right."

Josie took the keys from her pocket. But Hannah wouldn't leave it at that.

"I just couldn't tell you what really happened. You understand that, don't you?"

"I don't think I'll ever understand it. I can't imagine giving up my life for anyone, not even my mother," Josie said. She fiddled with the keys, knowing they had to have this conversation but somehow wanting to just skip over it, leave it behind. "If you're asking if I'm upset with you, I'm not. Everybody does what they have to do."

"You're not even mad about what she tried to do to you?" Hannah asked.

Josie twisted, sitting gingerly so she could look Hannah in the eye.

"I'm not exactly happy. In fact, I'm royally ticked off. I've never had anyone try to kill me before. But, Hannah, that's what your mother did and you are not your mother. I'm not my mother. How can I be angry with you for something she did?"

Hannah lowered her lashes, "Because I am her. I lied like my mother lies. If I told you the truth, then you wouldn't be hurt."

"That doesn't make you her, Hannah," Josie assured her. "You stayed quiet because you loved her. Your mom wanted to protect her money and her security. She was willing to gamble with your life and all the while you were protecting hers. There's a big difference."

Hannah's eyes were trained on the low-slung building where she could have possibly spent the rest of her life.

"I don't think she thought of it as gambling. She had a plan, but it just didn't work out the right way and she got scared. You know that snowball thing? First she figured she wouldn't get caught. Then she figured you would get me off. When you wanted to go to trial you just painted her into a corner. You have to understand, my mom has been scared her whole life."

"And you haven't been scared?" Josie asked quietly.

"Not the way she is. I've never been scared like that."

Josie touched the bill of her cap; she tipped her face toward the sun. It was so hot. It felt so good. She wanted to be on Archer's balcony. Instead, she was back in school, rooming with Linda Rayburn. Josie spoke more to herself than to Hannah.

"Your mom used to act like she had the world on a string. I don't know what happened."

"Nothing happened," Hannah answered. "She was always afraid of being alone, of having nothing. She used to curl up in a corner and cry when she didn't have someone to take care of her. I took care of her. That was my job because she gave me life. I would have taken care of her forever." Hannah sniffed. She put her elbow up on the window. "Who'll take care of her in there? Who'll take care of her when she's scared?"

"I don't know, honey," Josie said truthfully.

"I don't think she deserves to go to prison," Hannah whispered. "Not really."

Josie looked toward the prison. They didn't speak. They looked at that place the same way they had watched the stars in Malibu the night Hannah counted only to two. The night Hannah had touched Josie's hand and her heart and her mind. Finally Josie asked the question that seemed so obvious to her but had flown under Hannah's radar.

"Did you deserve to be there?"

Hannah closed her eyes and pulled her bottom lip under her teeth. So like her mother but so much her own, brave woman. Josie didn't wait for a response because it would be a long, long time before Hannah would be honest enough with herself to answer it.

Josie put the key in the ignition and started the car. Hannah opened her eyes. She put on her seat belt and looked straight ahead. Josie wondered if Hannah was well enough to see the future, or was just taking a last look at a place she never wanted to see again.

"Where are we going?" she asked as they turned toward the freeway.

"Haven't got a clue," Josie answered. "Let's try to figure it out at my place."

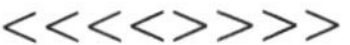

THRILLERS BY REBECCA FORSTER

The Best-Selling Witness Series

HOSTILE WITNESS (#1)
SILENT WITNESS (#2)
PRIVILEGED WITNESS (#3)
EXPERT WITNESS (#4)
EYEWITNESS (#5)
FORGOTTEN WITNESS (#6)
DARK WITNESS (#7)

BEFORE HER EYES
THE MENTOR
CHARACTER WITNESS
BEYOND MALICE
KEEPING COUNSEL
(USA Today Best Seller)

To contact me and to see all my books, visit me at:

RebeccaForster.com

36797812R00234

Made in the USA
Middletown, DE
11 November 2016